THE QUEST

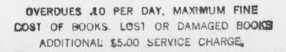

THE
CIRCLE of DESTINY
4

The QUEST

A NOVEL

by Jim & Terri Kraus

TYNDALE HOUSE PUBLISHERS, INC. | WHEATON, ILLINOIS

Visit Tyndale's exciting Web site at www.tyndale.com

Designed by Melinda Schumacher

Library of Congress Cataloging-in-Publication Data

Kraus, Jim.
  The quest : a novel / Jim & Terri Kraus.
    p. cm. — (The circle of destiny 4)
  ISBN 0-8423-1838-0
  1. College students—Fiction. 2. Cambridge (Mass.)—Fiction. I. Kraus, Terri, date.
II. Title.
PS3561.R2876 Q4 2001
813'.54—dc21   2001004108

Printed in the United States of America

07	06	05	04	03	02	01
7	6	5	4	3	2	1

Pittsburgh, Pennsylvania
April 1841

Jamison stood in the front room of the house and listened. The tall clock in the buttery-colored wooden cabinet ticked off each second, as it had ticked off each hour of each day of each week of each year, with the same slow, exacting precision for decades. The wide floorboards beneath him creaked and groaned as they had done all his life.

In the study his father removed a book from a middle shelf, and its leather cover murmured as he creased it open. Jamison heard him sit, the creaking of the chair hushed and muted. He heard the clink-clink-clink of spoon against china as tea was stirred in a delicate flowered cup. He listened to the rustle of the pages and his father's long, slippery swallow. His mother sat opposite her husband and did not cause a sound.

Jamison Pike, a modestly tall young man with reddish blond hair, an intense countenance, and dark eyes—so dark they looked as if they might see through mere flesh—gazed once again at the letter in his hand. With a painful slowness, he extracted the single page from the envelope. He placed it against the wall, just below the portrait of his unsmiling grandfather, the church's founding curate, and smoothed out the wrinkles with his palm.

Dear Mr. Jamison Pike,

We take great pleasure in extending to you the invitation to attend Harvard University for the academic year beginning on September 12, 1841. Your transcripts and recommendations were most impressive, as was your essay outlining your educational goals.

Please indicate by your earliest convenience your acceptance of this offer.

We await your reply.
With warmest regards,
E. A. Barach, Admissions Provost

Jamison entered the study, coughed politely, and with both of his parents' attention, read the letter aloud. Albert, his father, looked up over his glasses. If there was a smile in his response, it was held in check. He nodded to his son as if such an offer had always been fully expected and at the same time regretted.

Hazel, his mother, offered only the briefest of smiles. "I don't think you ever truly considered staying home. There are good schools here in Pittsburgh—good schools indeed. There is no need to run halfway across the continent. I don't understand. Why do you run away from what you have right before you? It is as if you are on some quest that never includes the spot on which you are now standing. What is it you are looking for? What?"

Her questions were painfully familiar. Jamison could never answer any of them to her satisfaction and did not attempt to do otherwise today.

"And Harvard, of all places. You will never fit in with those people. Not you." She glared at him with great politeness. "Don't smirk at me, Jamison. You have no right to smirk."

Jamison bowed his head in apology. It was a most familiar action.

His father laid his book across his lap and drew a deep breath, exhaling with some deliberateness. "I have heard that Harvard has a way of changing people," he said. "You must guard against that. You know the truth, young man. I have always taught you the truth."

Your truth, not mine, Jamison thought.

There was a subtle seasoning of anger sprinkled in with his father's words. "I agree with your mother—that Harvard and its liberal philosophy is no place for a man seeking the truth. But if you will not listen to reason, then go, but shun the evil ideas that spring up from a place like that."

Jamison searched for some suitable reply and found the right words lacking. He instead offered a shrug that he hoped would communicate both his awareness of the situation and an apology.

His father went back to his book and Jamison excused himself. He climbed the narrow stairway to his room under the eaves on the third floor. He sat on a tiny window seat and looked out over the street and the city beyond. From this vantage he could see people bustling about, heading into the city or out of it, carriages and riders competing for space on the dusty streets. Jamison stared hard at every person, occasionally using the telescope he had purchased at a secondhand store on Hill Avenue. He lost himself imagining the dreams that each carried in his or her heart. From the river beyond, he heard the sound of a steamer, calling out its departure. He imagined that he could see the puffs of smoke from the ship's fires as it headed west—west into the very heart of the land. He took out a thick, leather-bound journal and began to write.

FROM THE JOURNAL OF JAMISON PIKE

I have been accepted at Harvard. It is the outcome for which I have so strongly hoped. This will allow me admittance to a new society— a society denied to me by my birth and my geography. I am sure the parties there will be filled with bright and witty people.

And I am suited to Harvard. I know I am.

I have heard him preach—my father—on the Scriptures that admonish us to be as innocent as doves. But does not that same exhortation also admonish us to be as wise and clever as serpents?

I know much of the innocence of doves.

I believe it is now time to learn the ways of the serpent.

CHAPTER ONE

Pittsburgh, Pennsylvania
September 1842

Jamison shouldered his way into the small shop. It was barely dawn and already a crowd of people pushed along the bar, calling for coffee, bread, and sweet rolls bathed in honey. At the edge of the crowd, a few well-worn men called out for beer, whiskey, a slice of jerky, and a hard-boiled egg. A maelstrom of smells swirled about. Jamison felt an elbow at his back. He hefted his bag closer to his shoulder.

"Coffee!" he called out and imagined at that moment how delicious the world might be if populated with far fewer people.

He held his cup above his shoulder and snaked his way back out to the street. There he could drink his breakfast without fear of being jostled in midsip.

The Strip District, hard by the Allegheny River, was coming alive as sunlight began to edge over the glass plants, foundries, and factories. The smoke cast a gray pall over the area, keeping it bathed in almost permanent dusk. He sipped slowly, closing his eyes, leaning against the brick building, and let his heavy canvas satchel fall to the brick sidewalk.

His image was caught by the dawn in a large glass window at the corner. As with mirrors, Jamison was always surprised by his reflection. The man Jamison saw in the wavy glass was bigger than what he felt. The face on the image was more handsome than what he felt inside. He stared back, a luxury not permitted at home.

"All is vanity," his father would say, as he hurried past the tall mirror in the dark hallway.

He stared for a very long moment, wondering how to live up to that reflected image–and whether or not the people of Boston and Harvard would notice.

He pulled off his cloth cap and let his hair fall across his forehead. His features were precise and almost angular. Jamison's smile could be expansive but most often was held, like his father's and mother's, in reserve. On a bad day, one might describe him as pointed and hard. On a good day, he would be hawklike, with an intensity that would be as focused as a flame on dry tinder.

It was a look that came most naturally.

A carriage driver turned the corner no more than twenty feet from where Jamison stood, slapping at the reins, screaming out a long, creative blast of invectives and curses. Jamison drank the last of his coffee and smiled again. Only here in the belly of the city would the dawn be greeted in such an ignominious manner.

He returned the cup to the shop and ordered a large portion of cheese, sausage, and half a loaf of dense rye bread. He gathered up the food into his satchel, wrapping it in a linen handkerchief.

The pocketwatch flipped open in his palm. He would need to hurry if he was to catch the early eastbound train. The station, newly constructed, sat just south of the river. A tangle of freshly laid track snaked out of it, heading in all directions. The first train headed east, through Johnston, Altoona, Harrisburg, and then to Philadelphia. There he would switch trains and head to Boston, and then on to Cambridge to start his second year at Harvard University.

The station was set on a slight rise at a bend in the river. Jamison stopped at the entrance and wiped his sleeve across his forehead. He could see the jumble of buildings clustered at the point of land where the Allegheny and Monongahela Rivers met to form the Ohio River. Barges and flat-bottom keelboats jostled each other at anchor in the slow current. Early each morning, plumes from a hundred fires would billow into the still air. To the west of the city rose The Hill, the sharp incline of land that pushed away from the rivers that all but surrounded it. This was where Jamison had come from, the far west edges of the Hill District. Beyond that, beyond Jamison's neighborhood, was becoming the domain of the rich. Along Forbes and Fifth Avenues, mansions had begun to spring up, cultivated by the newly prosperous merchants and industrialists.

A bell tolled eight times, ringing and echoing from north of where he stood. He pulled out his watch again.

"My watch must be early," he said softly, "or God's bells are late this morning."

He wiped his forehead again.

"And we all know that cannot be."

Shouldering his bag, he made his way inside the vast station, searching out the eastbound train.

The engine jerked forward, and a sharp, metallic series of clanks and jostles started at the front of the train and cascaded along the cars until they reached the last car—the car that Jamison had selected. He always picked either the first car or the last. Never once did he purposefully take a car in the middle of the train. He had no reason for his choice—save that he would not feel comfortable elsewhere.

The last car smelled of cigar smoke and cabbage. It was not an unfamiliar smell, and Jamison selected a window seat near the rear of the car and forced the window open. He knew that until the train left Pittsburgh, he would not taste the scent of clean, unsullied air. Yet even colored by factory smoke, that air was more desirable than that which filled the train car.

The seat in front of him was empty. He tossed his bags there and then stretched out, laying his feet alongside his luggage, glad that he

3

had cleaned his shoes just prior to leaving, as his father had insisted. He rested his arm on the windowsill. In only a few moments, the train rumbled to a slow, jerk-and-pull start, then began clacking away the miles east.

He thought back to the last day with his parents. His father had gone on and on again about the "truth," as if it were a commodity that could be bartered and sold.

"You know the truth," the elder Pike had bellowed, "and I will not have this Harvard convince you otherwise."

"They won't," Jamison said quickly, though with little conviction. *I will need no further convincing on the truth of your truths,* he thought.

His mother had said but a handful of words to him over the course of the last week, so great was her disapproval. She alternated between sighing and brooding and rising when he came into the room, slipping out of his presence with a haughty, angry sniff.

It was not unexpected behavior, and it increased as if her actions might cause him to abandon his plans.

They did not, but it meant that his last week under their roof was a downright chilly affair, filled with the sounds of cutlery on china and the soft swallow of thoroughly chewed food.

Jamison sighed, closed his eyes for a few seconds, then opened them to stare out the window.

Pennsylvania had so quickly become a tame land, he thought, watching as neat farms and villages slipped in and out of view, filled with settlers who wanted no more than a good crop and a dry roof over their heads.

Jamison sighed again. The tracks followed the natural lay of the land and skirted past hollows, along the flat bottoms of valleys. Each hollow and valley harbored a handful of tiny cabins, often nestled tightly together in the ravines. Streams poured and rolled, filled with the cold water from the Allegheny Mountains above. Small farm plots had been hacked and cut from the trees and dense brush: a few cows, a yard filled with chickens busy pecking at the earth, a goat or two, a weather-worn farmer and mules tending the rows of corn and pumpkin and squash, and a couple of dogs lazing on the porch. As the train rumbled past, the hunting dogs would howl and offer chase, oftentimes followed by a young child or two, laughing and calling for the engineer to offer them a blast of the steam whistle.

As the train puffed and strained up the not-so-gentle incline through the mountains, Jamison stood and stretched. He took the bread and cheese and sausage from his bag and spread them out, pulling a penknife from his pocket. He sliced off a thumb's thickness of meat and began to chew at the peppery, fatty mix.

There were only a dozen passengers in this car designed to hold at least fifty. Close to the front, an elegantly dressed man stood and stretched. His clothing was expensive and thoroughly wrinkled. It appeared as if he were sniffing the air, tracing a smell.

He turned back and his eyes caught Jamison's.

The fellow offered a smile. Jamison did not avert his eyes. Instead he nicked off another slice of sausage and held it out, as if tempting a great friendly dog with a treat. The fellow smiled with a broader grin and, trying to match the swaying of the car, made his way back toward Jamison. Jamison gauged the man's age to be nearly forty.

Jamison removed his feet from the seat in front and wiped it with his free hand. As the fellow came closer, Jamison realized that a small dusting would in no means have offended the stranger. His clothes, when new, were no doubt purchased at great cost; now they appeared immensely creased, with a myriad of stains and discoloration abounding.

"I trust your friendly gesture was indeed an invitation and not simply a cruel tempting of a famished man," he said.

"Please," Jamison replied, offering the sausage slice again, "help yourself. I purchased more than I could ever eat."

The stranger took the slice and tossed it into his mouth, chewing enthusiastically. "Name's Edward Hisker. On my way back to Philadelphia." He also gladly took a wedge of cheese and, between bites, added, "Apologize for my disheveled state. Lost my suitcase and most of my attire in Cleveland and rather than get a backwoods tailor to fashion a bad suit coat for me, I decided to simply head home with what I had on my back at the time."

Without waiting for an invitation, he tore off a handful of the bread and chewed silently. Then he swallowed noisily.

Jamison offered a vague gesture in response—a gesture he hoped might impart that the state of a stranger's wardrobe was of no great consequence.

Edward Hisker leaned forward. "Now don't tell me your name, son—or anything else. This is a game I play with most everyone I meet. Using only my mental powers, I would wager that I could discern a great deal of your life. Are you game?"

Jamison hesitated, then nodded with a tentative smile.

Hisker tilted his head and examined Jamison through narrowed eyes. "You're not a farm boy—that much I know," Hisker said, almost as if Jamison were not present for the conversation. "Your hands are too smooth, too clean. Not a farmer, but not quite upper crust either. Your suit coat is almost smart. Almost, not quite."

Jamison held his grin. He had purchased his suit and shirt only weeks ago. The tailor, making the last adjustments, claimed that this style and cut were all the rage on the Continent. *He didn't say which continent,* Jamison had thought.

"No offense, young sir. Just making observations," Hisker said in a backhanded manner of apology.

"No offense taken," Jamison replied.

"And you were born and bred in Pittsburgh. Your accent gives you away."

Jamison looked more disappointed than insulted. All of last semester, he had worked hard at dropping the telltale drawl and cut words that marked the residents of his hometown.

"It's not a strong accent—like you have been working at it. But you have a touch, and a touch is all I need to hear. That means you are a young man seeking an education. Why else would you try and lose the drawl save for bettering one's position?"

Jamison offered a hesitant grin. "Mr. Hisker, you're very good."

Hisker extended his hand for another slice of cheese and sausage. "And I know you aren't traveling on some business. Your bag is too big for a traveling man. You're heading off to school." Hisker chewed thoughtfully. "And your parents . . . or maybe just your father . . . is a strict man and sets high standards for you. He expects only the best from you."

Jamison did his utmost to hide his increasing surprise.

"And by your bearing and the manner in which you hold yourself, I would lay odds that you're heading off to some well-established college with a reputation."

This time, Jamison simply stared in blank amazement.

"But say no more . . . let me guess." Hisker made a great show of pondering and conjuring. "And I would say the college you'll be attending . . . no . . . returning to is Harvard University in Cambridge. For your second year." He sat back with a smug look.

Jamison fell back against the hard seat. "Well, Mr. Hisker . . . you have completely surprised me. That's right. How did you ever know? Are you indeed a mystic of some sort?"

Hisker laughed so hard that small bits of cheese dropped out of his mouth. He held up his hand as if asking for a moment to compose himself. Then he slapped his hand on his thigh, still chuckling. "Normally, I don't give out my trade secrets. But with you—seeing as how you're a fine, upstanding young man—and you offering me a grand breakfast—I'll make an exception." He leaned forward and Jamison leaned in to hear his whisper.

"Your bag there—" Hisker pointed at it with a glance—"has a folder marked 'Harvard University' on the spine. How many people carry a folder from Harvard? None, I imagine, save those working or attending there. And you don't look like a professor just yet."

Jamison smiled. "But how did you know it was my second year?"

"*Oration and Prose, Volume II.* Who would read the second volume unless having been forced into it? And it looks to me from the pristine condition of the spine that you haven't yet cracked that book open. A requisite course, no doubt."

"It is, indeed. The professor operates under the following treatise: If the literature is boring, then it is cultured. If a man cannot endure it without falling asleep, then the work is high culture, indeed."

Hisker laughed until he collapsed into a series of racking coughs.

He reached into his breast pocket and pulled out a small flask, unscrewed it, and tipped it back. He closed his eyes, made a face, and coughed again. He offered the flask, which smelled of strong, raw brandy, to Jamison.

Jamison shook his head.

Hisker took a deep breath. "You certain, young man? It is good for any ailment known to man and beast."

Jamison declined again.

"Do you always play this game with strangers?" Jamison asked. "And are you always so good at it?"

"I am. I watch people. They give away their life stories without knowing it. Like you. Your clothes. How you sit. The fact that you're in the last seat of the last car. If I were of a mind to, I could take great financial advantage of people thinking I was a mystic from a foreign land."

"Well, are you a little bit of a mystic? You had much of my life pegged quite well. How did you ascertain that my father was strict?"

Hisker canted his head in a wry manner and took another large swallow from his flask. "A mystic? Land sakes, no. I'm not a mystic. I'm a reporter."

"A reporter? But how do you know about my father?"

"Two clues: Your handkerchief is neatly pressed. And your shoes are very polished. It seems that young men today don't care about such subtleties as clean shoes and pressed handkerchiefs. The fact that you do—well, to me that means your father insisted on it. And such fathers are strict, more often than not."

Jamison smiled. "You are good, Mr. Hisker. You are very, very good."

"And you say you're a reporter as well?" Hisker asked, taking another sip from his flask—a flask that never seemed to run dry.

Jamison had let slip the fact that he had written a few pieces for the *Crimson Review,* the student-run newspaper on campus.

"It's nothing much," Jamison insisted. "An odd article now and again."

"Well, being in print, with your name above a torrent of words—that is never to be described as 'nothing much.' I've been doing this for years and I still get a certain quickness of pulse when I see my name on the front page. Nothing like it."

"Well, yes, I enjoyed it," Jamison admitted, "but they were only small articles in a student newspaper. I'm sure that such activities will not amount to much. And I'm sure my father would have apoplexy if I even hinted I was seeking out a career as a reporter."

Hisker waved his hand in a grand gesture that might have had several interpretations of his intended meaning. "No small articles. No small papers."

Hisker's voice was becoming wobbly and cursive, if words could be spoken in a cursive tone.

"And don't listen to your father—and the advice that I am certain he gave you to abandon this foolishness of writing. Strict men often live in very small worlds. Don't let that happen to you. You have a look of . . . of destiny about you. You have it. I can see it. There's a noble quest in your future, lad. It's your eyes. Hard. Sharp. Your father will insist on a life no different from the one he leads. That would be a waste. You're more than that. I can see it. Women will see it, too. You will drive the women to distraction—if you haven't already."

He took another large swallow, then rattled the flask, as if hoping for a liquid sound. "I'm not a mystic. I'm not. But I know what I see."

Closing his eyes, he sipped again. "And there is a hint of anger in your eyes as well. The young ladies of Cambridge must seek refuge when you draw near."

Jamison tilted his head. "I don't think any of them have noticed."

Hisker snorted. "My good man, they have noticed. I can tell you that. Pay attention. You'll see. They are watching."

Hisker held his hand out to the windowsill and steadied himself. Both men stared at each other briefly, each realizing they had shared far more of their inner thoughts than they had anticipated. There was an edge of embarrassment in their eyes.

Hisker broke the mood by burping loudly. "When do we get into Harrisburg?"

Jamison slid his pocketwatch out and snapped open the gold cover. "We should be there in twenty minutes or so," he answered with relief.

Hisker snorted. "Less time than that, lad. Railroads set the schedule deliberately late so when the train arrives early, everyone is happy. You know why? So we won't complain about the terrible seats and gut-clenching rattling and bouncing. It's all a trick, lad. A trick to keep the peasants happy."

Hisker curled his finger, bidding Jamison to draw closer. Jamison did and felt, more than smelled, the pungent tightness of the brandy.

"Mr. Pike, you appear to be a good fellow. Smart. Have to be smart to be at Harvard. But I want to offer you some instruction—teaching you won't be getting at school. And this advice comes for free—from a man who has been there and back. I wish my father had told me this a dozen years ago. But he didn't. So I feel under obligation to tell it to young lads like yourself."

Jamison nodded and waited.

"Life is as big as you make it. The rich and privileged take the cream—but there is a lot left over for the rest. It's best to make life as big as possible and get all you can. And that's the gospel truth. I have seen too many fellows who get stuck somewhere that they never planned for. You see it in their eyes, lad. They say, 'I'm trapped and I'm going to die here.' It's like a scream that you know is in their throat but you can't hear a bit of it. Don't make that mistake, lad. You've got to live life in order to know life. No one is going to find out anything about life from some book. It just isn't going to happen. Got to be lived. You've got to get out there and live! The truth is inside you. It's up to you to find it. A noble quest—don't you think? Live life to the fullest—that's my motto."

Hisker drew a deep breath. "And the advice, my lad, is free."

The train hissed and shuddered. Both men were tossed forward as the brakes grabbed and held tight. A cloud of steam whispered its way to the back of the train.

Jamison looked out the window. "Harrisburg. We're in Harrisburg."

"How long till we leave again?" Hisker asked, his eyes now watery and more than a bit unfocused.

Jamison pulled out a printed schedule. "We have an hour at this stop."

Hisker stood, wiped a small avalanche of crumbs off his chest, and announced loudly, "I'm off to find a proper watering place. If they add liquid to a train to ensure its operation, why not the same of a man?"

And with that he spun about and stumbled to the rear door. Jamison watched him as he disappeared into the station.

Jamison remained seated for several minutes. He heard the gritty sound of coal being shoveled into the coal tender. He heard the splash of water and shouts of the engineer. Porters called out. Peddlers offered food and drink to those still on the train. The general hum of the station filled the air.

His pocketwatch showed four o'clock. A pleasant breeze found its way past the buildings and engines and crowds. Jamison thought he smelled lavender. He closed his eyes and imagined himself staying on the train through the night and waking the next morning outside New York. He imagined himself waiting for the scent of the sea as the train rumbled into Boston.

His eyes snapped open.

You have to live life to know it.

Jamison sat at the edge of his seat.

Off in the distance he could see Mr. Hisker leaning against a post by the freight office. In one hand was a large stein of ale. In the other was his silver flask.

The afternoon sun danced off the flask a dozen yards away and sparkled into Jamison's eyes. He blinked and then watched as Mr. Hisker took another long swallow.

And that is how one lives life to the fullest?

Jamison sighed and slumped into the hard wooden bench. He pulled out his textbook, *Oration and Prose,* and did not look up again until he heard the conductor call out, "All aboard!"

FROM THE JOURNAL OF JAMISON PIKE

The Destiny Café had not changed a whit over the summer. I imagine that the Indians said the same thing when they ate there. As a businessman, the owner is doing what is proper, I imagine–he makes money without sacrificing any of his capital. Why spend more money to make the same amount of profit? If he painted the place, all the charm would be lost. And the unique flavor of the coffee would be altered. If a patina lends a certain glow to a well-worn object, then the patina of years of coffee boiled in the same pot adds a certain flavor as well.

The room was filled with students, all telling tales of their summer adventures.

I had no tales to tell. Forced to take the position at my father's church over the summer, I spent every moment penning letters, drafting notices, posting accounts–clerical work that could have been done by a trained monkey.

I have taken some solace in the fact that I have already told him I will not follow him into the ministry. He did not express any untoward surprise. He was not dismayed or angry or relieved. I am not certain what emotion was behind his eyes, for he simply stared, nodded, then walked away.

He did not ask why. For that I was surprised. Had he asked, I believe I would have told him. This stand has not just happened but grown, like a tree in my heart, over the last few years.

I have hardened because it is all a charade–acting by those not meant to be thespians. No other reason can be more compelling. If God finds his voice in the people who ostensibly speak for him, then he has chosen an odd lot of interpreters. It is not that I do not believe in God in some sense, but I do not take kindly with his earthly crew–cold, hardscrabble, judgmental. All are emotions I have grown up with, and all emotions that I sense are less from God and more from man.

Perhaps there is a God who watches us with detached bemusement. Yet how could he smile with those in charge of "keeping his flock"? They say God is in church, but church is of man . . . and there is the rub that would callous the most resolute soul.

It is easier for me to observe, to watch, for I can no longer participate in this convoluted and Byzantine charade.

Unlike my most boring of summers, Gage Davis–of the wealthy New York Davis family–went on and on as he explained his duties working for his father in high finance. Hundreds and thousands of dollars flowed through his hands.

Gage, with his dark gray eyes and darker hair, would be an odd bird in Pittsburgh. Not from his looks, of course–there are handsome men in my hometown–but because of his bearing. There are a sense and a style that the rich possess that are so lacking in the common man. He smiles and others will smile, almost involuntarily. He has mastered the firm handshake coupled with a piercing look–as if you are the most important thing in his life when he greets you–even if he has another dozen or so friends still to greet.

It is as if the nature of wealth was like air–an element to which he was born to partake.

And yet, despite our differences, I find him a grand friend.

He is funny and self-deprecating and generous . . . and from what I can tell, well liked by the ladies.

Other fellows spoke of their trips abroad or to the shore or to the mountains.

What saved this night from completely self-indulgent storytelling was one member of the audience.

Hannah was there.

Her name is Morgan Hannah Collins, and we met near the end of last year. I have read of falling in love at first glance and never once believed it until I first saw her.

I say that not knowing for sure if such a thing is truly real. I know it is the stuff of books and poems–but my heart does something . . . something different in my chest when I see her.

She is not classically beautiful, yet her imperfections are perfected. Like Gage, when she meets you, her smile is offered for you alone.

Her blonde hair appears like dappled sunlight on a summer day, and her eyes are filled with secrets.

She was more stunning than she was last year—if such a thing is possible—but was surrounded by a table filled with admirers and charming fellows—all with better stories to tell than me. As a result, I only waved at her and exchanged nary a word.

As I walked home I berated myself soundly for my reluctance.

Did not Mr. Hisker say that life is to be lived?

And lived fully?

And just how do I do that?

CHAPTER TWO

Cambridge, Massachusetts
November 1842

Jamison looked up. A wall of granite and limestone shouldered into the sky, the mass broken by a few small windows. Since a gray layer of clouds hesitated only a few feet above, whatever life and vitality the stained glass might contain remained hidden on this day.

St. Barnabas Episcopal Church lay just off the river in Cambridge. Jamison did not feel well today. A headache nudged at his temples, and his belly rumbled in annoyance at the lack of breakfast.

He pulled out his pocketwatch and snapped it open. The gold softly nestling in his palm was a small daily pleasure.

"I have ten minutes," he said softly.

He set off at a run. Two blocks north and one block east lay a small greengrocer who sold coffee and rolls in the morning.

Jamison, an habitual early riser, knew every early-opening shop within a three-mile radius of campus. He gulped down a thick coffee, cooled with half a glass of cream, and grabbed a thick crusty roll. As he sprinted back toward the church, he tore off one bite of the roll, then another.

Just as he mounted the steps of the church, the low rumble of the prelude began. The organist, a small, energetic man from Bristol, England, bashed at the keys with a somber intensity. Jamison jammed the last of the roll into his cheek and found his way to a pew—right side, two from the back, near a small window.

The entire pew was empty. Jamison slid in and bowed his head. After a lifetime of being instructed to bow first upon entering God's house, Jamison found the habit most difficult to cease.

The last few notes crashed about the hard surfaces inside the church. There was nothing subtle about the music here, he thought, but it was so much improved from the trebly, reedy organ in his father's church with its nearly terminal, anemic sounds. The associate pastor, a recent graduate from Harvard, rose to the walnut podium, pulled out his spectacles, and after taking a short eternity to place them on his nose, began to read from the Old Testament.

Smiling, Jamison wondered if the fellow had ever taken a course in public speaking. He was quite certain he had not, so stilted and oddly paused was his reading. Jamison allowed himself to relax. Sunday morning had never been a peaceful time growing up. Even though the Pikes lived only a block from church, Jamison as a boy was always being dragged by his arm in order to arrive at the church doors on time. And yet now, away from the demands of his father, Jamison still hurried to arrive before the music started, always huffing as the music began, never once achieving the quiet introspection his father demanded.

He settled back, pushing his feet toward the unoccupied pew in front. Placing his arm on the back of the seat, he rustled about until he found a most comfortable position. The passage today was exceptionally long, and Jamison had not bothered to note its location nor to pay attention to the words as they were spoken.

He peered through the small window at his right. It was higher than his head, only a foot or two square. From where he sat, Jamison could see the sky through the rippled glass panes. The clouds of this morning had become even more gray. He stared up and out. A storm approached, for Jamison could see the reflection of lightning flashes. He felt rather than heard the first coilings of thunder from a distance to the west.

He closed his eyes. The choir took its place on the platform. Their selection today was an Austrian work that Jamison had never heard. After the first few measures, he understood why. For a man not well schooled in such things, Jamison thought the music awkward and jarring, almost atonal.

A quiet shuffling followed as the pastor mounted the steps to the podium, his hands holding the dozen pages of today's message. He stood with a grim expression, glaring out balefully. He raised his hands, cleared his throat, then called out in a voice that was too loud, "Let us pray!"

Almost as an exclamation point, a crack of lightning and a roll of thunder ended his call. Most of the congregation jumped in their seats as the white light exploded through the windows.

A fitting beginning, Jamison thought. *Now let's see if he can match his theatrical opening.*

At the conclusion of the service Jamison stood and edged his way toward the back with quick steps. He had attended this church with some regularity during his first year at Harvard. He would have been hard-pressed to explain why he came here, or any church for that matter, since he claimed at one time to be in opposition to nearly everything his father stood for. Church attendance was highly cherished by his father. As a pastor, one could not expect differently. The elder Pike could, after preaching a sermon, without a single failure name every person in attendance at the service, whether they stayed awake or not, and their attendance record over the past three months.

The reason Jamison attended this specific church was that no one else from Harvard appeared to ever darken its doors. In the dozens of Sundays he had sat in the rear right of the church, he had yet to see any familiar face among the smallish crowd. The anonymity suited Jamison well.

On this day, with the sky still laced with a thick, chilling mist, Jamison looked up, grimaced, and stepped out onto the front steps of the church, tightening his collar about his throat. He was about to hurry back to the Destiny for lunch when he heard his name called out.

His stomach tightened into a fist.

No one here is from Harvard. I am certain of that. No one I would know, at any rate.

For a heartbeat, he considered simply sprinting down the steps and running back toward campus, hoping that whoever called would simply think he had not heard and hurried to get out of the nasty weather.

"Jamison Pike!" the voice came again. "Over here, young man."

He closed his eyes. He knew he had to turn and identify the call.

From across the broad expanse of steps, between a pair of columns, stood Professor Miller Donletter, wearing his familiar tweed coat. Perched on his head, like a large, ominous bird of prey, was a hat that appeared at least one size too large. The brim rested neatly on his bushy eyebrows.

"Well, don't simply stand there, young man. Come over here and get out of the rain."

Jamison closed his eyes again. He mentally shrugged in acquiescence and turned back to the covered portico of the church.

"Well, let me be tied and shipped to Africa!" Professor Donletter exclaimed. He had a habit of mixing his phrases in an odd, disjointed manner, much to the secret mirth of his students. Professor Donletter taught English Prose. He was a most flamboyant professor and could often be seen strolling the campus with six or so students in tow, hastening to retrieve his every word. "I would never have thought Harvard's premier skeptic would be caught darkening the doors of a house of worship. You are filled with surprises, Mr. Pike. How fortuitous that we meet. I had been meaning to send for you ever since the term began."

Donletter waved his hands when he spoke, as if batting away a persistent fly seeking to buzz into his open mouth.

"Skeptic?" Jamison asked, genuinely confused. "I'm not sure . . .
I mean . . . I never thought myself . . . sir?"

"Land sakes, Mr. Pike, I'm certain I'm not telling tales after class.
Skeptic. Doubter. You know what it means. And you are Harvard's
premiere."

A splash of rain swirled about. Jamison felt the drops at the back
of his neck. "Yes, sir, I know what the words mean. But Harvard's
premiere? I truly am at a loss."

Donletter tipped almost backward, held his hand to his chin, and
stared down at Jamison. Donletter was a very tall man. "Well, I have
baffled you. I see that in your face."

He slapped an arm about Jamison. It was a gesture born of equals—
and a gesture that all but frightened Jamison.

"Well, lad, I daresay I do not know how you would have been
befuddled. After all, did you not write those pieces for the *Crimson
Review*—the articles on Brook Farm? The articles that so lambasted
George Ripley?"

Jamison wanted to duck away from Donletter's arm, which began
to feel ponderously heavy across his shoulders.

"Well, sir, yes, I did write the articles. But lambasting?"

Donletter stared at his former student, then brayed out a laugh.
"You don't see it? Truly? No objectivity here?" He slapped Jamison's
shoulder again. "Gadzooks," he laughed, "an innocent. A virgin mis-
anthrope at Harvard. How delicious."

Professor Donletter again stared at Jamison. Then a look of contri-
tion crossed his face. "I mean no harm, young man. Let me buy you
lunch. Make amends for poking fun."

Jamison wanted nothing more than to leave, but he gulped, then
shrugged. "I would be honored . . . I guess."

Professor Donletter laughed again and began clipping down the
steps of the church with as much grace as a hobbled packhorse, with
Jamison a few steps behind.

"And since you mentioned honor—let me take you to a place of
high honor, Mr. Pike. A place no student sets foot in—at least volun-
tarily."

"That was almost palatable," Professor Donletter whispered as he pushed his plate away. The serving girl smiled broadly and seemed to take a very long time in removing the plate streaked with gravy and crumbs.

As she made her way to the kitchen, Donletter kept his voice at a whisper and added, "The food at the Faculty Club is barely edible. But I do so like the scenery and ambience. Having a pleasant smile returned is most rewarding—especially to an old bachelor teacher like myself."

Jamison had accompanied Professor Donletter to the Harvard Faculty Club, a ramshackle and musty building on the far east side of campus. It was all but hidden from view by a tangle of evergreens that had been allowed to grow thick, nearly covering the structure. The public rooms were filled with myriad creased and worn leather chairs, leather-topped desks, and several dozen lanterns. Stacked in piles about the chairs and tables were books in abundance and newspapers as high as a man's knee. In the rear of the building was a large dining hall. Jamison had not even been aware of the building's function before today.

"And she has a sister who works here as well," Donletter continued with a sly nudge, "who is even more enthusiastic than this one—if you catch my meaning. Makes all the food taste better, I might say."

Jamison nodded but did not speak. In fact he had spoken only ten or so words since being set upon by the professor after the service.

Donletter pulled out an antique pipe and stuffed it full of tobacco that smelled of autumn and silage. With an elaborate, expansive ritual, Donletter tamped and poked and lit and puffed and drew until his head was all but lost in a great cloud of acrid, stomach-turning smoke.

"So then," he coughed out, "you truly do not register a bit with my appellation of you being a cynic? Truly and forsooth?"

"Professor Donletter," Jamison replied, "during all of lunch I have puzzled over your remarks. I thought I was being an honest witness to what I saw and wrote those articles as I saw that reality. I do not believe I colored any scene with my own partiality or bias."

By now only Donletter's pipe and nose were visible through the smoke. The pipe danced and stuttered in the air as he talked. "And, Mr. Pike, you were as honest as the driven snow when you wrote. Your words described what you saw. No implication of duplicity or deception on your part, I am sure. But your description of that crazy man Ripley and that odd beard of his—as 'a man wearing a vest full of petulant bumblebees'—well, I laughed so hard I nearly slipped from consciousness. And I am certain such words brought the poor Mr. Ripley to the brink of distraction."

Jamison took another sip of coffee. A sip at a time was all any man could tolerate without choking. It was not strong so much as biting and curdled.

"But that is not a cynical view, sir. Perhaps it was simply a sopho-moric turn of a phrase—a phrase I thought a clever way to describe a man."

"Oh, it was clever, all right. I heard the same repeated by several of Cambridge's literary illuminati—as if they themselves had coined it."

"Truly?"

"I heard old man Longfellow say it—and then take credit for that same specific turn of words."

Jamison was astonished into silence.

"But a clever phrase does not make a social agnostic, Mr. Pike. It is one's outlook."

And with that, Donletter disappeared into the smoke again. "I read the articles, Mr. Pike. You never came out and said so exactly—but I knew from the flow and tone that you thought the whole Brook Farm experiment to be balderdash."

Jamison neatly tensed only his legs and kept his face unmoved. "But in truth," he replied, "my report was balanced and fair. I never said it was balderdash."

"No need to have actually said it, young man. And perhaps that is your native genius at writing. A perceptive reader—such as myself, of course–could spot the critique. It was part and parcel of your style and panache as author. And hinting throughout your writing–like a fine wine over a leg of lamb–is your delicate and fine-honed anger."

"Anger, sir?"

Donletter coughed out a laugh. "You are such a sweet innocent, Pike. It's there. The haves versus the have-nots. The elite versus the rest of the world. The gay and witty versus those who must toil for a living." His voice dropped to a smoky whisper. "You are like me. We are not joiners–but observers. The world needs us. Impartial. Harsh. Honest. Truthful."

Jamison tried to nod, but his head refused to move.

Donletter swept the air again, cutting a swath through the smoke. "Now to be sure, I agree with you in your assessment of Brook Farm. Those muddleheaded fools over there will be bust in a year at most. No man serves another without expectation of compensation. No man is noble when his stomach growls or his wallet falls fallow. There is always a brighter star in the constellation, and the rest of the dim lights will revolt."

Jamison sipped at the coffee one last time. He could drink no more. "But I never said any of that, sir."

From the smoke came Donletter's voice. "No need, son. It was all there in your tone. I believe those articles to be the high-level mark in student journalism here at Harvard–well . . . since I have been tenured."

Jamison could not help but flush at the high praise.

"I mean that sincerely, young man. You have a gift. A gift of see-ing the world as it really is and not how people say it should be or might be or ought to be. If you are as naturally misanthropic as your words promised, you have been called upon to do battle with our world. Expose it. Throw a light upon the darkness. Place a mirror up to man and reflect back the true reality behind the nobility of a man's actions–or the glaring lack of all nobility. A wondrous quest, if I say so myself."

He puffed again, the hissing embers snapping and glowing in the midst of the smoke. "The truth, Mr. Pike. You are searching for it–

I can see that. But the truth about truth is that to everyone's surprise, truth is in yourself. Trust your own internal monitor. That is where the truth resides. Nowhere else but inside one's own being."

Jamison sat in stunned silence. The only noise was the hot warble that came from Donletter's pipe as he drew great clouds of air through the burning tobacco.

"I tell you this because I wish someone had told me as much so many years ago. I would be on this exact same quest rather than teaching about it—teaching it to inconsequential students of well-born families who do not truly care to learn or discern."

From the distance, Jamison heard the tower bell strike two. He shuffled forward in his seat.

"You are leaving?" Donletter asked.

"I do have some assignments to begin, sir."

With a wave of both hands, Donletter sat forward as well. The smoke around him cleared as if cut with a scythe. "One last question, Mr. Pike. What were you doing in church? I would have thought that such messy matters like religion and spirituality would be anathema to a man of your sensibilities. I mean to say, are you looking for God to give you something? Are you one of those pious supplicants who truly believe God grants poor fools the things they yearn for?"

Jamison hesitated for what he thought was a very long moment. He began to speak several times, then tightened his mouth.

He swallowed once. He had no reason to attempt to impress Professor Donletter but felt powerless to stop. Without truly realizing the import of his words, Jamison replied, "I was researching, sir. For an article I might write. Research, sir."

Donletter smiled, his lips twisted just so around the pipe. "I thought as much. A rational man such as yourself has no business in church. A crutch for the weak and feebleminded. For such a writer and thinker like yourself to be caught on their knees in supplication . . . well, that juxtaposition would be too jarring. I only attend church because my father stipulated in his will that I must go every week or his money disappears. It makes no difference which church. I simply note the name of the church and the topic of the message for the administrator of my trust fund. My father was a clever old coot—and I sense him laughing at me from that great beyond. Yet I dutifully check in, in order to receive my monthly stipends. And then I laugh back at him. You know, I have never considered this—but I suspect that one might say God has given me what I needed."

His giggle sounded high and almost delicate, as if he had shared one secret too many. When his eyes caught Jamison's, Jamison knew the revelation was most unexpected on both their parts.

"You do have a way of encouraging disclosures, Mr. Pike. I don't know what it is, but I have seldom mentioned that situation to anyone—and would appreciate your discretion."

Jamison nodded. "Of course, sir."

Donletter took another series of liquid-sounding puffs on his pipe and was again nearly lost in smoke. "Perhaps I will see you at church next week, Mr. Pike. Unless your research is complete?"

"No, sir. Not yet. And perhaps you will."

The Destiny was quiet, unusually so for an unpleasant Sunday afternoon. Jamison observed that when the weather was most inclement, the crowds were largest—as if the students gathered together seeking safety in numbers. On sunny weekend days, most students would be out strolling along the campus walks or by the river. But today barely a handful of his classmates braved the blustery winds and rain.

Jamison did indeed have assignments to begin, but after his lunch with Professor Donletter, those assignments seemed most insignificant. The words of the professor all served to put Jamison in a daze of sorts—as if he had just been told that an immense and unexpected fortune had arrived on his doorstep.

He was praised by a well-respected professor—praised and then praised again. And all for his supposed misanthropic view of the world.

Am I really such a person as Donletter described? he wondered to

himself as he drank his fourth cup of tolerable coffee that afternoon.
An angry doubter and skeptic?

Melinda, one of the serving girls at the Destiny, poured a fifth
cup of coffee for Jamison. She smiled at him, more than usual, and
Jamison felt a sudden redness in his cheeks.

"All alone today?" she asked, pushing a strand of hair from her
face. Wrinkles etched the skin around her eyes—wrinkles that belied
her young age.

He nodded, not sure what to say.

"And where is our Mr. Davis? He's usually here all day on Sunday."

Jamison shrugged. "I haven't seen him for a few days. He might
be back in New York."

"More the pity," Melinda sighed. She looked around the
sparsely filled restaurant, then pulled out a chair and sat opposite
Jamison. "Hope you don't mind, but my feet are not as happy as
they might be."

Jamison half stood as she sat. "No . . . go ahead. You can sit. I
don't mind. I mean, that is . . ." His cheeks flushed hot.

She laughed and tilted her head back, as if stretching the muscles
in her neck. "It's all right. You college men are all alike. Filled with
sound and fury until a woman actually comes over and talks with
you. Then it's all at sixes and sevens, and you act like you've never
spoken with a woman before."

Jamison tried to smile in response but did not think he did a good
job.

"So, Mr. Pike . . ."

Jamison was actually quite surprised that Melinda knew his last
name.

"Will you be writing on the Harvard *Crimson Review* again this
year?"

"Well . . . I guess . . ."

Melinda stared hard at him. "You didn't think I read, did you?
You didn't think I knew who you were, did you?"

He tried to form a reply but could find no words.

"Well, I do, and with all the copies of that paper that get left here,

I've seen your pieces a dozen times if I saw them once. You write good, Mr. Pike. I liked them."

"Thank you, Melinda. That is kind of you."

"You're welcome."

She sighed again and was about to get up when Jamison spoke. "Melinda . . . ?"

Her reply was a half smile, wary and thin.

"You say you read what I wrote."

"I did. I especially like those few about them foolish people up on Brook Farm. I actually served Mr. Ripley here on several occasions. I read your description and laughed for an hour."

"But I never said they were foolish, did I?"

She smiled as if she knew his secret. "You didn't have to. I could tell you thought they were all fools by the way you wrote it. I liked it. It was as if I were there, peeking around corners, overhearing things. Like I . . . like I knew who those people were just by reading the words."

Jamison leaned forward. He saw the creases beginning to form over the small bones in her shoulder. "Melinda, be honest with me. Do you think I am a cynical person?"

"Cynical?"

"That I distrust the noble motives of mankind."

She scowled at him. "I know what the word means, Mr. Pike. I may only be a serving girl, but I am not stupid."

He reddened further. "I'm sorry," he mumbled, unsure of what words might be appropriate.

"No matter. You're not the first. And yes, I would use that word to describe you."

He spread his hands open. "Why do you say that?"

Someone in the kitchen called out Melinda's name, and she stood and dusted off her apron.

"I'm not sure why, exactly, Mr. Pike. But you seem weary of all that goes on around you. I see you at the edge of conversations, never in the middle. Like you're watching, evaluating, waiting for people to reveal themselves somehow. Sometimes I think you are a little angry at everyone. But land sakes, Mr. Pike, you have nothing to be angry at. A handsome boy like yourself. Now, me, on the other hand . . ."

The voice called her name, louder this time.

"I'll be there in a minute!" she shouted back and looked down at Jamison's upturned face. "Do not despair, Mr. Pike. It's not a bad thing to be what you are. There's an air of mystery about you. I bet there are young ladies out there who want to find out who you truly are."

The voice called her name again, this time very loudly.

She shrugged and hurried off toward the kitchen.

Jamison sat for a long time, until his coffee had grown cold and bitter.

FROM THE JOURNAL OF JAMISON PIKE

I suspect, after being labeled a cynic twice in the same day–from two such wildly divergent people–I must conclude that perhaps they are correct. But angry? I'm not. I am not really angry. At least I do not think I am.

And Melinda said I was handsome. I believe that is a first for me– at least from someone other than a relative.

It is confusing. I have never considered myself handsome or a natural skeptic.

Having grown up watching the pious on Sunday act like the lost the rest of the week gives one pause to describe man as a good being. And through my father's eyes, I suspect, I watch and carefully consider exactly why people do what they say they do. Is it to gain favor with some supreme being? Is it to find favor with some professor or pastor? Is it to find an advantage with some young woman? No one does anything for pure motives, my father has always said, especially the ones who say they do. Those are the worst, he says, those who wrap their motives in righteousness.

I agree with that.

So many things are done in the name of nobility and goodness that simply are not.

Perhaps I see this more clearly than most. And perhaps that is why I write with some sharpness.

Melinda says that my "air of mystery" is attractive to the fairer sex. I have never considered that a possibility.

Air of mystery?

Perhaps I have managed to conceal my confusion with a mysterious air. It is not intentional, I assure you—but a pleasant serendipity.

Harvard Campus
Two Days Later

On a very warm November day, lying nearly prone on a bench beneath an elm tree, Jamison propped up his *Critical Prose* textbook on his stomach and tried, for the fourth time, to begin the assigned chapter. He had attempted reading in his room, but the two fellows living in the next small apartment were in the midst of some argument over a missing sausage. For nearly an hour they shouted back and forth, each accusing the other of some manner of perfidy. Jamison, tired of hearing the dull echo of their insults, had first run off to the library.

There he found a very quiet corner off by the foreign language section, into which, apparently, no student ever set foot. But after fifteen minutes, the room and space grew too quiet and Jamison kept looking up, thinking he had heard a sound when no sound was present. Then he tried the Destiny, but it was nearly full; several sculling crews, in full argument over the best boat, occupied three tables. In exasperation, Jamison grabbed his satchel and book and made his way out onto the campus. He found a lone bench, not too quiet, not too noisy, and began to read.

Perhaps no more than a page into the chapter, a shadow fell over his face and he blinked in some surprise. He turned his head to a female form, outlined by the sun.

In the shadow was the faint, sweet hint of lavender.

"Jamison Pike, reduced to sleeping on park benches. How sad."

He nearly fell from the bench in an effort to sit up and straighten his coat and shirt at the same time. His book fell with a papery clatter to the ground.

Jamison ran his hand through his hair. "Miss Collins . . . how nice to see you."

Hannah Collins stood between Jamison and the sun.

"And you are sleeping out here because . . . ?"

Flustered, he repeated his tale of attempting to find a proper place to read.

"Sausage, you say? An hour's worth of argument over a sausage?"

Jamison felt a curious warmth as her voice hinted at laughter.

"They may have come to blows by now. If the constable asks, I will have to say it would be a case of the missing links."

Hannah's laughter was as clear and precise as a bell sounding out the hours over a winter's landscape. He felt heartened to have been the man who had made her laugh so.

"For a cynic, Mr. Pike, you have the gift of making me laugh. I find that most attractive." She stared down at him. "Well, I must be off. Advanced Biology is at two, and I must not be late again. Perhaps we will see each other at the Destiny."

Jamison nearly fell again as he stood. "Yes, that would be most . . . most . . ."

"Enjoyable?"

He blushed. "Yes . . . enjoyable."

As he watched her walk away, he realized that the assigned chapter would have to wait for another day. He sat down and breathed deeply.

The faint scent of lavender lingered in the air.

And he knew, without admitting the truth to himself, that in a small edging of his heart, he would never be worthy of that woman. As that thought surfaced, he also vowed to himself that he would do nearly anything to prove it wrong.

CHAPTER THREE

Cambridge, Massachusetts
November 1842

Jamison never returned to his reading. He watched Hannah's every step until she turned the corner, more than two blocks away. The only thought that came to his mind as he sat there was what he might say to her that evening at the Destiny. Her invitation was not exactly an invitation, but Jamison was somehow certain she would be there. And he would be there as well.

The bell in the clock tower rang three times. Jamison shook his head slightly to clear the fog. He had sat here on the bench for nearly a full hour, cradling his book in his arms, never turning a single page or reading a single additional word.

"Jamison!"

He looked up and saw Clarence Edmonds heading toward him at nearly a trot. Clarence, majoring in Greek, wore tiny spectacles and expensive Continental clothing.

Jamison liked him in spite of his affectations.

"For the last three days I have searched all over campus for you!" Clarence exclaimed. "I do not know why, but everyone I ask claims to have just seen you. And yet when I look in that last place, I find nothing–not even a wisp of Jamison remains."

"I'm not that elusive," Jamison answered. "It cannot be that bad. Have you ever tried my room?"

Clarence sighed so deeply that he appeared to have deflated. "I have. I have left notes and messages with those two louts who appear to inhabit the rooms to the side of you. How they ever managed to gain entrance into this institution is beyond me."

"They have never said a word to me about your requests. Are you sure they heard you?"

Clarence gestured with a wide sweep of his arms. "Am I sure? Yes! They heard me–but whether they understood is another question altogether. I imagine that those two are only barely aware of their own existence. No doubt they failed to recognize my speech as English."

Jamison laughed. "It helps if you feed them. That usually brings their attention around."

Clarence twisted his lips into a polite and practiced sneer. "I shall bring some biscuits the next time I call."

"Raw meat works better," Jamison replied.

"I even stopped at Odd Duck Donletter's office, thinking you, as class pet, might have checked in. But he was as ignorant as your two loutish neighbors. He suggested I stop at St. Barnabas."

Jamison winced and tried to hide his expression.

"Of course I laughed at his suggestion. Jamison in a church? A rational man such as Mr. Pike in supplication in the last bastion of bad logic and twisted thought? Preposterous. A logical, truthful man like Pike would not seek the truth where it cannot be found. That is for certain, I told him. Yet he continued to jabber away as if you did."

Jamison did not answer.

Harrumphing one last time, Clarence readjusted his spectacles. "Have you eaten? Would you like to have dinner? I have matters of import to discuss with you."

"How about coffee instead? I think I may have a dinner date."

"*May* have a date?" Clarence said, his eyebrows arched. "My good man, either you do or you do not. How can one think he might have a dinner companion?"

Jamison gathered up his books. "It's a complicated matter, Clarence. I'm not sure I could explain it quickly."

Clarence rocked back on his heels. "The only equation I know of that yields what you describe is the sum of one very interested partner and one who might not be quite so willing. And yet I am too much a gentleman, Mr. Pike, to inquire as to who the young lady is who has not exactly said yes to your charming yet cynical nature."

Jamison did his best to hide his emotions. "Clarence, there can be other sums to the equation, you know. You are in liberal arts, not mathematics."

"Yes, but I know my additions and subtractions, Mr. Pike. I may not be Kepler, but I am observant and a shrewd judge of human foibles. You know what I mean and know that I am correct."

The two walked along for another block.

"Not the Destiny!" Clarence exclaimed as they turned the corner. "I am so fatigued with that place. The food all tastes as if it had been prepared last year and only now did they get around to serving it. Does not this town offer any other meeting place? Or is it written in the student handbook that all have to suffer through the distress of the Destiny?"

The two wound up at a small booth at Modar's, a quaint store that offered coffees, drinks, sundries, fabrics, toys, books, and an often outlandish assortment of men's furnishings. Neither Jamison nor Clarence could ever recall any customer actually purchasing an item other than coffee and a pastry, but they assumed that the owners had a small but curious clientele in order to stay in business.

Clarence, with great deliberate strokes, poured four heaping teaspoons of sugar into his thick coffee. He slurped and added one more.

"So, you have been looking for me for days," Jamison ventured. "And what might your efforts be for?"

Clarence leaned back and sighed. "To teach you better diction, for one. Do you often end sentences with prepositions? But I must remind myself that you did receive your education in Pittsburgh. I must make allowances for that."

Jamison slurped his coffee even louder for comic effect. He would not have done so had there been any other customers in the store.

"That is noble of you," Jamison said between slurps. "Considering how elite and sophisticated Hopewell, New Jersey, is."

Clarence, born and bred in Hopewell, played at bristling from the implied insult. "Many good things come from New Jersey. And at least I seldom end sentences with the offending preposition. And our address is now New York City, as you well know."

Jamison knew that Clarence was indeed offended by his misuse of the language. He was that precise and methodical sort of fellow who relished the safety and protection of rules and regulations.

"But, Clarence, be reasonable. Language changes. People bend it and twist it to fit the needs of a modern culture. You impose strict rules on the usage and you wind up with . . . well, you wind up with Latin. Elegant and fixed and very, very dead."

Clarence clutched at his heart. "You cad! Next to Greek, there is no other language to compare to the preciseness of Latin."

Jamison dismissed his comments with a wave of his hand. "We are not here to discuss language, I am quite sure. Just what is it that you wanted to see me about?"

He smiled as Clarence winced again at the ending preposition.

"For one, I wish there was someone with as much talent as you— who might be more obsequious. I thoroughly dislike any fellow who is so skilled that even he is aware of his talents."

Jamison squinted at his friend. "I am lost. What is it that you are asking . . . of, or about?"

"Land sakes, man, I am talking about the *Crimson Review* of course."

Holding his palms open and out, Jamison replied, "You have me, friend. I am still lost."

"You know that they have made me editor, did you not? You knew that Stanley Whitcombe had taken ill and headed west, I heard, for a

spell in dry weather. Is California a place? Or was it some other deso-
late place out there? No matter. He's gone. That's the key element.
There was an opening, my boy, and the *Review*'s advisers met and
unanimously, or nearly so, selected me to replace him."

"They did? Congratulations. And no, no one has said a word to
me."

"Gads," Clarence snorted, "you lead such a provincial, insulated
life. Whom do you talk with on campus? No one who is in the least
literate, I am certain."

Clarence drained the last of his coffee and snapped his fingers
in the air, calling impatiently for a second cup.

"And now that you are editor, why are you deigning to speak
to me?" Jamison asked, an edge to his voice.

"I have a proposition for you," Clarence said, reaching for the
sugar bowl on the table next to theirs.

"And that is?" Jamison asked, suddenly serious.

"The *Review* is most often tripe. You know that and I know that.
Young callow men have nothing to say, no voice in which to say it,
and most often can write no better than a baboon with an unsharp-
ened pencil. You, my friend, are different."

"Better than a baboon? I am greatly flattered."

"As well you should be."

Clarence drained his second cup of sugared coffee and wiped his
face with the back of his hand.

"I have reread every issue of last year. Did you know that your
articles have appeared in virtually every issue for the past year? And
even this year, you already have done a dozen pieces—more than
any other student—save myself. The reason for my research is that
I intended to make a list of all those contributors whom I wish to
keep this next term. Unfortunately that list was very, very sparse.
My name was on it. Your name was on it. And the barest sprinkling
of others."

"Well, then . . . I suspect I am flattered again."

"And properly so. I don't want to waste your time on the standard fare—the insipid politics of this institution, the boring array of

pedestrian speakers that are paraded in front of the classes, all the usual humdrum of life at Harvard. Of course not. I want you to write a regular column . . . in which you describe the world as you see it. There will be no subject that is taboo. You may feel free to comment on any or all of what you see as interesting."

Jamison sat back in great surprise. No one but upperclassmen ever wrote an individual column such as this. "But . . ."

Clarence wiped his forehead with his sleeve. "You are interesting, Mr. Pike. You have a naturally critical eye. I want that. I want a unique voice. Say you will agree to this."

"One column a week? Every week?"

"Well, three a month if four is too many."

"Every week? Really?"

"Say yes."

Jamison hesitated only a moment. "Yes."

Clarence exhaled a great sigh of obvious relief. "Then you owe me your first column by tomorrow morning. Five hundred words. No sentences ending with prepositions."

Jamison laughed until he saw that Clarence was not smiling at all. "You are serious?"

"I am. Have it written and on my desk by noon."

Clarence stood and tossed a handful of small coins on the table. "And remember, this is the last cup of coffee that I pay for."

Clarence was halfway to the door when Jamison shouted after him: "That ended with a preposition!"

FROM THE JOURNAL OF JAMISON PIKE

THAT SAME DAY

A writer must write and that is what I will do, chronicling the stuff of my days here at Harvard. I do not expect great literary events to unfold, but the discipline of a daily journal will serve me well. It worked for Boswell and Johnson. I hope it works for me.

This night has not been the first that I was present for the closing of the Destiny. But it was the first time I enjoyed it as much as I did. To be concise, there were four of us at a lonely table at the Destiny when midnight passed the land—and nothing but a flickering candle or two lit our faces.

I shall present an intriguing mix of characters:

Gage Davis—of the New York Davis clan. Rich. Very rich. How many students attended Harvard with a personal valet in their employ? Gage is adroit with men, fancy with the women, and adept at nearly all he attempts. He is full of wit and charm, and there is not a fellow who, after only five minutes in his presence, doesn't consider him a lifelong friend. It is his gift, I suppose, his treasure, that he will slide through life with nary a worry, nary a concern, and take his place as a titan of industry. He is handsome and aware of his attractiveness. Women are smitten early and easily. And yet, as much as I envy him, I also dislike him—all for his very easy life. He will have no struggles. It is not fair that such men are so blessed and that others are not.

Joshua Quittner—of the poor Ohio Quittners. I have seen him about campus, but tonight was the first time I have spoken to him directly. For a poor farm boy, the lad is one handsome fellow with a strong jaw and hair the color of corn silk. He has a natural intensity that I am certain strikes women on a deep, visceral level. I watched as our serving girl stared at his face with great, nearly hidden, yearning. He is a quiet young man whose good looks belie his goal—and that is to be a preacher and carry on his family tradition of preaching to poor farmers in the backwater of southern Ohio. To be honest, even after our brief meeting, I think that such an assignment would be a squandering of his talents. I cannot imagine him being satisfied behind a small pulpit in a small village. I am not sure why I say that—but there is something in his manner that alludes to a restlessness.

Morgan Hannah Collins—of the once-wealthy Philadelphia Collinses. The rumor is that her father lost the fortune in a series of ill-advised investments. I am at a loss to ascertain why I am so intrigued—and attracted—to this woman. Hers is not the classic face of beauty—

there is an odd asymmetry to her features—yet all her imperfections add up to a stunning impact when first a man gazes at her face. It is her laugh and form and her wit—and all manner of smaller thrills that make such a sum. A woman on campus is rare enough, but such a handsome woman—with poise and brains and charm—is rarer still. At the end of a long evening, she admitted that she plans on pursuing a degree in medicine. She wants to become a doctor! If any woman might attempt that and be able to live up to that promise, it would be Miss Collins.

Yet while she sounded most adamant, I do not think she will achieve those goals. A woman has no business in attempting to be a doctor. Where will they try next—the pulpit? An intelligent man—or woman—must be a realist after all.

Jamison Pike—of the Pittsburgh Pikes. I am not certain of how to describe myself, for as I gaze into a mirror I see a man whom I often do not know well. I suspect that what Melinda once said about me being pleasant looking is true—although I seldom feel handsome. I have been instructed, from birth it seems, to be satisfied with whatever life presents. Now that I am no longer under my parents' roof, I find that notion harder and harder to take. There must be more to life than a small job in Pittsburgh. There is a world beyond the confluence of those three rivers. While I know I may disappoint my parents, I must explore and discover it on my own. Politicians and statesmen speak of the manifest destiny of our country. Does not a man have a manifest destiny of his own? Do I not owe it to myself to seek out that destiny?

I believe I do.

I am pledging now—not to God, who would not care—but to myself that I will commit our lives to paper. As a young child, I imagined writing a book, creating a world from wisps of paper and pen. These three characters—and myself—will provide grist—substance—to that dream. During this time of study and writing and all manner of literary activity, I shall take notes of our lives. I shall record events with impartiality. I shall report. I shall journal. For I am curious to know if we shall become the people we imagine ourselves to be . . . or will life be some haphazard occurrence? An accidental life instead of one that is lived intentionally?

At the end of this evening, when all four had talked for hours of their plans and hopes, Miss Collins stood up and brushed at her sleeves. She said that an honest woman should not be seen on the streets so late without proper escort. She claimed that the only proper escort of this evening was all three of her gentleman friends. Gage stood immediately and offered his arm to her. She smiled and took it. Then for her left arm, she actually reached down and took hold of Joshua's arm, encircling it with her own, and pulled him to his feet. He blushed a furious crimson as she held him close to her side. Jamison stood back and walked behind the trio, berating himself that he did not move more rapidly to take her free arm.

In the dark shank of that night, Jamison lit the lamp on his desk. He drew out a single sheet of paper. He gathered a quill and nicked it carefully with his penknife. He stared out at the dark and silent landscape that lay before him. The moon had robbed his sight of all color, save for the colors lit by his lamp. The trees, all but bare, clacked and groaned under the freshening winds. The night had turned cold, and a sharp breeze came upon the city from the north.

Jamison knew it was the harbinger of winter, that first nipping wind of November. He walked to the window, creaked it open, and leaned out. He let the chilled air wash over his face, taking great gulps of it into his lungs. After only a few moments, a chill tacked at his cheeks. He withdrew into the room and lowered the window to within a few inches of closed.

He stopped for a moment. Sniffing the air, he smiled.

It was the scent of sausages coming from the rooms next door.

And with that scent fresh in his nose, he sat down, dipped his pen in the inkwell, and began to scratch out the first column, written under his name alone, that would appear in Harvard's *Crimson Review.*

CHAPTER FOUR

Cambridge, Massachusetts
End of January 1843

Normally Jamison spent as little time in the library as possible. He did not like the thick, quiet dimness; the leaden air scented with paper and leather; the leaned, hushed conspiratorial conversations. It made him feel as if everyone sat about with books in laps, plotting to do some nefarious deed. Sitting in a room too quiet made Jamison feel like he was back in his father's study, being silently examined for some manner of youthful transgression.

Instead he sought out the vitality of noise and commotion. He would find the book required, carry it to the student union hall or to the Destiny. There he could read in peace amidst the noise and clatter.

But this one afternoon, as a winter chill swept across the campus, Jamison took refuge among the silent stacks. He could not find the tome he wanted and instead wandered about, tilting his head to the side, reading title after title. Perhaps, he thought, he might read this afternoon for simple pleasure. But he remained unsatisfied. Not one book spoke out to him as a book that might be interesting to read.

He carried his *Oration and Prose, Volume II* with him, thinking he might have to settle for its stuffy tone.

Just then, as he turned a corner, he spotted a glimpse of vibrant green—the color of a dense jungle, he thought. He stopped and ducked backward, remaining hidden.

From even that brief glance, Jamison knew who it was.

Hannah.

She was sitting alone in an out-of-the-way alcove on the second floor. Sunlight poured in through a tall window above her and she was bathed in gold—like a buttercup nestled in a wall of English ivy.

Jamison did not move. He simply stared at her from the narrow slit in the shelves of books. He was quite certain she could not see him.

Since that wonderful evening at the Destiny, his path had not crossed hers. He had seen her on occasion as she bundled about the campus in the cold but had not been within hailing distance. And he had not felt as if he could just run up to her and exchange pleasantries.

She would know it was all contrived, he told himself.

But today was different. They were in the same room, with no distractions and seemingly no other student within earshot.

I should go over and talk to her.

He nodded to himself but did not move.

But what would I say to her?

She looked up as if she had noticed or felt his eyes on her. Trying not to make a single sound, he stepped backward again, farther into the shadows.

Hannah pushed a strand of hair back from her face, and it fell in a ringlet on her neck. Jamison could not help but stare. She shrugged and returned to her reading.

I could ask her how her studies are going, he thought. Then he silently smacked his forehead in frustration. He shifted his books to his other hand. *I could ask her of her activities over the recent holidays.* But he shook his head. Everything felt forced—and the words fabricated and false.

Hannah lifted her head again and scanned about, staring hard in Jamison's direction. He was certain she could not see him.

She returned once again to her book.

He stared from the shadows.

Hannah looked up again, this time appearing most perturbed and anxious. Calling out in a loud voice, she asked whoever was there to identify himself.

Jamison's heart stopped, then leapt into his throat. His stomach tightened and his forehead began to sweat.

She called out again, demanding that the hidden party come forward. Jamison looked about, frantic for an escape route. But the only way off the floor and away from this section was past the place where Hannah sat.

"Come on, now," Hannah called out, her voice strict and tight. Finally, Jamison shuffled out, a most sheepish expression on his face.

"Jamison Pike! You were spying on me?"

FROM THE JOURNAL OF JAMISON PIKE

She had me by the throat. I now know how a rabbit feels as the jaws of the lynx slowly close about the jugular.

Hannah asked if I was spying.

I smiled and said that *spying* was such an ugly word. I claimed, in a calm and collected tone, that I was merely observing.

Where such an explanation came from I do not know—it was as if I were divinely inspired. What other reason would there be? Because as I spoke, I noticed that her features softened into a polite and welcoming smile.

I launched into a long dissertation about how what I was doing might be likened to watching a bird. I told her that she was, as a woman, a rare bird at Harvard and that she warranted further observation.

I marveled at my own aplomb. This witty banter came from me? I scarce believed it myself.

She asked me what was birdlike about her.

With a pounding heart, I said she was a most pleasing-looking species and "to also be so beautiful is a rare trait."

Those were my exact words. My thoughts raced, and my heart began to beat faster. I was being the sort of gentleman–like Gage–whom I so often envied from afar.

Then she pinned me to the wall with the most tantalizingly direct gaze I had ever felt. As her eyes found mine, I felt their impact in my heart. Its pounding echoed like a bell throughout my entire body.

I could think of no other words. Panic flew into my eyes. My throat became dry. I began to sweat even more.

I managed to croak out a few words about having a class to go to–which of course was a lie–but enabled me to scurry away like a frightened rodent. I do not think she laughed as I beat my hasty exit, but she could have.

What is it about her that so affects me?

And will I ever do more than feel like an idiot in her presence?

Women! Is there a way a mere man might understand them?

I have asked myself again and again what it is about Hannah that so flummoxes me as well as intoxicates. Is there a magic ingredient, a specific element that draws one particular man to one particular woman? Tentative couples must often ask this question–is this the woman (or man) I am destined to be with? Or are they merely a diversion, a teaching moment as it were, that I will stumble on and my heart will then learn what it truly seeks?

Gads–I have been reduced to stuff of romantic poets by this woman.

And while I have not known her for long, nor have I talked to her at great length, I still feel . . . overwhelmed by her.

She is pretty–although not classically beautiful.

She is smart–but not in an offensive way.

She is aware–and I think it is that quality, above all others, that stirs me. She is simply aware. Aware of everything, it appears–without being pretentious. She knows of current events. She knows of the campus gossip. She knows of things held private by men–like our false bravado, for one. No other woman I have met has seen through the male's bluster and thunder as she has—knowing we are as uncertain and as unsure as a young boy most of the time.

And yet, while she is aware of the truth, the reality of the world, she offers a sly and knowing smile that shows she knows your thoughts—and perhaps even sympathizes with you.

To be so aware is a rare gift.

There are more beautiful women out there, but I have not met any whose focus is as broad as hers, whose abilities are so great, whose empathy is so distilled.

Gads . . . speaking of romantic poets. If I go on further, I will be sullied by their effete reputation.

Suffice it all to say she has me enamored.

And yet . . . I am a realist.

Perhaps what I yearn for will never be. Time will tell of my destiny, I am sure.

February 1843

"Jamison!"

He spun about, searching for the source of his name. He was midway between the administration building and Crawford Hall, his hands clutching his lapels to fight off the icy chill.

"Over here!"

It was Gage, half out of the door of a carriage. The tasseled ends of his brilliant scarlet scarf fluttered like butterflies in the wind. "Come join me."

In a moment Jamison hoisted himself in and tossed a fur throw over his legs. The carriage started with a lurch, and Jamison grabbed at the cold leather of the seat.

"Should be legislation against weather this brutal," Gage said, cupping his hands about his mouth, blowing into them for warmth.

Jamison nodded.

They rode in silence for several minutes, their breath misting and icing in the frosty interior. As the carriage turned a corner, both men leaned to the opposite side.

Jamison scraped at the frost on the window, trying to peer out. "I suspect I should have asked before," he said.

"Asked what?" Gage replied.

"Asked as to your destination."

Gage laughed. "Does it really matter? I rescued you from the cold and from the frustration of your oratory class. That is where you were headed, was it not?"

Jamison nodded. "But perhaps this cold would have improved the professor's lecture. He would be forced to move about just to stay warm."

"Old Glory Petersen? Not likely. And his voice will be even further muffled by the mound of sweaters he loads on for a day like this."

"Then best that I was diverted," Jamison replied. "Yet, may I ask of our destination?"

Gage fluffed the collar of his coat about his cheeks. He offered a weary sigh, his breath a great resigned cloud of vapor. "I thought we might have lunch at the Boston Club. I think we will be able to snag one of the tables by that massive fireplace. Just thinking about it makes me a bit warmer."

Jamison had heard of the Boston Club, had passed its ornate brass doors gleaming in the sun, passed by the uniformed doorman. The name of the club was carved into the granite rock that made up the archway and portico—but ever so discreetly. Jamison had imagined the very scent of money as he'd walked past the open windows.

"The Boston Club," Jamison sniffed. "Well, I suppose. But I don't want to make this slumming a regular habit."

Gage's laugh was muffled by the fur about his face.

There was a hollow sound as the carriage rolled across the bridge over the Charles River. Jamison looked out at the flat ice. The wind snapped the snow into little drifts and whips.

"I hear you have been watching a bird," Gage said.

Jamison tried not to jump to attention, but he was certain that he did. "Watching a bird?"

"In the library of all places," Gage added. There was a curious twist to his voice—not malicious and not playful—but a jabbing tone.

Jamison stared at his friend, nearly hidden in a great swath of buffalo fur. "And you heard this from . . . ?"

Gage lightened his words. "Don't be so suspicious."

"Why? Were you there? It was only Hannah and I."

Gage pulled the fur from his face, swatting at it as if it were a swarm of insects. "No . . . and do not think ill of our Miss Collins. She tells a close friend in confidence—as friends do. Now the friend may tell another close friend in confidence—as friends do. The third party has no real allegiance to the secret and that third party delights in repeating this confidence to a person who finds such tales delicious. And then . . . here we are. Tales of watching a bird in a frozen carriage. Such a curious itinerary for such an amusing incident, don't you think?"

Jamison didn't know if he should be upset or hurt or amused. Amused seemed to be the best tactic, so he tried to laugh as authentically as he could. "Yes. I was watching a bird. And I thought I did perform quite well under pressure."

The carriage lurched up the narrow streets of the Back Bay.

"Pressure? From our Miss Collins?"

Jamison sighed. "Well, she is a very pretty woman."

"Miss Collins? Well, I suppose she is, in her own way."

The carriage jostled left and right as it clumped over the ruts in the cobblestone streets. Both men reached up to grab the leather straps.

"What do you really think of her, Gage?" Jamison asked. "I mean, aren't your families acquainted somehow? Don't you know her from before?"

"Acquainted? Well, yes, a little. The Collinses are old money and most of it is gone, I hear. And I may remind you that the Davises are new money—those two circles seldom intersect, I am afraid. We talk about each other—each one envying what the other has."

"Envy?"

"We envy the social standing. They envy the money. What goes about and all that." Gage scratched at the glass. "Almost there. A block or two away. Hannah will make a fine catch," he admitted. "But not for you."

Jamison was taken aback by Gage's flippant dismissal.

Gage added brightly, "Besides, Joshua is the one who is really in love with her. You are just infatuated. It will pass. I am willing to wager that a proper lunch with all the accoutrements will be just the thing to make you forget all about her. Lunch and a fire, that is."

And by the time Jamison had formulated his clever and reasoned reply, Gage was out of the carriage and nearly inside the massive brass door.

During the winter months, student life at Harvard often followed the patterns of nature. Many students emerged from their rooms or apartments only to scurry to class or to forage for food, as it were. Seldom did groups congregate—at least outside. Even the Destiny, a few blocks off campus, was less attended when the winds grew bitter. It was easier for most students to take their meals in the student union—easier, but not more palatable, to be sure.

Jamison hesitated at the open doors of the student union. A waft of smells rushed past him, and all that came to mind was the color brown. Brown bread, brown food, brown gravy, brown coffee. He stood as students milled about, jostling him politely as his indecision hindered their progress.

He shook his head and turned away from the swell. As he did, he collided with Joshua Quittner, wearing a coat that had obviously once belonged to Gage Davis. It was well tailored, smart, and obviously not a product of southern Ohio.

"Joshua," Jamison said in a manner more friendly than usual, "I do not think I can dine here today. Would you care to accompany me to the Destiny?"

Joshua shuffled his feet. "But I'm cold. . . . The Destiny is blocks away, and I am here now."

"I am not fond of dining alone," Jamison said, hoping he could convince Joshua. It was obvious that he had not, so he added, "And let this meal be my treat."

Brightening, Joshua spun on his heels. "Let's go. The only reason I eat here is because it costs less."

Jamison broke into a run following Joshua's hurried footsteps.

The windows of the Destiny were coated with steam and frost, small rivulets of moisture coursing down, creating a chilled, wet spider's web. The place was nearly deserted. They selected the table farthest from the door and closest to the kitchen, hoping it would be warmer.

When they sat, Joshua bent down and unlaced his boots and drew them off his feet. "I know. I know," he said in defense, "a man should not be taking his attire off at the table. But these boots leak. Perhaps by the time I return home, my socks will be dry."

Jamison tried not to be obvious as he scanned Joshua's worn boots and socks, darned a dozen times, and most certainly uncomfortable. Jamison had thought of himself as a poor student until he compared himself to Joshua.

Joshua's pride did not stand in his way of his dinner order—soup, stew, cheese, bread, two pieces of pie, and a large pot of coffee. They spoke little as they ate, enjoying the crisper and cleaner taste of their meals—at least as compared with those the college provided.

"Well," sighed Joshua as he leaned back for the first time during the whole meal, "that was a most agreeable diversion. Again, friend, I thank you for your largesse. I did not expect such a gift—and I daresay that I should not have imposed on you in such a manner."

Jamison smiled as he reached for the coffee. "A tad late to tell me now that you shouldn't have eaten. The damage is done, and I do not think it retrievable."

"I have heard a few preachers say that it's most polite—and profitable—to turn down a gift with your hand already upon it. Makes it embarrassing for the offer to be withdrawn. I don't think I'm that type of preacher though," Joshua said as he sipped his coffee.

"I don't think you are either," Jamison agreed. "And yes, I know some men of the cloth who are. Their mouths say no while their appetites say yes."

Joshua placed his feet up on the empty chair between them. He fussed with his socks for a moment, adjusting the bunched-up places where they had been mended. "Almost dry," he said softly. He looked up at Jamison. "Your father is a preacher, isn't he?"

Jamison nodded. "Presbyterian."

Joshua nodded back, his eyes indicating he knew more of Jamison's life than Jamison had ever shared prior.

Jamison watched as Joshua turned his coffee cup with the handle pointing away from him. He did this every time he was about to ask a question. Jamison was certain it was unintentional.

"You're not in seminary."

Jamison nodded in quiet agreement.

"Why?"

Jamison offered no more than a shrug. He had explained it a thousand times to himself and was tired of the vocabulary of regret.

"I couldn't have done that," Joshua said. "Not to follow my father's footsteps would have caused him so much pain."

Jamison shrugged again and felt a surprising surge of anger in his heart.

Why do I need to explain this to him?

Joshua turned his mug about and now the handle faced him. "You still go to church, don't you?"

Jamison nodded, feeling the desire to talk all but gone.

"And you still believe in God, don't you? You haven't listened to those at Brook Farm, have you?"

"No, I haven't. I think there is a God. It is church that I find so disconcerting." Jamison answered the second question with dispatch and ignored the first.

Joshua laced his hands over his stomach. Jamison expected his eyelids to flutter shut, but they didn't.

Joshua tilted his head back, as if he were remembering some incident from long ago. "I know how it feels . . . growing up the son of a preacher. I feel that I have paid my dues and no further work is needed." He leaned forward, the chair groaning and creaking. "But that isn't enough; you know that, Jamison, don't you? A pedigree is not enough."

I didn't buy you lunch for a sermon, Jamison thought, not allowing his anger to show. "I know," he finally said. "And I know what you mean about having paid dues. I feel like I have heard all there is to say about God. Takes the challenge out of church."

Joshua laughed in reply. "Then you should find a better church," he said. "Church, like life, should always be a challenge. It keeps things interesting."

"Mr. Pike, as I live and breathe."

Jamison jumped at the words. On his knees, pawing through a stack of newspapers left on the floor of the student union, he clearly did not expect to be greeted. As he turned about, he lost his balance and fell to his side, the papers shushing and hissing underneath him.

He looked up, into the light of the afternoon sun, shielding his eyes with an outstretched palm. "Miss Collins?"

Her throaty laugh filled the air.

"Do you always grovel so?" she asked as she extended her hand to him and helped him to stand. "A gentleman of your standing should not stoop so low."

He brushed at his knees. "I was looking for a clean copy of the paper."

She merely arched her eyebrows and he felt compelled to explain.

"I save them. I mean, not all of them. The ones in which my column appears. And I don't have the current edition. I mean, I had it and . . ."

She held her hand out near his face and extended a finger to almost touch his lips, bidding him stop. "I understand. Souvenirs. I save things, too. Helps one remember what was once important, don't you think?"

He nodded, hoping she was not making light of his actions.

"Speaking of newspapers," Hannah said, "are you planning to cover Miss Lucretia Mott's appearance at Harvard?"

"Miss Mott? I don't think I have heard of her," he said with a note of anxiety, not wanting to disappoint Hannah.

Hannah placed her hand on his forearm and he fell silent. "It's all right. She is one of those 'women' who go about rabble-rousing and threatening all sorts of mischief for the sake of women's rights. A gentleman might never have heard of her. And I forgive you for that."

He gulped and wondered why he always felt so off balance in Hannah's company, as if a false word or action might cause her to turn away in anger.

"I have not heard. But if you say her message has import, then by all means, I will attend."

She extended her hand to him. He stared at it as if it were some odd creature until he finally realized she was extending it to shake his hand in farewell. He did so but felt as if he lunged at her in a most clumsy manner. His hand grazed the lace wrapped about her delicate wrist.

"I will drop you a note with details," she said. "I do so hope you find her story interesting enough to include in the paper."

"If you say it is, I am sure I will as well."

"Do not fawn, Mr. Pike," she said with sweetness. "Just say you will cover her appearance at Harvard as a journalist."

As she turned and walked away, he hoped she did not see his cheeks redden from embarrassment.

All during class, Jamison fidgeted and squirmed. Not that the class was boring—far from it. Not all classes kept his attention, but this class on the plays of Shakespeare taught by an English fellow, not much older than Jamison, was lively and filled with a great deal of Socratic give-and-take. That Jamison liked, rather than the long, tedious lectures that many of the older professors employed.

But on this day, Jamison could not concentrate. The class discussion swirled about him.

"So the motivation of Lady Macbeth was . . . ? Why did she push her husband to kill as he did?"

Students' hands shot up.

"To be rich."

"So she could be the queen."

The professor, Ian Maclaret, nodded and paced about the platform, pointing to one student, then another. "And why did her husband listen to her?"

"He had no other plan. Hers seemed logical at the time."

Another student spoke up. "Even though this was written hundreds of years ago, Shakespeare is remarkably current."

Professor Maclaret stopped his pacing and propped himself against his desk. "And why is that, Mr. Lucas?"

Phillip Lucas, a short, phlegmatic student from upper New York State, stood up. "Lady Macbeth wanted power, pure and simple. She wanted power that, by rights, only men had held. She knew her husband was a weak man and that she could lead him to do almost anything. So she did. And once she had what she wanted, all manner of terrible things began to happen. She saw that power is not a panacea nor does it provide comfort. It can be evil and corruptive. She goes mad as a result."

"And as to your point that this play is a comment on contemporary society. . . how do you draw a connection?"

Lucas stepped forward and gestured to the class. "Well, all of you know that women are meeting and attempting to gain the power to vote and run for public office. You have read in the *Review* the events they are planning. Even the columnists are in an outcry about it. I have heard that these women are seeking a redress of all manner of gender inequality. I am afraid that they will seek to run the family home and hearth wearing trousers, quite possibly! They are like Lady Macbeth— they may get what they seek, but the power will drive them mad."

"It already has," called out a student from the back of the room. The rest of the students erupted in laughter.

Professor Maclaret laughed with them, then held up his hands for quiet. "Perhaps so, but that is another class altogether–I mean women as another class."

"And another species," called out a student, the class nearly drowning out the sound of the bell by another wave of laughter and catcalls.

Jamison laughed with them but could not shake the uncomfortable feeling that dogged him the entire hour. He stood, shared comments with a few friends, and began to gather up his books. He looked over his shoulder again, feeling as if there were a hidden presence glaring at the back of his head. And when he looked he saw the flash of blonde hair and the unmistakable profile.

It was Hannah.

Jamison gulped and slowly made his way up the steps and to the door. Ten or so students milled about by the entrance. Jamison imagined that they might have lingered on purpose. As he grew closer, he could see a fire in Hannah's eyes.

He knew what was about to happen.

He had written on just such a subject in this week's column. It was an interview of sorts with Mildred Oswalt, an assistant to Lucretia Mott. Jamison had judged his reporting to be fair and unsullied by his gender–until Clarence read it. As he read, he guffawed loudly in places and smiled during the entire time.

"What was funny?" Jamison had asked. "I thought the piece was fair. I made no attempts at comedy–just reporting on Miss Mott's and Miss Oswalt's plans."

Clarence had removed his tiny spectacles and wiped his eyes. "No, that was fine, Pike. But your descriptions–they were priceless–as always."

"Descriptions?"

"'Miss Oswalt, wearing a frock that came only a step away from being cruel . . .'"

"That was funny?"

"Hysterical," Clarence had said, then added, "and this one . . . 'Miss Oswalt appears to have the patience of a hungry bulldog with a biscuit on its nose–and the same temperament as well.'"

"But that is just a turn of words. I meant no disrespect, Clarence."

Clarence had waved him off with another laugh.

And now Jamison met a very stone-faced Hannah. He forced himself to look down. In her fist was a tightly crumpled copy of the current *Crimson Review*.

Jamison nodded. "Hannah," he said softly.

Hannah did not speak but glared at him harder.

Jamison suddenly became more aware of the small but hushed crowd surrounding them. He knew he could not back down from his words. He knew he could not play Macbeth to her Lady Macbeth. Even though he did not want this battle–especially with Hannah–he knew he would be forced to defend what he had written.

Hannah took a step forward. Although Jamison knew she was very, very angry, she had never looked more beautiful to him.

"The temperament of a bulldog?"

"A clever turn of words, Hannah."

"A cruel frock? You described Miss Mott's dress as a cruel frock."

"You met her, Hannah," Jamison replied, attempting to defend himself. "If you do not admit her apparel was hideous, then you are fabricating a new reality."

Her eyes narrowed. "Oh, I see. When a man speaks to us in a stained and threadbare suit, you call him colorful and eccentric. But when a woman does exactly the same thing, you call it ugly. That is not right, Jamison."

"I write as I see, Hannah. You wish me to do otherwise?"

Jamison knew Hannah had little room to argue. She had met Miss Oswalt and had been put off by her appearance as well. She had said as much to Jamison after the meeting. In fact, Jamison had used Hannah's own words–"a cruel frock"–without attribution.

"You could have been kinder," Hannah hissed.

Jamison wanted to ask forgiveness but could not with the audience. "And I could have quoted others. I did not. If I did, I daresay you would not be here–angry with me."

It was evident Hannah knew what he meant.

Her lips tightened and her jaw worked so hard that the muscles twitched. Finally she let out a gruff exhalation, threw the paper to the ground, and stormed toward the entrance of the building. She turned back to them and called out to Jamison's fellow students, none of whom had moved an inch during their confrontation, "Aren't you all so happy that none of you will have to marry a woman? That you men are so above us? Since we are such inferior creatures, that is."

And with that she banged open the door and hurried away.

Jamison knew he could not follow, but he prayed the hurt was only temporary. When he turned back, the rest of the students looked at him with a mixture of surprise, anger, and admiration— not sure which of the three emotions might be best expressed.

They were surprised Hannah had stood up to Jamison. They were angry for being tarred with the same brush used on Jamison. And yet they admired Jamison for his courage in taking such a stand—especially with an attractive, unusual woman.

Jamison waited until they all had left, then reached down and retrieved the crumpled paper. He carefully smoothed out the pages and slipped it inside the pages of his leather journal.

Jamison stood on the porch of Hannah's aunt and uncle's house, where she was residing while taking classes at Harvard. He did not realize just how nervous he was until the time came for him to actually reach for the door. He watched, as if his hand were a separate species, and his fingers trembled and fluttered inches away.

Jamison assumed that Hannah could not afford private lodging on campus and was forced to live with relatives. Their home must have once been elegant, but the years had not been kind. Paint that might initially have been a canary yellow had faded to a ghostly tint. Bushes grew wild and untamed about the porch, not having seen a clipper for years.

He swallowed once more, closed his eyes, and knocked politely on the wooden door frame. A chip of paint came off against his knuckles.

He strained to hear any movement.

And he waited. A sheer lace curtain on the glass door prevented him from seeing inside the house.

He rapped on the door again.

There was a rustle of uncertain footsteps, and a small triangle of lace curtain was pulled to the side. Jamison saw an eye blink once and then withdraw. He heard the solid sound of the tumbler of the lock being turned.

The door opened a few inches.

"Yes?" The voice sounded scared.

"Is Hannah Collins available?" Jamison was not certain if the person lurking behind the door was Hannah's aunt or a servant.

"Who is calling?"

"Jamison Pike. I am a friend of Miss Collins. From Harvard. Are you Mrs. Granger?"

The door snicked shut and Jamison stood befuddled. Was Hannah there? Was she being told of her guest?

He waited another long minute until the door swung open completely. Hannah stood in the dim interior. "Yes?"

"Hannah . . . ," he said, feeling his neck grow prickly and beads of sweat form on his forehead.

"Yes?"

"Hannah . . . I wanted to apologize."

From behind Hannah, there came a furtive hushing, then Hannah turned and nodded. "Please, come in," she said and stepped back from the door.

She led the way into a sparsely furnished parlor. A lantern flickered on a table. The room, laced heavily with lavender, felt as if it were a stranger to bright light. Jamison sat at one edge of an uncomfortable sofa. Hannah took a seat in a high-backed wooden chair.

"Hannah, since you came to my class . . . I really did not intend on the article causing such discord. We are friends, are we not?"

He watched her face for any hint of softness, then glanced at his feet. Noticing the frayed edge of the rug, he slid his foot to cover it.

"We are friends," she said. "At least I thought we were."

"We are," Jamison said softly. "But we are both at fault."

Hannah rocked back in her chair. "Me? I'm at fault?"

From the corner of his eye, he saw a slip of brown hasten past the door. It must have been Mrs. Granger. Jamison knew he was being observed. "Yes," he said firmly. "You said the words *cruel frock*. I merely repeated them. And I did not mention your name."

He stared and kept his hands folded in his lap.

After a moment, he saw the edges of her mouth quiver and turn. She brought her hand up to her mouth, as if hoping to stop her giggle. She was not successful.

Then, in the quietest of voices, she said, "It was cruel, wasn't it?"

And with that, Jamison's heart started again, and he basked in the light of her smile, brilliant in the darkness of the room.

FROM THE JOURNAL OF JAMISON PIKE

Following is a brief accounting of the last few months' highlights:

JANUARY 1843

For the *Crimson Review* I have interviewed William McNaught, who is attempting some advance to the steam engine. I did not comprehend the engineering, and the fellow was a shambling, disorganized inventor, but he provided a most colorful interview.

Gage and I toured Boston once again—on his resources and at his insistence. I never knew that many late-night establishments existed. Without a person like Gage, I would never have the wherewithal to gain entry to this rarified world.

FEBRUARY 1843

For the *Review* I spoke with John Roebling, who is *planning* to span Niagara Falls with a wire bridge. Some men dream large dreams. I could not imagine the bravery—or foolishness—it might take to be the first man across such a roaring deluge.

Debated with Gage long into the night the virtue of staying either here or New York—or heading west to discover the riches of the new land. Gage claimed he would never leave New York. I said I might. Gage said there is no sure money out west—but there is in New York.

MARCH 1843

Interviewed Samuel Morse, who is working on some manner of electrical communication through wires. Mentioned this invention to Gage, who said he knew all about the scheme. Has he invested money? I should follow his lead but never seem to have more than a dollar or two to spare at the end of any month.

Weather has been miserable. Rain, sleet, snow, gray—with a bone-chilling edge to it. No one ventures out unless forced to. Classes are often half full. Even the Destiny has empty tables at all hours.

Was contacted by an editor at the *Boston Globe* asking if I might write freelance for them. I agreed, but only as my time allows. Being paid for my words—I am a most fortunate fellow.

APRIL 1843

A real coup for the *Review* . . . Using Gage's contacts, I managed to meet Charles Dickens, the English novelist of some note. He is almost famous here. But in England, they tell me he is all the rage. I have read some serializations of his work but do not care for his style—too emotional. His stories are brimming with pathos that panders to the reader. Even hired a fellow with a bellows contraption to take a photograph of him.

MAY 1843

I met a most interesting fellow this month, a chief of a tribe called the Cherokees. He was wearing a modern suit yet had a full head-dress of eagle feathers and beads. And he was barefoot. A rugged-looking interpreter, in buckskin and boots, helped with the language. Some promoter was selling tickets for an evening with this Indian man and filled every hall, every night. It gives me pause to truly head west someday. Indians! The very thought quickens the blood, does it not?

JUNE 1843

Summer in Pittsburgh—working for my father again—scribing and posting. Besides the work, there is nothing occurring in this town that is worth noting. This house is the quietest dwelling I have ever entered. At night, it is like a tomb.

JULY 1843

Have never imagined that a single month could last this long.

AUGUST 1843

Father and Mother journeyed for two weeks north to Lake Erie for a short sabbatical, leaving me alone in the house. It was a delicious freedom. I ate dinner after dark and had coffee all throughout the day. They would see such behavior as scandalous.

Got together with a few old friends from my childhood. Most seemed astounded that I have ventured to the East. Most have no idea of the larger world around them, and one said he would never have business that took him across the river. Such a small environment.

Renewed acquaintance with Neta Hill, a young woman who attended secondary school with me. She is petite and has very dark hair, which she parts in the middle and wears tied with a bow. Her smile is easy, and she found my school exploits amusing. She promised to write, as did I. Our time together was a most pleasing interlude during an otherwise horrific summer. I did not remember her as being quite so attractive. Of course, she is not Hannah, but most cheerful and amenable. I am sure she sees me as quite the catch—for in Pittsburgh, I am quite the sophisticated bon vivant. And it is pleasant to be so considered.

SEPTEMBER 1843

Back at the *Review* and at Harvard. Classes are much the same—the required ones are stultifyingly boring. I spend more time at the

Review now and find I am receiving a better education from those experiences than in class.

I have met a small group of men and women who are about to set off for a new settlement in Oregon–that is a territory on the Pacific Coast near Canada. I sense their great fervor and wish I could go with them.

Received a very nice letter from Neta, signed "With affection." Does she truly mean that? And why would she find a man like me attractive?

OCTOBER 1843

Lunch with Hannah. Happened by chance at the Destiny. We spoke of schoolwork and campus gossip. She was most distracted. Mentioned a fellow by the name of Robert Keyes and asked if I had ever heard of him–in business circles. I said no but will make an attempt to find out now. It sounded to me as if this fellow has taken to asking her out, which is not a pleasant consideration.

Interviewed the fellow–a self-trained physician–who has developed a new gas to render patients unconscious so that operations can be performed without pain. Unlike other inventors and schemers I have met, this fellow was quite precise and fastidious. Demonstrated on another student–an underclassman, of course. Actually cut into his skin–removed a small growth–with no pain or screaming. The patient slept as if a baby. Fascinating.

Cambridge, Massachusetts
November 1843

"I do not believe how warm Novembers are here. In Pittsburgh, we would be wading through snow at this time."

Clarence rolled his eyes. "If I hear another word about Pittsburgh, I shall dismiss you from the staff. That is all you have spoken about since you received that letter from . . . from whom?"

"Neta," Jamison replied.

"Neta." Clarence harrumphed. "I can't for the life of me understand why parents go to such great lengths to give their offspring such cumbersome appellations."

Jamison and Clarence were seated on a bench outside Harvard's administration hall. Clarence had called for a meeting and Jamison had insisted on being outside.

"And I suppose she wrote that it is snowing back home? And that there are snowdrifts blocking her doorway? And that there are wolves skulking about devouring those in the storm?"

"Yes, she said all that, Clarence, and then she inquired as to how I stand working with such a pompous young fool as yourself. I told her all about you, you know."

"How deft," Clarence replied with a smirk. "And now may I go back into my office? I have passed on your assignments."

"If you wish. Go back into your tiny office. But how often do you get such wonderfully warm days? It is November, after all. The cruelest month."

"I think the cruelest month is April. And today may be warm, but there are leftover insects from summer flitting about. Insects I do not like."

Jamison gathered his books and papers and slipped them into his well-worn leather case. "Then go back inside, into the stuffy air of your office. I am going to enjoy this day. Soon enough we'll be trapped by the desperate cloud of gray that happens every winter."

"For a writer with cynicism to spare, you are most chipper today," Clarence huffed. "I must say I don't like it much. You should remain true to form. You upset people when you appear . . . normal."

Jamison laughed again. "Even a cynic has his good days, Clarence. They may be few and far between—and this is one of them. It is a time of adventure. A golden day indeed. Do not dampen it with your innate and nearly overwhelming pessimism."

With that Clarence huffed again, swatted at a bug flying by, and then hulked back toward the *Review* offices, located on the third floor of the administration building.

Jamison turned around and nearly collided with Hannah Collins. Hoping he might not blush, he stammered a greeting. "I had no . . . I mean . . . I did not expect you . . . that is to say . . . how are you . . . Hannah?"

She tilted her head just so. There was a hint of music in her voice. "Well, I must say, overhearing your words to your friend, I have been emboldened. This is a beautiful day. More precious than gold, correct?"

He nodded, unable to respond.

"Then by all means, we should take advantage of it, should we not?"

He nodded again, mute.

It was as if she knew, sometimes, of the power she had over men. She did not smile, but in her eyes Jamison could see the words, hear her voice: *I understand.*

And then she did something that totally surprised Jamison. He would think of these few moments for years to come.

She placed her gloved hand on his forearm and gave it the slightest squeeze. She leaned in close to him and whispered in his ear, "If this is a rare day, then we should do something just as rare. Let us . . . let us abandon our classes for today and do something . . . do something wicked."

Jamison had all he could do to keep from fainting.

FROM THE JOURNAL OF JAMISON PIKE
THAT SAME DAY

She kept her hand on my arm for another moment, then took my hand in hers and began to pull me along—me looking like a lost puppy, I am sure. How dainty her hand felt in mine—yet how possessed of power it was.

We rushed (she rushed and I followed) down the walk, past the administration, past Wendell Hall, past the Keating Science Facility, and on toward the buildings that housed the seminary classes.

"We must rescue Joshua!" she exclaimed. "He needs liberation as well."

I suppose it was destined to be this way—her adding Joshua to the mix, as if not content to be with me alone. Why would I think she had some plans for an afternoon with only me?

We located Joshua's class, and I will not endeavor to describe all that went on, save when the commotion was over, I had tumbled to the ground when Hannah stepped backward to escape the swinging door from which Joshua had exited. We bantered back and forth in a most familiar manner. She called me a prevaricator and I accused her, in jest of course, of being the mastermind of this day's activities. She laughed and I grabbed at her foot, and my hand found purchase on Hannah's ankle.

And to make this even more convoluted, Professor Wilcox looked on with both bemusement—and I think great surprise. I am certain he could not have thought Joshua capable of being involved in such a display.

To make a long story shorter, we all three tumbled out of the building and rushed along and did not stop until we found ourselves on the banks of the Charles River, with pretzels slathered with rich mustard, sitting in the grass, watching the muddy water, talking of our future.

Joshua made certain of his plans for the ministry—and chastised both Hannah and me for our lack of certainty. He spoke of some manner of personal involvement with God. I find that emotional approach to faith to be unbecoming and would have said so had Hannah not been in our company.

Mark my words, Joshua will not cleave to such a dogmatic faith forever. There will come a time when he will stumble. All men of such high and uncompromising principles are destined to lose their grip at some hardship or temptation.

There is truth in the world, and man finds that truth by examining his own soul. It does not descend like gentle rain from heaven. Truth is how we see and describe the world. Perhaps God is there, but he leaves us alone to work out our lives.

And near the end of this golden afternoon, a carriage pulled up
at the small park. We heard our names called. There is no one else we
know who can afford the luxury of hiring a private carriage and driver.
It was Gage, of course. He alighted from the cabin and in a most animated manner, invited us all to be his guests in New York City for a
week of thanksgiving—as the president has called the country to do.

A week in New York!

With Hannah!

How much more perfect can one day become?

New York City
Thanksgiving 1843

The coach was dark, lined with a rich thickness of leather, and
perfumed with the scent of recent cleaning and roses. Joshua and
Gage sat facing backward. Jamison and Hannah sat in the rear
seat, facing forward. For five days the quartet had scoured the city,
heading from glittering cultural events to the depth of the Bowery
and raucous taverns populated by sailors and street merchants and
all manner of what were thought to be the unsavory elements of
society.

The carriage rocked softly, protected by large metal springs.
Gage only hired carriages so outfitted. "If you ride in one of the old-
fashioned hacks, your backside will protest for hours," he insisted.

The dark felt like velvet to Jamison, and the gaslights flickering at
the street corners looked like diamonds, then stars in the heavens.
This night they had been at a small restaurant that specialized in
French food. Jamison had never tasted such delicate and intricate
flavors. Each sauce and gravy seemed to possess a specific magic.

"Joshua is struck unconscious by the richness, I am afraid," Jamison
said as he nodded to Gage. Joshua had closed his eyes early in the
ride and now slumped against the back of the seat, his head lolling
about.

Gage smiled, reached over, and nudged him so that he fell into the corner, his head coming to rest against the back cushion. "Let the innocent sleep," he said, then nodded to Jamison.

Hannah's eyes were shut and at one rut in the road, she was jostled toward Jamison. She slipped against his side with her head on his shoulder. He lifted his arm just so and she nestled like a kitten against him. He could not think of ever taking a more perfect carriage ride—even if the destination might be paradise.

"We have lost another one."

Gage seemed to know every person at both the top and the bottom of service, and they all treated the young man with friendly deference. Jamison noted that he seldom entered any establishment without palming a coin or a bill into a half dozen hands—waiters, maître d's, serving girls, owners, singers, musicians, and conductors—anyone who might possibly make the evening more glittering.

And the evenings were a kaleidoscope of sensations.

Jamison loved every moment of every day and of every night. Yet as much as his soul and heart were thrilled with what he saw and heard and did, it would have been hard to determine his evaluation. He maintained a calm exterior, reacting only at the most extreme circumstances.

Gage proved the perfect host, varying their itinerary so greatly that no one had any idea of what might be planned next.

One morning Hannah sat at the massive mahogany table facing her breakfast of currant scones and hot tea. Gage came into the room, swirling about, filled with bubbling excitement.

She looked up and sighed. "Do I have to change my attire again?" she protested. "At every event this week I have felt either over- or underdressed. Please, Gage, you must take pity on us. Today tell us beforehand where we will be spirited off to."

Both Jamison and Joshua looked up, surprised.

"Do you mean there are people that actually alter their attire depending on the event?" Jamison asked.

"And there are people who have more than one suit of clothing to change into?" Joshua added, his eyes wide and doelike.

"And you mean to tell me there are people who are so vain that they truly think that other people care what attire they are wearing?" Gage added. "Joshua, isn't that unbiblical, somewhere?"

"I think it is," he replied.

"And if it is not, it should be," Jamison said.

The trio of grins surrounded Hannah as she hid her face in her hands and pretended to wail in reply.

Jamison slouched just so in a huge leather chair in the vast Davis library. The sun was lost behind the buildings to the west, and Jamison wrestled the chair closer to the window to catch what light he could.

He settled back down, and rather than open the book in his lap, he simply stared out the window. He, like Hannah and Joshua, was overwhelmed at Gage's wealth. They all knew he was of means. But his massive home with its seemingly hundreds of rooms, each dripping with opulence, made each of them, Jamison was certain, regard Gage in a different manner.

The latch clicked, and the door, nearly two stories tall, edged open.

"Hello?"

It was Hannah.

"In here. I think Joshua and Gage are still at the cathedral."

Hannah swept in, wearing the new frock she had purchased that day. It was the palest blue in color and of a thick material that almost shimmered. It was as if Hannah were illuminated from within. Since the dress flowed down to the floor and trailed slightly at the back, she appeared to glide across the vast expanse of the room. Her delicate ankle boots made a soft sound on the thick Turkish rug.

"But Joshua is not Catholic. Why would they be at a Catholic cathedral?"

"Gage said something about its being a replica of St. Peter's in Rome. Hearing that, Joshua could not be stayed a moment more."

"But he's not Catholic," she stated again.

"Does one need to be Catholic to appreciate fine architecture?"

Hannah slipped past a chair and trailed her arm over the top, her fingers all but dancing along the gleaming brass studs. "I suppose not. But I thought a preacher took a vow not to do that."

"What? Not to see what the competition is doing?"

Hannah stiffened, then laughed. "I suppose he can visit."

Jamison straightened up, and without thinking, adjusted his straps and collar. "That's gracious of you, Hannah."

She faced the open window near Jamison. After a minute of silence, she sighed loudly. "Do you like all this?"

"All what? New York? This house? The air?"

She glared at him the way a sister glares at a pesky brother. "All this wealth, you tease."

Jamison looked around as if seeing for the first time. "Oh . . . this? Well, I admit that it is a lot smaller than my home in Pittsburgh, but I suspect that in time one learns how to adjust to living in a tattered hovel such as this."

Hannah placed her hands on her hips. "You men are just impossible. The odd thing is that I do not know why I am so shocked. None of you ever rise above the level of a child."

"It is because," he said as he stood and walked to the fire, "you are such a pleasure to tease. You respond in just the right manner of outrage. If you would ignore us, we would simply disappear."

She laughed. "You are right, of course. I suspect I like the banter as much as you do."

The fire hissed and popped.

"And no," Jamison replied, "this does not bother me."

"What?"

"All this."

"Gage's wealth?"

"I'm a little jealous. Maybe a lot jealous. But they came on it through hard work."

"Gage? Hard work? He is clever, perhaps. But he does not work hard."

"Being clever is hard work. It is," Jamison insisted.

Hannah slowly circled the room. Jamison followed her with his eyes, watching her closely.

"Will you take the position?"

"Position?"

"On the *Post*. Or the *World*. Or the *News*. Which is it? Gage's newspaper. The one he spoke of at lunch. The newspaper where the editor practically fawned over you—though I am certain I do not see why he did so."

"Talent. He recognized sheer talent."

Hannah dismissed him with a wave. "So which is it?"

"The *World*."

"Will you take it?"

"Maybe. Perhaps. I don't know for sure."

Hannah turned to him. "You'll take it. You'll take it and become famous as a writer. You have a way of seeing the world that I like."

"You like it?"

"I do."

"And you're sure that the world will like it?"

"I am sure."

She leaned closer to the window, and Jamison saw her reflection in the glass. It looked like a painting, ready to be hung in a gallery. There was a translucent quality to both Hannah and her reflection.

"I see their carriage. Gage and Joshua's."

Jamison held his smile. He had hoped the two would never return. But that would be in a perfect world.

And New York did not exist in a perfect world.

Cambridge, Massachusetts
December 1, 1843

Joshua slowed his walk, as if matching the more careful strides of Jamison. The weather, as Jamison predicted, had turned harsh. A cold wind swept down from Canada, bringing freezing rain that coated Cambridge with a glittering layer of ice. Dozens had fallen and dozens more were trying to skate across sidewalks and streets, laughing and braying at their clumsy antics.

Joshua appeared at home with the slick surface. Jamison was not, holding his hands out like a man on a tightrope, balancing high in the air.

When they came to a corner, Jamison stopped and grabbed the pole of a gaslight. "This is the first time I've felt secure since leaving the house," he quipped.

Joshua smiled. "To be honest, I feel this way all the time."

"On ice?"

"I mean that in a spiritual sense. I feel like I am always about to tumble, have my feet splay out beneath me."

"You?" Jamison said, surprised. "You have cleats on your shoes. And cleats on your soul as well. How could you tumble?"

Joshua shrugged.

Jamison was not accustomed to this manner of intimacy. Yet since returning home from New York, all four had felt a closer bond, a certain kinship that comes from time spent together.

"I could. Being in New York felt for the world like I was dancing at the edge of sin every moment."

Jamison tilted his head. "Truly?"

"Truly. Did you not feel that New York was an evil place?"

Jamison shook his head. "If anything, I felt I did not dance close enough to its soul—like I was too far from the center."

Joshua crept toward the curb, placing his feet just so on the ice. Jamison followed and, in an instant, grabbed at Joshua's sleeve as his feet took off in two directions. In the next second both Joshua and Jamison were at the curb and in the frozen gutter, arms and legs akimbo, laughing and wincing at their fall at the same time.

CHAPTER FIVE

Cambridge, Massachusetts
January 1844

The Destiny closed at half past eleven. Jamison had
listened for the eleven o'clock bells and hurried when they rolled
across the empty campus. For the past three hours, Jamison and
Clarence had argued and fumed over what would be included in the
next issue of the *Review*. It had become a routine. Rather than spend
the hours ensconced away in the newspaper offices, they brought
galleys and notes and spread them across a table near the kitchen.
And now they were finished. Neither of them was completely satisfied with the results—but such was the nature of the newspaper business.

They gathered up their papers and slipped out into the night. The
air was cold, yet not numbingly cold. Bundled up in heavy benjamin
coats with wool scarves and gloves, the two students huddled along
in the silence.

As they crossed the wide commons by the administration building, Jamison stopped in the middle and stared up. With the moon
absent, it seemed the air amplified the light of a thousand stars.

Clarence only glanced up, stamping his feet and blowing into his hands for warmth.

"Not one for stargazing, Clarence?"

Clarence offered only a snort in reply.

Jamison added, "Have you grown too old to see the wonder of this all?"

"Tarnation, man. It's almost midnight. It's as cold as the heart of a critic. I am weary. I believe I have an examination in Great Epochs of the Western World—for which I have not even opened the book. And you ask why I do not see the wonder in this all?"

Jamison spun about one more time and began to walk again. "You are the cynic, Clarence, not me."

Clarence tucked his hands under his arms. "Perhaps in the spoken word—not the written word, for sure."

Three blocks away, the bells began to toll out the quarter hour. Jamison was sure that even those in Boston could hear the chilling peals. He stopped walking again. "Clarence?"

Clarence spun about, exasperated. "Now what, Pike? I'm tired. Shall I leave you here to wonder amidst the darkness, posing your odd questions to the cold?"

Jamison acted as if he did not hear Clarence's comments. "Do you believe in God, Clarence?"

"Sakes alive, Pike, that's not a simple question that can be answered when one is chilled to the bone."

"But, Clarence, it can be. A yes or no. Simple words. That's all it takes. Do you believe in God?"

"Are you asking because of that Joshua Quittner fellow—the farm boy? The one who's always muttering this or that about God and faith and all that bunkum?"

Jamison shrugged. "Maybe. Why do you ask?"

Clarence stomped his feet. "He's a friend of yours, isn't he?"

Jamison nodded. "Not best of friends, but we meet and talk some nights."

"I have heard that once he stands behind a pulpit he talks as smooth as honey," Clarence said, affecting a Southern drawl. "And that us Northern folk find it sweet."

Jamison scowled. "You make a terrible yokel. And you haven't answered my question."

"And you haven't said why you're interested."

Jamison shrugged. "I don't know exactly. We talked some about this recently. He asked me about it. That's all. I've been thinking about my answer . . . the answer that I gave him."

"But, Jamison—you of all people! Don't you know the Bible? Isn't your father a minister? With that pedigree, how could that Quittner chap not think you are a Christian?"

"He says knowing about something is not the same as believing in that something. He said I know the truth but do not really *believe* the truth."

Clarence snorted. "Listen, I don't know why you want to know—but the answer is yes. I believe. There is some sort of Supreme Being out there. Maybe he's interested in us. Maybe he isn't."

"Really?"

Clarence drew his scarf tighter about his neck. "I will answer this one last time, and then I am heading back to my snug little apartment. There is probably some sort of God. Hard to think otherwise. But I have seen far too many men of God pontificating and drawing their own rules up and making people generally miserable. Life is too short for rules. Life is too short to deny one pleasure. Any pleasure. All pleasure. Jamison, our role is to question those rules—poke holes in them. Most of religion is done with chicanery. It makes the poor, ignorant church people remain subjugated to the frauds of preachers and priests. You have gone on and on about your father and how cold and distant he is—is that what God is like? Is that what the Supreme Being wants? If it is, I want no part of man's religion. God perhaps, but man's God, no."

Clarence wiped his nose with his glove. "And now I am more than just cold—I am near to death from freezing. Will you accompany me home? Or shall I leave you out here to freeze to death?"

Jamison hesitated a minute, then followed Clarence, who made his way through the frigid night.

Jamison lived in a small room carved out of unused space on the second floor of a saltbox house. The owners, former professors at Harvard, rented out a half dozen tiny rooms. One professor did all the interior work himself, and it showed in walls that tilted and doors that seldom latched with the first attempt. Jamison's room held a bed, a nightstand, a desk, a chest of drawers, a chair, and little else save the window that looked over a jungle of trees and shrubs at the rear of the house.

The light from the match created a halo of gold in the dark room. Jamison lifted the glass mantle and notched up the wick a finger's width. When the flame caught, he blew the match out, lowered the mantle, and began to take off his heavy winter attire.

He hung his coat on a nail in the door. Unlacing his boots, he wiped the wetness off the leather with an old rag he kept in a small box by the door.

As he did, a slip of white at the bottom of the door caught his attention. It was not a torn slip of scrap paper–Jamison was too neat for that. It was a sharp edge protruding just a hair from the darkness below the door. He bent down and touched it with his forefinger.

Then he reached out farther and pulled it into the room. It was a letter from home. On occasion, his neighbors might stop at the university express office, and if they saw an unclaimed letter for Jamison, they would bring it home and slip it under the door.

He looked at the return address. Pittsburgh. Setting it on the nightstand, Jamison finished readying himself for bed. He selected his extra thick, extra long nightshirt because of the chill. Adding a full shovel of coal to the fire, he made a mental note to bring up another scuttle before tomorrow night. He carefully laid out his trousers on the top of his dresser, painstakingly edging along the crease, then stacked books on the fabric. In the morning, the trousers would have a clean crease, with no ironing needed.

Only after all this was completed did he return to his bed and slip under the thick down comforter. He kicked at the sheets, rubbing them furiously with his feet to warm the cold bed. After a moment he felt he could lie down without risking a chill.

He carefully broke the letter's seal and slipped out the pages–dense with writing on both sides. It was written in a very tight, very precise hand–his mother's. Every line was equally distant from the line above and below. The elegant curves and swoops were all well within the proper boundaries. Each paragraph was indented just so, and each period well marked, the pen almost piercing the thick vellum.

Jamison began to read, taking his time with each word, just as his mother had taken time in writing each word. She wrote of the happenings at church. A guest speaker from England had taken a recent Sunday, and despite his esteemed education, most congregants said later that they would have preferred to hear his father speak.

She went on to describe a recent church social.

At the bottom of the letter, a word jumped out of the page well before Jamison's eyes had a chance to find it. That word was *Neta*.

No longer holding each word like a jewel, Jamison began to hurriedly scan the page. He read quickly and flipped the page over.

And who should be at this social? It was a most improbable guest–Glenna Hill, the mother of Neta Hill. And as we chatted over a delightful sassafras punch, she informed me that it was so nice of my son to be in correspondence with her daughter. She claimed that my son writes the most witty letters detailing his life at Harvard. She claimed that my son has told her daughter all about the fascinating people he has interviewed for the student newspaper. She claimed that her daughter so looks forward to receiving yet another letter from my son. She claims that nearly a dozen missives have been exchanged.

Neta Hill! Of all people! Neta Hill!

*Why did you do this to me? Why did you hold this information from
me? Do you not realize that the omission of facts is much the same as a
bold-faced falsehood?*

*You are still our charge and as such should not be carrying out these
affairs without our knowledge. And if you had asked, I would have said
that the Hills are simply not our type of people. I admit that Neta Hill has
a certain base charm—but she is not worthy of your attentions. I ask that
you cease correspondence with her posthaste.*

*And your father has worried that this flirtation is symptomatic of a
deeper problem—and that is your being tainted by the worldliness of that
university. Are his fears true? Are you listening too much to the world?
And working on a newspaper? I pray every day that you remain unsullied
by the evils that abound—and now it appears you have deliberately
disobeyed us once again.*

*We both agree that your association with the newspaper will have to be
terminated. One day you will have to return to Pittsburgh and with that
sort of reputation following you, how would you expect to find a suitable
position for a young man of your standing?*

*Think before you act and please stay away from all those scoundrels who
would drag you down to a base and pedestrian level.*

Yours,
Mother

Jamison lay there in the dark for a long time. He heard the bell
tower call out twice. Before the last echo died in the cold air, Jamison was up and out of bed, grabbing at his clothes, pushing through
his belongings to find a warmer shirt and sweater. He snatched his
coat, turned the wick of the lantern down, and stepped out the door
into the hall.

Jamison did not stop walking until the very faint etching of dawn
nicked at the eastern sky. It was nearly five in the morning. He had
walked for hours, not truly observing where his path led. He came to

the river and crossed the bridge. He wandered along the narrow streets of Beacon Hill in Boston. He walked to the east to the ocean. After a while, he stopped and stared out at an oily, cold Atlantic. Eight ships gently rocked in the icy water, tethered to the piers and wharves. Behind him lay the city, not yet awake.

The darkness was cold yet comforting. It was as Jamison expected. He could not allow that letter from his mother to simply lay on his thoughts all night. He had to try and cast out the demons. So far, the distance walked had not been enough. The words kept bubbling up through his thoughts.

The piers and docks were deserted. Jamison stared perhaps fifteen minutes to the east, watching the blackness slowly twist to purple and scarlet. Finally he stomped his feet and blew into his cupped palms.

It is cold.

He looked down the pier, the pilings appearing like the giant jagged teeth of a great sea beast. To the south was a warm glow from a small shanty.

And that looks warm.

A ragged sign nailed at an angle above the door read Depert's Fine Provisions and Alehouse.

Jamison, shivering, grabbed for the door. Ten or so tables lay inside, yet only a single man with a great explosion of gray hair about his head sat at the table closest to the window. In front of him was a cup of dark liquid with steam rising into the air.

A thin black fellow came out from behind a curtain. His wide eyes had a question in them. "You for breakfast, sir, on this chilled and dark morn?" he asked in an odd but pleasant singsong accent.

Nodding, Jamison slid out a chair.

"You do best if you take my recommend of the usual fare, sir. Most take it."

"Well . . . I guess if it's the usual fare, I'll take it."

In a few minutes, the black cook returned with a huge platter of biscuits, gravy, and ham. It looked to be a breakfast for three people, not just one.

"I'll be here until lunch," Jamison laughed as he reached for his fork. He took a large bite and smiled. "This is very good."

The cook beamed.

Jamison ate slowly, staring out the darkened window at the black water and furled sails.

I am not ashamed of writing to Neta. There is nothing to be ashamed about. I like her. She's pretty. Maybe as pretty as Hannah. I can imagine what advice Gage would offer: She's a bird in the hand. Hannah will forever be lost in the bush. Neta is a good woman. Good women don't come by all that often. And he's right. I have known old bachelors who have lost early at love and never found it again. Maybe there isn't that spark about her like Hannah. But if I wait for that spark—will I be waiting forever? Is everyone entitled to that spark?

"And you being finished, young man?" the cook queried.

Jamison blinked and looked up. "Yes . . . I guess I am. It was very good. Thank you."

"Be most appreciating your words, sir. I like when anyone smiles as they finish."

Jamison fished in his pocket for coins. He carefully counted out the price of the meal, then another tall stack of coins for a tip. Finding refuge tonight was worth extra, he told himself.

He pulled on his coat and adjusted his hat. The black cook watched, careful not to be intrusive. As Jamison neared the door, the man sang out, "Thank you, sir, kindly, for the extra. I be most grateful."

Jamison kept his hand on the doorknob but did not turn it. "Have you been working here long?"

The cook stared at his feet. "More years than be remembered, I imagine."

Jamison looked into his eyes and asked, "Are you happy?"

"Lawd, sir, that be a big question for this early," the cook replied, appearing startled.

"Forgive me, then," Jamison said and turned the knob. A slice of cold air slipped in.

"Be a big question, sir. But not one that don't be answered."

Jamison held the door open an inch.

"Being happy, sir, is finding out what the good Lord be giving you—and then finding happy in that. Sailors be most customers here. They all have sad eyes. They don't have what they thought they wanted and then they be searching the world to find it. Ain't there. I know it. Good Lord gives what you need. He don't give what you can't be having and then laugh at you. No, sir. He gives what you need."

Jamison's smile was lit by the early gold of the dawn. "And that's the truth?"

"Be true, sir. You find happy with what the good Lord gives. Don't be worried 'bout what he ain't giving you. You plan on waitin' for what he ain't going to give you—well, that be enough to make any man sad."

Jamison nodded, then slipped out into the chilled light of daybreak.

Cambridge, Massachusetts
April 1844

Hannah stepped into the Destiny, and an imperceptible hush settled across the room. Heads turned and virtually everyone in the building turned to follow her walk. Jamison heard the words *woman* and *cadaver* whispered as Hannah came closer. Everyone staring at her knew that this was the day her anatomy class first ventured into the realm of dead flesh and began their autopsy on what was formerly a live human being. News of a woman's presence in that heretofore all-male domain swept across campus as a wildfire before a dry wind.

"Hannah," he stammered as she drew close to his table. He sniffed as if expecting to smell formaldehyde on her person. "I did not expect to see you this evening."

She sat down without speaking. As patrons jockeyed for position, chairs groaned and squealed. No one was willing to be blatant, but every ear was canted in her direction.

Jamison looked about, then to Hannah. "Have you contracted some sort of rare disease?"

She shook her head.

"Or committed some sort of unusual moral lapse? An interesting one that is particularly offensive?"

She shook her head again.

"Then it must be that you must have done the unpardonable."

She refused to smile, though Jamison offered her his best screwed-up, professorial face.

"And that is?" she asked in her most innocent of voices.

Jamison took extreme delight in the sweet facade she maintained. "You have learned the secrets of a man," he said, hoping all around could hear his stage whisper. "You have seen how we work."

He watched as a smile crept onto her lips. "And it was not a pretty sight now, was it?"

She hesitated an instant, then her deep throaty laugh rang out in the quiet room. A minute later many others around them joined in.

Jamison hoped she would have seen in his eyes the great yearning in his heart, but he wondered if she'd ever know.

She stayed at his table for another hour, telling her wonderful tale of knives and flesh and fainting.

She was adamant that all the fainting in class was done by the stronger of the species—the male—and that even being in the front row, she had maintained a most professional demeanor throughout.

Walking home that evening Jamison felt a tight constriction in his heart. He was laughing and talking with the woman who had so captured his imagination and interest. And at the same time, though Jamison had devised intricate and elaborate fantasies of the future, his cynical and pessimistic side often took over. And when it did, his mood would come crashing down with a deafening roar. He would berate himself for ever having hoped that a woman like Hannah would ever deign to think of him in any manner of romantic way.

He would all but shout as he walked that only a fool like himself would hold out hope for something more.

But then, spiraling out of the ashes, a tender spark would ignite—fueled by the memory of her smile and laugh and perhaps even the gentle touch of her hand on his arm as she laughed at his observations. Then an alternative future would unroll—a future in which he and Hannah were somehow together.

And on this evening, Jamison let the two sides soar and plummet, trying to corral neither one nor the other. He reveled in the positive feelings, yet let the desperate, lonely emotions run their course.

As he opened the door to his room, he heard a papery rustle. He stepped to the side and lit the lantern. An envelope lay at the far sweep of the door. He held it up to the light. It bore a Pittsburgh return address and the gentle sweep of Neta's handwriting.

After the back-and-forth battles of his future with and without Hannah, he was happy to have something less taxing and less complicated to consider. He sat down in the lone chair in the room and turned up the wick.

Sweet Jamison,

Your last letter, which lies before me, is such balm to my heart.

Spring appears delayed here, and all we see are gray skies and chilled rain and sleet. Oh, to see the bud of a flower!

Your descriptions of your friends are so delightful that I am believing that I, too, have attended Harvard. You write with such a clarity that I close my eyes and I can see, with great precision, the scene exactly as you have lived it. I have said it before—but that is a gift.

Mother and I have been to Kaufmann's this morning to look for new linens. The streets are so horrid and muddy that it took us nearly all day to complete the trip. How I yearn for warmer weather. I will luxuriate in the first warm spring day—like a kitten in a warm puddle of sunshine.

There is one thing that I yearn even more for than that.

The object of my desire?

Your return from Cambridge.

I know that we have had only the shortest time together last summer.

Our few minutes together over Christmas were so agonizingly brief as not to count. Drats on families that managed to keep our schedules separate.

But this summer . . . well, such should not be the case.

You will be here.

I will be here.

I cannot begin to tell you how warm I am made by the thought of this.

I will close now.

I look forward to your next letter. I am certain that all my words will pale in comparison to yours.

Yours, in waiting, waiting to be warmed,

Neta

Jamison let the letter fall to his chest. Closing his eyes, he saw Neta's dark hair lifted by a summer breeze. He heard her laugh, energetic and enthusiastic.

Then he opened his eyes with a start. He sniffed. From somewhere, a hint of lavender found purchase in the air.

It was the scent Hannah had worn tonight.

And again his heart tightened.

"Good Lord gives what you need. He don't give what you can't be having and then laugh at you. No, sir. He gives what you need."

Jamison wondered why of all the sermons he'd heard preached and all the philosophies he'd heard examined, these few words from an old black cook sprang out of his thoughts.

He gives what you need.

CHAPTER SIX

Boston, Massachusetts
May 1844

A fine spray, like jewels in the sun, lifted into the air as the boat sliced through the gentle waves. Jamison counted another fifteen small sailboats bobbing along the waters of Boston's Back Bay. It was not his first time on a small sailing vessel, but nearly so. He stood at the bow of the ship, holding on to the rails. He smiled and laughed and hoped he did not betray the queasiness he felt.

Gage, in one of his more expansive moods, had chartered the sailing vessel and crew to take him and Joshua and Hannah on an afternoon cruise and lunch.

"I don't do this sort of thing often, old friend," Gage had told Jamison as he invited him along, "because word gets around. Feelings get hurt. You know—questions about who was invited and who wasn't. That sort of triviality always besets my best intentions. So I only invited my three best chums, for I know that all are the soul of discretion." Gage slapped him around the shoulder. "And I know there is little I can do that truly impresses any of you—you all know my foibles all too well, I'm afraid."

Jamison had laughed as expected. And now as the boat bounced and tossed as the afternoon winds picked up, Jamison regretted one more time his acceptance of Gage's offer. He consulted the sun. The water on the teak decking glistened like jewels.

It must be near four. Don't we go in at four? Isn't that what he said?

As Jamison tightened his grip on the mahogany rail, the varnish well worn by both firm hands and salt, he heard Gage's laughter from the cockpit of the craft. He had been there by the large wheel for most of the afternoon. Hannah sat next to him and Joshua sat on the bench opposite them both.

How that farm boy does it is beyond me, Jamison said to himself. *He's never been on the open seas either. Yet here he sits, as relaxed as a dandy—as a man born to the sport. Gads! How I dislike them all right now.*

From the corner of his eye, he caught a great frown from Gage. He had pulled out his silver pocketwatch and snapped it shut with a flourish.

"Drats! Jamison!" Gage called. "They tell me we have to head for home. Care to take a spell at the wheel—or rudder—or reins—or whatever it is sailors call these things?"

Jamison waved back. "No, not today."

When the boat slapped down a deep green wave, a feathery spray washed over him. The cool water felt good on his face. Gage waved back and made a great pantomime of dragging Hannah to the great wheel and forcing her to place her hands on it. All the while she laughed and resisted and blushed.

Just get us back to the dock—now!

As the boat slipped closer to the Cambridge dock, Jamison breathed a sigh of relief. It had been an interesting afternoon—and the first hour or so was pleasant. Then the winds had come up, making the ride rough.

It was most apparent to Jamison that Gage, despite his innocent bluster to the contrary, was a man at home on the water—as if he had sailed every summer of his youth.

Why are the rich like that? he wondered. *To play at being less privileged than they are?*

As they docked, Gage unwrapped a bottle of champagne for all as a reward for making it back to dry land, he said. Both Hannah and Joshua declined—Joshua for moral reasons and Hannah because she claimed she must study for an upcoming test. Jamison only took a small fluted glass, hoping it might settle his still-rolling stomach.

It did not.

In the carriage ride back to campus, Hannah and Joshua became involved in an animated discussion on the merits of decorum and style. Joshua held that a man's and a woman's position in all areas of life were spelled out in the Scriptures, and Hannah argued that culture is the determining factor.

It was a familiar argument, so Jamison leaned back against the smooth leather seat and closed his eyes, hoping the ride would be brief.

Gage smiled as the two talked, then turned to Jamison. Jamison felt his stare and opened his eyes.

"Have you made plans for the summer yet?" Gage asked.

Jamison blinked. "Summer?"

"Yes, the month after this? Summer? Hot and sunny?"

Hiding his scowl, Jamison answered, "I know the season. I just wasn't expecting the question."

"Well, have you? If you haven't, I am sure there would be a temporary posting at *The Post* or *The World*. You want me to ask?"

The question and offer took Jamison by surprise. It was not that his summer had not already been planned—more of the same clerical duties at his father's church. It was that the offer came so late and so near the start of Harvard's summer hiatus.

"I think . . . no . . . for certain I will be returning home to Pittsburgh. My father has accumulated what he describes as a mountain of correspondence for me to handle."

"Correspondence? Truly?"

Shrugging, Jamison tried to form a reply but could think of nothing that might lessen both their disappointments.

"Well, then . . . there is always Neta, isn't there? That will make the months more pleasant for you."

Jamison's heart caught. He had mentioned Neta once or twice to Gage, describing her as a most attractive and comely girl.

Gage offered a knowing smile.

Jamison shot a panicked look to Hannah. It was obvious, to his immense relief, that she did not hear that name.

"Neta?" Jamison whispered. "I suppose . . . I mean . . ."

Jamison was certain that Gage saw his desperate look to Hannah and yet refused to take that not-so-subtle hint and withdraw the subject.

"Pittsburgh will be a more pleasant place this summer for you, Jamison, than stuffy New York. I can offer no such diversions. Forget about the posting. Enjoy yourself."

In that one grasping of time, Jamison absolutely hated Gage Davis. Till this moment, Hannah and Neta were of two different worlds, never commingled. A world with Hannah had no Neta in it. A world with Neta precluded Hannah. And as the name of Neta was mentioned, his two worlds collided with an immense, mute crash.

"The sooner you find a good woman like that, the quicker you will find contentment. And isn't that what we all seek? A woman of sturdy stock with no illusions," Gage commented.

And then Jamison hated him even more. He simply nodded, hoping Gage would simply not say another word until they returned home. Jamison knew that Gage was clearly indicating, in a subtle manner, that Jamison did not exist in the same sphere as Hannah. If Gage supposed Jamison should find himself content with a woman of his own sphere, then would not Hannah think the same?

It was those thoughts that swirled about Jamison's head for the rest of the ride, the rest of the day, and the rest of the week, if the truth be told.

Cambridge, Massachusetts
June 1844

Summer did not creep into Cambridge this year, but leapt upon it, with claws and teeth flashing. Shimmers of heat radiated from the streets. Leaves were held motionless, as if catching their breath, waiting for a cooling breeze, but caught only a hesitant breeze at best.

Jamison slowly made his way to campus. He felt the scratch of his shirt against his back, the cloying of his trousers. He wished again that Harvard would relax the coat-and-tie rule during the hot months at the end of term, but the administration made no motions to that end. He ran a finger around his collar, already wet from his short walk.

Everyone he passed seemed to operate as if walking in water, with slow movements, slow greetings. Even the horses plodded along in slow tempo.

How could he endure his final classes inside, since he was hot, bored, and anxious to leave?

He turned onto the commons yard. The area was shaded by trees and in the afternoon, the wall of buildings to the west shaded most of the lawn. The brick cliffs halted the heat of the sun while eliminating the breeze as well. The commons would be bathed in a hushed shade.

Students would first gather in the lee of the building and slowly edge east as the shadows lengthened.

I truly do not want to go to Oration and Prose today, he thought as he wiped his brow with his sleeve. It was too hot for the niceties of a handkerchief. To his left he heard a familiar tumble of laughter. It was Hannah, sitting on the lawn, her dress pooled around her legs. She was leaning against the coarse bark of an oak tree. Sitting beside her was Joshua, tossing a green acorn in the air.

Class will have to wait.

"Is there room in the shadows for another?" he called out.

"By all means," Hannah said, sounding as if she were happy to see him.

Jamison tossed his bag to the ground and stripped off his jacket, letting it tumble without regard to wrinkles and dust.

He flopped down and lay on his back, perpendicular to Hannah.

"If it gets much hotter, Joshua, you'll have no more sermons to preach on hell. We will have already lived through the fires."

Usually gracious about such good-natured jesting, Joshua stiffened in response instead. "I think hell will be a sight more unpleasant, Jamison. And making light of eternal punishment is not a well-conceived habit."

Hannah smiled at both men. She had grown used to the small rivalries between them and acted as if she enjoyed watching them spar.

"I do not make light of it," Jamison replied. "But to think a loving God punishes with such harshness—well, I would imagine the liberals on the seminary faculty have taken that old dictum to task, have they not?"

Joshua's expression tightened further. "They have and have failed. Man likes to think he will get what *he thinks* he deserves—but remember this as well: Man's ability to delude himself is infinite."

Jamison rolled onto his side. "Well, that, my friend, would make a great sampler. Perhaps we might have Hannah here embroider it."

She kicked at him with her foot. "And now you are willing to anger us both with your tedious remarks?"

As she kicked, Jamison saw that the top three buttons of her boot were undone and a flash of her calf was exposed. He was sure she knew of the exposure but did nothing to cover herself.

"I am tedious—but it is the weather to blame. How we are expected to study in this oppressive heat is beyond man's abilities," Jamison grumbled.

Joshua wiped his face with his palm. "Thanks for reminding me. I must take my leave. Class awaits."

A quiet slipped around Jamison and Hannah. She leaned against the tree and braced her palms behind her head as a pillow.

"What do natives on some tropic island do in such heat?" she asked.

Jamison lay on his back again and tried to shrug. "I don't know. Perhaps they wear fewer clothes?"

Hannah snorted. "You men are all alike."

"I only surmise from what I have read. Grass skirts and all that."

"Truly?"

"From what I read, yes."

Hannah sighed. "Do you think that you'll travel to those tropic islands someday? You talk as if you will."

Jamison shrugged again. "Perhaps. Or perhaps I will be forever chained to my father's desk, writing letters about roofs and coal."

"Not you, Jamison. You won't do that. You'll see. You'll visit those islands someday. I do not think I will—but you will. Of all of us, I am sure you will."

He closed his eyes as she talked, reveling in the sound. He felt the tickle of grass at his neck and the musty smell of the earth.

He turned to look at her. Her dress had ridden up another inch or two and a hand's width of her bare calf showed. He tried not to stare. Hannah looked off into the afternoon sun. Sunlight diffused through the leaves dappled at her face.

She sighed as if struck by a wave of melancholy. "Well, Jamison, will you think of me this summer?"

He wanted to ask why she asked. He wanted to ask if she would think of him. He wanted to ask if they might write.

But all he did was nod and tell her that he would.

FROM THE JOURNAL OF JAMISON PIKE
LATE AUGUST 1844

Summer in Pittsburgh was as I thought it might be—at least part of it. Again I suffered silently as I acted as correspondent and assistant to my father. It is quite inconceivable to me how much brain-numbing minutia goes on at a church. Correspondence mounts up like a wave threatening to overwhelm me. This afternoon alone I sent out nearly twelve letters—all merely asking for bids on the upcoming winter's coal service. When bids are received, all will need be summarized and presented to the elders for a vote, then twelve more letters sent out accepting or declining the offers. And that is if the elders choose not to ask for additional quotes—or shift the heating to split wood.

Of course the work is beneath my abilities—and I have said as much to Father. That is always cause for a sharp exchange of words. He claims no man is better than any job. I do not agree. Some men are not suited to write letters asking the price of a scuttle of coal. If they do, then their true potential is lost.

No matter the logic of my argument, it is an argument I will not win this year. The air this summer in our home has been occasionally nicked with tension. No one seems to smile much—including myself—at least while I am forced to do such menial work.

Yet the summer has offered its moments—mainly because of Neta.

Upon coming back to Pittsburgh for the summer, my mother made me all but promise that I would never see Neta again. She had assumed, of course, that I had ceased writing to her after her own vitriolic letter regarding my interest in Neta. I had not. My mother must have spoken for an hour on the crassness of the Hill family and how they were not much removed from being plain river rats. I chose not to argue, of course, and nodded at the right moments.

At the end of her talk with me, she folded her arms and said she was glad this unpleasantness was all settled.

Since she never specifically asked me to make a vow to stop seeing Neta, I did not feel any obligation to actually do so. No vow was made, so there was none to be broken. I simply did not mention my activities. And what was more surprising is that both my mother and father did not ask much of what and where I was going after working hours. Perhaps it is because I am now older. Or it might have been because they were afraid of what I might tell them.

I did not visit Neta until the first week of July, so busy was I with my summer position. I sent a note to her house requesting her company for an afternoon stroll up to the Allegheny Cemetery—not the most romantic situation, but the new gates, the manicured landscape, and reportedly exquisite statuary have truly been the talk of the town since the grounds opened this spring. To my pleasure, she immediately sent back a note saying she would be delighted. (I had to wait by the door to intercept her note lest it fall into my mother's hands.)

It was a most wonderful day.

As we strolled among the very elegant headstones and memorials, Neta made wry and witty comments on many of the families resting there. A few of Pittsburgh's mayors lay in peace–and it appeared Neta was familiar with not only their public image, but the less polite image behind that facade. She slipped her arm in mine as we walked and talked as if it were the most natural thing in the world to do. At one point on our first summer encounter, she asked to rest on a shaded bench. I escorted her there and stood as she fanned herself, her eyes closed to the sun. I was able to observe all facets of her charms without embarrassment.

She is truly a very pretty young woman.

After our walk, I hailed a carriage to take us downtown to the Diamond Market. We bought fish sandwiches and ate them out-doors with napkins spread across our laps.

It was a most delightful day after so many days of dour tedium in the tomb of the church office.

I inquired as to the time she needed to be back at home and she smiled. "Why, my mother and father have gone for the evening. They won't be back till midnight."

She said that with a most coy smile on her face, almost a smile of invitation. I am sure my expression gave my thoughts away.

"They are very open-minded people, Jamison. And I am a grown woman."

I'm not sure what I said, but I do recall dropping a bit of hot fish into my lap.

As dusk edged at the sky, I mentioned we should avoid the poor roads from downtown to the Hill District in the dark. We hurried to her door and arrived there as the bells of the church sounded out nine.

Other than Hannah–and my mother and relatives–this was the latest I had ever been alone with a woman.

We sat on her front porch for a long time, talking and exchanging thoughts. She is most interested in what goes on at Harvard. I mentioned Gage and Joshua to her. She seemed most fascinated by the wealthy Gage, but not in the way I have seen other women become. Mention a rich, eligible young man to some females and their eyes get hazy as if somehow they might meet him instead of you. Not so with Neta. She asked about his activities and what he does, but never once did I imagine that she might rather be pursuing him.

I lost all track of time and the bells called out ten.

I told her I must go and she nodded, then turned her face to me and all but demanded that I kiss her good-night. I did but I was shocked.

As she stood at her door, she clutched my arm, then demanded–I think–another small kiss before she went in.

I did not offer any protest–nor did I hesitate.

As she closed the door, she whispered, "You must call on me again. And I will be discreet in my response. I know that the name Hill on a note might not be well received in some homes."

I managed to see Neta another dozen times before I had to return to Cambridge for the fall semester.

Our final good-bye was tearful–on her part, and modestly passionate.

Neta is a fine woman. There would be many a gentleman who would strive to have her on their arm. Yet while I am with her, my mind contrives against me, whispering the name of Hannah into my ear. Neta is as comely as Hannah. She seems to truly appreciate my company.

Neta looks at me like Hannah never has–with admiration tinted with a shading of awe. And for a woman to so look at a man is rare.

He gives what you need.

Those words keep ringing in my ear.

Do I need a woman like Neta? Am I merely being tempted and teased with Hannah?

It is indeed a quandary. My leaving Pittsburgh and Neta and returning to Harvard and Hannah has brought no answer to the question.

He gives what you need.

November 1844

"I wish we could repeat our journey of last year at this time," Joshua said as he removed his coat and laid it across an empty chair. The Destiny was as quiet as a church on Monday.

Jamison nodded. "I did enjoy New York. Would it be presumptuous of us to invite ourselves to Gage's for thanksgiving?"

Joshua appeared surprised. "You would do that?"

"Of course I wouldn't," he said. "Unless you think it would work, that is."

Joshua ordered a hot cider and a butter biscuit.

"Eating light? That's not like you."

Joshua smoothed at the table with his palms. "Eating poor," he said with no trace of bitterness. "As the month comes to a close, so do my resources."

Jamison arched his eyebrows.

"But God always provides," Joshua added in a hurry. "He always has, and I have no reason to doubt him now."

Jamison wanted to cover his roast beef but could think of no polite manner to do so. Instead he continued to eat, but he tried to hide his enjoyment of the taste. "So you think that God gives you what you need?"

Joshua carefully broke the butter biscuit into four pieces, piling the crumbs into a small mound on the plate. "He does."

Jamison laid his fork down. He would have stopped eating sooner but felt a compulsion to finish everything on his plate. He pushed it to the side. "May I ask you a question? Does God ever test you by placing a goal that seems out of reach, yet he wants you to strive for it?"

Joshua chewed thoughtfully. "I think he might. But he also closes doors when a person seeks something that is harmful."

"So an obstacle might be a test—or simply God's way of saying no?"

Joshua took another bite and nodded. "But, Jamison—a just man on a noble quest will not be denied. You will know the truth. God will lead you on the right path."

Jamison sat back. "Thanks," he said calmly. Then he lifted his hand to signal for Melinda. "And as thanks, God will use me to provide for you tonight. Order something more substantial than a biscuit. The month is nearly over, and I still have coins in my pocket."

Joshua did not argue with his request.

December 1844

The weather snapped cold the first week of December, and students scurried about campus with a great sense of chilled purpose. It was not knowledge they were seeking, but escape from the winds sweeping off the Back Bay, biting and nicking at exposed flesh.

Clarence and Jamison rushed into the great hall of the student union and were amazed to find two empty leather chairs. They immediately claimed them as their own and dragged them into a close proximity of the fireplace at the west side of the room.

"I am so glad to be indoors," Jamison said as he drew off his gloves.

"And into the smoke and drafts," Clarence added. "One would think with the tuition as it is that this university might afford a decent place to come in out of the cold."

Jamison smiled. Clarence seldom spoke an encouraging word. Jamison had learned not to attempt to talk Clarence out of his dislikes and grievances. He found that if he let them be spoken, then they were as likely to be forgotten quickly.

Clarence made a great show of removing his greatcoat and smoothing out his long green scarf with the delicate tassels. Only after all his outer garments were placed just so would he sit. And that he did with slow deliberateness. "Ahh . . . this is much better," he said as he stretched his feet out toward the fire.

"Shall I get coffee for us? A cider?" Jamison asked.

Clarence reacted as if bitten by a disagreeable, though not poisonous, reptile. "Here? A drink here? Surely you jest. The Destiny is bad enough–but the student union makes the Destiny seem like the Tremont in Boston." Clarence shrugged. "But if you must get something, then cider might do."

Jamison was back in a few minutes, balancing a large sweet bun and two mugs of cider.

The fire cracked and hissed as they drank. He was not sure why two of his best friends at Harvard also happened to be among the school's wealthiest. Gage was new money–he being only the second generation. Clarence was older money. It was more dignified, he claimed.

"I'm not even sure how it came to be," Clarence once admitted. "No one says. I have a feeling it was selling whiskey and guns to the Indians–but if that truth was ever told, my father would disavow me as part of this illustrious family."

Jamison got up and pulled out two logs from the carrier by the fireplace, tossing them into the grate.

"Ye gads, Jamison," Clarence snorted, "the university has servants to do that. Do you want to be mistaken for a servant?"

"No, I just want to get warm," he replied, rubbing his hands in the rush of new flame. "And besides, my father says there is no job beneath any man."

Clarence rolled his eyes. "I have heard you say that before and the concept is preposterous. Some men *are* better than others–and the survival and success of the more advanced man is most obvious."

Jamison waved his hand, dismissing the argument.

"You'll see that I am right, my friend. Once we graduate from this place, the one with the intelligence and cunning will go the furthest. Those pious types and the sluggards will be left behind in our dust."

Jamison screwed up his face. "And you are placing yourself in the most advanced category?"

"Of course. And you are there as well. You should be grateful."

Laughing, Jamison pushed his chair back from the fire. The flames had grown hot. "I suppose I am, Clarence. I suppose I am."

The two remained in their comfortable old leather chairs, talking for nearly an hour. Then Clarence, as if the time had slipped passed him, sat bolt upright and began grabbing at his belongings, saying he had all but forgotten a late-afternoon appointment.

In a huffed rush, he was gone, and Jamison sighed. He looked for Gage and Joshua, who had been holed up in a corner for most of the afternoon locked in an animated discussion. They were gone. In fact, only a handful of students remained. He heard the soft moan of the wind and imagined that most had returned home and had forsaken their afternoon classes. The main doors of the union banged open, but it was a polite banging, as if they had been snapped away by the wind. A smaller figure hurried in and pulled them closed.

Jamison blinked. It was Hannah. He had seen little of her the past weeks. He waved and she waved back. "You just missed them," he said.

"Missed who?" she answered, looking about.

"Joshua and Gage. They were here all afternoon."

Hannah turned her head just so, and the faint afternoon light lit up her eyes in a smoky, dusty manner. "Don't either of them have classes anymore? I keep seeing them about campus, often in the middle of some heated dispute or another. What were they contending today?" she asked.

Jamison had no idea. He had only waved at them and had not exchanged a single word. "The same as always, I imagine–the meaning of life," he answered, certain it was the truth.

Hannah's laughed filled the room with music. "Money or God, right?"

Jamison smiled. "Exactly."

Hannah slipped off her finely worsted wool coat and scoop bonnet and leaned back in the chair. Her hair was pulled up into a topknot with small ringlets cascading down the back of her neck. Jamison tried hard not to focus on how beautiful she looked.

Suddenly a puzzled look came over her face. "Where did these chairs come from? Florence and I were in yesterday, and I don't recall them here."

Jamison looked down as if seeing the chairs for the first time himself. "A friend of Joshua's was tossed out of Harvard for cheating. That's the story I heard. He had them stashed in his room."

"A friend of Joshua's? Cheating? How could that be? Doesn't his goodness rub off on all those nearby?" she asked wryly.

"So where's your Valkyrie friend?" he replied, changing the subject.

"Who? Who's a what?"

"Valkyrie. The tall blonde woman. The woman I always see you walking with on campus."

"She's a Valkyrie?"

"Yes," he stated.

Hannah's eyes tightened. "Do you know what a Valkyrie is?" she asked.

Jamison rubbed his chin, hoping he might sound clever. "I'm not sure, but it sounds tall, blonde, and Swedish."

Jamison's joy withered at the continuance of Hannah's hard gaze–until she leaned back and laughed out loud again.

"You're right about the tall and blonde–but she's English."

He felt a sense of great relief. "Close enough."

Smiling, Hannah replied, "Well?"

"Well, what?"

"You asked about Florence."

"Who?"

Hannah reached down and removed the current issue of the *Crimson Review* from her books and threw it at him. He ducked, laughing, as the papers sailed over his head.

"You are simply impossible, Jamison Pike! I do not know why I put up with you. Honestly! A simple conversation with you can lead a person to distraction."

Jamison hoped his immense relief would not be noted. His verve returned in a flash. "Is that outside Boston?"

Puzzled, Hannah replied, "Is what outside Boston?"

"Distraction. You keep saying I could lead a person there, but I've never set foot in the place."

With that Hannah jumped up from her chair, grabbed Jamison

about the shoulders, and proceeded to shower a flurry of friendly blows to his arm. His face was turned from her, but his smile could be seen across the room.

As a lonely dog barks in order to receive attention—if only a beating—Jamison relished this moment of connection.

"Joshua! Joshua!" Jamison shouted as he chased him down a snowy street. The Christmas holiday was still two days away, yet the campus had an odd, abandoned feeling. Jamison had decided that winter travel entailed too many risks—not so much in eventually getting to Pittsburgh, but in the odds of becoming trapped there by snow or storm. It was too great a risk to take.

As part of his own Christmas gift to himself, he'd spent an afternoon in a Boston bookstore with a five-dollar bill and instructed himself to spend it all.

The impact of one of his treasures spurred him to pursue Joshua even faster. Joshua, bundled from the cold, could hardly walk upright nor most likely hear or see.

Jamison came to a sliding, slipping halt just alongside him. "I was calling your name for the last two blocks. Your ears are too buried."

"Better that than to fall off from frostbite," Joshua said as he loosened his scarf. "Ohio never seemed this cold. Why were you trailing me for two blocks?"

Jamison scrabbled about in his coat for a moment, then triumphantly withdrew a small book.

"And?" Joshua eyed the book.

"Read the title."

Joshua leaned forward and squinted. "The *Emigrants Guide to Oregon and California*. Oregon? California?"

Jamison held himself to keep from bounding about. "It's the future, Joshua. The future. Oregon. California. The West."

Joshua leaned close to Jamison. "You haven't been drinking, have you?"

"Not a drop. But this book, Joshua–it's filled with all sorts of adventure and maps and hints of treasure. When we're done at Harvard–we have to head west."

Joshua carefully retied his scarf and turned his collar up and buttoned it tight. "Is it warm there?"

Jamison, puzzled, flipped through the pages as if he expected to find the answer. "I'm sure it's warmer than here."

"Well, I doubt I will ever go there. But if I do, you'll be the first to know."

And with that Joshua walked away toward his apartment, leaving Jamison on the corner holding the small book next to his heart, shouting out, "But it's the future. . . ."

FROM THE JOURNAL OF JAMISON PIKE
DECEMBER 1844

I will go on no longer about the *Emigrants Guide*. I have bored all my friends to tears. Why do they not see this as I do–a marvelous chance for a future unencumbered by the past?

Well, no matter. Eventually I will get there. I have no idea of how or why–but I will.

Speaking of pioneers and adventurers leads me to a most jarring juxtaposition.

I received a note from the editor of the *Boston Globe*. We had met when he toured the campus some months back. He passed on his card to me with a scribbled note on the back. He wrote asking if I could attend a gala banquet at the Kensington Club as a reporter. All manner of politician and dignitary were to be in attendance. The editor asked if I might write a story on the affair–and he would supply the tickets and enough money in advance to rent a formal coat. (He understands how meager the typical college budget is.)

I accepted at once–an article in a major newspaper is quite the coup, as Clarence would say. The affair was as I anticipated–much posing and primping and circulating about, chatting away in the smallest talk possible. I did meet the mayor of Boston, two ambassadors—one from England and one from Portugal—and many folks pushing James Polk and Henry Clay for our next president. Once they heard I was on assignment from the *Globe* they came at me like flies to a split watermelon, so anxious they were for the *Globe*'s endorsement.

The speeches were fine—some stirring, some tedious. The food was grand. How they manage to serve more than two hundred dinners at the same time is an unbelievable feat!

But what was most remarkable about the evening is that Hannah was there. She was accompanied by that Keyes fellow. Why she sees him is beyond my comprehension. He is sallow, shallow, and his eyes are of the devious type. He is not suited for her at all.

It was late in the evening. All the important people had long gone—now it was left to those seeking free drinks. I was told to stay until the bitter end, so I had no recourse and my story need not be filed until the afternoon of the next day. I had already composed most of it in my thoughts, so writing would be a simple matter.

I took a seat in a small, dark alcove of the hall, sipping a cup of very good coffee. Who should stroll past unescorted but Hannah.

She asked if she might sit. There was a single strand of pearls about her neck, and they caught the light as if illuminated from within, casting small round globes of illumination on her skin. She smelled of lavender. Her hair was done up, coiled and turned, in a most attractive manner.

She asked me what I thought of the evening.

"Full of sound and fury, signifying little," I said. That was true. For a moment I saw such deep sadness in her eyes that I wanted to embrace her and tell her all was fine.

Then I heard a man's voice calling her name. It was that Keyes fellow. I think he had one too many ale cocktails. And I looked at her again and that spark was gone. I saw a sadness in her smile as she rose to leave and bid me good-bye.

Women. Why are they so hard to fathom?

CHAPTER SEVEN

Cambridge, Massachusetts
April 1845

FROM THE JOURNAL OF JAMISON PIKE

It hardly seems possible that my student life of nearly four years here in Cambridge has passed like an ephemeral wisp of the wind. In only a few short months, my classes will be completed. I will be issued a sheepskin with all manner of Greek or Latin inscriptions and be told, in polite terms of course, to get out and get on with my life.

Being here, cloistered behind the bricks and ivy of Harvard, there is a sense of splendid isolation. We are the privileged few.

I have reviewed much of my journals written while a student here and found that I have seldom mentioned any classes or professors or serious debates on ideas, and that is because there have been so few memorable ones. Most are content with a repeat of whatever lecture they presented the previous year. It must be impossible to remain excited about ideas when they are in their fourth and ninth and dozenth retelling.

Have I been shaped by my experiences here? Perhaps. But it is because of the people I have met rather than the facts I have been taught. Nowhere else in the world would I have met such wonderful and amusing and challenging characters as I have met during my four years here.

Yet not all characters are quite so wonderful. The two gentlemen in the next apartment have resumed their argument of this morning—and that is debating who has consumed more of this morning's coffee. One claimed no more than a cup . . . perhaps a cup and a half. The other said two and that is all—yet a full eight cups of coffee were brewed. Each accuses the other of underestimating their consumption.

If ever I wish to make a point of the baseness and ultimate hopelessness of mankind, I will simply think back to these days and my neighbors' insufferable arguments.

Why does mankind not live in peace?

I will tell you why—because one man has taken too many sips from the coffeepots of the world without telling the other—and therein lies the cause of all wars.

In one of my columns in the *Review* a few months ago, I made a not-so-veiled reference to my two chums next door. They battled for nearly a week over the loss of a fruitcake—or an earlier-than-anticipated consumption thereof. Words went back and forth in a heated manner for days. (I think mice are the true culprits.) Whenever I think too highly of my fellowman, I will remember their stunning debates over food—and all this in a land of plenty. If the fruitcake was gone, both could purchase a new one a thousand times over.

But back to the point—my column made reference to these two louts, and I described their actions and possible motives. A day or two later one of them leapt from his room while I was locking my door. He had a copy of the *Review* in his hand.

"Is this supposed to be us?" he asked. I hesitated with my answer, for he was the larger of the two and could have pummeled me if he chose.

"No," I replied, trying to remain calm. "It's about some others I know."

And to my great surprise, he simply nodded, satisfied. "Good. These two yokels are blooming idiots."

And with that he returned to his rooms.

How could they not see themselves? How could they be dissuaded by my simple denial?

That is the way of the world, I imagine. No one admits to his own frailties and no one recognizes his own portrait—especially when painted in brutal and honest colors.

A case in point: I visited Gage as he prepared to leave campus. He began his preparation early—for he, of all students, had a great deal to pack and catalog. Boxes and crates and trunks littered his rooms, as if tossed helter-skelter by a giant's hand. He was slouching, without socks, shirt loose and unbuttoned, on an uncovered couch, eating an orange. There was a half-moon of peels around his feet. When I entered the room, he lifted his arm and offered me a section—which I took.

I have never seen Gage appear anything but in charge and in control. Yet he was neither of those this day—as if he were being tossed about in a storm and swept to a place of unknown trials.

My recent meeting with Hannah still weighed heavy on my mind, and I asked him again of Hannah and what he thought she might do with her life. I know I should simply have asked Hannah, but I cannot.

Gage offered a weary, knowing smile. He said that women are vexing. He said that a man finds value with his position. If his woman is too strong, he explained, then the man will be seen as weak. "That is Hannah's fundamental flaw—she is too strong. Even that Keyes fellow, despite his wealth, will be overshadowed by her. No man can endure such diminution."

I thought for a moment, then asked if *diminution* was indeed a word.

Gage laughed and threw another section of orange my way.

And as he talked, I found myself agreeing with him. Perhaps Hannah's star shines too brightly. Perhaps I would be best served with a good woman like Neta—a dimmer star perhaps, but a better star for me.

From a Letter from Neta Hill to Jamison Pike

My dear, dear Jamison,

How I wish that salutation could actually portray my true feelings. But it cannot.

These months have gone by with exceeding slowness. Your letters to me are the only high point of my days. I wish you would write more often; then I rebuff myself since I know you are swamped with many other worries and studies and reports and the like.

Jamison closed his eyes and massaged the bridge of his nose. He took a deep breath, then began to read again. The next three pages of the letter were filled with news, some bordering on gossip, from the goings-on in Pittsburgh. For not having an extensive education, Neta was a natural storyteller with a great eye for detail. Jamison smiled as he read and excused her the occasional misspelling.

His eyes slowed as they came to the final paragraphs.

Again, dear Jamison, how I miss your presence. On any given night there are several affairs and galas and parties in the city. I attend only a sprinkling of them–I do not like to attend unescorted–though hosts often insist that I do. If you were here we could attend all of them, my sweet. How delicious I would feel to walk into a room in a new ball gown with a bustle and a feathered hat and shoes that match, with my arm in yours. You would be wearing a new suit, of course–from one of the smart new tailors on Pitt Boulevard–with a gaily colored waistcoat. We would make such a handsome couple! All eyes would turn on us, I am sure–and there would be jealous stares from many.

Please come home soon. I know your education will be over soon–and then it might be you and I in a whirl of parties and receptions. How I look forward to that day. How I look forward to being in your strong arms again. How I look forward to all the rest as well.

Write soon.

I remain yours.

With great affection,
Neta

Jamison sat in the student union, slowly folded Neta's thick letter, and slipped it into his pocket. He walked to the front doors, propped open with a battered chair, and inhaled deeply. The rush of air into his lungs did not lift his somber mood. Neta's letter lay heavy against his chest.

As he walked toward the Destiny, he tried to imagine how he would respond. He decided to wait a day or two before taking pen to paper. Perhaps by then some thoughts would come.

As he turned the corner, he nearly stumbled on the curb as he caught sight of Hannah bounding up the steps into the Destiny. As he hurried the last half of the block, he all but forgot about his possible reply to Neta.

A Day Later

"Are you certain you have to leave now?" Jamison asked. "Another month or two should not make that much of a difference."

Joshua Quittner shook his head and sighed. His features were lost in the gray afternoon, the sky dark and low under a leaden scud of clouds. The two of them hastened along the sidewalk toward the Destiny. Leaves skittered about, hurried along by a freshening breeze.

"It might, Jamison. My mother's letter made it appear that my father was at death's door. I cannot in good conscience wait any longer."

"But there are final examinations and graduation ceremonies . . . and all the parties and celebrations. Surely they would not have you miss all that?"

Joshua waved his hand in an indistinct gesture. "My professors have stated that the final exams could be missed without damage to my grades. Graduation I will miss taking part in. The parties and all that, I will not."

"But surely your mother and your father cannot expect you to give up on your life to help them," Jamison continued.

Joshua stopped walking almost midstep. His leather soles squealed on the cobblestones. "But they do. And I will. Gladly. For that is as the Scriptures require."

Jamison held his hand up, bidding him to stop. "I know. Honor thy mother and thy father and all that. But giving up your life for theirs is not what the words mean. It cannot mean this level of sacrifice."

Joshua started walking again and Jamison hurried at his side, trying to match the soon-to-be preacher's hurried gait.

"Jamison, I appreciate your concern, but I would be traveling back to Ohio in a few months regardless."

Now it was Jamison's turn to stop. "But a fellow with your skills. You could have your pick of churches!"

Joshua turned around, then softly laughed. "Have you ever heard me preach?"

Jamison could not help feeling small and a bit guilty. "Well, not exactly, but everyone says you are one of the best."

"Then you should have heard me."

"But I did. Every night at the Destiny. You preached all the time. To Gage. To me. You warned us poor sinners that our debauchery will lead to naught."

The wind began to shift and the northern breeze mixed and pushed with a warm, humid whisper from the south. There was a hint of the Back Bay in the air and of salt water and of rain.

"But you never heard me. Your father being a minister and all— that always surprised me. That you no longer attended church, I mean."

Jamison did not look up. "I heard enough growing up. It's the same words over and over, you know. Be good. Don't sin. Give to the church. Avoid enjoying life," Jamison said in a weary tone. "That's the truth of the Scriptures, right? That's what preachers get paid to say. The same worn theology over and over."

Joshua stopped again and Jamison stumbled.

"Gads!" Jamison laughed as he found his footing. "If you are going to play start-and-stop with me, let's find a place to sit down instead."

"Jamison, I am sorry for stopping—but what you say just is not true. You know the truth and yet you do not want to submit to it."

Jamison resisted getting angry. He simply shrugged, and they continued on to the Destiny.

Jamison ordered coffee and pie for them both—without asking and knowing that he would pick up this check.

"You truly want to go back to Ohio?" Jamison asked as he stirred sugar into his coffee. "Aren't there any number of churches around here that would extend a call? Couldn't you send money home? I'm sure a church here would pay a sight more than what you can expect back in Shawnee."

Joshua nodded. "All that is true. But that's not honoring my parents as God would have it. That is the easy road. To write out a bank draft and think that covers a son's obligations? That is not the way I must be."

"But it is your life—not theirs."

Joshua reached up and smoothed his collar. The shirt had been Gage's—Jamison could tell from the tailoring. He wondered if Joshua would once again be comfortable with harsh, homespun fabric.

"No matter," Joshua said as he leaned over. "I will do what God commands. To follow him is my destiny. Such is the price of being a true believer."

Jamison stabbed at an errant slice of apple and did not reply.

"We have danced about this subject before, Jamison, but I never had the courage to ask. Now that I am leaving, I grow bold. I suspect those on death's door have much the same boldness."

"Boldness about what?"

"About your heart, Jamison."

"My heart? Are you like Hannah, practicing medicine?" Jamison said with a weak smile.

"No. And you know what I mean."

"Faith?"

"Yes. Faith in God."

Jamison's neck muscles tightened, holding in his anger. "So you are starting to practice what you will soon be preaching?"

"I've always preached it. You have chosen not to hear it. But you saw how faith is to be lived, I hope."

Jamison shrugged, then softened. "Yes, I suppose I did."

"And you didn't answer me either."

Jamison shoved his plate away–the pie half eaten–and laid his hands flat on the table. "I don't know. I know all of God and his doings. With my father, how could I help but know it all? I know the Scriptures. I can name all the books of the Bible. There is not much mystery."

Joshua waited, then said softly, "You still haven't answered."

Jamison bowed his head. He took a deep breath and looked up. "I don't want to answer."

Joshua waited a minute, then spoke again. "You don't want to answer because you know your answer is . . . a condemnation. You know the truth and have turned away from it."

"That isn't it at all. I am *not* condemned," Jamison snapped back.

"You are. You can call it what you will. But it is a condemnation. Not to decide is the decision of condemnation, by not acknowledging the truth."

Jamison glared at his friend, then looked down at his hands again.

"Listen, Jamison," Joshua said. "It is time for me to leave. Both this place and Harvard. I have to pack now. But I have to tell you one more thing."

"What's that?" Jamison replied, his voice gone reedy and thin.

"You are a gifted writer. You have a way of seeing the clarity of truth in a world gone cloudy. You are a truth teller, and yet you cannot see the truth right before you. If you are angry at your father, let that anger be with him and not with God."

Jamison sat bolt upright. "I am *not* angry with him."

It was Joshua's turn to shrug. Then he leaned close and spoke very calmly and slowly. "You cannot give up on the truth."

Jamison drew his hands from the table.

"I have heard a saying," Joshua continued. "When a student is ready, a teacher will be there." He stood up and extended his hand.

Jamison stood as well and offered his hand back.

"When you are ready, Jamison—and I know there will be a time when you are—look for the teacher. God will have him there. God will give you what you need."

Jamison stared back, struck at Joshua's parroting of the old black cook's words.

"I know you loved Hannah," Joshua said softly.

Jamison heard the words but did not truly believe Joshua was speaking them.

"I know you did—because I did too. And now that I'm leaving, I know that I will never see her again. And my heart is telling me that you will not either—after you leave here, that is."

Jamison could think of no words to reply, so great was his surprise.

"I say this because I am certain, beyond any doubt, beyond any human uncertainty, that Hannah came into our lives at the proper time—and is leaving at the proper time as well." Joshua drew closer. "We both must get on with what God has prepared for us—for the life he wants us to lead. Listen to him, Jamison. Listen with your heart. God will give you what you need."

With that, Joshua nodded, as if offering a coda to the conversation, and smiled a tired, heartfelt smile. The two shook hands. Joshua slowly walked to the front door, turned, offered one last wave, then stepped out into the swirling breeze.

He did not look back.

May 1845

"I cannot believe how much detritus has accumulated here," Clarence sniffed as he pitched a raft of papers toward the fire. Some of them fluttered to the floor like cheery blossoms in a breeze. The bulk of them, however, landed in the flames with a soft thump and a shower of sparks that hissed and popped.

"You're burning your files?" Jamison asked as he spun about in the rickety chair Clarence had used for three years. "Are the Hessians at the gates of Cambridge? Are we in danger of being overrun? State secrets must be destroyed, or what?"

Clarence wiped the sweat from his forehead. "I'm burning my papers, my good man. There is only so much memorabilia a man can possess."

A handful of students occupied the suite of rooms used as the offices for the *Crimson Review*. Only a few weeks remained of the school year, and all seniors had been instructed to clean out the desks to make room for next year's staff.

"You're not keeping anything? When you write your memoirs, you will have nothing to show for these golden years," said Jamison.

Clarence flipped through a handful of papers. "The second draft of a third-rate piece on a fourth-rate play performed by incredibly bad amateurs? That is stuff for my memoirs? If that is all I have, I shall have no business penning them."

He dismissed the rest of the papers in his hand with a scowl and tossed the lot into the fire. As the room grew hot, Jamison lifted two of the large windows. He had cleaned out his small alcove in the office a few days earlier. He had spent much more time deciding what to keep than Clarence, who was now gathering up great armfuls of material and feeding the blaze. Jamison had looked at every paper and made three stacks—one to discard, one to keep, and one to decide after seeing all the material. In the end, the undecided stack was three times the height of any other and forced him to spend another several hours in painful review.

When he had finished, a large Saratoga trunk was filled with his notes, final copies of articles, and samples of clipped old *Crimson Reviews*. He anticipated needing all of them to prove to some editor that he could indeed write well.

Now Jamison could relax as he watched others in the midst of the same decisions. He sat at the broad mahogany window seat that overlooked the campus. Staring out, growing oblivious to the increasing mayhem in the offices, he watched as students dallied about the commons. With lectures and final examinations soon to be completed, most students became much more cavalier about their schedules and class attendance. Small knots of fellows drifted here and there on the grass. One group tossed a ball about. Another group, made up exclusively of pipe smokers it seemed, gathered in a hazy, smoky circle on the lawn. Others lounged about near the doors of the student union, hailing chums, joining in small intense conversations or leaning back in loud braying laughter.

Jamison took a deep breath and sighed. He knew he would miss this place. He was happy and sad and nervous and confident and filled with regret all at once, with no emotion taking precedence.

Clarence broke his meditative mood by thrusting a stack of papers in his face. "You want these?"

Jamison shuffled through the wrinkled papers. He immediately recognized the story. The subject was Hannah Collins and her quest to become a physician. Jamison had interviewed her for hours—many hours more than the article required—and had crafted a detailed portrait. He knew it was not his finest work, for he had been much too personally involved in the story. Yet it was his favorite of all the stories he had written.

"I suspected you would. Is she still planning on pursuing her medical degree? Or will she marry that dolt from Boston—the one with the money?"

Jamison shrugged.

"You don't know?" Clarence cried, feigning shock. "You've loved her from afar for nearly four years, and now you don't know what she is planning? Mr. Pike, I am disappointed in your lack of tenacity."

Jamison turned red in a flush of embarrassed anger. "I have not loved her from afar for nearly four years," he said in protest.

"Three and a half, then. You probably didn't meet her right off, did you?"

"Stop it, Clarence. You have no business meddling in what doesn't concern you. No business at all."

Jamison turned away and stared, unseeing, out at the campus. Fully aware Clarence had not moved, Jamison didn't look at him but softly spoke. "I suspect you are right. I did not think it was obvious to everyone, that's all."

"I know. Such things are most hidden from those in the midst of it. But I did not mean to sully your feelings with such a cavalier remark. I know about unrequited affection. I do."

Sighing, Jamison stared down at his open palms. "She will probably marry that fellow from Boston, as you said."

"The handsome dolt?" Clarence asked.

Jamison nodded.

"Women. Who can understand them?"

Jamison shrugged. "I can't."

After several minutes of silence, Jamison asked, "Am I foolish for feeling the way I do? Am I just a simpleton who will never face the truth?"

"No, Jamison, you are not a simpleton. But after I heard you talk of Hannah Collins and then I met her, I realized that you two would never be together. Your quest would be forever denied. She is from a world inhabited by the beautiful and blessed people who lead charmed lives filled with indulgences brought on by their good looks, and free from pain and petty diversions."

"And the rest of us? Are we doomed?"

Clarence smiled. "No. It is just that we will observe those chosen people from afar. Perhaps we are allowed to mingle with them but not to be part of them."

"But, Clarence, you have been born to wealth. Surely you are part of this world more than I."

Clarence shook his head slowly. "No, I am rich and witty, but I am not a charmed individual as she is—and as that dolt from Boston is. Look at me. Am I a handsome fellow?"

Jamison looked at his friend as asked. "To me you are acceptable. Not a paragon of male beauty, but acceptable, nonetheless."

Clarence laughed. "You are most judicious, my friend, and generous. I may have some attributes but not all. People like Hannah have them all. And therein lies the gulf we cannot breach."

"And that is the truth?" Jamison asked quietly.

"It is. But take heart. Those Olympians are few and far between. What is left to the rest of us is satisfying enough. That Neta woman you have gone on about—she waits for you, doesn't she? She sounds most comely and agreeable. That match would be right. The gods will never match you and Hannah."

Clarence sounded so sure, so positive, so rational.

"And that is a surety?" Jamison asked.

"It is, my old chum. Now, please, help me burn the rest of my past here, or I will be trapped in this inferno for another day."

And with that Jamison sighed again, stood, and marched toward the fire.

CHAPTER EIGHT

Cambridge, Massachusetts
June 1845

Jamison sat in a worn chair in his room, doing little but gazing out the window, feeling, at times, melancholy. Tacked to the wall, tilted a few degrees off horizontal, his calendar displayed the ominous reality. Classes would be complete at the end of the week.

Three days left.

He had three days remaining as a college student and three days left with his friends.

For the past two weeks, as darkness lay across the campus in the evenings, Jamison had walked in the warm silence, walking without destination. He walked to the church that he most often attended—without ever once telling anyone of his actions. He walked past the Destiny, dark and empty after midnight. How would he replace that in his life—the gathering place of ideas and thoughts and friendship?

He walked past Hannah's residence—more than a dozen times. He never stopped nor even slowed. Only allowing himself a furtive glance, he hurried past the dark porch and windows. If he had been viewed by Hannah on his midnight constitutionals, he knew he would burst from embarrassment.

Gage and Joshua's residence loomed like a ghost in the dark. Gage occupied all of the second floor and most of the third, leaving Joshua shoehorned into a tiny attic room. That room, as well as the rest of the house, was empty and still. Occasionally Jamison would see a lantern flicker in Gage's suite. He thought of stopping and tapping softly at the door, but he did not do so. He would have to explain the why and how of his visit—and to be truthful, he could not.

The last night he found himself by the Charles River, standing on the bridge that led to Boston's Beacon Hill. A scattering of lights shone in a few homes, and the gas lamps on the bridge were reflected in long slivers of light along the oily waters.

Jamison leaned against the stone rampart and focused on the water, then out toward the sea. His thoughts continued to swirl. In every scrabbled image, in every whirling thought, there was the hint of Hannah. He heard her laugh, saw her eyes, felt the velvet touch of her hand—as if her image had fractured into a thousand pieces in his thoughts, each tiny bit containing an element of her reality.

At last the rough stone edged into his chest. He lifted his eyes to the heavens. Only the brightest stars shone through the haze of the city.

God will give you what you need.

"But shall I wait until he gives it? Do I simply wait with out-stretched arms?" Jamison whispered.

He took a deep breath, then turned and began to walk back toward Harvard, each step a little quicker than the one before. After a block he began to run.

He didn't really understand where he was going or why. He wasn't sure if he was running toward something—or away from something.

That morning, feeling a jangled sense of awareness from lack of sleep, Jamison hurried about the campus. He was looking for one particular person. He was seeking out Florence Galeswhite, Hannah's friend—the one he had once called a Valkyrie. Her tall form was easy to spot, standing a full head taller than some of the gentlemen around her on the steps of the administration building. He came up to her from behind, took her by the arm, and led her to a quiet alcove by the door.

"Tell her to meet me tonight," he said, hoping his voice conveyed enough mystery and passion and urgency for Florence to actually carry the message home.

He watched her surprised and bewildered look.

"Who? Where?"

Jamison stared at her. She actually leaned back from the intensity.

"You know who, Florence. And she will know where."

Florence swallowed, then nodded. "I'll tell her. I promise."

She tried to remove her arm, but he wouldn't release it.

"Will she marry him?"

"Who?"

Jamison winced. "You know who. That Keyes fellow from Boston."

Florence, to her credit as a loyal friend, bit her lip as she considered her answer, leaving a red mark. But under Jamison's glare, she weakened; then a pained look came upon her face. "I think she will, Jamison. He has asked her. At least I think I am sure he has asked her for her hand. She has not told me exactly–but how could it be otherwise?"

"And she said yes?"

Florence hesitated again as if she saw something in Jamison's eyes that held her words in check. "I don't know. I mean, she once told me she would say yes. Last year she said that . . . that she would say yes if he asked. I think she will."

Jamison loosened his grasp and looked down at the ground.

Florence rubbed her arm where her flesh bore a slight red mark from his grip. "I'm sorry. But he is handsome and will be very rich."

Jamison turned away and then back again. "Is that what she wants? Is it really?"

Florence lowered her eyes.

Jamison had his answer.

And now the day was gone. Night had come, and the laughter of students faded into the porcelain evening.

Jamison paused at the steps of the Destiny. He stopped and looked behind him. The street was empty, the sky dark. He took a deep breath and entered.

She was not there. Silently he made his way to a table in the back. He sat down and waited. The server brought coffee and cream. He nodded and did not smile.

There was no anger on his face, nor annoyance—but an undeniable look that mixed dread and expectation, joy and fear in one nearly blank expression.

He waited for a long time. He heard the clock tower sound ten.

"Jamison?"

It was Hannah. She had slipped in and was behind him. Her voice was as soft as the fog.

He had known what to say for weeks, perhaps years, and now felt his throat tighten. He gulped and forced himself to speak. "I didn't want all this to end and not have time to talk with you once more," he said evenly. He hoped his voice was calm, not reflecting the urgency he felt in his heart.

She smiled curiously and sat without waiting for an invitation.

He watched her sit and fix the folds of her dress, then place both hands, fingers barely touching, flat on the table in front of her.

"Coffee? Pie? Both are fresh," he said.

She nodded, though he realized she was merely being polite. With eyes averted, she spoke. "You'll be leaving at the end of the week?"

Jamison nodded.

"Where to? Someplace exotic?"

His laugh was chilled. "Hardly. New York. The position is on Gage's paper—the one that his father owns a portion of."

Her expression went serious. "Is that where you want to work? Do you really want to be beholden to Gage?"

Jamison took a deep breath. Whenever she spoke of Gage, there was an edge to her words—as if his money was ill-gotten. Perhaps some of it was, Jamison thought, but wasn't she seeking out her fortune just like Gage by marrying Keyes? Why was her pursuit of wealth more noble than his? He told her it was a job offered on his abilities–not connections. And the salary was more than what even his own father commanded.

Hannah turned her coffee cup in her hands. "Then that's good."

"I'll get to travel the world. I'll get to see exotic places. I'll have my dream. And I'll get to do what I love–write."

He stared at her as he spoke, trying to decipher what was behind her eyes. He could tell that his gaze at times unnerved her. He closed his eyes and let the words come–words he knew he should never voice. "Are you going to marry him?"

Her lips tightened. "And who might you mean?"

There was no turning back. "You know who."

"I do?"

"You do."

"I am sure you are mistaken, Jamison," she said with forced civility.

Jamison felt a familiar surge of anger. "All right, then, I'll play the game. Keyes. Robert Keyes. He asked you to marry him."

To her credit, Hannah did not respond with anything but politeness. "He did? You think I'm going to marry him?"

Jamison wanted to jump and shout and bang on the table. But instead he merely shrugged. "I've heard."

Hannah moved her coffee cup a few inches to the left. Then, without any provocation, she leaned back, extended her arm, and punched Jamison's shoulder with all her strength. She rocked forward, and he rocked back. It was not a polite, good-natured, brother-sister tussle. Hannah meant to hurt him–and she did.

"Jamison Pike," she shouted with no care as to who heard or observed, "do you believe everything Florence tells you? You believe every bit of gossip?"

He grabbed his arm, sure that it would be black-and-blue in the morning. "Then it's not true?"

"It is neither your concern nor hers," she hissed.

"That is not an answer," he hissed back.

"It is the answer that you will have. It is the only answer that you deserve."

He stared at her, staring at him. There were three small pools of light in the room. Her eyes were almost lost in the deepening shadows.

They sat motionless for several minutes.

Then Jamison moved first but somehow knew Hannah would move as well . . . and she did. He sat up straight, began to lean forward, and did not stop. After only a heartbeat, Hannah did in kind.

They came closer and closer. He placed his hand on her shoulder, marveling at the firm warmth. Without hesitating he slipped his hand to the bare skin at the nape of her neck.

He saw her eyes flinch, but only for an instant.

He drew close to her and found her lips with his. There was no hesitation on her part either, and for that one, clear moment, the world stopped for Jamison. All activity ceased in a thundering silence. He placed his arms around Hannah, enveloping her in a fierce, nearly angry embrace. Both of their chairs tipped toward each other.

Jamison had felt lips before and knew what a kiss might be—but all of that exploded in a tremendous ache of passion in this one moment. With the greatest of reluctance he leaned back ever so slightly, tasting the hint of lavender in the air as her perfume intoxicated his senses.

Her hand flew to her heart, as if to calm its rapid pulsing.

The world would not stay silent.

"Don't," he could only whisper. "Don't marry him."

And with that he could stay no longer in her presence, for both the promise of pleasure and the guarantee of pain were too strong, too sure, too absolute to allow him another minute in her company.

He stood up, his chair clattering to the floor behind him. Reaching into the breast pocket of his coat, he removed a thin envelope, laid it on the table, and walked away in the night. Never once did he look back, although every bone and fiber in his body cried out for such a glance.

FROM THE JOURNAL OF JAMISON PIKE

I am not now even certain what I wrote in that small note. It was something to the effect that she must not give up on her dream of becoming a doctor. I think I called her a bright and able woman and told her she must not abandon her dream—for it would be a loss I could not tolerate.

Two days after that night I am still at a loss to explain my actions. There is no reason I can determine for my boldness and my impudence. Perhaps the only person more outraged and shocked by my actions—other than me—is Hannah.

To be true, we have had many conversations in the past four years, but most of them were more contentious in nature than friendly. I so enjoyed sparring with her, and I am baffled to see how sparring leads to romance and affection.

But it has. I realize that Hannah holds such a place in my heart that I am in terror that she will marry this Keyes fellow. And to be honest, what chance might I truly have had? I am not rich and most likely never will be. I do not think I am what most women would call handsome. It is not likely I will ever travel in her social circles.

So why am I moping about these last few days—moping about a woman I could never possess?

I do not know—save for the fact that Hannah has captured my heart in a way I had not expected—and that part of my life is now over.

And in order to move past this, I am going to write my sweet, innocent Neta.

I wonder if life is ever going to be easy, the answers ever apparent. I look at a fellow like Joshua who has all the answers. Even if he is wrong, at least his life will be peaceful and orderly. After all, what sort of adventure and confusion could lay in store for a peaceable man of God, for whom the world offers no lure and temptation?

I should think Hannah will be what she is—a vision I can never attain—and let her simply be part of my past.

I should face the future with clarity.

And now—how is that done, exactly?

From a Letter to Mr. and Mrs. Pike

Dear Mother and Father,

I trust that all is well in Pittsburgh. You were right in not attending my graduation exercises. The trip and the expense would have been too high a price to pay to watch me step upon the stage for only a few seconds—as you wrote in your last letter. I do not harbor any regret at your absence. The actual day of graduation proved to be most hot and humid. Rain remained a threat but kept away through nightfall and the end of all the festivities. It was a crowded affair made more confusing by being held out of doors—since the auditorium was not yet complete.

Can you imagine hundreds of parents and well-wishers all crowding each other out to get a glimpse of their sons (and a few daughters) marching across the stage to receive their sheepskin diplomas? A great deal of effort was undertaken for those few moments in the limelight.

And because of the celebrations, the town's hotels and inns were filled. I believe many of them charged a premium. I know that would have shocked both your sensibilities and pocketbook.

My four years of education are now over. I have a diploma and have been certified by this institution as a man of letters. It is a most curious feeling—to be recognized as an intellectual sort of fellow.

After graduation, I spent several days packing and handling many details involved in closing my bank accounts, paying rent, returning borrowed books, and the like. Now that classes are ended, the town of Cambridge seems much slower and smaller.

I will not be returning to Pittsburgh. At least not now. This news may not be a total surprise to you, but it is a decision I have spent many hours pondering. If I were to return home, no doubt you, Father, would want me to work with you at the church. And quite possibly, in the future, attend the Bethel Park Seminary. You have said as much on several occasions.

That is a course that I, in good conscience, cannot take.

I do not believe you will be shocked by these words and this decision. The quiet, bloodless battles we have fought over this in the past no doubt served as a predictor of my choice.

The truth you tried to teach me as a child was not enough. I have seen, even though I am not so experienced yet, enough of this world–and I know that the "people of the world" are not as evil, nor are "Christians" as innocent, as you think and as you taught.

What I learned as a child I have had to unlearn as an adult. Good people with wonderful hearts are not believers. Horrible people with venal hearts claim the Bible as their own. Does that make sense to you, Father? To me, it does not.

I was ten. You preached on the evil nature of man and the difficulty of finding our way to heaven. Your arms flailed about. You loomed above me and your shadow cut across my face. "The road is narrow and the travelers will be few," you bellowed. Even then I felt inadequate. How could I measure up? How could I dare think I would be good enough for God when I was not good enough for you?

I couldn't then. And I have not improved upon my position since, I am afraid.

It is with both regret and relief that I write these hard words.

Since I will not return, I have decided to make my home in New York City. I have been offered a job at one of New York's leading newspapers–and they have offered me the sum of $55 a week to begin. That is the actual salary to be paid per week–not per month. I can scarcely believe it either.

I know you may be disappointed in me. But I must strike out on my own and make my own way in this world.

As a journalist, I have promised to seek out the truth. Perhaps someday I may see all of this differently. But for now I must attend to my own life.

Your son,
Jamison

From a Letter to Miss Neta Hill

My sweet Neta,
I have struggled with this letter for days now. I have been in receipt of

two of your lovely letters and have not formulated a single page of response. I might blame it on the busyness of the end of classes and the like, but I would know that to be a falsehood. There is never a day that passes when there is not time remaining for a short note to be drafted.

I read of your activities in Pittsburgh with great interest. It appears as if the town has grown so since I left for Harvard.

I would like to think of myself as a gentleman, and as such a person, I must be frank and honest—even if such frankness might cause some consternation.

Neta, I am not returning to Pittsburgh. Instead I will seek my fortune first in New York City. We have never truly discussed what might occur to both of us in the future—and I do not want to tie your hopes up in a man who will not soon be at your side. Perhaps I have taken too great a liberty concerning this. Perhaps you had no inclination to be more than a friend to me. If the latter is true, then I have become the fool and not the gentleman.

Yet I do not wish to hold you to a hope that will not be realized.

However, as I write these lines, I am also aware that more and more young women are striking out on their own and finding their way to places like Boston and New York. I am sure with your wit and charm there would be no end of things you could find to do. If so, you must promise you will inform me of your plans at the earliest opportunity. I may not be a native New Yorker, but I have a fair knowledge of how to get around in such a metropolis. It would be a wonderful privilege to be your escort.

I wish to be included in your continuing correspondence. Even if you are unable to venture to New York City, it will be most possible that I may be traveling through Pittsburgh at some point in the future. Such is the life, they say, of a journalist.

As always, your great admirer,
Jamison

The breeze rattled loudly at the leaves as Jamison walked along the main path through campus. As the bell in the clock tower sounded out ten, his stomach rumbled. An inveterate early riser, Jamison had allowed himself the luxury of staying in bed till well past nine o'clock the past few days. With packing completed and last-minute errands finished, Jamison was left with little to do. Nearly every student, save those forced into remedial summer courses, had long since departed, and the campus and town had fallen into a subdued quiet.

The editor at the *World* wrote and said it would be best if Jamison would begin work on September 1–more than two months from this day.

He wondered if he might first travel some. However, he soon discovered that while he had the resources to live, and live comfortably, until winter if needed, he did not have nearly enough to indulge in frivolous travel.

Moreover, there was no one he truly desired to visit. His friends were all too recently departed to welcome visits from a fellow classmate. He thought at first of returning home, but that would entail discussing his recent decision for days on end. Whatever pleasure seeing Neta again might offer was more than offset by the pain of the confrontation with his parents.

The library remained open, so he thought he would indulge himself in that fashion, perusing all the books and novels he had found no time to enjoy during the last four years. He spent much time reading and rereading the *Emigrants Guide to Oregon and California*, plotting out the suggested routes on a map he purchased in Boston. He found it most alluring that much of North America between the Mississippi and the Pacific Ocean was unoccupied, unexplored, and unsettled.

That same book, now in tatters with creased and folded pages, was tucked under his arm. He was on his way to the Destiny for a late breakfast, or perhaps an early lunch. At that time he could enjoy the quiet; he was often the only customer for hours.

Settling in behind a large stack of pancakes, with a side of fat, greasy sausages, Jamison folded back the book to a familiar section, forked a slice of meat into his mouth, and began to read. He had gone no more than three pages and two sausages when he heard his name being called from the street. It was Clarence, with his face pressed against the window.

Jamison laughed and waved him in. "Come join me, Clarence," he called out. "I thought you had left."

After brushing the chair off with his handkerchief, Clarence settled in. "I had left. I thought for good. But I am back."

"So I see. For any reason in particular? Why return to Cambridge? Weren't you in New York?"

"Indeed, I was. But I return with news—news of import to you, my friend."

Wolfing down another forkful of pancakes, Jamison waited for an explanation as he chewed.

"My grandmother."

"Your grandmother?"

"Yes. It's because of her."

"And why is that?"

"You know she is rich."

"So you have said. Many times," Jamison replied, recalling that Clarence often said the words with a mix of anger and humor.

"She has a magnificent mansion in New York City."

"She does?"

"A couple of dozen bedchambers. A ballroom we could play baseball in."

Jamison chewed thoughtfully. "And . . . ?"

"She's old, Jamison. And does not relish being there alone with only servants around her."

"Why don't your parents move in? Or some other relative?"

"There aren't any who could tolerate her for more than a few hours—inheritance or not."

Jamison nodded, then held his hands up in surrender. "But why are you here? Why are you telling me this?"

"She has requested me to live there with her—in my own wing, of course—and have an occasional meal with her."

Jamison could not think of another question that might be pertinent.

"She asked if I knew of anyone else. There is an entire wing that no one uses. Everything is covered with white sheets."

Jamison looked puzzled.

"You don't get it, do you?" Clarence asked.

Jamison shook his head.

"You could live there with me and my grandmother in a truly grand style that you would never be able to afford in your wildest dreams of fancy! That's why I am here. I am offering you a place to stay when you get to New York."

Jamison's fork tumbled from his grasp and clattered on the table.

"I am serious, my good friend. If you can pack by two o'clock this afternoon, we can catch the next train home."

More than a minute passed before Jamison spoke. "How many rooms in my wing?"

Clarence laughed. "More than you would ever need, my friend. Now shall we gather your belongings?"

Jamison was standing before Clarence had finished talking.

God gives what you need.

CHAPTER NINE

New York City
November 1845

Jamison stretched his arms over his head and yawned
expansively. Blinking his eyes, he squinted over to the window. The
heavy damask curtains were snugged tightly together, save for a tiny
triangle in the middle of the window. A petulant beam of sunlight
poured through that triangle and onto the bloodred wool carpet.

Jamison groaned and stretched again.

He propped himself up in bed and instead of drawing open the
curtains, struck a match and lit the lantern on his nightstand. It was
no ordinary lantern, Jamison noted as he slid the chimney back into
place, but a delicate fluting of etched glass, tinted with red and gold,
its base silver. He had to turn the wick up in order to force more
illumination through the decorations on the glass. At last, satisfied
with the light, he reached down to the floor and retrieved yesterday's copy of the *New York World*.

Working on a newspaper infrequently allowed time to actually
read a newspaper.

He paged past the front-page news of the political scene in New
York and only glanced at the machinations of the crowned heads of

Europe. He leafed through the stories, quickly perusing headlines, mentally critiquing the style and substance of five other articles until he came to his own byline. Then he stopped, sat up straighter, folded the paper in half, then in quarters, and read his own words for the dozenth time.

The story was small. Jamison had heard of accusations of bribes and all manner of illegal payment over at Ellis Island–not from the immigrants, but from and to contractors paid by the government to do repair work on the structures. He had spent several days on the island talking to over thirty people. He found, to no one's surprise, that virtually no one would reveal anything, except in cryptic, veiled remarks. He did find two fellows who claimed they had to pay a portion of their wages to the foreman to do masonry work on the facility. Jamison mentioned no names, but the quotes were colorful.

He sighed when he finished reading. It was a satisfied sigh. To see his name in print continued to prove most gratifying. He read the article twice more, thinking of different ways to turn a phrase and alternatives to the progression of the facts.

It was then he heard a curious screeching–a mixture of the cry of an angry cat and rusty wheels being dragged over an iron grate. It continued for a long moment, then was followed by a crash that echoed throughout the house . . . and a muffled stream of invectives and curses.

Jamison closed his eyes and pinched the bridge of his nose.

"It is time to arise anyhow," he said as he dressed quickly. The shouting emanated from the entrance hall, which Jamison considered a long walk from his bedchamber. He headed north for a while, past a gallery of dark oil paintings of dour ancestors in the Edmonds family. He turned right at the bust of Homer, which he imagined was purloined from a Greek temple during someone's tour of the Continent. Then he marched down the "carpet" hall, as he called it– a long broad hallway covered with two thicknesses of rugs, one peeking out from the other. He had no idea why anyone would have a fifty-foot by six-foot rug–let alone two of them in layers. But Clarence's grandmother did, and on mornings as chilly as today, he was grateful for the extra padding underfoot. The servants had been up for hours, he supposed, and had lit only every other gas lamp. Their oily hissing always made Jamison think of walking through a den of serpents. Finally, after what seemed like hours, Jamison reached the top of the stairs overlooking the grand expanse of the foyer and entry hall.

Jamison admitted, when he had first surveyed the home, that the Edmondses were more than just a few dollars wealthier than Gage Davis and family—and they were even more willing to provide evidence of their wealth. He once asked Clarence, after a long night of conversation, who was wealthier—the Edmonds clan or the Davis family.

Clarence turned up his nose and sniffed. "Good heavens, man, those people are peasants compared to what my grandmother owns."

"Then why didn't anyone at Harvard know that? You never played the part."

He sniffed again. "The truly wealthy never do."

But this morning Clarence looked anything but the wealthy son of an aristocratic family with "old money." He was in evening coat and hat, but to call him merely disheveled would have been kind. His white shirt was stained, with a few buttons undone, and his coat actually appeared muddy.

"Clarence, what on earth . . . ?"

He stared up at Jamison. "No lectures, my good man. Just help me get this in the house."

Jamison began to pad down the grand staircase that wound about the circular entry. "It's already in the house, Clarence. But what is it?"

Clarence straightened up and peered behind him. "Good heavens, it is in."

Jamison came close and nudged the apparatus with his foot. "Were you out dredging the river?"

The contraption appeared to be an amalgam of wires and wooden struts with the proportions of a middling-sized horse.

"Dredging the river, that's a rich one," Clarence snickered. He yanked off his coat and stumbled toward the kitchen but seemed to be sucked into the vacuum of the drawing room. Before Jamison could react, he heard a hollow thump. Clarence had simply toppled over in the middle of the floor, and by the time Jamison knelt beside him, his friend was fast asleep. He nudged at a shoulder and got no response. He shook it harder but only received a snort from Clarence.

Jamison sighed, stood up, and went to the bellpull by the door.

In a scant minute Alan, the manservant, appeared in the shadows just beyond the drawing room door. "You rang, Mr. Pike?"

Jamison tilted his head to the now sound-asleep Clarence.

Alan sighed loudly. "It appears Mr. Edmonds has enjoyed himself greatly last evening."

Jamison offered a weary smile. "Apparently."

"And what might that be in the hallway?" the servant asked, as if it had been ordered by Jamison. "It looks like a lobster trap for equines."

Jamison laughed. "It might be, Alan. It does look like he dragged it from the river."

"Shall I take it to the basement with his other finds?"

"I suppose, Alan. But first, call for the liveryman and let us take our friend to his bedchamber at least."

Since moving in with Clarence at his grandmother Edmonds's mansion, Jamison and Alan had repeated this same duty at least ten times. And every time had been preceded with Clarence hauling something home. Twice it had been a park bench, another time the front seat out of a carriage. Jamison could not figure out why Clarence did what he did when overimbibing, and Clarence simply refused to talk about it after his head cleared.

Alan and the liveryman, whose name Jamison could never quite recall, came down from the north wing of the house, wiping their hands and showing as much exasperation as any servant could dare without risk of termination.

"Sir, shall I call the cook to prepare your breakfast? Or would lunch be better suited?" Alan continued, a certain edge of insult in his words.

Jamison let the words pass without comment. After all, he *was* a guest in the house. A long-term guest to be sure, but a guest nonetheless. "Breakfast would be wonderful. Thank you, Alan. Tell her I will dress first and be down in fifteen minutes."

"As you wish. In the dining room?"

Jamison sniffed. There was still a pungent air remaining from Clarence's entry. "No, I'll eat in the kitchen, actually. It's warmer and not nearly as much work for everyone. And the light is better as well. I may read while eating this morning."

If Jamison's magnanimity impressed Alan, he did not show it. His impassive face, his winter pallor, remained unchanged.

Fifteen minutes later, as Jamison slid behind a table in a sunny corner of the massive kitchen, Hilda, a wonderfully pleasant lady who was as wide as she was tall, placed a plate of eggs, ham, and potatoes before him with a warm smile. "You eat now, Mr. Pike. Eat good."

Jamison smiled as he forked in the first taste of eggs. He had carried with him the newspaper and a few current magazines. "Thank you, Hilda."

"Toast ready now too. Jam? Butter? Sugar?"

"Yes. I mean, jam is fine, Hilda. Thank you."

She beamed at him.

Clarence would never have taken a meal in the kitchen. In fact, Jamison was near certain that his friend could not find the kitchen, even on a good day.

He stabbed at the ham, cut thick as he liked it, and flipped through the pages of the magazines as he scanned the articles.

Jamison ate his way through both slices of toast and then began to sip his warm coffee. Leaning back, he took in the small phalanx of cooks and maids that attended to washing and scrubbing and cooking. Jamison could never understand the need for such a large staff. After all, there were only the two of them in residence now that Clarence's grandmother was on a short trip to Savannah to visit a distant aunt. There was little for the servants to do but clean and polish. By now every surface in the house gleamed.

Jamison was certain by the time he finished breakfast and returned to his bedchamber, it would be stripped of all used bed linens and covers and clean ones installed. There would be piles of fresh, fluffy towels provided–even though he had not used them the day prior– and every surface would be cleaned and dusted and swept.

Nearly every day Jamison would shake his head in absolute amazement at his wonderful good fortune. How many others would have sold their soul to live in such luxury? It would be a very simple matter to grow very accustomed to this level of service and the prestige that came with it. He now began to understand, at least to a small degree, why Hannah often seemed focused on finding a suitor who might provide her with a continuing high standard of living.

Jamison selected a most modest outfit–a brown suit, a brown tweed coat, and a brown Bollinger hat that was all the rage in England, or at least so claimed the haberdasher. He recalled hearing several tailors and outfitters claim the same thing–as if Americans could not help getting attired without first looking to the grand styles abroad.

But he liked the hat.

The weather was chilled as expected for mid-November. He set off to the north. He had thought many times of walking to the Davis home. After all, they lived in the same neighborhood, the houses only a mile apart–one at the north edge of the best section of town, the other at the south. Since Harvard, Jamison had vowed to visit at least once during every week, but had yet to fulfill that vow.

Today was different. Gage had sent a note requesting Jamison's presence at lunch. Jamison was looking forward to the chance to catch up on the latest news from his old friend.

He walked into Nutley's, a restaurant he often passed on his walks but never once entered. "If an establishment does not post its fare– and prices–outside," he had said, "then it is too rich for my blood."

Nutley's did not offer such a posting, and in fact resembled more a discreet club than a restaurant. It was just the type of place Gage would favor.

Inside, the air reeked of expensive cigars, walnut paneling, and money.

Jamison spotted Gage immediately. Gage waved his menu in the air, evidently delighted to see Jamison.

"My, my," Gage exclaimed as Jamison sat down, "our intrepid reporter has deigned to break bread with a mere capitalist. How charming."

Jamison offered a good-natured scowl.

"I see your name splashed across the pages of the country's premier newspaper," Gage continued, "and I wonder how you find time in your busy day to eat, let alone meet with old friends."

Jamison grabbed a crusty roll from the silver basket in the middle of the white linen tablecloth. "Gage, at Harvard you were known for stretching the truth until its origin was confused–and that trait has not left you after graduation."

"You wound me, Jamison. You do. I have followed your career, and for a journalist so soon from Harvard to have garnered handfuls of front-page stories is amazing."

Jamison's face showed his consternation. "You actually saw my stories? You paid attention?"

"Of course I did. We own part of the paper, you know. I pay attention to all my assets, my good man–especially ones that will pay off."

The waiter, in starched white shirt and morning coat, took their orders. He merely nodded at each request, as if a skilled waiter had no need to commit their desires to paper and pencil. Then, nodding one final time, he sidled off to the kitchen.

"So, Jamison, things going well for you?"

Between bites of crusty bread, Jamison reported to Gage the latest news and gossip from the editorial side of the newspaper. Jamison had been surprised at the sheer number of rumors and innuendos that swept through the newsroom on any given day. He had thought reporters might be immune to such wild-eyed tales–but it was obvious they were not. More often than not, such innuendos found their way to the pages of the paper–most often disguised as facts or shadowy truths.

"That's what I like about your writing," Gage said. "I never get the feeling that you have passed on one single rumor as truth. Makes your words unique—substantial."

Jamison, embarrassed, looked down at his soup in reply.

"You're still living at the Edmonds mansion?" Gage asked midway through the lunch.

"Well . . . of course. You sent your note there, remember?"

Gage rolled his eyes. "Yes, I know where you live. But I was hoping you might have come to your senses in the last few days and moved on."

"But it's a mansion. And it's free," Jamison said, puzzled.

Gage pursed his lips. "My friend, it does not cost you hard currency, but I am sure of one thing—there is nothing free. Your address will cost you dearly if you stay."

Jamison propped his elbows on the table, nudging at the heavy silverware. "What do you mean? Cost me dearly? What have you heard?"

Gage leaned in closer, as if about to share a harsh secret. "You must know of Clarence's excesses. If I have heard of them, then for certain, half of New York has heard. He lives there. You live there. That relationship is bound to hurt your reputation."

"But it's not like that. Clarence is a good friend. He just overindulges on occasion."

Gage shook his head. "More than that, Jamison. If it were simply a fondness for drink, I would not offer a warning. It is more than that."

"What then?"

Just then the waiter slipped to the table. "Dessert? Coffee? An after-dinner libation, perhaps?"

Gage evaluated Jamison with a curious stare, then requested a pot of coffee for the two of them.

After the waiter left, Gage simply added, "Jamison, I have heard things that are not savory in the least. Be forewarned, old friend. Clarence may have been an old Harvard chum, but I believe he thinks money will quiet any tempest. It won't."

Jamison knew from the look on Gage's face that he would provide no more information.

"Well, I suppose it would not hurt to find a place of my own," Jamison replied. "Your paper pays me enough."

"If they do," Gage laughed, "I should talk to them about such extravagances."

"If you do," Jamison laughed back, stirring a spoonful of sugar into his coffee, "I will begin investigating Davis Enterprises."

Gage held his hands up in surrender. "Let's change the subject. I want no part of your dogging my steps—friendship or not."

"Speaking of old friends," Jamison said, "have you heard anything from Joshua?"

Gage shook his head. "Not a word. But I did not expect it either."

"Why?"

"He didn't want to go home. I think he was embarrassed."

"He didn't want to go? But what about his speech on loyalty and obedience to his parents?"

Gage spread his palms on the table. "That's why he did it. I understand that. But I don't for a minute think he truly *wanted* to do it. There is a big difference."

Jamison focused his attention on the windows facing the street. All he could see were hats of tall men. The rest of the street scene was blocked by the thick damask draperies.

"Have you heard from Hannah?" Jamison's words fell softly.

Gage shook his head again. "I haven't, and again, I don't expect I will. I don't think she ever considered me as a confidant. Joshua maybe. Not me."

"Joshua?"

"He was safe. She knew he would go back to Ohio. She could flirt with him and never have to worry about entanglements."

"Seriously?"

Gage shrugged, then leaned over the table and whispered, "Yes. Perhaps. Or perhaps not. I don't know for sure anything about women. A mystery, all of them." Gage offered a knowing smile. "Jamison, you need to forget about Hannah. You need to focus on that Neta woman. She seemed to be terribly nice. At least from what you told me. Sounded like an intelligent girl. And you said she was quite pretty, didn't you?"

"She is. But . . . why does that Robert Keyes fellow have such a lock on Hannah? Is she bound to marry him? Regardless of how she feels?"

Gage swallowed the last of his coffee, making an odd face. "I think she will. I think she will marry him. I think she will make herself believe that she does truly love him."

"Why?" Jamison had never really discussed Hannah with Gage– especially after Gage had all but dismissed Jamison as a potential suitor to her.

"Money is part of it. She came from money and now it's all gone– or most of it. I think her parents expect her to save them from their poverty."

"Are they really that poor?"

Gage waved his hand, dismissing the question. "Of course not. They have enough to live on–just not as much as before. It's difficult to go back after tasting the good life. That's another reason why you should leave the Edmondses. You'll grow to expect the niceties. Then, regardless of how much the paper pays you, it will never be that much."

"Are you sure?" Jamison smiled.

"Positive."

The waiter, on a cat's silent feet, slipped up to the table and left the check on a far corner, almost treating the tab as some wounded, dangerous animal.

Gage was quick, snapping up the leather billfold. "My treat," he demanded, as if he expected resistance from Jamison. He slipped a few bills inside and patted the cover closed.

Neither made an effort to stand.

"Are you sure about Hannah?" Jamison asked again, with the tiniest hint of desperation.

"I think I am. A woman like Hannah will never be satisfied. I know she painted a great picture of how she is a modern woman and all that Lucretia Mott nonsense–but she isn't. None of them are. Given

138

the choice between love and money, ninety-nine out of a hundred will snap up the money. If a good-looking rich man approached our Miss Mott, she would stop her fuming and fussing and settle down like a cat in the summer sun on the porch."

Jamison did not speak. Nor did his expression give light to any of his thoughts. Then he stood and waited for Gage to do the same.

As they made their way to the front, a woman's voice called out. The sound was like silk rustling against silk. Then a woman came to Gage and pecked his cheek, smiling at both of them. Gage spoke a few words and offered a brief introduction to Jamison, but the noise of the crowd and street overcame his words. Jamison simply nodded as if he had heard.

The woman smiled again, her eyes caressing Jamison for a minute. She was slight with an air of complete confidence. Her very dark hair spilled in tight coils about her face. Even her eyes seemed to glow darkly, like embers of coal, against her very white skin. She lowered her eyes, seeming to survey what Jamison was surveying. Then she looked up, her lips now slightly open, as if acknowledging the power of a woman well aware of her assets. Finally she turned and walked away, as if she knew Jamison would be staring after her.

Jamison whispered to Gage as she slipped into the crowds, "What was that woman's name again?"

"Eva. Eva Rikler."

"Rikler?"

"Yes."

"My lands, I didn't hear that. Is it really Rikler?"

Gage smiled as if he were a cat holding a fat bird. "Yes, my old friend. She is indeed the daughter of Dexter Rikler. And the last time I checked, Mr. Rikler is your editor, is he not?"

And with that, Gage turned into the crowd and slipped from view.

Jamison stood for several minutes, a confused and almost happy look on his face.

From a Note to Jamison Pike from Eva Rikler

My dear Mr. Pike,

How nice to bump into you yesterday. I had no idea that Mr. Gage Davis and yourself were classmates at Harvard. I should scold him for not introducing us earlier.

Ever since my father hired you, he has been telling tales of his newest find—a jewel of a reporter who can actually write a coherent sentence, complete with subject and verb—and who actually knows something of the culture and society around him.

You have no idea how he rails against less-skilled reporters. It is as if he must virtually instruct them in how to do each step of their tasks.

On the other hand, he has confided in me (and you must promise never to reveal this confidence) that he can trust you from assignment to comple- tion—with nary a worry of lawsuit or embarrassment.

High praise indeed, Mr. Pike—and you know how sparse my father is with praise.

We should make plans to meet again. Perhaps I will mention to my father to pass along to you as he sees fit invitations for a gala or two. Perhaps you might ask me to accompany you.

Yes, I know that at this moment your eyes are wide in amazement at the forwardness of this woman whom you have just met.

A hussy, you say? No, not at all.

This is New York. And I am a most modern woman.

Expecting to hear from you soon.

Yours,

Eva Rikler

There was a note on his desk when Jamison arrived at work the next Monday.

Come see me. 9:00
  —Rikler

Jamison stood outside the office at 8:50.

"If that's you, Pike, come on in. No sense in waiting for the clock," a voice boomed out.

Jamison let himself in. The office was not large, but expensively furnished. One wall was floor-to-ceiling volumes of books in mahogany bookshelves. Opposite was a leather couch, a chair-and-table arrangement with a lantern and a stack of newspapers. In fact, there were several stacks of newspapers spread around the room. Most were competitors from the city, though Jamison spotted some foreign titles as well—mostly from London, it seemed.

"Sit down, Mr. Pike," Rikler said.

Dexter Rikler's coarse features belied his ability to produce such a beautiful daughter. His hair was dark, though not at all curly, but thick and coarse. A lantern jaw offset a small, narrow mouth and close-set eyes. Of short stature, Rikler often could be seen squaring his shoulders and standing erect and stiff, as if that would make him more powerful. He reminded Jamison of a not-so-handsome medieval prince who might quickly resort to Machiavellian politics to survive and flourish.

Jamison sat as he was told and fussed for a moment with the sleeves of his jacket.

"You like working here, Mr. Pike?"

Jamison did not hesitate. "I do, sir. Very much."

"You like the stories you're doing?"

"I do, sir. Very much."

Mr. Rikler stared at him from behind his massive desk. The morning sun reflected off it like a mirror, forming a halo around his face. "Good. You think you're being paid enough?"

Jamison swallowed. He had no idea what all these questions meant. "I do, sir. I mean . . . what I get is fine. More would be better."

Rikler's intense stare withered Jamison's last few words even before he spoke. Then Rikler cocked his head back and guffawed loudly, like a man after his third libation. "Good! I like a man who's honest."

Rikler reached into the top drawer of his desk and tossed an envelope toward Jamison.

Jamison caught it as it hit his lap.

"Two tickets to the opera. Take my daughter. She said a friend of hers introduced you at lunch. She knows a great many people, it appears. Regardless . . . the opera . . . well, you can write about it–but don't go taking notes while you're with her. Remember what you need as it happens."

Jamison stammered, "I will, sir, I mean, thank you . . ."

The editor waved his hand as both a dismissal and an acknowledgment. "Pike–I like you. You are one of the few reporters here who knows how to write. I saw that in the stuff you did at Harvard. You have a good slant on things. Clever. Turn a phrase well."

"Why . . . thank you, sir," Jamison replied, looking down at his feet, suddenly embarrassed.

"One word of advice, though."

"Sir?"

"When you quote somebody, make them sound better than you do. Your quotes make the people sound like dolts."

"But I write what they say."

Again Rikler waved his hand. "That may be, but I don't want dolts in my newspaper. Fuss them up some and make them sound at least halfway intelligent."

"But, sir, wouldn't that–"

The editor gave another wave. "Maybe. But it's my paper. Not yours. Smart people sell better than dolts. Understand?"

Jamison nodded.

"And take care with my daughter. She can be a handful."

Jamison nodded again. "Thank you, sir. I mean, I will. I mean, I know."

And with that Jamison stepped out of the office, closed the door, and breathed a great sigh of relief. Only then did he look again at the tickets. There was a wet circle on the envelope from the sweat of his fingers.

CHAPTER TEN

New York City
July 1846

Clarence and Jamison sat in the cushioned stillness
of the grand drawing room of the mansion. There was a surplus of
furniture in the room, with delicate carvings on legs and arms—all
muffled with crisp white linen slipcovers for the summer. All of it
seemed to hover like ghosts. Clarence had ordered two massive
leather wing chairs brought down from the library upstairs. Around
the chairs he placed a series of tables and lanterns and hassocks and
drew the whole arrangement close to the fire in the winter, and
farther away as the days grew warmer.

Holding his newspaper just so, Jamison caught the last light of the
afternoon.

"Land sakes, man," Clarence sniffed from his chair nearly five
yards away. "Is that all you ever read? Newspapers? Don't you get
enough of them during the day? You have to bring them back here
with you like some homeless dog?"

Jamison peered around the open newspaper. "I need to watch the
competition. And to borrow ideas."

"You are too involved, my friend," Clarence said disdainfully.

"You need to develop a life outside the newspaper office. You should read this." He held up a copy of a magazine.

Jamison squinted. "What is it?"

"I shouldn't tell you."

"What is it?"

"A new magazine."

"What sort of magazine?"

"No, Jamison, I do not want to cause you to sin. I am fairly certain there is some manner of extra punishment involved—in the biblical sense—with leading an innocent astray."

Jamison placed his hands on the arms of the chair. "I am tired. Tell me or not—it truly does not matter."

Clarence giggled, gathering the magazine tight against his chest.

Jamison sighed. "Well?"

"Well, what?"

"The magazine?"

"Oh, this rag? Just some gentleman's magazine."

"Gentleman's magazine?"

"One could call it that. It has a usual selection of stories, and a sprinkling of the odd etching."

"Of what?"

"That is what I shall not show you, my innocent friend. The illustrations are most racy. I have heard that in Boston they have issued a warrant for the arrest of the publisher, should he happen to visit the city. Indecent, they claimed, and purple with moral turpitude."

"What!" Jamison exclaimed. He had heard of such magazines but had never yet seen an example. "Where did you get that?"

"A friend of a friend of a friend who thought I might be interested in such things. And they were right."

"Let me see," Jamison said as he stood up and took a step toward Clarence, who had the magazine still tightly grasped in his arms.

"No!" Clarence shrieked. "Too corrupting."

And Jamison stopped for a second. The last few hints of sunlight filtered into the room and caught Clarence full face. And in that moment of clarity of light, Jamison saw how pallid his friend had become since their days at Harvard, how the flesh on his face seemed to sag, almost as if the skin itself suffered from great fatigue. His eyes, squinting in the sunlight, were dull and nearly as lifeless as Jamison had ever seen—and he had seen, in these past few months, more than enough lifeless eyes—cold as a wagon tire. In that instant the sun dipped another degree. Dimness returned to the room, and Clarence's features returned to normal. Jamison stepped back, almost frightened by his friend's transformation.

"Well," Jamison managed to laugh, "perhaps you are right. Perhaps I should not partake. One cad per house should be sufficient."

Clarence eyed him with a curious grinning frown. Then his brow furrowed and his countenance shifted to petulance. "Besides, Jamison, there is nothing here that you have not seen. I'm sure of that. What with your many evenings escorting Miss Rikler about the city."

Jamison picked up his newspaper and was about to leave the room. "Clarence," he said sternly, "that is enough. Miss Rikler is a very fine woman. She is a decent woman."

Clarence snorted again. "And the daughter of your employer, correct?"

Jamison fumed but did not reply.

"Jamison," Clarence said with a wave of his hand, "go peddle your righteousness somewhere else. I hear things. I hear lots of things. You have been seen in a great many public places with that woman. And if only a fraction of what I hear is actually true, then you have nothing to be indignant about, my friend. Nothing at all."

Jamison stopped in the doorway. He was suddenly very, very angry. He glared at Clarence. "I will not argue with you, Clarence. I am a guest in your grandmother's home. But I know what the truth is."

Clarence waved him away. "Ah yes, the truth. Indeed. You know the truth. The ephemeral and mercurial truth."

And as Jamison walked out of the room, he heard Clarence mutter, "And I am the queen of the May."

The two men sat down together at the massive table in the dining room. The slick mahogany surface would hold three dozen elaborate china and silver place settings, complete with elegant crystal water goblets, wineglasses, and champagne flutes around its ornately decorated centerpiece.

Clarence sat at one end and Jamison at the other.

Jamison felt like a complete fool on these evenings when Clarence insisted they take supper in the formal rooms of the house. Conversation was limited, for they both nearly had to shout to be heard across the expanse. Servants scurried about behind them. Six of them were required to serve a full meal, as well as a full complement of kitchen help and chefs.

If a choice had been given, Jamison would have eaten in the kitchen with the cooks. It was much more comfortable and the light was better, not to mention the aromas and conversation.

The soup—some sort of cold concoction—had been whisked away. While Jamison knew cold soup was an indicator of fine dining, it was a dish he had never quite warmed to.

"What about that woman . . . ," Clarence near shouted, the last few words lost in the not-so-silent clatter of metal warming domes on china.

"What woman?" Jamison shouted back. It was not a shout exactly, but he felt like it was.

"That woman from Pennsylvania. The one you said might visit. Why hasn't she?"

He was referring to Neta, of course. Jamison regretted ever telling him of his relationship and correspondence with Miss Hill. Clarence used that knowledge at carefully selected opportunities to prick and jab at Jamison.

"She might."

Clarence held his wineglass in the air, waving it slightly. The cut crystal caught the light in a wobbly dance. "Truly? She might visit us? We must tidy the place before she arrives."

Tired of Clarence's antics, Jamison once again promised himself that on the morrow he would begin searching in earnest for new living arrangements—luxuries be ignored.

"She might. She wrote that her father had business to attend to out east and that she was attempting to persuade him to allow her to accompany him."

"Attempting to persuade? She should simply go. She is of the age of consent, is she not?"

Jamison sighed with great weariness. "She is. And if she does plan a visit, I will be certain to let you know."

Clarence's eyebrows raised in question. "I know you won't, you cad," he answered, taking a long swallow from his wineglass. After a moment, he brightened. "Does Miss Rikler know about Miss Hill?"

Taken aback, Jamison did not reply.

"Your silence implicates you most directly, Jamison." Clarence drained the last of his wine. "But I shall be the true gentleman, Mr. Pike. If Miss Rikler ever hears of Miss Hill and your entanglement with her, the rumor shall not have come from my lips."

"There is no entanglement with either, Clarence, and you know it."

"So you say, Mr. Pike. So you say."

From a Letter to Neta Hill

August 1846

My dear Neta,

I was both heartened and discouraged with your most recent letter. Heartened, of course, to hear from you. Anytime a letter arrives with your distinct handwriting, my day promises to be better. But discouraged that you will not be traveling with your father. I understand, of course, that your safety is a most precious commodity and that no father would ever place a daughter in jeopardy.

Yes, traveling can be harsh. I trust that in the spring of next year, your father will have a change of heart and allow you to come to New York. I so want to see you again.

I have no time today for a longer missive so will simply say that I will write longer on the morrow.

Perhaps I shall travel back home for Christmas. It would be a pleasure to spend time with you again.

Your friend,
Jamison

FROM THE JOURNAL OF JAMISON PIKE
SEPTEMBER 1846

Miss Rikler has returned from her summer cottage on Long Island, though I am quite certain to call it a cottage is a disservice. She sent me a note the day of her return. We had not corresponded over the summer, and I had not ventured out onto Long Island. I indeed was busy and did not have any time to spare. As a substitute for older reporters taking vacation, I was kept quite occupied.

Eva said she is not much of a letter writer.

Her note to me was brief: *Meet me at Brennons tonight at 9.*

And I did. I wore my new fall waistcoat and shirt, and she remarked as to their sophisticated cut and tailoring. I did not think she would notice and was pleased she had.

As I dressed I wondered at her allure. She is not as smart as Hannah or Neta. While she has great command of the city's gossip, her knowledge is limited and not very deep. Yet she is a beautiful woman. Perhaps that makes up for her limited awareness of cultural matters?

And she is bold. I have never before spent time with such a forward woman and must admit that such boldness is an intoxicating lure.

She had selected a tiny booth near the back of the restaurant, in the shadows actually. Her dress was of some blue shimmery material I had never seen before, with a similarly colored lightweight woolen burnoose about her shoulders.

She asked of my summer and I told her of my activities. I asked her of hers, and she laughed and dismissed it with a wave. "Hot. Sunny. Boring."

Our meal was delivered—veal Oscar with parslied potatoes.

What she did next was both shocking . . . and perplexing.

Before she picked up her fork and knife, she leaned over to me (it was a small booth as I mentioned), placed her hand behind my neck, and pulled me to her. She kissed me with great vigor for a full moment, then released me from her grasp, smiled, picked up her knife and fork, and began to eat as if nothing odd had transpired.

I sat there bewildered—astonished for several minutes. She smiled at me again and asked if I was going to eat my food before it got cold.

Numbly I managed to cut and chew through most of it—though it could have been shoe leather for all I remember of its taste.

Later that evening, still in a state of great tumult, while awaiting our carriage I asked her why she had acted so bold earlier.

She pulled the hood of her burnoose over her hair and answered, "Bold? That was not bold, Jamison. I saw something I wanted and took it. That is reality, my sweet man—the reality of the world. What you need, you take."

I had no answer, no response, so I simply nodded as if it made sense.

Does she find me attractive? Can that be? A beautiful woman with great wealth—could she be interested in a plain man like myself? One with potential, I imagine, but not on the same social level as the Riklers, for certain.

I am so drawn to her world. I find a woman who clearly states her desires and then grabs them to be most attractive.

There is a fascination here—troubling, yet terribly compelling.

If my parents had observed that incident, they would assume I had taken leave of my senses.

Perhaps, in some way, they would be correct.

New York City
November 1846

"Sir, your father is in the drawing room."

Jamison was at the desk in the library surrounded by books and papers and inkwells. He did not turn.

"Sir. Mr. Pike?"

Only when hearing his name did he raise his head. "Pardon?"

"Your father. Mr. Pike. He is in the drawing room."

Jamison at first stared blankly at the servant. Then he asked, "My father?"

"Yes, sir. He is downstairs. He said something about a letter."

Jamison blinked his eyes several times, as the announcement had come as a complete and total surprise. "A letter?"

From the far corner of the library came a soft harrumph.

"Clarence?" Jamison said, his tone rising sharply. "Do you know anything of this letter? My father? Downstairs?"

Clarence offered a shrug. "There might have been a letter. Maybe there was. I don't recall exactly. But . . . there might have been. I suspect I did not mention this to you, did I?"

Jamison was on his feet, tucking in his shirt, straightening his suspenders. "No, you did not, thank you very much. My father? I don't believe it." He bent under the desk, searching for his left boot.

Now Jamison hated himself for not seeking out his own residence and promised, once again, to find a new home on the morrow.

"Shall I go down to meet him first?" Clarence asked. "I could keep him occupied until you're fully dressed."

"No!" Jamison barked out from under the desk.

Clarence was lounging in a satin-collared dark blue velvet robe and satin pajamas. It might have been acceptable after ten in the evening, but it was no later than half past four.

"No. I will go down. You stay here."

Clarence sniffed. "As you wish, but do bring him up so I may meet him. Will he spend the night with us? Shall I ready the guest wing?"

Jamison shrugged this time. "I don't know. Perhaps. It is always ready, isn't it?"

Jamison seldom ventured to that side of the house but assumed that servants dusted and cleaned there with regularity.

His footsteps echoed in the hallway and slowed as he neared the bottom of the grand staircase.

What is my father doing here? What could he want? he thought anxiously.

Correspondence between parent and child had continued—strained as it was—but with irregularity.

The massive French doors to the drawing room had been closed, so Jamison swung them open. A squeal sounded from the heavy brass hinges.

"Father," he said calmly, even though his heart was beating rapidly.

Albert Pike, dressed nearly all in black save the narrow white ecclesiastical collar, turned slowly to face his son. "Jamison," he said in a low, gravelly voice, "do you always make visitors wait so long?"

Extending his hand, Jamison lowered his eyes. "I didn't know you were coming."

"I sent a letter. Months ago. I named the date and time. How could you not know?"

The questions took Jamison back to his childhood. They were questions he had no answers for, yet ones that kept coming, in a barrage that often left him speechless, shamed, and near tears.

"I never received it. I would have been waiting if I had known."

The elder Pike let go of his son's hand after a very brief moment.

"What are you doing in New York City?" Jamison asked. He could imagine no reason for his father's journey, so harshly did the elder Pike speak of traveling about, wasting money on room and board when it existed at home.

"The general assembly."

Jamison held his hands open, not understanding the import of the answer.

"Of our denomination. Every five years they meet to elect officers. They invited me to speak."

"Why, that is a great . . . honor, isn't it?"

The elder Pike made a face, as if he had taken an entire lemon into his mouth. "Days of travel at great expense and discomfort for an hour of words? Hardly seems an honor to me."

Jamison held his tongue. "Well, I am glad to have you in New York, then. You will be staying here, won't you?"

He shook his head. "They have secured rooms for us in private homes. I am staying near the meeting hall. A small room on the top floor."

"But we can meet for dinner or lunch."

Albert Pike shook his head again. "Had you read my letter you would have known that this afternoon is the only free time I have. With assembly duties and the like, I am otherwise occupied until I leave this Monday."

"But you have traveled all this way. Surely we can find a moment or two."

"Those moments would be now, Son. I am due at an evening session at six."

"But it is now nearly five."

The elder Pike shrugged again as if to say the brevity of their time was out of his control and he would do nothing to change it.

"Then let me offer you some coffee or tea. I can call the cook and have her make refreshments. Let me call the manservant."

His father waved his offer away with a small sweep of his hand. "No. There will be food at the session. And since when does a Pike have a cook and a manservant?"

"I don't. The house does," Jamison replied, feeling his throat grow tight. "I mean—the owner of the house."

"And who is that?"

"Mildred Hauser Edmonds. She is quite wealthy."

"That much I can see. Is she here?"

"No, not exactly." Sweat formed on Jamison's brow and he brushed it away. "She has not been well. She is staying in New Jersey."

"And why are you here?"

"I was asked to stay here by her grandson. He lives here. He was at Harvard with me."

"And you do everything this fellow asks?"

Jamison's hand tightened into a fist. "It is not that way at all, Father," he said hurriedly. "And besides, you are only here for a little while. I do not want to argue."

The elder Pike spun around, his eyes glaring. "Who are you, Jamison?"

"What . . . what do you mean?"

The elder Pike took three quick steps over to the leather chair by the fire and grabbed at a magazine, holding it as if it were a poisonous reptile, shaking it in the air. "What is this?"

Jamison closed his eyes. The pages of one of Clarence's gentleman's magazines flapped malevolently in the air.

"It is not mine," he said softly, knowing its ultimate ownership would have made little difference to his father.

"But it is in the house where you live, is it not? Is not that pantry filled with bottles of spirits? Someone has been drinking them," he shouted as he pointed at the expansive bar tucked into the corner of the room.

Jamison could only nod.

"And this house . . . or mansion, I should say, is filled with such crass signs of wealth and material riches, I can barely stand to breathe the same air. And you come down wearing the costume of a dandy, smelling of tonic and wine."

"It is not wine," he called back, both his anger and his shame growing.

"I came here thinking I would find the son I once thought I knew. And that son would have fled from a home in which this was so proudly displayed." He took the magazine and tossed it at the fire. A cascade of sparks showered the grate and hearth. "You tolerate such perdition around you? That is evidence enough to me that you have changed, Jamison. I will not tell your mother of this, for such news would eat at her heart. She still loves you and holds out hope for you."

Jamison took a step toward his father. "Because there is a maga-zine of some baseness in this house—you assume *I* have fallen? Isn't that rash, even for you?"

His father's hand raised and then dropped, as if he were consider-ing striking his son. "You shall never talk to me in that manner. Never."

And with that the elder Pike grabbed his coat and hat and stomped to the door of the drawing room.

"Wait," Jamison called. "Father, please wait. Please understand. This is not my home. I have no control of what is in here and what is not."

"But you do have control of whether you stay or not, don't you?" Albert growled. "And that is enough. To see you living in such deca-dence pains me more than you know. You know the truth, Jamison. I taught you the truth. And anyone who holds the truth dear could not stay in this place."

"That, Father, is unfair," Jamison retorted.

Visibly shaken by the tone of his son's reply, the elder Pike stated, "It is not. I have seen sin, and I exhort you to repudiate it as well."

"You have seen nothing!" Jamison shouted back. He heard a creak from the stairway out in the entry hall and knew Clarence had edged close to eavesdrop. Yet having an audience was not nearly enough to dissuade Jamison this afternoon. "After such a long journey, you can only spare a brief afternoon for me? I think that inappropriate as well."

His father pulled on his coat. "It is the only free time available to me. I am about God's work, you know. I am not lounging about in some fancy mansion with wicked books and alcohol at close hand."

"I do not partake of that," Jamison fired back.

"Then why do you live amongst it? Does not the brush that paints the true owner paint you as well?"

Albert stomped out into the entry hall. Jamison followed.

"It does not," Jamison insisted flatly. Then, in a flash, he lost all energy and passion for the argument. It was as if he had known for years that all would come to this moment. That there would be nothing he could do to dissuade the path of his history. It was as if it were destined to be his father and himself, arguing over a matter Jamison could scarcely grasp.

"Is it not true?"

Jamison hung his head. His father fussed with his scarf and top buttons. Once again Jamison heard the stairs creak. Clarence must have moved up a step or two to avoid detection when they left the drawing room.

"Father," Jamison said softly, knowing his father was seconds from leaving, "will you answer me one last question?"

In the faint light of a winter afternoon, his father looked lined and drawn, more so than Jamison's memory recalled. A sharp trio of wrinkles arched over his eyes, as if he had scowled for years.

"What?"

"The truth you talk about—what is it?" Jamison asked.

Albert reached for the brightly polished door handle. "Is this some sort of game?"

"No game, Father," Jamison said with an almost unnatural sense of calm. "I simply want to know what you call *truth*. You claim I do not seek the truth. I want to know what the truth is, and that is all."

Albert Pike grabbed the door and flung it open. "The attitude is what I find most intolerable," he snapped. "Your mother said that you might have changed after making your own way in the city. I thought otherwise—and I was right. It is that condescending attitude that always drove me to distraction."

"It was a simple question," Jamison shouted back.

His father leaned away in surprise.

"What is this truth you claim to have passed on to me? Why do I not feel it? Why does that truth seem like a mist? 'Find the truth,' you shout. But you never show me what the truth is. How does that work, Father? Tell me how I find the truth when all I hear are words? Don't I need to see it *lived?*"

The two held each other's glare; then Jamison's father narrowed his eyes and walked out the door. Jamison heard the scramble of feet on the porch.

Jamison followed his father to the front door, remaining several steps distant. "Father, I ask that you tell my mother I inquired about her."

Cold wind gusted through the open door, sending leaves scudding down the hallway.

"I will tell her that," Albert said as he stepped out into the darkening cold.

Jamison did not move. The door was pushed shut, and the brass latch snapped into place. He heard his father's footsteps click down the granite steps. Then he lowered his head and sighed once.

From the landing halfway up the stairs came Clarence's chuckle. "The truth? That was wonderful, my friend. You make a living of looking for the truth and he accuses you of abandoning it. Such delicious irony."

Clarence's high-pitched giggle echoed in the cold room.

Jamison did not answer or respond. He simply reached for his overcoat on the rack in the entry hall, slipped it on, and followed his father out into the darkness.

New York City
December 1846

"So you never caught up with him?" Gage asked as he hustled his mound of packages into the carriage. Pine and holly scented the air.

"No," Jamison replied. "I think he truly was an specter and simply vanished into the night."

"Truly?" Gage replied, settling in on the seat.

Jamison laughed, taking the seat opposite. "Of course not, Gage. I am not some sort of pansy who believes in evil spirits. It was him in the flesh, all right."

The two old friends had bumped into each other during the week before Christmas along New York's Fifth Avenue, lined with fash-

ionable shops and hundreds, if not thousands, of people out in winter finery looking for Christmas treats. Jamison followed Gage as he
spent hundreds of dollars purchasing gifts for a long list of clients
and associates. Jamison was buying for no one this year, save a few
trinkets for the staff at the Edmonds mansion.

"But couldn't you track him down at his meetings?"

"I could," Jamison answered, "and almost did. I found out where
it was being held and got within two blocks of the place—but just
couldn't force myself to enter and find him."

Gage shook his head sadly. "All this because of a little bit of wine
and a little bit of women."

"Not to mention my shaving tonic." Jamison laughed. "And the
wine and women were not mine to begin with. I have nothing to do
with what Clarence drags home."

Gage replied, "The sooner you are out of that place, the better. I
warned you. You heard me warning you months and months ago."

"I heard you. It is just hard to leave such luxury."

"Exactly as I cautioned, Jamison. Leave before you can't."

The carriage turned the corner on Fifth Avenue and Forty-second
Street. Jamison reached up and grabbed the leather strap.

The two remained quiet for a while.

"Have you seen Hannah?" Jamison asked. Seeing Gage reminded
him of how much he missed seeing her.

"I haven't. I haven't heard much either. She is keeping to herself
back in Philadelphia. Still attempting to follow a medical path from
the little I have heard. Foolishness, if you ask me. Not really the
place for a woman."

"But didn't you help her at Harvard? That was all the gossip back
then."

Gage shrugged. "I might have. But I never thought she would take
it this far."

The carriage turned again and several gaily wrapped packages
tumbled to the floor.

"I should write her," Jamison said softly. "Maybe visit. I could arrange a trip for work. Must be a story or two to investigate down there."

Gage grinned. "As part owner of the newspaper, I should be shocked. But I'm not. Done all the time, isn't it?"

"More than you might think."

The carriage slowed at the wide steps to the Edmonds mansion.

"My stop," Jamison said.

"We should get together after the holidays," Gage said with cheerfulness. "Drop me a note. We'll have dinner at the club some night."

"I will."

As Jamison descended from the carriage, Gage shook his hand.

"Jamison," Gage said quietly, "Hannah has not changed. I am certain of that. Don't think more of her than an old friend. I can see it in your eyes. It will only lead to heartache."

Jamison glared.

"I know that sounds harsh, but if you go to see her, all it will bring is hurt. You need to get on with your life up here."

"That's not for you to say, Gage. It's not your business." There was a chill in Jamison's words.

"I know. It isn't. But what I said is the truth. You loved her. So did Joshua. There are things that are not meant to be. For neither of you. It's true. I'm not being mean-spirited—I am simply telling you the truth."

Jamison stepped away from the carriage. "Seems like everyone knows the truth except me." He took a deep breath and waved. "Have a good holiday. I will drop you a note," he said with no trace of rancor.

Gage was a man who seldom spoke with maliciousness, and Jamison knew there was none present today.

The carriage clattered away. Jamison watched it turn the corner. Instead of entering the house, he slipped his hands into the pockets of his coat and began to walk. After a while he came to a small plot of land, narrowed between two homes, covered by a thin, pocked veil of snow. He could see cornstalks poking through the snow, and a rustle of cabbage leaves and beanpoles left out in the winter weather.

At the edge of the lot was the stump of a tree. He brushed at the snow and sat down. All he saw were dead plants.

I have heard enough of truth to last me a lifetime, he thought, *yet it seems everyone knows the truth, save me. My father clubs me with his truth. Gage tries to deliver me from pain with his truth. And in all of this, I do not know for certain–with absolute certainty–what the truth truly is. I know facts. I know quotes. I can re-create a scene with words that so mimics the original as to be remarkable.*

But what of the greater truth? And does it truly matter?

Perhaps Clarence is right: that since life is so short, we may as well attempt to enjoy all the pleasures offered.

Perhaps Joshua is right when he says the truth is out there, waiting for me to be ready to believe it.

And my father's truth–I will have nothing to do with.

A gray wind swirled about his frame. The tree branches clattered above. Smoke from wood and coal drifted through the air. He took a deep breath, turned his collar to the wind, and began his cold journey home.

And is it true God gives us what we need?

CHAPTER ELEVEN

New York City
January 1847

New Year's Day broke leaden and colorless and cold. The wind came off the Hudson in a bitter howl, driving the snow into waist-high drifts, and kept the streets nearly empty of human form.

Jamison sat in his bedchamber, wrapped in a triple thickness of blanket, counterpane, and throw. Even though the fire was crackling and full, the room was chilled. The windows rattled from the wind, and from the rooftop came an unearthly moan.

The storm had begun to lash New York a day prior and had dampened a thousand planned New Year's Eve celebrations.

Jamison had no disappointment to hide, for he did not relish being trapped in a room with a band of raucous libertines, all intent on overimbibing. The garish, brittle laughter of these affairs caused him to wince, almost as if in pain.

Earlier that day, when the storm had seemed to be at a peak, he sent a note to Eva Rikler, who had invited him to a fete at the New York Club. He hoped the note had gotten through. Even if it hadn't, he was certain most, if not all, of the revelers had been forced to rethink their plans for the evening. Eva would understand the cause of his absence.

Even the bells tolling at midnight were lost to the whip of the winds.

Clarence had departed a week earlier to a family celebration in New Jersey, so Jamison had the entire house to himself. The solitude was delicious. Once again he promised to seek out another residence. Yet he also knew the luxury of a full staff and cook would be hard to duplicate on his own.

Jamison reached out into the cold air of the room and retrieved a sheaf of letters left on his nightstand. He turned up the lantern and settled against the velvet headboard, adjusting the pillows around his head and shoulders.

Slipping his finger under the flap of an egg-colored envelope, he tore at the crease. It was stamped *Pittsburgh*. He knew it was from Neta; the gay and scrawling penmanship gave her identity away.

He smiled as he scanned the first three pages quickly. He would reread it later but knew her style was to include every jot and tittle of gossip from Pittsburgh almost as an introduction. Jamison never admitted to liking that part of her letters, but it was interesting to hear of the goings-on of people he knew–and some he did not.

Neta had a true knack for making even the most mundane meeting or shopping excursion a most interesting, though trivial, tale.

His eyes slowed as he held the final page in his hands. He lifted the sheet closer to the light, to avoid confusing any of her words. He knew that her level of intimacy increased the longer she wrote, and this letter was a five-page affair–which meant she would be even more expansive on the final page.

He smiled. The writing took on greater flourishes, with swooping letters and coiled ends, as if she were finally free.

All the men in Pittsburgh are such boys–especially when I compare them with you. Father invited the son of an investor to the house, and while he was wickedly handsome, he could not hold a candle to your light, Jamison. I suspect I should be ashamed to go on so about you, but my heart will not allow itself to be fettered. Our time together was so short, and I yearn to be held in your arms again. I will wait for you, Jamison. Please hurry and become a famous reporter so you can send for me. I will come.

   Your dearest friend,

   Neta

Jamison read the last lines several times. He smiled and held the page close to his face, inhaling the still-pungent aroma of her scent.

After reading the letter one more time, he folded it carefully and placed it back in the envelope.

He reached for the next unopened letter. It was postmarked *Philadelphia*. His heart lurched. He had not noticed the mark yesterday when he picked up his stack of mail on the marble table in the massive foyer.

It was from Hannah.

Jamison held the small card and stared at it. He had sent Hannah, a few weeks prior to Christmas, an engraved card—all the rage in England. The card carried a pleasant winter scene of skaters on a frozen pond. He included a greeting and a few lines of his current activities.

And she wrote back.

Her note was brief, thanking him for the card, telling him of her family activities over the holidays and little else. She made no mention of her plans to continue seeking medical training. And he also noticed she made no reference to Robert Keyes either.

He tried not to think more of this omission than it warranted, but he was not successful.

   Washington, D.C.
   May 1847

The room echoed and rolled with conversation. The walls were covered with mirrors twice as tall as a man, gilded about the frames, with gas lamps above. Each lamp reflected a thousand times in the mirror on the opposite side. In the center of the room ten tables were lined up in a hesitant circle. Each one, draped with a crisp white tablecloth, was piled with food—roast beef and hams and turkeys and jellies and a whole table piled high with dense rye breads and rolls and crackers.

"You notice those who have never left the tables are reporters," Jamison whispered. "There's Evans from the *World,* and Thompson from the *Gazette,* and Husker from the *Republic,* and Stotler and Arch and . . . well, you see what draws us journalists to events like this."

Gage Davis, who was standing next to the English ambassador, grinned.

The event, held in a Washington, D.C., ballroom, was the opening fete of a new institution—a museum of sorts, being underwritten with the grant of some Scottish fellow by the name of Smithson. The invitation heralded the planned facility to be the rival of any European enterprise. Jamison would not have gone except for the personal request of Mr. Rikler. The editor had begged off the invitation, issued by the senator of New York, claiming such affairs were "boring, tedious, and too far from home."

Jamison had been glad to find Gage in attendance as well.

Gage introduced Jamison to the ambassador and several minor European counts and vice-princes, all of whom seemed suitably impressed that Jamison worked for one of the largest and best-known papers in New York.

The English ambassador seemed most keen on giving Jamison his government's view on the skirmishes between the United States and Mexico. The government called it a war, Jamison heard it was nothing less than a military fiasco, and the Englishman was pressing him to editorialize in his paper for peace. Jamison nodded at all the right moments yet knew little of any foreign matters. He paid attention to local politics and to the state's political machinations, but none more wide-ranging than that.

Later, after the echo of the raft of speeches had died down and the reporters had picked the last meat from the turkey carcasses, Jamison tapped Gage on the shoulder. The crowd in the room had thinned, and the noise and bluster of Washington conversation had abated.

"Gage," Jamison said, "do you have a moment or two?"

Having spent all the afternoon glad-handing nearly everyone in the room, Gage looked tired and wan. "For an old friend, I have time," he said. "Are there any drinks left, or have the servers packed up their wares?"

"I'll get two coffees."

After receiving their cups, Jamison motioned for Gage to follow him. They walked toward a door on the far wall, then wormed through the crush of people about the dessert buffet. Making their way through the double doors, they found themselves on a long, empty balcony overlooking the street below. Dusk was falling, and the air felt brisk with the rich chill of spring.

Both men were quiet for a long time. Jamison felt relieved to be silent. He had not expected to run into Gage and had not spent any time formulating the proper queries.

Jamison stared out at the streets and the lights as the carriages and wagons clattered by. "I can see why you love New York," he said. "Compared to this town, there is so much going on—I sometimes am reluctant to go to sleep because I know how much I will miss."

Gage nodded. "The hustle and bustle can be infuriating, but there is no city like it in the world. But I know you didn't ask me out here to compare cities. So what is it?" Gage asked.

For the first time, Jamison heard a weary tone to his words. At Harvard, even after the parties and studies kept Gage awake for days, he had never sounded tired. He did this day.

Jamison turned his coffee cup, as Joshua often did—with the handle pointed out. "I have heard things," he said flatly.

"Heard what?" The weary tone was quickly replaced with anger.

"The blood of a newsroom is gossip," Jamison replied. "I hear things all the time."

"About me?" Gage's smile had evaporated. "I doubt that whatever it is, is true. You know how gossip is."

"Gage," Jamison said, "I haven't even told you what this is about."

It was obvious to Jamison that Gage knew already. What other explanation could there be for his anger?

"But they are things that I don't believe," Jamison added.

"Don't believe? Then why tell me?" Gage asked.

"Because the stories have to do with you. That's why I don't believe them."

"Me? About me?"

"I have heard stories about that invention you represent—the one purported to make the telegraph obsolete."

Gage shrugged. "That is true. And it is not news. It has been in the papers."

Jamison looked at his hands. "Someone is claiming you have over-sold the stock in this venture by one hundred percent. I have heard that the invention itself has yet to be finalized, but investors are handing you money because of your reputation for an honest deal." Jamison hesitated. He could feel an actual pain in Gage's glare.

Then Gage's face softened, as if he found an answer that felt right. "I have heard that, too. Rumors get started by all manner of competition. Some are simply jealous of another man's success. It's done all the time."

"Then it is not true?" Jamison asked, hopeful.

"No," Gage said. Then he added, "You have my word on it."

Jamison smiled in return. The smile did not last long, though, for he knew that when a man said, "You have my word on it," it meant something was amiss. For after all, wasn't a man's word his bond? Did a man need to swear a second time on the truth?

FROM THE JOURNAL OF JAMISON PIKE
NEW YORK CITY
JUNE 1847

Astounded and *disappointed* are not words enough to describe how I feel. What Gage assured me was a lie—was not.

In Washington I confronted him with the rumors of overselling stock—and he insisted it was merely gossip emanating from his competitors. But the whole sordid affair was not idle gossip—it was the truth.

Gage, while not charged or convicted of anything illegal, has stepped down from the leadership of the company his father founded. No one admitted anything, but I am told that when a man steps down from a position of power, it means he is guilty—and unwilling to go to jail.

I called on him several times, and he refused to see me. His valet said he was busy—though I imagine it was shame that kept him from meeting me.

I persisted and forced a confrontation with him just before he left town. He was a broken and contrite man. Even though his transgressions were relatively minor compared to other corruptions I have covered, they were enough. Once a man's honor is lost, so is the man.

I have seldom quoted my father, but he often said a lie is like poison—it only takes a small amount to kill a reputation.

I feel so sorry and ashamed for Gage.

I asked if he could fight these charges. He is not a man without resources. He does have interests in several newspapers. He could use them if he so desired. Public opinion is shaped by public media, and the public can be made to accept a sin.

He waved the suggestion off like it was a fly at a picnic, claiming he would not degrade the proud Davis name into a protracted and most likely ugly battle. It was better, he said, to face the truth, realize its power, and depart, rather than take a stand and perhaps cause both sides to taste bitter defeat. This way it was only he who would suffer and no one else.

Such are the results of a mistake.

And I am proud, in a perverse way, that he has chosen not to defend a lie.

At the end of our conversation, when I asked him if he was going to tell Hannah, Gage spoke softly. "No. I hadn't planned on it." What he said with his eyes but couldn't verbalize, I already knew—of all the friends he had once had, it was Hannah's shame he most feared. I knew this instinctively, since I felt the same way.

I promised I would not tell her either. But I did tell him such news travels quickly, especially by way of those who love to traffic in gossip. I could see Clarence writing a scattering of notes to his friends about this.

Gage sighed. "I just don't want to . . . disappoint her. Sounds foolish, doesn't it? Just don't let her hear it from you."

He said he was heading west, he thought. To Chicago, then to New Orleans. Perhaps he will be able to make a fresh start there.

I hope he can.

And I hope my heart returns to normal soon.

As Jamison penned these lines, sitting cross-legged on his bed in near darkness, a tap at the bedchamber door interrupted his work. A servant stood in the hall, at half bow it seemed, carrying a silver tray with an elegant ivory card nestled in the exact center.

"He is awaiting a reply, sir," the servant said with precise softness.

"Who is?"

"A powdered-carriage man, sir. He said a short answer would suffice."

Jamison tore open the envelope. It was from Miss Rikler.

She wrote:

My sweet Jamison,

All work and no play is certain to make Jamison a dull boy. Especially in Gotham in the summer. Come to our summer home this Wednesday for a very long weekend. My father has waived all your duties at the paper. Our carriage will return for you at noon tomorrow. Pack your evening attire, for we are expected at the Astors on Saturday night.

You must not disappoint me.
Eva Rikler

Jamison nodded to the servant. "Tell the fellow yes."

Jamison rode in the Riklers' carriage to the edge of Manhattan Island. He could have taken the bridge at the southern edge of Manhattan Island, but a ferry was faster and Jamison dismissed the driver with a smile and a tip. He took a small passenger boat across the brown, languid water. A short hansom cab ride brought him to a tiny train station that provided passenger service between the river and the far eastern end of Long Island. Crates of lettuce sat next to pens filled with chickens and geese—all destined for Manhattan grocers. A boxcar full of noisy cows sat off on a siding close to the station. Jamison slipped his ticket into his breast pocket and hefted his bag, then found a seat near the end of the train heading back out toward Montauk.

He soon lost interest in the book he had brought with him and instead gazed out at the landscape. The ride out led past crowded tenements along the river, past stately homes with grand manicured lawns, and into the farmland of the island. The landscape was neatly divided by fences, barns denoting one farm from the next.

The rich have a long ride to escape, Jamison thought as he stood for a moment and stretched. *To make this journey every week would be such a tiring effort.*

The letter from Eva was in his pocket and he unfolded it again—almost as if to ensure that the invitation was still in effect. It was not that he had never tasted the "good life." He had—often as the guest of Gage Davis. With Gage as a friend, Jamison had entered more exclusive clubs and restaurants than he even knew existed. His current residence was a spectacular mansion with scores of servants. Yet in all of this, Jamison seldom felt truly the invited guest—but rather the fellow who stumbles into the wrong party and everyone is too polite or too afraid to ask him to leave.

And now he was being asked to dine with the Astors–a family with such a storied heritage that Jamison had read about them in his history books as a student.

Gads, he thought as he leaned back in his seat, *how far I have come from provincial Pittsburgh.*

He thought of Eva.

While Hannah seemed to be aware of everything that happened around her, Eva seemed most aware of her impact on men. There was something in her eyes, Jamison thought, that said *I know why you're staring–and I appreciate it.*

Jamison had never once acted in an ungentlemanly manner with Miss Rikler and had no intentions of changing that. But he also was well aware of how his heart tightened whenever she drew near to him.

I must be honest with her . . . and with Miss Hill as well. While at Harvard I once admonished Gage for having more than one love interest at a time, and I shall not fall into that same trap. I view Miss Rikler as a friend. After all, her father is my employer–and I have no desire to jeopardize that arrangement.

Never once had Jamison imagined there might someday be *two* women interested in him. And thus he found his current circumstance both bewildering and complimentary.

As the miles clicked on, he wondered if either woman could fill that hollow feeling just inside his heart.

Long Island
June 1847

The small sailboat cut through the waters of Long Island Sound like an aquatic animal. The bow would dip slightly as it crested the waves and dig into the trough at the bottom, spraying jewels of seawater in the brilliant sunshine.

Jamison pushed the rudder and edged the vessel around the point, skirting by the rocks, leaving only a hand's width between them and disaster.

Eva, sitting with her back to the mast, her hands flat on the slick deck, tilted her head back, closed her eyes, and laughed. It rose from deep in her throat—the sound of diamonds rustling together in the darkness.

"You are such a danger," she called out over the sound of the waves, "and I love coming to the brink like that."

It had not been intentional; Jamison had not seen any rocks. If he had, he would have steered well away.

She turned and pointed. "Over there—see those two small islets?"

Jamison nodded.

"The tide's coming in. There is a gap between them the width of this boat and not much more. Run it through. The swell will fly us faster and higher than you have ever been on a boat."

He pulled the helm and skirted the boat around.

Jamison truly was not a skilled sailor. After overcoming his initial queasiness, he had watched Gage pilot a sailboat on several occasions and the previous summer had paid a fellow to teach him the rudiments of the sport. The fact that he had taken them almost into harm's way was strictly accidental. Jamison was simply tacking into the wind and had overestimated his abilities and underestimated the power of the breeze. Now Miss Rikler was asking him to do a daredevil stunt. If he carefully considered, he would never attempt such a thing. But her laugh and her smile and her confidence in him gave him all the assurance and motivation he needed.

He aimed the bow where he thought the wind was taking them, and a great slapping well of seawater pushed the small boat through the strait between the islets. It roared down a river of a wave, like running down a long staircase of water.

Eva screamed with joy, and Jamison hoped his fear was masked by his relieved laughter.

Later, as he tied the boat to the pier rambling out into the calmer waters in front of the Riklers' summer home, Eva sat and watched. From the wooden decking, Jamison pulled the ropes tight and then extended his hand to Eva. She took a long moment to respond, slowly raising her hand to his and grasping it. Then she slowly tightened her hand about his, much like a snake caressing a small woodland creature to breathlessness.

"You are such a surprising man," she said, her voice all but a purr. Her hair had been touched with sea spray and was mottled into ringlets about her face like a dark halo.

"Surprising? And why is that, Miss Rikler?" Jamison asked as he hoisted her to the deck.

She took his arm. "At times you are like a schoolboy," she said, smoothing his forearm with her free hand. "At times you act as if the world is still chaste, and every incident in your life is new. At times I feel as if I am making tracks in a meadow of unsullied snow. Then there are the times you go on and on about truth and how it is our perceptions that shape truth. I admit I do not always pay attention, for your words are too deep for me."

He did not answer, for he did not know what she was attempting to say.

"And then there are moments like on the water this day—when the world is as small as that boat and as immediate as the rocks and the wind and the water. *Enthralling* is the only word I can use. Enthralling . . . and alluring. You skimmed the vessel so close to drowning us today—as close as the hunter skins his prey. No man has ever sailed me through those islets before. It was as if I was in a separate world—in one that you had complete power over."

She stopped and turned to him, taking both of his hands in hers. Her grip was surprisingly hard, nearly unfeminine. "Who are you, Jamison Pike? What manner of man are you? Are you an innocent? Are you a man who tempts fate? Who are you?"

And then she pushed herself toward him. He did not retreat and felt her rise on tiptoe to place her lips on his. She held that embrace longer than Jamison was comfortable with, considering it was daylight and they were in full view of the house and anyone on the rear porch.

Then she backed down and in a small voice asked again, "Who are you, Jamison Pike?"

He swallowed once and tried to measure his words slowly. "Whom do you want me to be?"

"California!"

Most of the guests jumped as Ian Guster slammed his palm on the dining-room table. Wineglasses skittered about, and ripples were even noticed in pools of gravy on nearby plates.

"That's the future, Rikler. That's where the brave young men of this land will head!" Guster looked about to ascertain the mood of the guests, then slammed his palm again. Most expected it, so this time no one jumped or even flinched in the slightest.

Mr. Rikler took a long swallow of his wine. Then calmly he replaced the empty glass in the exact same spot. He cleared his throat. "California? Indeed?"

"The future is out there. It awaits the intrepid and the brave."

Ian Guster, a sailor of some note, had returned only weeks prior from a voyage to the West. It had taken him months, and he had terrified the ladies and entertained the men during dinner with tales of the wild natives of Tierra del Fuego–the "Land of Fire"–and the howling storms his craft endured. He had claimed any hardship would be worth the risk, seeing as to how close to paradise the California territory was.

"And to think, not one of your reporters has ever set foot there," Guster opined. "In fact, I don't think any of your men have ever set foot farther west than the Hudson."

A general wave of giggles followed.

"A reporter? Out west? Whatever for?" Rikler asked. "How many folks are out there? A few hundred? Hardly worth the trip."

Guster leaned forward, fixing the publisher in his stare. Then he spun about and pointed straight at Jamison. "Ask your own man here, Rikler. Ask this young fellow if a grand adventure is worth the tale. Ask him about facing danger. Ask him if the poor readers of your papers don't yearn for that. Let the poor people live through someone else, Rikler. California is the future, my man."

Rikler picked up his wineglass again. Lifting it into the air, he coughed. A servant scrambled from the shadows to fill it.

"Is that right, Pike?" Rikler asked. "Adventure? You want danger? My daughter says you are quite the helmsman. Right at the edge. Dangerous waters and all that."

Jamison squirmed, and his expression tightened. "Well, sir . . . I suppose readers might like to read about such things. Perhaps I could do a piece or two on Mr. Guster's travels."

"A piece?" Rikler bellowed out a laugh. Then he slapped the table. This time Jamison jumped in his chair. "No! Not Guster's travels. That's secondhand stuff. I mean no offense, Ian."

Ian smiled and shrugged.

"I mean *you*, Pike," Rikler continued. "Are you game? You are a bright young man. You can write and spell. Your articles make sense. Are you game?"

Jamison's stomach twisted. From the corner of his eye he saw Eva stare at him in unashamed admiration . . . or perhaps some other emotion altogether. He would have sworn that she fluttered her eyelids at him.

"Game, sir?"

"Game!" Rikler half stood at his chair. "To go to California! Have an adventure or two. Write all about it. Indians! Shipwrecks! Pirates!" He slammed his hand on the table again. "Gads! Why didn't I think of this before? Pack your bags, Jamison. You're going to have an adventure!"

And like the tide of this morning, Jamison felt the waters about him break and swell, carrying him toward a strange and unfamiliar shore.

Later that evening, after a dozen of the Riklers' brandy and wine bottles had been emptied, Jamison excused himself from their company. He had not taken a drink, content to sit at the edge of the swirl of conversation as the volume grew louder and speculations on what Jamison might encounter grew wilder and more shocking.

He stepped out onto the rear porch and took a deep breath of the dark sea air, hoping to rid his lungs of the gulps of cigar smoke he had been enduring for the last several hours.

The sea was as black as a tiger's eye, and the sliver of the moon a ghostly vapor above the water's edge. Gulls called, and from far out to sea, a delicate wisp of a bell's sound slipped across to the shore. He placed his hands on the railing and breathed in again, tasting the salt carried by the breeze.

And just then two hands came about his waist, like a serpent striking from the dark, thick grass, and clasped him hard.

"You are such a brave man."

"Miss Rikler," Jamison sputtered and attempted to turn around.

"It's Eva. You promised months ago. My name is Eva."

She loosed her grip, allowed him to face her, yet did not release her hands from around his waist.

"Eva, then."

Without any hesitation, she nearly threw herself at him, seeking out his lips with a hunger Jamison would later liken to a wild animal seeking after food.

It was several moments before she spoke a word. "I have never been more fascinated by a man than I am now," she whispered with a growl. "I have never been this close to such a brave and willing man before."

And then she threw herself at him once again.

Jamison no longer thought about danger that night, nor about California, nor about opportunity, nor about Eva, but merely the reality of a new perception.

He was becoming who they thought he was.

New York City
July 1847

Jamison understood how the shipwrecked must feel, how those trapped in floods and avalanches must think. For since the dinner party at the Riklers', he had been carried along by a powerful current, lifting him, bouncing him forever forward, ever to the West.

Rikler insisted that the paper outfit Jamison with the best equipment available. He was provided a new wardrobe. Some promised to ward off a blizzard's cold; others promised escape from tropical heat.

Rikler made him purchase a tent and equipment made for camping in a rather high style. At first Jamison protested, saying he would not be able to carry it all and that porters may not always be available. His protests were ignored. By the time he booked passage on a steamer heading to the West Coast, there was a small mountain of equipment, each labeled very neatly with his name and address.

The first night in his cabin, he undid his personal satchel. It was there he carried his journals and pens and paper. At the very top lay a scarlet envelope. It smelled of roses.

My dear Jamison,
 I can barely stand to see you go. Remember that I await your return. And as with all homecomings, there will be quite the reward.
 Waiting patiently,
 Eva Rikler

The scent of roses lay heavy in the cabin as Jamison tried to sleep.

From Just off the Coast of California
November 1847

Jamison stood gasping, knee deep in the surf, pulling a trunk after him, water dripping from his arms and chin. He turned and watched the mast of the schooner that he had been on only moments before snap off and tumble into the water. He watched as the heavy swell lifted the vessel and crashed it once again into the rocks a hundred yards off the shore.

As the ship had floundered near the rocks, Jamison, the only paying passenger on board, realized that it would be every man for himself. The crew seemed to take the perilous situation in stride, as if many of them had crashed in the same rocks before. Jamison pulled his sea trunk to the deck. Many of the crew grabbed what might float best and tossed themselves into the roiling waters. Jamison watched the captain of the craft toss in a cotton bale and dive in after it. The shore was no more than a quarter mile distant, and Jamison hoped that the men would make it to shore safely. As he hit the water, a swift current seemed to take hold of the trunk and pull him south from the crash. He did not notice any of the crew near him.

When he was close to shore, he dragged the trunk, digging a deep vee in the wet sand. He continued pulling it until he reached dry land, then slumped onto the top of the trunk and looked around.

Scrubs of palmetto and some sort of dry brush clumped together in small stands. A bluff rose from the shore and down the beach, and Jamison could see a cluster of structures at the edge of that same bluff.

An hour later Jamison finished his three-page recap of his journey to date. Liberally using the newspaper's money, he had arranged for a trio of fishermen to take those hastily written pages, wrapped in waterproof oilskin, back down the coast to the larger harbor he had left days earlier. He instructed the fishermen to get his package to a large ship making a southerly voyage. On the outside of the package was written in French, Spanish, Creole, and English the following words: "Whoever delivers this package to the offices of the *New York World* newspaper in New York City will receive a reward—in gold— of 500 dollars U.S." It was signed by both Jamison and the owner of the newspaper.

He paid the fishermen a five-dollar gold piece and watched them scramble to their boat, attempting to make the retreating tide.

Had Jamison been in the newspaper office a month later, he would have watched the editor drop his jaw in amazement at the motley crew of sailors and wastrels that brought the package into the editorial offices, each claiming a portion of the five-hundred-dollar reward. In fact, one of the original fishermen made the entire trip alongside the parcel.

And Jamison would have been heartened to see the headlines in the following day's newspaper.

REPORTER STAYS ALIVE
THROUGH LATEST TRAGEDY

TALES OF TREACHERY AND INEPTITUDE

AFTER INDIANS AND JUNGLE WITCH DOCTORS
COMES SHIPWRECK

SINKING OFF VERA CRUZ DOES LITTLE
TO DISSUADE OUR INTREPID REPORTER
FROM HIS JOURNEY

Report by Jamison Pike

As I write this I can still view the hulk of my ship crashing and grinding against the rocks of Vera Cruz. As the waves broke over the bow of our ship, with men crying out to the Almighty, I wondered again had I tempted fate once too often? Had the gods decreed that this was as far north as I shall prevail?

I, Jamison Pike, a reporter for this newspaper, have been on an epic journey these past months. I have been at sea and in jungles. We have sailed past pirates and skirted around bloodthirsty natives, who lurk in the foliage, silent and unseen.

I tell this tale with truth and veracity–and all that you will read has occurred as I journey from New York to the shores of golden California.

Jamison would have been disheartened to read further, for the editors took his leaner, sparse prose of the report and embellished it with all manner of florid and ornate imagery.

In fact, for weeks the newspaper had run banner headlines, promising the next installment of the story of its reporter's trip to California, much to the dismay of other newspaper editors who wished they had thought of the idea first—but to the great enthusiasm of the paper's readership.

San Francisco, California
January 1848

After the shipwreck, Jamison made his way up the coast of California, stopping in the fishing village of San Francisco. There Jamison spent three nights and days eating, sleeping, bathing, and sleeping some more. After a month of being without most of the accoutrements of civilized life, he was greatly relieved to enjoy them once again—even if the bath was shared with the entire floor of the hotel.

"Does this city ever get warm?" Jamison asked as he slid his chair closer to the fire after eating dinner.

"Not until the summer," the fellow at the front desk said. "And even then it ain't all that comfortable. My advice is to hike on inland. The fog and the sea air is what make this town so cruel."

"Inland is warmer? Even now?"

The clerk smiled, showing several gaps in his teeth. "Yep. It may snow, but it won't feel this cold at all."

Jamison edged closer to the flames. A spark shot out and landed on his sleeve. He smacked at it. "And if you were a traveling man, where would you head?"

The fellow scratched his chin. "I ain't really a man who goes in for that. I like my normals. Get up. Have coffee. Walk to the docks. Normal sorts of things."

"But if you were heading out?"

"Well maybe towards Sutter's Mill on the American River. I hear tell it's quite pretty. And Sutter is one interesting fellow. They say he's trying to start his own little country out there."

"His own country? Isn't it part of America? Can he do that?"

"They tell me he's about to try."

Three days later, Jamison was on a horse, with a packhorse trailing behind, carrying a tent and six blankets.

"A man can't be too warm," he said as he stacked his purchases from the general store just around the corner from his hotel.

No one had a map of the area, but he asked over twenty people how to get to where he was going—standard procedure when heading into unmapped territory. He was instructed to ride along the southern edge of the bay. Eventually he would come to a large, muddy river, the San Joaquin. The locals told him to follow the largest branch around to the north—a day's ride perhaps. Then the river split again, and he was to head south on the Mokelumne. Another day's ride, perhaps two, would take him to a small lake and the next creek to the north past the lake would be Sutter's Creek.

Jamison amazed himself by finding the ranch with no doubling back.

The day broke cold but clear as Irish crystal. A slight frost dusted the meadows and larch trees. And before him lay the sprawling ranch and estate of George Sutter. Situated on a wide meadow bordered by two creeks, the setting could not be more idyllic.

Jamison stood in the stirrups and looked east. A mile or so down the trail lay a large paddock area, barns, corrals, and a huge white house positioned up on a knoll. By the river stood a waterwheel, catching the morning sun as it turned slowly.

As he rode, Jamison carefully considered all the questions he might ask Sutter.

But as he turned a bend in the river, he came upon a group of Spanish-looking men, shouting and gesturing wildly, standing in what looked to be very, very cold water.

Jamison had no idea that this scene would not only change his life and the lives of his friends, but the destiny of the whole country.

Jamison knew enough Spanish to order food, find a room for the night, and make some sense of conversation—as long as the words did not speed past.

This day the words flowed in a great flood.

Jamison quickly dismounted his horse and ran to the edge of the water. At first he thought there might be an injured man there, so great was their obvious agitation. But the shouts were not of concern, but rather of glee or joy.

The men were gathered about a shallow scarp of rocks and stone in the middle of the river, where the cold water ran ankle deep. They were all bent at the waist, splashing through the frigid flow.

Jamison edged into the water, feeling his toes quickly go numb. He called out to the men, *"Qué es?"*

One fellow held up a glittering rock in his hand and shouted back, *"Oro.* Gold!"

Jamison hurried closer. Each moment another man would call out, stand, and hold a glittering nugget to the sun, shout, smile, stuff it into his pocket, then bend into the water again.

Jamison neared the group and looked down, just as they did, bending at the waist.

He saw it immediately.

A small rock, the size of his thumb—gold, pure—its glinting unsullied by the rush of waters fresh from the snowfields higher in the mountains. He reached down and his hand was shocked by the pain of the cold water. But he found the nugget and lifted it up. It was surprisingly heavy for its size. And as he picked that one up, another came into view and he reached and grabbed that one, too.

He stood and did exactly as the men he watched. He held the gold up to the morning sun, catching its warm metallic color. He smiled, laughed, then quickly stuffed it into his pocket and bent to look for more.

By noon they all clumped from the river on feet so numb that all feeling had departed. One of the men sparked a fire with dry grass and tinder and in a flash, all had boots off and socks steaming in the flames.

"Is this real?" Jamison asked one in his best Spanish.

His question was met with a puzzled stare.

He pulled out a nugget and pointed to it. "This is real, isn't it? *Es oro, sí?"*

The man broke into a wide grin. *"Sí,* senor. It is very real *oro!"*

They all returned for hours of sloshing through the waters, pulling out what lay near the surface. Jamison was no expert on gold or its value, but from the sagging weight in his pockets, he knew he carried a small fortune with him.

They all retreated to the fire once again.

"Too cold," Jamison said.

One of the men nodded. "Very cold."

"Springtime will be better."

They all laughed; then silence caught them all. They looked at each other. They looked at the river. They looked at Jamison as he looked at them.

And in that instant, Jamison knew what they all knew: that when spring came, so would others. News such as this was not merely interesting–it was tempting, alluring, bedazzling! Not one of these men, Jamison included, could leave this river and not, in the span of a day or two, blurt out his story, show a handful of the glistering rocks and nuggets, and grin like a fox let loose in a henhouse.

They all knew this day would never occur again.

The sun tipped toward the tree line. The other fellows scrambled down the riverbank and into the water once more, splashing and pawing through it as if they could push the water clear of the rocks below. Jamison stood and was within an instant of joining them. He patted at his pockets. There must have been twenty pounds of gold stuffed into them. He had had to cinch his belt tighter twice to keep his trousers from falling from his hips.

And in that short time, as he watched the men splash in the afternoon sun, he considered what direction his life might take from this moment on.

He might very well just stay here and take as much of this gold as he could and return home in a year, a wealthy man. Or . . .

Smiling, he walked slowly over to his horse and filled one saddlebag with the nuggets, tossing out his second set of clothes to make room.

He lifted himself in the saddle, waved to the men still standing in the river, now bathed in deep shadows. "Adios!" he called out.

Only one man stood, returning his wave and adios. The rest stayed in the water, eyes never leaving the surface of the water, searching in the last glints of light.

FROM THE JOURNAL OF JAMISON PIKE
ON BOARD THE REFLECTION
SOMEWHERE SOUTH OF THE PENINSULA CALLED BAJA
JANUARY 1848

This has been an epic journey—an epic journey fraught with dangers—yet almost tolerable with the money and resources made available by my newspaper. Gold and the promise of more gold is a keen motivator of men.

As I travel, besides the reports I have sent back to New York, I have kept a daily log of my adventures. So voluminous are my notes that when I return, all I will need to do is a slight edit and I will have a book ready to be published. From my sailing to the Caribbean Sea and my trek across the jungles to the shipwreck and my adventure leaving Vera Cruz and how I made my way to California—all are tasty fodder for a grand book. And the gold! Perhaps that is the true crux of this story.

The journey itself may not be unremarkable if all goes according to what was planned. Yet I think not one journey goes as planned.

There are Indians, pirates, bandits, and so many curious people who populate the route that a writer's material could never be exhausted. And there is gold.

California may not be a paradise, but it is a unique and fascinating culture. There are Spanish folks who claim the land for themselves. There are American adventurers who seem to think this land is their manifest destiny. There are Russians, with their harsh and incomprehensible language, making claims to the territory too. There is beauty, and as William Blake wrote of the tiger, such beauty has a terribly savage side as well. And there is gold.

The journey has changed me. I know what fear is—true heart-shaking, soul-twisting fear. But I have faced it all and have come through on my wits, my skills, and my nerve.

I know my parents would scarce recognize the man I now am as their son. The sun has baked my skin and hardened what is inside me.

When I return to New York, I will return as a man who has grown stronger, more sure, more resistant to the softness of society. I look back and see what a weak man I was.

My search for the truth? I laugh at my sophomoric thoughts. Life is not lived on the streets of New York. It is not lived in the drawing rooms of high society. It is not lived in the coldness of the church.

Life is out here—in the face of nature and all its unthinking cruelty and beauty.

Oh . . . what a book this will be!

New Orleans
February 1848

Storms and squalls dogged Jamison's ship as it left Panama and headed for New Orleans. The winds and the rain made travel miserable but fast. Cooking on board, even in the best of times, was difficult, and when fighting through high swells, most day's rations were nothing more than cheese, hardtack, and bad water.

On every voyage, at least for the first few days, Jamison suffered wretchedly from the rolling and pitch of the waves. But before the initial week was up, his stomach seemed to right itself, and his "feeling green around the gills" all but vanished.

When they finally arrived in the calm waters of the port of New Orleans, Jamison and the rest of the crew rejoiced.

Jamison had his story and was in a race to get home.

In New Orleans he agonized over the choice of sailing north in the shallow waters along the eastern coast or taking a steamship up the Mississippi. The spring rains had not yet fallen, and the river was navigable the entire way to Ohio—and perhaps into Pennsylvania. The voyage along the coast was faster by days, but the captain and others declared the weather omens to be unfavorable.

"Storms heading up from the Carib'," one said. "You'll be lucky not to go aground off Hatteras. I lost two ships in weather just like this last year."

So Jamison, freely spending the last of the newspaper's money, booked passage in a large stateroom on a fast paddle-wheeled steamer headed north. The elegant quarters boasted a copper tub, with hot water right in the same room. It was a luxury he could not pass up—especially owing to the deprivations of the last months.

Jamison watched Natchez fade into the darkness and distance as he soaked in that copper tub. The water at first was hot enough to boil eggs. He was forced to kneel next to it, stirring the steaming water with his hand, like a giant's bowl of soup. Eventually he slipped in with a great, happy sigh. He leaned back, fixing his attention on the lights along the shore.

If Jamison could have painted his recollections of this trip, the canvas would be a smudge of somber colors, washed and splashed into an eruption of brown and gray and lead.

Accommodations had been spartan at best. Food was most often abysmal. Jamison felt in constant danger—from pirates and shipwreck and angry natives and disease and bandits. Law and order and justice remained mere concepts in most places. Even in these primitive locations, men found women and alcohol and gambling–as if those were the only comforts of home worth bringing along.

And yet, he thought as his skin began to wrinkle from the hot water, he had never once felt so alive as he had on this trip. He was journeying to places where few white men had ever ventured. Around every corner and in every harbor an explosion of new landscapes awaited him, a swirl of new sights and people.

It was as if the world were unveiling itself to him.

Jamison found it hard not to smile at every moment, so great was his pleasure at the unwrapping.

March 1848

The ship plowed north through the muddy and chilled waters of the great Ohio River. In places it was still cold enough to have to dodge ice floes from smaller rivers that fed the great stream. During the day Jamison often bundled himself in layers of jackets and blankets and watched as the gray and dead winter landscape passed in colorless monotony.

He monitored the ship's progress on the captain's map in the ship's wheel room. Every day a new section of the river would be traced in red pencil. The route led along the southern edge of Ohio. The captain promised that, unless the ice increased, they would be able to steam, under full power, into Gallipolis, Ohio, within two days.

Jamison knew he had to disembark. There was one person he had to see.

FROM THE JOURNAL OF JAMISON PIKE
SHAWNEE, OHIO/GALLIPOLIS, OHIO

Six months ago, had you shown me the expression on Joshua's face when I first appeared at his church during a Sunday service, I would have wagered a year's salary that no man could exhibit more surprise.

It was, in some nostalgic way, a most wonderful time with Joshua Quittner. I scarce recognized him, to be true. He had grown more lean and more intense since I had last seen him. I wish I could have paid attention to his sermon, but my thoughts have been in such a tangle for so long that I admit to merely staring at him as he spoke. I assume he spoke on *something* from the Bible that day.

He treated me to food and shelter and a hot bath, of all things. Even the best accommodations on a riverboat do not often include a hot bath.

We reminisced some. I told a few stories that I knew would excite and please him. I made myself out to be braver and more sure of myself than I am. But do not all men do that? The truth gets glossed over in places and expanded in others. It is the privilege of a writer to embellish some.

We talked a bit more. I slept.

The next morning I departed with Joshua's hearty farewell. I left him the tattered *Emigrants Guide* with a long note explaining the best routes and procedures.

Then I did something I have no explanation for. I left him the largest gold nugget I possessed. It was a choice, shiny, heavy one— the size of a pig's foot, if I had to guess.

I don't know why I did that.

Well . . . I do. I suppose I do, anyhow.

I left it to tempt him. Joshua, with the perfect life of service to God, in the perfect little church, and his perfect new lady friend— I left the gold to show him otherwise.

My heart has not been settled for years.

I stepped out into the cold again, knowing that I left the glistering temptation of gold and the promise of untold wealth behind—plus a map on how to get there.

And my heart was less settled than before.

Now I am but a few days away from New York City.

My great fear is that all too soon, like Joshua, the people there will see behind me and know what a great imposter I have become.

Pittsburgh, Pennsylvania

After visiting Joshua, Jamison hurried back to the river and continued on to Pittsburgh. He debated on what he should do. He felt a tremendous obligation to return to New York posthaste. He had a final few installments of his journey to write and, no doubt, a very anxious publisher waiting for him.

Pittsburgh presented a dilemma.

He knew he should stop to see his parents, but since his father's visit, only an occasional letter had passed between them—and none of them could be described as friendly. He truly desired to see Neta—but if he did, he knew, without question, that his visit would be the stuff of great gossip. And as much as his parents decried gossip in all its forms, he also knew they would hear of his visit in short order.

Even as the ship pulled up to the river docks, its steam boiler hissing under an enormous plume of vapor, he had not decided.

Hoisting his bag to his shoulder, he hailed a hackney. The driver reached around and opened the door. Jamison tossed his bag in.

"Where to, sir?" the driver called in an unmistakable thick Pittsburgh accent.

Jamison stood on the carriage step.

He could have said the train station on the north side.

He could have said the Pike residence on Forbes Avenue.

He hesitated as the horse stomped on the ground.

"Sir?"

"The Hill residence on Fifth Avenue. By the bluffs. The yellow house with the white columns. Do you know it?"

The driver appeared wounded. "Sir, of course I knows it. Be a simpleton not to know of the Hills."

The carriage pulled away with a jerk, and Jamison held on tightly to the leather strap, hoping not to be jostled more than necessary.

Had he known, he would have covered his ears when he tapped at the entrance to the Hill residence. Neta peeked around the edge of the heavy door, and he was certain her high-pitched squeal could be heard for blocks. Mr. and Mrs. Hill came running, fearing that Neta had been attacked or worse. When they saw their guest, they too cried out and surrounded him in a hurricane of slaps and handshakes and hugs and even a kiss or two.

Jamison felt as if he had left one storm and entered another. Within minutes a meal appeared, as if by magic, and Jamison did not have to be coerced into seconds and even thirds of a proper home-cooked dinner.

While he ate, questions from all three—Neta and her mother and father—flew fast and furious. They were all familiar with his exploits since copies of the New York papers generally made it to Pittsburgh, though two or three days past the printing date.

Jamison realized quickly that his tales of the journey—especially when he confronted a dangerous situation—had the three of them leaning forward, enthralled and enraptured by his exploits.

Neta seemed lit with a glow from within as he spoke.

For Jamison, being the center of such focus was both embarrassing and a bit exciting.

But what made them all howl with displeasure was his insistence that he must catch the late-evening train headed to New York.

"If I don't get back, my editor will have my hide," he explained. "Next time I will stay for a week, I promise."

Jamison did not even wince as he fabricated that story. If he stayed the night, he knew he would have to visit his parents. And that was a trip more daunting than the whole of the journey to California.

Mr. and Mrs. Hill insisted that Jamison take the family coach and driver to the train station. And, of course, Neta insisted on accompanying him.

Jamison found no reason to argue.

"I can't believe what you've done," Neta cooed as she slid her arm into his. The carriage was dark. Both were wrapped in a warm thickness of buffalo pelt. "You are the talk of all of Pittsburgh. Everyone is simply spellbound by your epic journey. And I can't believe I am sitting next to you again."

"Please, Neta, I am not a man prone to blushing, but I am not famous."

"But you are," she said as she hugged his arm. "I heard several strangers in town talking about the stories. They went on and on about how brave you sounded. I wanted to march right up to them and tell them that I know you."

"Did you?" Jamison could not have been more shocked.

"No. But next time I will."

The clock tower pealed ten times as the carriage sidled up to the station. Jamison's train left at quarter past.

"I should go. If I miss this train," he said, taking her hand, "I would be forced to spend the night."

Neta smiled and pulled him to her, wrapping her hand on the back of his neck, pulling his lips to hers. He let it last only a heartbeat or two.

He would have preferred longer but thought he may be taking advantage of the situation had he done so.

"I am so happy that you came," she said as she hugged him. "And I am so angry that you're leaving so soon. Next time, you must stay longer. You must. I need to hold you longer than this brief moment."

And she squeezed him so hard that his chest hurt. He felt her fingers entwined behind his back.

"I will," he gasped. "I promise."

"If you don't, I will come and track you down, Mr. Jamison Pike." She pecked his cheek again.

He smiled. "I am trusting that you will."

On the Train to New York City

The train hissed into the night, and Jamison sat staring at the blackness reflected in the window.

Who am I becoming? he questioned the darkness. *I am so terribly perplexed. There is a woman I love. There is a woman I desire. And there is a kind, sweet woman I respect.*

The car jolted to the side and he banged his forehead on the glass. He leaned back and closed his eyes.

I can grow to love her. I know I can. It is not a counterfeit emotion. The heart feels what the head insists.

He blinked his eyes open.

The landscape was lit with the thin chip of the moon.

God does give a man what he needs, doesn't he?

And isn't Neta what God is giving me?

> *New York City*
> *July 1848*

Jamison stopped dead in the street. He closed his eyes, then spun about and sprinted back to the shopwindow he had just passed. Normally, if he passed a bookstore, he would take a moment and go inside to examine their offerings on display tables in front or in the windows. Since his return, he had done little idle viewing.

But today was different.

He stood in front of Young's Books and stared and stared. Stacked in the window, thirty or so copies deep, was a snug little volume. A large, handwritten poster leaned against the top of the stack. It read: *"You have read of his journey. Now read the secrets behind the story!"*

There was a tall stack of books—copies of *A Western Odyssey*. The sign read: *"Exciting words by a gifted young writer—Jamison Pike."*

He smiled. He had known for weeks that the book was due to be in the shops at any time. And now that the reality had come, all he could do was look and offer a wry smile, betraying only a small portion of the emotions that exploded in his mind.

He wasn't sure how long he stood there. Eventually he felt compelled to continue and made his way slowly to the offices of the paper. Since his return, he had been treated with great deference by the other reporters. The older ones treated him as returning royalty, and the younger members hardly spoke to him at all, so great was their awe.

At least Jamison hoped it was awe.

During the weeks it took his book to find its way into bookstores, he packed up his belongings from the Edmonds residence and had them shipped to his new apartment. Clarence had begged him to stay, but Jamison was quite certain it was his newfound celebrity Clarence desired, not a return to their old friendship.

He saw Eva Rikler a few times during the weeks following his return. She had been overjoyed to see him once again, but he could not share her enthusiasm. He knew that his celebrity would have given him great liberties with her—or any number of society women. But a relationship based solely on desire did not satisfy the hollowness in his heart.

If one had asked him only a few years prior, could he have ever imagined spurning a woman such as Eva, he would have laughed. "Unimaginable," he would have replied.

Yet that was exactly what he was doing.

And he did not know exactly why, save that he knew he had to.

Philadelphia
October 1848

"Hannah?"

The woman whom Jamison had so long imagined standing before him was doing just that. And both were surprised beyond belief.

Jamison had been sent out on a short tour of a few major eastern cities to promote his book. His publisher had given him a tight itinerary, complete with names of every editor to contact and every bookstore to visit between New York and Charleston.

He had been on the road for only a week when his travels took him into Philadelphia. He knew, of course, that Hannah lived there but vowed he would make no attempt to contact her.

Now, in a small bookstore in Philadelphia, their two disparate paths crossed.

Hannah had managed to spin about in the crowded aisle, stare at Jamison for a moment, mouth his name, then crumble to the floor.

Jamison dove to her side and lifted her, expecting to run with his precious baggage to the nearest doctor or hospital. Instead, the owner of the bookstore, an owlish little man, corralled Jamison and the unconscious Hannah into a back room. Jamison laid his delicate burden on the couch with tender care. He was surprised at her slightness, knowing he could have carried her for miles, if needed, to find aid.

A tumbler of cold water appeared, and Jamison tilted her head and shoulders forward. She lay soft and warm in his arms. He managed to slip a trickle of water into her mouth and watched her, his face tight with fear and concern.

Then she coughed once, her eyelids fluttering like a butterfly after a storm. She opened her eyes and, like a dream, reached out with a wavering hand and touched his cheek. She gently called his name.

Later, after Hannah had recovered, Jamison could not have imagined a more perfect evening. He managed to convey the why and how of his journey and convinced her to have dinner with him at a nearby restaurant.

The evening slipped past like an ephemeral mist, Jamison thought, and in an instant, he was forced to hurry to the station to catch the next train and complete the next leg of his trip. After all, his publisher had gone to great lengths to arrange his tour.

As the train pulled from the station, Jamison could scarce keep his thoughts coherent. He was agitated and anxious.

It was not until hours later that his breathing regained its normal pacing.

Yes, it was so good to see her, he told himself. *For now I am sure of my future. What was in the past is in the past. And we are friends forever—but there can be no more than that.*

He sighed.
God gives us what we need.
He closed his eyes.
If I now can force my heart to believe it.

From a Letter to Hannah Collins

Dear Hannah,

How wonderful it was to be with you in Philadelphia. A book tour is a lonely journey, and yet this segment of my trip was made so bearable by seeing you again.

It was such a welcome serendipity running into that bookstore. Who could have planned our meeting?

Our dinner was a highlight of my year–even more memorable than any of the tales in my slight book. I was happy to afford a signed copy for you.

I trust we shall continue to write. I so value your friendship.

Yours,

Jamison Pike

New York City

"You're leaving again? You have barely been back in the city two weeks. The book tour hasn't worn you out?" asked Benjamin Grossman in a concerned tone.

Jamison slouched farther into the chair. His head was barely visible over the arm. "No, not at all. And haven't I been back for months now?"

"Rikler doesn't think so. He isn't thinking about sending you out again. You're probably less expensive to him here than on a journey." Benjamin snorted out a laugh.

"Rikler? He only thinks of selling papers."

"But why go off again?" Benjamin asked.

"My journey sold a lot of papers, didn't it?" Jamison asked. "And it's nice to be famous. Or almost famous."

"You know a dozen other papers are sending out reporters just like you. There'll be competition out there," Benjamin replied.

Jamison raised a hand above his head and waved. "But none of them have my experience. And first is always best, is it not?"

Benjamin smiled.

A few months after returning home from California, Jamison invited Benjamin Grossman to share his apartment. The space was large enough for a family of four or five. Not far from the newspaper office, the rooms were bright and airy and quiet.

There were four bedchambers and a spacious living area with a formal drawing room and a large dining area. Jamison was certain he would travel again and wanted the rooms occupied by someone he trusted. Benjamin was a fellow reporter at the *World*, a likable fellow from Richmond who possessed an easygoing nature and a slow and steady approach to his work.

"I might head back to California," Jamison added.

"What? You've done that," Benjamin replied.

"I'll take a different route. Overland perhaps. I'll meet some Indians this time. Scalping and buffaloes and all that."

Shuddering, Benjamin shook his head. "How can you jest about this? A fellow could wind up very dead on a trip like that."

It was hard for Jamison to shrug from such a slouched position, but he did. "I could write another book. I truly did not see much of California nor spend much time in the town they call 'San Francisco.'"

"And that is bad?"

"It is part of the territory. It possesses a wonderful natural harbor. Anyone with an interest in shipping would be interested."

Benjamin stood and carefully picked up his cup and saucer. He had brought with him a complete set of his mother's best china, imported from France. He did not have any sisters and, as such, was destined to receive all the family heirlooms.

He hesitated, shuffling about in the shadows by the kitchen door.

Jamison knew there was a question in the air. "What?"

Benjamin cleared his throat. "It is truly not my intention to intrude ... nor is it my affair ..."

"But?"

"I am not sure how to say this, but you of all people should understand. You go on and on about the truth and how important it is. So I trust you will understand if I tell the truth—at least how I see that truth. And to me, it appears you are running away. Ever since you came back from Philadelphia, you have paced about here and the office like a caged beast of some sort. And now I see your face light up when you talk about departing again. You are almost famous now. You have many friends and a wonderful apartment and could be the talk of the town for months. Yet it appears you don't want any of that. It appears to me you're running from something."

Jamison waited to answer. "I truly do not owe anyone, even you, an explanation," he stated.

He heard the cup rattle against the saucer in Benjamin's hand.

"I only meant ... I mean ..."

"No matter, friend."

Benjamin did not move. He waited and stared at Jamison with a most curious look on his face—a mixture of sadness and sympathy.

Jamison cleared his throat and pushed himself upright. He ran his hand through his hair, then rubbed his face with his hands. "Perhaps it is true," he confessed. "Perhaps I am running."

After a moment Benjamin asked softly, "From what?"

Jamison shrugged. "I'm not sure. And when one is on a journey, one has no time for such weighty thoughts."

"Truly?"

"The advice I have oft given is to pack light," Jamison offered with a soft laugh.

Benjamin opened the door to the kitchen. Having such a large kitchen was also an oddity in an apartment building and another reason Jamison liked the place.

"I will make some fresh coffee. Would you like some?" Benjamin asked.

"Do we have any cream?"

"I think so."

"Then, yes," Jamison answered.

The room fell silent after Benjamin's departure, and Jamison massaged his temples. He did not have to take another journey. Rikler had not insisted. In fact, quite the opposite was true. Rikler had increased Jamison's salary and offered him a position that would never require travel.

But Jamison knew he could not stay.

The few moments he had shared with Hannah in Philadelphia were immensely powerful, causing a flood of emotions to rob him of sleep and peace.

He would not indulge in alcohol.

Religion was not a comfort.

But travel–movement–silenced the turmoil and the questions.

As Benjamin puttered about in the kitchen, Jamison forced himself out of the chair and to the small writing desk near the fireplace.

He quickly scratched out the following note:

Dear Hannah,

I am once again on a journey. I am traveling to . . .

He stared at the blank wall for several minutes. He could most likely name the destination, and based on his previous success, Rikler would underwrite any journey.

. . . California again. There was so much there I did not have time to examine and other routes and approaches to explore that I feel obligated to journey once again.

And my publisher wants a sequel. Publishers! They are the bane of the writer, I assure you.

All my best. I will write as I can. If there is anything you might ever need in the city, please contact my new roommate and fellow reporter, Benjamin Grossman. He is a kind chap out of Richmond and a good fellow to know if you need a favor in New York.

Always,

Jamison Pike

CHAPTER TWELVE

New York City
November 1848

Grossman says you're planning another trip?"

Jamison clicked Mr. Rikler's door shut and stepped toward his desk. Sunlight was not kind to his office. Stacks of newspapers tilted into corners; papers and books littered his desk and bookcases. There was a motley assortment of coffee cups—none seeming to match—and many from the restaurant on the ground floor. An ashtray was heaped with the wet, ragged ends of cigars.

Rikler pushed aside one deep stack, cleared a space on his blotter, then leaned back and slapped his feet there. A few small thumbnails of mud fell off as he did so. His chair creaked as he pushed backward.

"And don't blame the man. The whole newsroom seemed to know of it before I did. Grossman was just a handy fellow to ask. And I trust him. More than I can say for most of the people who work for me."

Jamison tried to hide his smile.

"Didn't mean you, of course. You're different."

"Thank you, sir," Jamison replied.

The two men eyed each other, Rikler chewing on a very black and gnarled unlit cigar. "You don't have to go anywhere, son," he said evenly. "No one here is pushing you to go. With the book and all, you'd never have to leave again."

Jamison had his speech ready for some days now. "Yes, sir, I know. But there were a lot of places I missed and experiences I didn't get around to recording. It won't take more than six months. I'll do a second book. It will sell a lot of papers. I want to go, sir."

Rikler reached into his vest pocket and fished out a box of matches. With some ceremony, he lit the match, warmed the cigar end, and then drew into it, creating great white clouds of thick, aromatic smoke.

"Well . . . ," he said between puffs, "you're right about it selling a lot of copies. Since your stories ran, we have nearly doubled our readership."

"I've heard, sir. That is good news."

Rikler let his feet fall from his desk and stood up, hitching his pants in such a manner that Jamison thought he had hurt himself.

"But something's troubling me, son."

Another series of smoke clouds added to the disorder of the office. "Sir?"

"Don't rightly know how to say this. Never had to before."

"Sir?" Jamison asked. He thought he knew what was coming.

"It's about my daughter. Eva."

"Yes, sir. Your daughter."

"I understand a lot of things in this world—politics, how a newspaper gets written, printing, typesetting machines . . ."

"Yes, sir."

"But that list doesn't include women."

"Yes, sir."

"Seems my daughter is smitten with you for some odd reason. Truth be told, I never understand why any woman bothers with us as a whole. We're cranky and have odd habits and tendencies."

"Yes, sir."

"But they do. And ever since you got back to the city, Eva has gone on and on about this. And me without her mother, God rest her soul. None of it makes sense."

"Yes, sir. I mean no, sir."

"So what do I say when I tell her you're leaving again? Or do I let you tell her?"

Jamison had rehearsed this response as well. He had anticipated it. Since his return, he had escorted Eva to several events. Each evening ended with Jamison fending off her advances–advances that had grown more and more aggressive. He knew a lesser man would have been most ungentlemanly with her.

"Sir, I think the world of Miss Rikler. She is a terribly sweet girl. But I am a reporter. A poor reporter at that–when compared to what she has grown up with, I mean."

"You wrote a book. That should help."

"Sir, aren't you a publisher?"

Rikler scowled for a second, then grinned broadly. "You have a point there, son."

"And, sir–I am still young. I have no plans of settling down just yet. To lead any young woman on would be callow of me. And I could not expect a woman as poised and beautiful as your daughter to scuffle about the house, lonely, waiting for a man like me to return. She could do so much better, sir."

Rikler eyed Jamison carefully. "Well, I understand what you're saying. I daresay she won't. She can be impatient. But you will tell her of your plans, won't you? You don't expect me to bear bad news to her, do you?"

"Sir, of course I will inform your daughter. I am a gentleman. But I want you to understand why I have to do that."

"Good lad, then," Rikler said, puffing thickly. "And you're all prepared for the next adventure? Leaving soon?"

"Day after tomorrow, sir. I see your daughter this evening."

Rikler nodded. Just before Jamison stepped out of the office, he called out, "Then Godspeed and all that, son. We'll be here waiting for your dispatches."

"Thank you, sir."

"And try not to spend too much of the newspaper's money, would you?"

Jamison smiled and did not answer.

"So you see, Eva, I must leave again. There is another side to the story that must be told."

Jamison stood by the fireplace with his back to her. They sat in the thickly furnished drawing room of her father's house. The fire made his shins hot, but he was afraid to move. Eva hadn't said a word since he began his nervous soliloquy.

He could see her face bathed in shadows, reflected in the grand mirror above the mantel. He could see her expression in the dim light.

He could wait no more.

There was no doubt she was angry and hurt.

"But you have been back such a short time," she said, her voice nearly a wail.

"I know, Eva, and if I could stay longer, I would. But unless I leave now, the weather will make it more difficult."

He did not add that the weather, regardless of the season, could prove unpredictable and dangerous.

"You're leaving because you find me unappealing. That's why you're leaving, isn't it?"

Jamison leaned back in surprise. He had never anticipated that response. "No, not at all. It has nothing to do with our relationship."

Eva stood and ran to him, embracing him tightly. "You do care then, don't you?"

How could he say otherwise? he thought. "Well, for certain I do."

"I knew you did," she whispered into his chest.

Puzzled as to how she had forced him to this point, Jamison said slowly, "But, Eva, I will be gone a long time. I couldn't ask you to . . . to wait."

Wait? I never even considered asking her to wait. And for what? What am I saying?

"Jamison, you bounder, you," she said in a throaty whisper, "of course I will wait for you. There is something in me that finds a bad boy so appealing. And right now you have never been more appealing." She squeezed him harder.

"But I'm not worth waiting for," he insisted, realizing how weak the words sounded, even as he spoke them.

"You are worth it," she said. "You are."

When she squeezed him again, he felt trapped, as if he would never be released.

Her farewell was a far sight different than the angry good-bye he had expected.

Somewhere in the Jungles of Panama
December 1848

Jamison had been happy that the sleek clipper ship made short work of covering the miles between the New York harbor and the coast of Panama. At the port of San Cristobal Jamison asked, in his best, though rudimentary Spanish, for an English-speaking guide. A score of people offered the same recommendation: Braden Parker. Parker was a slight Englishman with a lisp who looked nothing like an intrepid adventurer. His blond hair exploded from under a worn helmet; his clothes appeared as if never having touched the power of soap.

But everyone said he was the best of the lot, so Jamison reluctantly offered him a sizable sum to take him through the jungle. The land separating the Atlantic from the Pacific was no more than fifty miles wide.

Parker promised Jamison he had made dozens of trips across the narrow land and had not lost a single customer. True or not, Jamison was happy to have someone there who spoke English and carried a big rifle.

Fifty miles back home was no more than a trifling journey. But fifty miles in a Panamanian jungle was a troubling and harsh distance indeed.

Now, three days into the crossing, Parker claimed they could not light a fire for fear of attracting the attention of one of six tribes that populated these dense jungles.

"Some of them still be practicing on eating their enemies. May not matter to you, Mr. Pike, but I don't fancy becoming a main course for a bunch of dirty and ignorant savages."

Jamison had no reason to argue, so now the two men and twelve porters lay on the damp ground. Protected only by thin blankets, they were at the mercy of massive swarms of flying insects and crawling, squiggling, white-as-wax worms and larvae. Jamison attempted to make himself as small as he could, to attract as little of their attention as possible.

Well past midnight, Jamison was awakened. Not by a call or shout, but by a firm grip on his shoulder.

Parker whispered in his ear, "Don't say a word."

Jamison strained to hear a sound, strained to see anything in the pitch-blackness of the night. He could do neither.

From his left came a muffled scream, then a louder scream. Parker rolled to his left. Jamison heard a mechanical ratcheting sound; then the darkness and silence were shattered by an explosion of flame and smoke. In that one illumination, Jamison saw Parker, silhouetted by the flash, holding his rifle at his waist, firing into the jungle. Farther from the flame, he saw the outlines of a dozen faces, painted in whites and golds and reds, and the sleek shadows of spears.

Flames exploded from the rifle again. A native was lifted off his feet and tossed back into the foliage, his arms splayed about. In that same instant, Jamison saw a spear protruding from the still form of one of the porters.

Parker fired again. "Thank God for five shots!" he screamed. "Grab your kit, Mr. Pike. Take hold of my hand."

Jamison, like most travelers, kept his most essential possessions in a small bag, seldom allowing it to be out of sight. He had his gold, his tablets, his pencils, a change of clothing, shoes, preaddressed oil-skin pouches, and his shaving kit all tucked into a hefty leather grip. He was using it as a pillow, so it was not hard to find. The rest of the supplies—food, bedding, tents, plates, medical supplies—were stuffed into large Saratoga trunks and always carried by porters.

Jamison found Parker's hand. Feeling the hot blast of the fourth rifle shot, he turned to see more natives swarming out of the brush, appearing as if by magic. The porters were up, screaming as they were set upon by the painted men.

The fifth shot roared into the night. One of their attackers flew backward from the impact.

"Hold the rifle!" Parker shouted as they began running. "I've still got six rounds left in my revolver."

Instead of standing and fighting, the two men ran. They hurried along the river where they had bivouacked and splashed in the shallow waters alongshore. The moonlight was brighter there, and they could see no one in front of them.

After perhaps fifteen frantic minutes, Parker slowed down and stopped, gasping, then turned to look behind. "See anyone?"

Jamison shook his head.

"And I don't hear any of them blighters either. I think they were satisfied with the porters, them poor buggers." Then Parker turned and began to slog up the river, pushing hard against the slow current.

"And we're just going to leave them?" Jamison asked, incredulous.

Parker did not hesitate. "And fight off a couple dozen of them savages? Just the two of us? If you think you can, Mr. Pike, be my guest. But like I said before, I don't relish the thought of becoming Sunday roast for these chaps."

Jamison wanted to wait, wanted to do something to save those unfortunate men, wanted perhaps to even say a prayer. He began to say the words, then stopped. He peered at Parker, who was already thirty feet ahead. Instead of praying, he hefted the bag to his shoulder and hurried to catch up.

Río de Jesús, on the West Coast of Panama

Jamison bid Parker, his guide across Panama, farewell. The trip had taken little more than a week, yet Jamison felt he had known Parker for years.

"I hope you make it back with fewer frights than occurred on this journey," Jamison said.

Parker hefted his rifle on his shoulder. Behind him, six native porters milled about. His client for the return trip, an English fellow, was having some intestinal difficulties and had run back into the hotel.

"I'm sure I will, Mr. Pike. Already heard that the Federales marched into that area and started lopping off hands. The politicals here don't warm up to that sort of disturbance. Bad for business, they say. I think we'll be fine. And it was a pleasure doing business with you, Mr. Pike, and with your newspaper. If I'm here for your return, I'd be honored to do the journey again."

"Not likely. I'm going to try to go overland this time."

"Through them mountains and all?"

"That is my plan."

Parker leaned close. "What I heard about them redskins makes the savages here seem like a tea party with the queen. Best be careful."

"Oh, I will, Mr. Parker. I will."

Jamison had to wait only two days until a small schooner that was headed to San Francisco stopped in port. He booked passage but had to sleep on deck.

It was on a cold Christmas Eve that Jamison stepped off the boat and walked up the steep hill to find an inn that would shelter a very weary traveler.

February 1849

Jamison was tired—more tired than he had ever felt before. He wanted to go home, to feel safe again. He hoped it was possible.

He had spent weeks crisscrossing California—from the Russian settlements to the Spanish missions. He stopped once again near Sutter's Mill. The word had spread about the gold, and now there were dozens of men setting up camp on the river's edge.

He spent an afternoon in a quiet pool and gathered up enough nuggets to fill two leather sacks.

Now he was done, he thought, and his story complete.

Jamison had all but memorized the maps in the *Emigrants Guide to Oregon and California*. He was attempting to follow the portions of the path suggested in the book—but only in reverse. He knew without question that winter was no time to be attempting a crossing of the mountains by way of Denver, so he headed south.

He traveled overland, south along the coast, and turned east just south of San Diego to head out over the desert, past Yuma and Nogales and Las Cruces. At the tiny, dusty town of El Paso, he looked for a fellow willing to lead him the entire distance to Kansas City. It was not hard. As in most frontier towns, there was an abundance of men calling themselves guides. To Jamison, most of them looked as if they could easily guide a man to the nearest saloon, but not much farther than that—at least not safely.

He thought he might have to make the journey alone until he ran into George Lambers. Jamison found George sitting in a rickety chair in the town's only barbershop. A sign tacked to the wall said: *"Guiding. The Most Experienced Man for the Job. Won't get kilt in Indian lands."*

Finding the sign both amusing and enchanting, Jamison asked of his qualifications for leading a man to Kansas City.

George thought for a minute. "You'll be crossing redskin land," he drawled. "And I bet there ain't one chance in a hundred you'd make it cross there with your scalp still on your head."

Jamison nodded. "Can you get me there in a month?"

George scratched at the gray stubble on his chin, scowled, then grinned. "You did say you were paying me double, didn't you?"

Jamison grinned back. "I didn't, but I will pay more for speed. And safety."

"I like a man with priorities," George said. "I'll get you there in a month–maybe three weeks."

And before dawn of the following morning, Jamison Pike and George Lambers, each on a horse followed by a pack mule, set out east, walking into the morning sun.

Somewhere in Kansas Territory

George loosened the saddle on his horse and hefted it to the ground.

Circling about the campsite, Jamison gathered up all the sticks and branches he could find. They were heading out on a southerly route, one that promised a better chance at warmer weather. For the past week, they had been most fortunate. There were no clouds in the sky during the day, and the sun warmed the air quickly. At night the temperatures and winds stayed mild.

In the matter of a half hour, Jamison had built a small fire and stacked enough wood to last them through the night. He pulled the coffeepot out from the bag on one of the mules.

"I'll be doing that, if you don't mind," George called out. "No offense, Mr. Pike, but coffee making is not one of your strong suits. You best stick with writing and them smart things you do."

Jamison smiled. He knew the guide was correct. He had tried cooking a few times and the results were edible, but only barely.

As George scooped coffee into the pot and set it near the fire to heat, Jamison rolled out his ground cloth.

"How much longer until we turn north?" he asked.

George stood up and scanned the country, as if the question were a novelty and might be discerned from a quick review of their location. To Jamison, the flat, nearly featureless land gave him no idea of where they were or how any man might recognize a landmark.

Pointing to the east, George replied, "There's a slight rise there. That marks the break tween the two watersheds. It's north right after we crest those hills. And we're here early. I feel the extra money in my pocket already."

The guide often mentioned his extravagance, Jamison noticed. "It's not my money." He laughed. "It comes from the newspaper."

Darkness crept up as the two finished their dinner of dried beef and potatoes mixed in with some cattails and wild onions George found by the banks of the stream.

"That was delicious," Jamison said as he patted his stomach. "This is the first time I've enjoyed the food as I traveled. You could be a cook if you had a mind to, Mr. Lambers."

"Not the life for me." Lambers guffawed. "Too confining. Four walls all day? No sir. I need to be out here. A man can breathe out here. Inside, the air gets powerful stale and a man dies a little every day."

Jamison leaned against his saddle like a pillow and threw a coarse blanket over his legs. "How long have you been out west, Mr. Lambers?"

"Nearly twenty years now. Left Baltimore when I was fifteen. Never went back."

"And you've been guiding travelers ever since?"

George almost spilled his coffee as he brayed with laughter. "Land sakes, no. I've done just about everything a fellow can do out here—from skinning mules to shooting buffaloes. Guiding started more recent. A lot of city folks heading this way have a tendency to get lost lickety-split. That be good for business, though. Bones, bleached white on the trail and all. People see that and ask for me."

From off in the distance a coyote barked and howled. The moon, half faced, was seemingly at arm's length in the eastern sky. It lit up the empty country about them like a brace of candles in a cellar.

"And you're always by yourself like this?"

George nodded. "I'm alone . . . but I ain't. Know what I mean?"

Jamison was about to agree, as he often did to help people talk more. But this time he paused, then replied, "No, I'm not sure what you mean."

George spoke softly, his words no louder than the hiss of the fire. "A man who might be right with himself never minds being alone.

A man who's tangled up inside, well that fellow can't stand to be by himself. Always has to have somebody with 'em or be doing something or drinking something. You try anything to keep that noise down inside your head."

"Noise?"

"Yep. It ain't strange voices or such like that. It ain't being touched. But a man who ain't right with himself always hears himself saying that you got to move on, you've got to have this drink, that you ain't no good, that this life, poor as it might be, is all that a man gets—all sorts of things that trouble a man's sleep."

"And you don't hear that noise?"

"Used to, Mr. Pike. Used to hear it all the time. Came out west 'cause of it. Drank up most of my money in bad whiskey on account of it. Chased women just so I couldn't hear it no longer."

Jamison was sitting up and leaning forward.

"It ain't like that voice is screaming all the time. With me, it was always loudest when I was alone and maybe at the edge of sleep. Whispers. Little nudges of thought. If life ain't any more than a smooth glass of whiskey and a friendly woman, then why not just chase those two things around? That sort of talk be easy to listen to, know what I mean, Mr. Pike?"

"I think I do."

"And now things ain't like that. I'm done with the lying to myself. And now I can be alone without being scared."

A slight breeze rattled through the scrub brush. A horse whinnied. An owl screeched as it found its prey in the dark.

Feeling a chill, Jamison rubbed his hands in front of the fire. He waited several minutes before he spoke. "What happened? Why aren't you scared anymore?"

He knew the answer before he had posed the question, yet was compelled to ask.

"Well . . . I found God. Or God found me. Yet it ain't like God had lost me. It weren't that he was having trouble finding me. He knew where I was all along. But you know he touched me at the perfect moment. You know about perfect moments, Mr. Pike?"

An image of Hannah, her face illuminated by candlelight, flashed in Jamison's thoughts. "I . . . think I do."

"Well, I didn't till it happened. I was in Dodge City, almost drunk, almost happy, and almost broke again. Then I heard it."

"Heard what?"

"The sound of God."

"He talked to you?"

George's laughter broke the tension. "Not really, Mr. Pike. But I heard these ladies singing an old church song down the street. Seems like they were trying to find some lost souls and were just singing by themselves, hoping God would show them some. I walked out of the bar and into their church. It was perfect for me and perfect for them. Ain't had a drink since, and ain't once been scared of being alone anymore."

"Never?" Jamison asked, his voice softer than the breeze.

"Been afraid plenty, but never once scared of being alone. That is the difference. God is with me now. And I ain't scared of myself any-more."

The fire popped, an arm's length of wood readjusted itself into the flames, and a shower of sparks cascaded into the night sky.

"A perfect moment," George repeated softly. "It be perfect 'cause it was set by God."

A breeze whipped down from the north, filled with the threat of ice and snow.

"Best be finding sleep early, Mr. Pike. We'll be cold by daybreak—and best be getting an early start. This still be redskin territory, and I ain't happy being here longer than I need be."

Jamison nodded, pulling a second blanket onto himself. "So God gives you what you need," he said quietly. He'd said or thought those words so often that they had begun to lose their meaning—like saying "God bless you" after a sneeze. Jamison never considered himself a religious man anymore, but he wanted to know how the God of granting a man's needs played into George's theology.

George laughed in the darkness. "No, he don't. Not always. I needed a drink for years, and God for sure didn't give me one.

Sometimes things like strong drink are things that make a man comfortable and stupid. It makes a man never hear God's voice. So don't go thinking God gives you what you need, 'cause a man don't always know what it is that he do need."

Jamison closed his eyes to the dark universe swirling above him and pretended he was asleep.

"Good night, Mr. Pike," George said in a voice as soft as a rabbit's fur. "Maybe God will talk, but you got to listen."

"You ever lose anything out here?" Jamison asked as they saddled up the horses and reloaded their gear onto the pack mules the next morning.

"Sometimes, Mr. Pike. A horse or mule runs off, and you can look for days and just not find it. Things fall off the pack. So . . . yes, I've lost things."

Ever since waking, Jamison had felt a strange foreboding. He spoke only a few words. He was about to cinch his personal belongings onto his horse, then stopped. He undid the leather catch that held the kit shut. He lifted the flap and peered inside. Two bags, each the size of a loaf of bread and filled with gold, lay at the bottom of the satchel.

"George," Jamison called out, almost in a surprised tone, "would you take one of these bags? In case I lose my satchel."

He hefted it out and George whistled as he took it. "What do you have in here? Gold?"

Jamison did not smile. "Yes. From California. From Sutter's Mill up from Stockton."

George whistled again. "I can understand why you want to get back so soon. There ain't nothing out here to be spending it on, is there?" He secured the canvas bag in his roll and tightened the hitches on his saddle. "And don't you worry. I'll give it back when we get to Kansas City."

"I never doubted that you wouldn't," Jamison said as he pulled himself up into the saddle.

Overhead the sun bore through a thin ceiling of clouds. Jamison found himself sweating despite the chill in the air. He took off his hat and wiped his brow with a bandanna. He flexed his back as the horses plodded along, hearing the cracks as his muscles and bones sought realignment. Not a skilled rider, Jamison was competent yet seldom felt truly at home riding a horse.

They had reached the bluffs by midmorning and had turned north. Jamison was sure the weather would grow colder and add to the troubles of the journey.

He twisted again and turned his chin over his shoulder, hearing a series of pops. In the far distance behind them, perhaps a mile or two, he noticed a cloud of dust, lit to gold by the sun. He shielded his eyes to stare, thinking it might be some sort of whirlwind or tornado. He had heard that the whirlwinds would lift up entire herds of cattle as they swept along the plains.

"George," he called out, "what's that behind us? Is that a whirl-wind?"

George stood in his saddle and turned to the rear. A second later he shouted, "Cut the mules loose! Cut the mules loose!"

He grabbed the knife at his belt and slashed at the leather strap that held the two animals together. "Mr. Pike! Cut the rope! Cut it now!"

Jamison fumbled with his pocketknife but managed to unsnap it and slice through the buttery leather.

Ahead of him George was spurring his horse furiously. Jamison did the same.

In a moment, Jamison pulled nearly alongside. "What is that? Why are we running?" His words bounced and chattered as they ran.

"Injuns!"

"Who?"

"Redskins, Mr. Pike!"

"What tribe?"

"Don't care and don't intend to find out. Any redskin that comes at a man that fast has nothing good to say. They ain't coming out to greet us, that be for sure."

The horse slowed for a little creek. George dug his spurs in, and the horse whinnied and threatened to buck. He slapped at its haunches with his reins. "Ain't no time for niceties, Mr. Pike. Them savages behind us got much better ponies than we do, you can bet on that." His words came harsh and fast, edged with urgency.

As Jamison did his best to keep up, the two of them ran side by side for nearly thirty minutes, past tree groves, over dry washes, around hillocks. Every few hundred yards Jamison or George would turn in the saddle. The evaluation was always the same. "Still there. Gaining on us if I had to guess."

By now the horses were in a lather, and Jamison knew they could not continue running much longer. "What should we do?" he shouted. "Split up? Take a stand?"

George shrugged as best he could while riding. "We split up and they do as well. They'll get to both of us in time. Taking a stand—well, all I have is this old revolver and that single shot in the rifle. It would be a mighty quick stand."

The horses had slowed to a fast trot.

"Been praying pretty hard since you saw that dust. Don't know what's going to happen—but I ain't all that afraid. God still be in charge."

Jamison's heart had not slowed since they first spurred their horses to a gallop. *Dying with God may be all well and fine for George,* he thought, *but I don't think I am quite ready for it. Not just yet. Not now, not here.*

George led them through another series of dry washes and shallow ravines, twisting their route some, hoping their pursuers might lose their tracks—even if for a few minutes.

In the tangle of elevations and trees and brush, Jamison looked a dozen times and could not see or hear their pursuers anymore.

George spurred his horse up a rise. He pointed north. "If we get to that brush line," he called out, indicating a deep green line of trees, "and head straight north for just a few more miles, we'll get to the river. Jump in there and float away from them—cold water or not. The current is pretty swift."

Jamison stared ahead, trying to find the best route north through the rolling washes. His breath came in great gulps, and his shirt and coat were soaked through with sweat.

Just then he heard the most curious thumping sound. It was as if a rock had been hurled into a patch of thick mud. Then he heard it again. He turned to George to ask what that might be.

When he did, his heart came to his throat.

Two arrowheads protruded from George's right shoulder. He was pawing at them, windmilling his left arm, not willing to make contact with them.

Jamison veered wildly to the side. Some fifty yards distant a lone Indian sat on a multicolored pony. Jamison stared as the Indian pulled another arrow from a quill at his back, notched it into his bow, and let loose. George tumbled from his horse, and the arrow, which would have struck him midchest, instead plunged into Jamison's horse. The horse bucked backward and stumbled off the hillock, leaving Jamison sprawled on the ground.

From a greater distance Jamison heard a rising curtain of shouts and whoops.

The lone archer turned and waved, calling back, pointing to where George and Jamison lay.

The arrows had snapped when George fell, leaving only a stub projecting out the front and back. With his left arm, George grabbed Jamison's hand. "Take my horse. Head to the river like I said."

"I can't leave you here!" Jamison screamed, surprised he still had power over his voice. "I'm staying. We can fight them. . . ."

George pulled out his revolver and pointed it at Jamison. "I ain't lost anyone yet, and this ain't going to be the first. I can't ride. Your horse is gone. They'll be here in a minute. A couple of shots will slow them down."

Jamison put his hand on the man's bloody shoulder. "But . . . I can't just leave you."

George swallowed hard. "I'm as good as dead now. Might as well make my life count for something. I'm ready. I know you ain't. Now git. You ain't got much time."

Jamison shut his eyes, feeling the salt of his tears. "God . . . ," he whispered.

"He will, Mr. Pike. He will. Now git!"

And Jamison turned, leaped on George's horse and grabbed the reins, spurred him once hard, bent down, and let him run. He did not rise or stop until he reached the river. As he rode, he heard the sound of five gunshots. He did not hear the screams that followed. He jumped from the horse, undid the saddlebags, slapped the horse on the rear flank, and dove into the iron gray waters.

Night was at hand when Jamison stopped moving. He had never once dreamed that what had occurred today could have happened to him. He kept seeing the image of the bloody arrowheads and George waving him away.

He found a spot on the north side of the riverbank after swimming and thrashing in the frigid waters for so long that he no longer felt his feet or hands. Clumsily he dragged himself out of the water and lay on the riverbank, gasping for air, trying to flex his fingers and toes. He held his breath, straining to hear the sounds of pursuit.

The air was silent—but for the faint, silky hush of the dark waters.

Shivering badly, he stumbled about, pulling together dried leaves, twigs, and sticks, kicking at them with leaden feet, pushing them into a pile. He pulled at George's pack, trying to undo the knotted and wet leather thongs. He bent down and tugged at them with his teeth until, finally, the contents spilled on the ground in front of him. He pawed through it, ham-handed, until a slender, silver capsule rolled into view. Using both hands like blocks, he managed to unscrew it, and a dozen matches poured out. He succeeded to force one between his frozen thumb and forefinger and struck it on a dry rock. It sparked. He struck it a second time and it came to flame. He carefully set it to the pile and only when the leaves caught fire did he breathe again.

The fire spread new life into Jamison. As he warmed, his fingers and toes screamed out in pain—but it was life-affirming, good pain. As the warmth and blood returned, he gathered up more wood.

"I don't care if they do see the smoke," he said through chattering teeth. "If I die, I am going to die warm."

But there were no observers to his fire.

George had been well prepared. In his satchel, he carried an extra outfit, wrapped tight and tied in an oilcloth sack. Jamison unrolled it and to his amazement it was dry. He stood, stripped off his wet and tattered clothes, and dressed in George's fringed buckskins. The chamois leather felt smooth against his skin, and he watched as the fringe made shadows dance. Then he swallowed once, fell to his knees in front of the fire, and began to weep.

He did not stop until sleep freed him from the pain.

Walking into Kansas City felt more like a dream than any dream Jamison had ever known. There were buildings and beds and restaurants and no Indians waiting with drawn bows, ready to launch their arrows at him.

He hired a boatman to take him down the Missouri River as quickly as possible. In St. Louis he found a stagecoach leaving for Louisville in the morning. Three days later, he was on a riverboat heading north. He booked a first-class cabin the entire way to Pittsburgh.

He knew he was well ahead of his dispatch sent by boat and had the luxury, for the first time in months, of relaxing just a bit and breathing a little easier.

There would be plenty of time to write his second book.

CHAPTER THIRTEEN

New York City
June 1850

Jamison's second book, *Western Blood,* sold at a brisk
rate and continued to sell even a year later. He was thrilled and
oddly puzzled the first time he saw someone carrying a copy of the
book. Easterners who never went inland more than a few miles from
the coast snapped it up, hungry for tales of the wilderness and frontier. The acclaim it brought assured him of a constant supply of
dinner invitations and social engagements. At Benjamin's urgings,
he accepted his first for-hire speaking engagement for the New York
Manufacturer's Club. The demand for his presentation was so great
that they relocated their meeting site to the Orpheum Theater
around the corner from Broadway on Fiftieth Street.

The fellow who had made the engagement had asked if Jamison
would be wearing his now-famous fringed buckskin outfit.

"They want me as a sideshow!" he complained to Benjamin. It
was a fine Sunday morning, and he and Benjamin were in their
apartment.

Benjamin, owing to his very detailed personality, had found it natural to help his friend with the arrangement of his speaking invitations. He had steadfastly refused to take an agent's commission.

"Nonsense," Benjamin replied. "It's simply that most of these people haven't traveled much farther than the park up north of us. They don't know what it is to see the stars or build a campfire. And they sure don't know what an Indian is. This will be like . . . an educational talk."

Jamison snorted. "Educational? No, they want to hear about the savages and bloodshed. Of course, I have been told that sort of melodrama is the stuff of great literature," he replied, pacing. Then he added softly, "I don't think I can go through with this."

Benjamin seemed ready for his reluctance. "They are paying you handsomely . . . and have paid half up front. Five hundred dollars is not a small sum of money."

Jamison turned away from the window. "Five hundred dollars? Really? I had no idea they were offering that much. I thought it was a few dollars' honorarium."

"Not for your story, Jamison. You are a sought-after commodity. And such commodities do not come cheap."

Jamison reached up and fingered the tiny gold nugget he had had fashioned into a pendant. It hung around his neck on a thin gold chain. "Well, then. I suppose I should honor their request. Perhaps it would serve me well if I had that outfit cleaned."

Jamison raised his arms and settled against the window frame, focusing on the traffic along the street below. "Or does it look better if it shows the stains and scars of actual wear?"

The Hamptons
August 1850

"The entire summer has slipped away from us. The fact that this is your first visit with us is downright unacceptable. Quite unacceptable."

Mr. Rikler had Jamison's hand in a tight grip, almost refusing to let go.

"Yes, sir, I know that summer is gone," Jamison said as apologetically as he could. "There were just so many demands on my time. I hardly had a free evening–and that was all summer. But I imagine the uproar will fade away soon enough."

Rikler nearly dragged Jamison into the foyer of his summer home and toward the rear porch. "Nonsense. People never tire of a good tale. And yours is quite compelling."

Benjamin trailed along behind, ignored by the host. But he didn't seem to mind. It appeared he was becoming quite used to being almost invisible as Jamison's right-hand man and agent.

"But I have told the tale once in the book. Anyone interested can purchase my words–and often for much less than the price of admission to one of these events. I do not think I will ever understand the public."

Rikler laughed loudly, as if he'd had a glass or two of wine too many. "Don't ever overestimate the public. They like seeing things in the flesh. They think you're going to tell them something you did not include in the book. They want secrets. You should always give them the impression that you are telling them some deep secret that has remained hidden until this one specific night."

Rikler had led them down the main hall of the house and out onto the veranda overlooking the waters of Long Island Sound. The broad porch was empty, though a scattering of glasses and plates inhabited the tables and chair arms.

"Blasted servants!" Rikler hissed, then shouted loud enough to frighten both Jamison and Benjamin. "Harper! Get out here! This place looks like a pigsty!"

In a moment a diminutive gray-haired man scurried out with a large silver tray etched with a huge monogrammed *R* in the center.

"Wretched oversight, Harper. Leaving all this out. Like this is some tavern or alehouse. Ye gads, man." Then Rikler turned away from his servant and, making no effort to lower his voice, said, "Servants aren't worth anything out here. Don't care if the place is tidy or not. If I had another, this one would be on the road out front right now."

Jamison nodded as if he understood the plight of household management—when he actually had no idea. Although he and Benjamin had a maid come in twice a week to straighten up, Jamison rarely saw her. But he always appreciated the fact that at least two days a week he would not notice soiled cups and misplaced plates about.

Harper finished his duties and scurried out.

"Sit down, gentlemen. You came at a quiet moment. Most of the ladies are in town. I think it's the final fete that the village holds during the last week of summer. There's a band, I think. And booths for food. I'm not sure. I never go. Blasted contrivance to make money. They have the audacity to charge a dime for beer. Can you imagine? A dime! When right across the street, it goes for a nickel! Do they think we are foolish? To pay twice the going rate? Just to drink it outside?"

Jamison nodded again, but his heart wasn't in it. He glanced at Benjamin, who, by the look on his face, was apparently thinking the same thing. *Why would a man who has millions, a sprawling house on the ocean, and a huge house in the city be concerned over a nickel's worth of beer?*

"Harper!" Rikler screamed again. "Bring us some cold tea! Now!"

Jamison stood. He was becoming too nervous to sit at the older man's side. Instead he walked to the railing and leaned out toward the water, taking a deep, lung-cleansing breath.

Rikler evidently noticed Jamison's action. "You're not thinking of leaving again, are you, Pike?"

Jamison laughed, but it was Benjamin who answered. "No, sir, he isn't traveling off again. Not just yet. I have him booked at lectures up and down the coast for the next four months."

Rikler stood up. "Harper!" he shouted. "Where's the tea?" Then he stepped to the rail next to Jamison. "I hope that doesn't mean . . . I mean to say . . . you're not resigning from the paper? I won't hear of it! I won't. You need a day or two off for rest, that's fine. But no resignation. The readers like you. We get letters."

Jamison stared out to sea and did not speak.

"So . . . no resignation, right? You are staying?" Rikler persisted.

Rikler did not turn his attention away from Jamison even when Benjamin spoke up from the couch. "He'll be able to work for a few days a week for the paper. Then he has lectures and talks."

Rikler spoke to Jamison even though Jamison was not speaking to him. It was an odd triangulation. "I can't allow that. You need to be in the office all week. If I let you do that, then everyone will want to."

"Then we're sorry. The lectures will take priority," Benjamin insisted.

Rikler put his hand on Jamison's shoulder. "But think of the precedent. A day here and there, perhaps. But not on a regular basis."

"We're sorry," Benjamin said again.

A trio of gulls swooped over the house and landed flat-footed on the sand. Then immediately they set upon each other, arguing over some bit of dead fish.

"Don't you see what sort of predicament you have me in?" Rikler hissed. "I can't let you leave. And I can't let you come and go as you please, willy-nilly. Do you have any idea of what sort of inconvenience this will cause me? I don't think you do."

Jamison turned and sat on the rail, his back to the ocean. He eyed Benjamin, as if trying to ascertain his thoughts.

For the past several months Benjamin had acted as Jamison's business agent. He had done such a good job that Jamison had drawn up formal papers assigning Benjamin negotiating rights, as well as setting commissions. Jamison disliked dealing with money and demands. Benjamin, on the other hand, did it extremely well. Benjamin had assured Jamison that Rikler would pay anything to have Jamison stay—such was his popularity.

Benjamin shrugged as if to say, *Anything you decide is right for me.*

"Mr. Rikler," Jamison began softly, "I am willing to work for you two or three days a week, and at my choosing. If you don't accept that, then Benjamin and I will take our leave now. There will be no more discussions."

It was very clear that Mr. Rikler was not used to being denied. He sputtered and fumed for several minutes, pacing back and forth on the porch, clenching his fists on occasion. "Blast it, Pike! You have no right. You can't come to me and lay out your terms. It isn't done."

"It is now," Jamison replied with only a hint of a grin.

"Blast you!" Rikler shouted, then grimaced. "All right! You can have your way. But I am not happy about this at all."

When Jamison extended his hand, Rikler hesitated, then took it. As they shook hands, Benjamin removed a contract from his pocket.

"Land sakes! You mean to have me sign this as well?" Rikler said, obviously perturbed.

"He does," Benjamin said calmly as he laid the pages out on the table. "He does indeed."

Benjamin and Jamison stayed for dinner at the Rikler manse, although neither felt particularly comfortable. Benjamin told Jamison he felt invisible, and Jamison imagined himself as a target. He had hoped Eva would be in town with the other ladies, but her father assured him she was home and most eager to see him again.

She was seated across from him during dinner and the width of the table made their conversation difficult and sparse. Her eyes and demeanor left little doubt in Jamison's mind that she wanted to see him later in the evening.

As the dessert plates were removed, Jamison said loudly, "Well, we have planned on catching the last train back to the city. That is at nine, is it not?"

Eva stood as she replied, "Oh, no. During the summer, they add one train at ten. And since it is only eight, will you do me the pleasure of accompanying me for a walk by the shore, Mr. Pike? I have not had a chance to talk with you for what seems like a lifetime."

He shrugged to Benjamin as she led him by the hand out onto the veranda and into the growing darkness at the edge of the ocean.

"I never imagined I would know someone as famous as you," Eva said as she clutched his arm. She had led him off the path to the dock to the east of the house, past a tangle of trees and a long sand dune twice as high as a man.

The air turned crimson from the sun, now disappeared behind the western horizon. There was just a hint of autumn in the breeze.

"I'm not famous at all," he replied, wincing as his arm was clutched even more firmly than before. "I am but a small ripple in the awareness of the city. Come winter I will be replaced by a new storyteller with a novel tale to tell."

Eva laughed and threw her head back. Jamison could see the white circle of her throat and beyond.

"Mr. Pike, do not delude yourself. You are famous, and there is very little you can do about it. I would suggest that you relax and enjoy the benefits."

"Benefits? What manner of benefits do you mean? Other than being thought of as a commodity, that is?"

Eva smiled into the darkness. Even Jamison could see it.

"Well, you are the toast of the town. There may be others, but the important people will want to meet you. They'll invite you to all the best parties. You will be seen in some of New York's poshest residences. And that is only the beginning."

Jamison stopped walking and Eva turned to face him. Her back was to the sea.

"That does not sound appealing at all. It sounds ghastly," he said.

Eva pushed at his arm in a playful manner. "Jamison, always the jester. You'll see. You will have a fine time being the number-one guest with so many hosts."

Jamison stepped to the side and walked to the edge of the sea. A small wave broke and the thin fingers of water slipped over his new shoes. He did not bother retreating.

Eva stared after him. "I know what you said to my father, Jamison. And I understand why you said those things. It was to protect me, I know."

She stepped closer but looked down at the sand, attempting to gauge where the next wave might stop. "I don't care why you said those things. It was a long time ago. Things are different. You will need an escort to all these galas. You simply cannot attend them alone."

"I can go with Benjamin," he replied quietly.

Eva laughed again, louder than before, then looked at him slyly. "We'll not have anyone thinking that of you, Jamison. Not a man who has faced death at the hands of red savages. No. That will never do."

She examined her feet, kicked off her shoes, then walked into the surf to face Jamison. "I forgive you," she said softly. "For everything you said to me before you left. I know you were under a lot of pressure and did not mean it."

He did not reply.

"I don't care what you said at all," she purred.

He remained silent.

"You are famous," she whispered, "and I find that particularly attractive in a man."

She giggled, then grew serious, and without waiting for any manner of invitation, pushed his arms aside and embraced him in a tight, grasping hug.

He did not push her away.

From the Journal of Jamison Pike
New York City
May 1851

I have less time now to write than I have ever had before.

Eva was correct. I was feted and indulged in dozens and dozens of the most elegant of homes over the fall and winter. After the first invitation was accepted—at the Astors, no less—the floodgates were opened. Benjamin, my most faithful friend and confidant, often did accompany me, as I told Miss Rikler he would. I need to have some-one on hand who handles the billings for my appearances and the like. For me to do that, well, is not beneath me in any way, but it certainly feels most awkward.

And Miss Rikler has been my guest to many of these affairs as well. She has a way of twisting me about so that saying no is a most difficult task. She treats these parties and gatherings as ambrosia, lapping them up with gusto. I see them as a chore to be endured.

Despite the fact that the second book has sold well—so the pub-lisher says—it is not on a scale of *The House of Seven Gables* or *The Scarlet Letter*. What with his books selling thousands of copies in just days, that Nathaniel Hawthorne has fame as well as great wealth. It appears I have only fame.

The speaking engagements continue and the compensation is more than adequate—but the money seems to dissipate like dew on a spring morning. Benjamin is my traveling companion and that doubles our costs, but I would have it no other way. I could not travel and handle the innumerable arrangements he manages. With my reduced time on the paper paying a reduced salary, the money seems to be about the same as it was before—yet I am expending a great deal more energy to achieve it.

Is this the give-and-take of the world?

Yet there have been other events that are even more worthy of note.

Hannah.

I have seen her again.

She wrote me a pleasant letter asking if I might visit her in Phila-delphia and at the clinic at which she works. I wrote back that I would be delighted, and dates were set. She was as lovely as ever, if not more so. We spoke not a word of her marriage, and I asked not a single question about her husband.

I did not want to know more than I knew already.

Her appeal in securing my visit was for me to investigate a series of manufactories and mills that employed children—very young chil-dren—and the appalling conditions under which they worked. Such things go on in every city where there are factories or mines—and in every city the very same story could be told.

And should be as well.

I spent a week there. It did not take long to gather the material and information I needed. I talked to a child of six, rolling cigars in the dank, fetid basement of a factory for ten and twelve hours a day. She was paid by the piece and her little hands were blistered and brown from her work. I spoke with a lad of no more than twelve—he did not know his age for his parents seemed not to care. He worked in a mill by the river, with looms that made rugs and canvas. He was missing three fingers from his right hand—a fast-moving shuttle had ripped them. He was fortunate. The mill foreman had allowed him to visit Hannah's clinic, where the worst of the damage was repaired and the bleeding stopped. Most would have wrapped the wound with rags and forced him to return to his position.

Heartbreaking as all these tales are, I met a woman working in a mill, bent over her weaving, with her daughter of no more than six running spools back and forth from loom to loom. The only inter-action between mother and child was the scant seconds they had as the little girl passed by the machine where her mother was stationed. A wave. A few shouted words. A smile. And that was all they had for ten and twelve hours a day and six days per week. For a grown man or woman to do such work is hard enough, but to steal the childhood of a young boy or girl seems criminal.

I wrote a series of ten articles on these factories, making each story as pathetic and tear-inducing as I could. Benjamin did not go with me but found a local artist who did fine drawings of the children that were later done as etchings for the paper.

Of all the words that I have so far written, of these I am most proud. A public outcry followed, and we even had ladies with pick-ets walking in front of our offices, demanding that something be done.

Of course words do not change the world overnight, but there has been talk in the state legislature of enacting laws that would prohibit such young children of only five and six years of age from working so many hours in such conditions. It is not a cure, of course, but it is a step.

And Hannah was ever so grateful. I let her read the pieces before they were printed and saw tears in her eyes. The day I left she insisted on taking me to lunch. I do not think I ate a bite. When I departed for the train station, she embraced me tenderly, then kissed me on the cheek.

Gads! Why did she have to marry that man?

And as I write those words, I realize that I have not given up all my past. It is a work in progress, I am afraid. For it is Neta I should desire and Neta who is my future. Our correspondence is warm, cordial, and filled with anticipation of what will come.

She knows she must wait for me and she has said she will gladly.

And as I ponder the future with her, my heart becomes more settled and quiet.

New York City
September 1851

"I see that look in your eyes again," Benjamin said. The two of them sat in an open-air restaurant overlooking Trinity Church off Broadway.

Jamison stirred his coffee and sighed. "You don't either. I am not that transparent."

Benjamin sliced through his roast beef and chewed thoughtfully. "But you are. You always have been. And since you came back from Philadelphia, that look has seldom left your eyes."

Jamison sipped his coffee. Since returning from Hannah and Philadelphia, he had lost weight and his cheeks were drawn a bit, his eyes more hollow. "That is not true. I have been preoccupied, is all."

Benjamin ate in silence for a minute, then pushed his plate away. The serving girl was out almost instantly, clearing the table, asking if they desired anything more. The exemplary service was due, in part, to Jamison being recognized as they sat down. He saw several patrons nod together and point or nudge each other in his direction. It did not happen often, and for that he was grateful. But his face, via a rather handsome etching, had appeared in several newspapers. He was amused for the first day or two to have passersby stumble as they met him on the street. But since then, the familiarity had become an increasingly frustrating distraction.

He did not like people walking up to him and extending their hands as if they had known him for years.

"Preoccupied with what?" Benjamin asked kindly. Then, distracted by the waiter, he paused. "I'll have a piece of apple pie, please."

Jamison laughed in spite of his dour mood. "Priorities are priorities, aren't they, my friend?"

When the pie arrived, Benjamin stabbed at an errant apple slice. "The moody and downcast we will have with us always, but fresh apple pie does not last forever."

"But doesn't the Bible say that man shall not live by bread alone?"

Benjamin nodded, then spoke with his mouth still full of pie. "Yes, man does not live by bread alone. But he does not live long without it either."

Jamison signaled for more coffee.

"Just admit it. It's that woman in Philadelphia. Since you returned you have done little except mope about. I'm not stupid, Jamison. I can see that visit has had an effect on you."

With a very calm move, Jamison placed his cup on the saucer, stared hard at Benjamin, then slapped the table. "Why is it any business of yours?" he whispered angrily and loud enough to startle Benjamin, but not loud enough to attract the attention of other patrons.

Benjamin returned slap for slap. "Because I am your friend. You appear miserable. I know she was at Harvard with you. I know there must be something more to your relationship than you have ever admitted. And I know she is married. I found a copy of the announcement in our archives."

Jamison glared at his reporter friend and agent. He wanted to strike the man or stand up and run away from this place. But he did neither. He knew just as surely that running or violence would not end the hurt in his heart. So instead he leaned back in his chair. "I was smitten. I had no recourse. She is married. And there is nothing I would do to weaken that vow. And besides, the woman is much too noble for me. I am but a word merchant who tells the same story over and over again. She is a doctor who saves lives. How do I think I could ever be at the same level as she is? I can't be. It was not meant to be, simple as that. Right? I accept the past and move on. Isn't that what you tell me? Accept. Acknowledge. Advance."

"I have said that on occasion. I suspect it might be appropriate here as well," Benjamin answered.

Jamison propped his elbows on the table. Pain and desperate longing shone from his eyes.

"Unrequited love is perhaps the most cruel of regrets," Benjamin said kindly.

Jamison nodded in agreement. He wiped his eye and hoped Benjamin did not see the tear. "What do I do? What do I do now?" he asked softly.

Benjamin bit his lip, as if in thought. "Well . . ."

"Travel keeps the pain at bay. It does," Jamison argued.

Benjamin sighed. "You can travel to the Continent. There are more than enough requests for your presence. Six months. Maybe a year."

Jamison stared at his hands, then looked up. "When can we leave?" he said, managing a brave though small smile.

"How quickly can you pack?"

CHAPTER FOURTEEN

New York City
September 1851

Tde cries of the gulls mixed with the curses of the
stevedores and the cackle of the fishmongers, all vying for attention
on a warm September afternoon.

Benjamin and Jamison followed a burly teamster along, with
Benjamin paying much closer attention than Jamison. Pushcarts and
wagons jostled for space on the narrow decking. Casks and barrels
stood sentry along the way, with bales of furs and crates stacked
higher than a man could jump. The walkway was a spider's web of
ropes and pulleys anchored on pylons that disappeared into the gray
water under the pier and beams that cantilevered overhead. Men
would toss down hooks as large as a man's chest and then strain at
the ropes, like the fisherman strains at the pole, and bring up a new
barrel or cask from the hold of the ship.

"A good day to depart." Jamison whistled. Ever since the decision
to travel had been cast a week earlier, his mood had brightened like
the dawn. And now, as their departure grew imminent, Jamison
had a swagger in his walk and an unmistakable aura of bravado.

Benjamin had accepted a dozen engagements in England on

Jamison's behalf—mostly in London and towns nearby. The money offered was enough for their accommodations, their tickets over and back, all their meals, Benjamin's wages, and a tidy sum left over, which would be Jamison's profit.

Aboard the Resolute on the Atlantic Ocean

Benjamin decided, or at least his constitution decided, that sea travel was most unpleasant. As soon as their vessel, a large and well-appointed clipper ship noted for its luxurious passenger accommodations, had cleared the breakwaters of the Hudson River, Benjamin had gone a shade green and had remained that way for the bulk of the crossing. He slept little and was able to eat only some broth, usually at breakfast.

He asked Jamison every morning to inquire of the captain as to how far was English soil from this day's position.

It was only a matter of time until Land's End came into view. Benjamin finally brightened and managed to stay at the rail until the ship was tethered at the dock in Portsmouth. Once on firm ground, Benjamin's normal vigor returned, and he and Jamison set out by train to London.

London, England
November 1851

Jamison stopped pacing and stood still. The footlights kept him from seeing the faces of those before him. Slowly he walked closer to the edge of the stage. A ghostly quiet settled on the audience.

In a tense whisper, Jamison described he and Mr. Lambers, on horseback, on the rise, just a moment's ride from the river and safety. He related the panting of the horses and their clamoring for their own breath. He spoke, in that same whisper, of the absolute stillness of all else in God's nature. No birds, no breeze, no calls from the foliage.

Then he stared out for nearly a minute, letting the tension build.

He clapped his hands twice, the sound reverberating in the theater. Some of the women in the audience jumped in their seats. And as he described the bloody arrowheads and the screams of the Indians as they attacked, the glint of their long scalping knives in the sun, and the desperate sounds of the pistol as he rode away, he saw women pull out their handkerchiefs and bury their heads in their hands, either out of anguish for the poor soul of Mr. Lambers or from the gruesome manner in which Jamison told the tale.

He knew it was a most practiced account, and on every retelling he would polish and turn the words just so, hoping to keep it both exciting and dramatic.

At the end, when he finished his story, when he reached white man's civilization again, the audience stood as one and clapped and cheered.

The applause was gratifying but always left him with a hint of violation in his heart—as if he had just shared too personal a secret.

London, England
December 1851

The headline read:

FIRE AT THE WASHINGTON, D.C. LIBRARY OF CONGRESS DESTROYS TWO-THIRDS OF COLLECTION

Jamison frowned as he glanced at the story, handing the newspaperboy a coin from his pocket. Then he tucked the paper under his arm.

"All those volumes—gone in a heartbeat," he said sadly.

"Doesn't the sun ever shine here?" Benjamin asked as the two of them walked along Booksellers' Row.

Jamison had just finished his eighth lecture in London. "Since we arrived, I do not think I could verify the existence of the sun," he answered. "And it's cold. No one said it was going to be this cold."

Benjamin's beaver hat was pulled down over his ears. He claimed it was the only thing that kept him from injury inflicted by the damp weather.

"No one told me either," Benjamin replied. "I would suggest returning to our rooms, but they are every bit as cold as it is out here."

Jamison laughed. "How do they do that?" He wasn't sure if Benjamin shrugged or not, for his bulky coat hid most small movements. "How many more lectures this week?" he asked.

"Two," Benjamin responded. "I've been approached by several gentlemen who would be willing to sponsor our travels up north—and even to Ireland. They claim you could keep occupied for six months, if you so chose."

Both men turned the corner and stepped into a stiff breeze off the Thames, filled with cold wetness.

Jamison shivered. "Is there a coffee shop nearby? Could we at least attempt to get warm?"

"I don't know if they have such a thing here. They have tea shops, I imagine."

"Whatever, then. Over there," Jamison said, pointing. "Is that one?"

"I think it is."

"And you have some of their odd money? I am befuddled by it."

"Yes, I have a pocketful of farthings and pence and whatnots."

They found seats near a smoky coal fire and ordered coffee—much to the surprise of their serving girl.

"Coffee?" she asked. "But, sirs, that's a drink for the evening."

"We'll take that risk," Jamison said with a laugh. "We're Americans."

At hearing that, she nodded, as if such erratic behavior was to be expected from the poor, lost colonists.

Two coffees arrived, in dainty cups and saucers. But there was also a full pot of coffee left on the tray, so Jamison was satisfied.

A delicate swirl of sweets and cookies was arranged like a fan on a doily next to the coffee.

"This is such a different place," Jamison said. "Tea, cookies, pence, and farthings. And cold."

"And very cold," Benjamin added.

They sipped quietly.

"No new bookings after these last few in London, right?"

"You've asked me not to, Jamison. I still can if you would like."

"No."

"What then?"

"I want to get warm."

"So do I."

Jamison swallowed the rest of his coffee. "I can swallow more coffee in one gulp than this cup holds even filled to the brim." He poured a third cup and added a sugar cube. "We need to go south. If we want warmth, we need to head toward the sun."

"South? Where south? The Isle of Wight?"

Jamison laughed. "No. I'm not sure where that is, but it sounds English."

"It is. It's south. In the channel," Benjamin claimed.

"Not far enough. I'm thinking–" Jamison leaned forward as if some manner of conspirator–"of Morocco."

Benjamin was silent momentarily, then asked, "Do we have to take a boat to get there?"

They did, of course, have to board a ship to reach Morocco. Benjamin agonized over the choice, thinking he might instead just remain in London for another fortnight.

"It is our great adventure," Jamison cajoled. "I'll not let you freeze here–and they tell me this journey is short. And calm. One seldom leaves sight of land."

"That makes it even worse. To see *terra firma* and not be able to stand upon it–such temptation would be vexing," Benjamin replied, turning slightly pastel in his cheeks, as if he were already imagining the slow roll and pitch of the waves.

But in the end, after several afternoons of desperate pleading, Benjamin finally relented and agreed to this one side trip. "And when we are done," he said, "we book passage back to New York on the biggest and fastest ship available—correct?"

Jamison readily agreed.

They left the people of London clamoring for more tales of the American West and its savage inhabitants. Jamison indeed could have been booked for many more lectures. The English were hungry for stories of intrepid pioneers and cowboys. Men in buckskins, in leather, fighting off the elements and red men with painted faces captivated audiences.

"When we come back, I should bring along an Indian chief or two, with a feathered headdress and bow and arrow and war paint. That would be the most desirable ticket in town, would it not?" Jamison asked.

"It might be, but once I return home," Benjamin stated with finality, "there will be little chance of me making this voyage again."

As they sailed into the warmer waters off the African coast, Jamison noted that the crew of the ship began to behave oddly. More men lined the decks, even when they went off duty. Instead of a single man in the masts on lookout, there began to be two and then three, and at one point a full ten men were to be seen perched in the high ropes.

A sense of nervous energy percolated throughout the ship.

"Captain," Jamison asked one fine though very hot and humid morning, "what has happened to the crew? I keep feeling an urgency about the ship—and I see no good reason for it."

The captain scanned the open deck, put his fingers to his lips, and pulled Jamison and Benjamin into the darkness of belowdecks and his cramped, fetid cabin.

"Pirates," he whispered. "From the Barbary Coast."

Upon hearing the word *pirate*, Benjamin looked immediately over his shoulder as if they might be in the room. "Pirates? Where? Here?"

The captain, a florid, ill-smelling fellow from Portsmouth, who had yet to button his coat in an even manner, held up his hand. "Not to speak the name so loudly, sir. If the crew heard you even say the word, they will believe you have caused a great curse to descend upon this ship."

"A curse?" Jamison asked quizzically. "Over the utterance of the word?"

"Indeed, sirs. And I have tempted the gods by uttering the word myself. These waters are rife with them. Parasites and leeches they are—ready to dispatch a man to the bottom for the slightest transgression. You best pray that we escape them this voyage. No telling what might happen if they come upon us. In fact, your own American naval forces fought with them years ago and had it settled then. But they have cropped up again."

Benjamin made his way to the small window at the bow of the ship.

"You'll not see them now, sir," the captain claimed. "They are like jackals and only strike under the blood of the moon."

Jamison could not help smiling. "Have you been assaulted before this sailing?"

The captain shook his head and rapped on the wood of his desk. "No. I haven't. But this voyage can always be the first. That is why no one speaks the name or of the possibilities. If we do, it makes it happen. That is the way of the sea."

FROM THE JOURNAL OF JAMISON PIKE
AGADIR, MOROCCO
MARCH 1852

There were no pirates.

Drats.

I was hoping for an exciting story to relate. I did, however, find several English sailors who were more than willing to tell their tales of encounters with the Berber infidels. The tales reek of exotic locals and bloodthirsty villains. Despite my desire to write only of my own experiences, I will use their tales in my reports. Somehow being drawn and quartered on ship is not an ideal way to experience life.

That is what the sailors claim is the preferred method of torture by the Berbers.

We have spent days wandering the town. I have never been in a desert town such as this. The sights and sounds are the stuff of dreams or fairy tales. The marketplace is filled with peaked tents and men selling hot tea from jugs they carry on their backs. Women scurry about, almost ashamed it seems, to be seen by men. They wear thick robes and veils on their faces. Only a narrow slit for their eyes is visible. Men in turbans swagger about, every one, it seems, with curved scimitars and daggers in his belt. From their expressions, I would say they would as soon chop a man's head off as smile at him.

That is the rule around here, I am told. For crimes like stealing and assault, the criminal loses a hand or a leg to the sword.

Gads. The prospect sends chills through me—despite the heat of the place.

I asked Benjamin about the churches here—mosques, they are called. He told me of the Islamic religion—or at least as much as he had read.

He then went on to tell me about his religious experience in England listening to a fellow by the name of Charles Spurgeon. Benjamin claims it was then he had some transcendental religious awakening. I nodded in all the right places, but I am in no mood to hear what God has in store for me. Up to now my life has not gone the way I had envisioned. God gives us what we need—what a foolish notion.

A few days after we docked we made acquaintances with the English consul general here, and he invited us to his official residence. He was a friendly chap and insisted on treating us to a lavish official banquet, complete with native dancing girls and a trio plucking away at some odd-sounding instruments. The port wine flowed freely—at least for the consul general. He may have been too far into his cups, but he invited us to meet the Dey of Agadir in his palace.

This was quite the coup, for the dey seldom holds audience with foreigners. He seemed like a nice fellow, surrounded by burly men in turbans and swords. I spoke not a word to him nor he to us. Yet it was a pleasant diversion.

As we walked back along the dusty street, with shouts of prayer coming from the minarets (I am told that is the word for the pointy structures), I wonder what is transpiring back home. I know Benjamin suffers from homesickness to a great degree. I have promised him that from here, we shall find the first ship bound for New York.

I have searched the entire city for a newspaper—one that I can read—and have come up empty.

New York City in the Newsroom of the New York World
April 1852

The office boy pulled out a copy of yesterday's paper. He scanned through the pages. DEMOCRATS TO NOMINATE PIERCE FOR PRESIDENT. SCHOOL ATTENDANCE LAW ENACTED IN MASSACHUSETTS. THOUSANDS READING *UNCLE TOM'S CABIN*. On the desk in front of him was a large wooden box with the name "J. Pike" scrawled on top in grease pencil.

The young office boy flipped the pages until he came to the obituaries. He ran his finger down the columns and then stopped. He pulled out his penknife and cut out a square. He tossed the newspaper into the basket next to him.

He read the heading again.

ROBERT R. KEYES, FINANCIER,
PASSES ON IN PHILADELPHIA

He scanned the list Jamison had left him. On it were scrawled eleven or so names. "If they ever appear in print," he had said, "you must clip them out and save them in the box for me. For when I return I do not want to read through months of newspapers."

The office boy had agreed and, over the months, had nearly filled the box with clippings. He placed the small square of newsprint in the box.

From across the room came a shout for a copyboy.

The young man sighed, stood up, and trotted away.

A slight breeze swept through the room, and the small obituary flipped from the box and fell to the floor, snugging under the desk, far underneath.

When the office boy returned, he did not pause, thinking he had already placed the small article safely inside. Instead he picked up the box and placed it on top of a large cabinet, where it would remain for another week.

By that time, the memory of one small article was all but gone from his thoughts.

CHAPTER FIFTEEN

New York City
July 1852

Benjamin and Jamison had found passage on
an Italian ship that had stopped in Agadir for fresh water. Their
berths were painfully small, but the food on board, in Jamison's
opinion, was second to none. Again, being on open water had
caused Benjamin great and continued discomfort. Jamison com-
miserated to a point but readily left his friend softly moaning in
their cabin when it was mealtime.

On the evening the vessel tied off at the piers on the southern
edge of Manhattan Island, Benjamin bent to the ground and
kissed it.

As usual, the return trip had allowed Jamison the time to turn
the story of their visit with a Berber chieftain into a very long
newspaper piece. He was certain it would be sliced into segments
for successive Sunday editions.

He was also sure it would hold the interest of the reader—
especially since he added in the pirates and a beheading or two.

Jamison and Benjamin were greeted warmly by their fellow reporters and editors. They wanted to know all the details of their trip. And Jamison obliged, amplifying his tale of the Berber dey and tales of the pirates. For an hour he went on about the trip, weaving in snippets of what he had heard with what they had actually done.

After so long a conversation, Jamison held up his hands. "You all have work that needs tending to. And I usually receive at least a dollar from every man who hears the story."

A series of catcalls and hoots greeted his humor, but the crowd dissolved and Jamison made his way to his desk. On top lay his box of clippings.

He began to flip through the stack.

On the very top was a handwritten note, done in a powerful scrawl.

Come to the Hamptons this weekend. Expect to see you on Thursday.
Rikler

Jamison smiled, folded the note in half and half again, then tucked it into his pocket. He looked over to Benjamin. His friend's head was lost in a thick stack of papers and aging correspondence. It was obvious Benjamin was not included in Rikler's weekend plans.

And Jamison, clearly, was not going to mention the offer.

Instead he continued his steady progression through the thickness of clippings. He paused occasionally to read a particular piece. After doing so, he would either place the clipping in the top drawer of his desk or crumple it into a ball and toss it in the general direction of the trash bin.

In two hours he had read everything in the box and had only a small stack in his top drawer. He pushed it closed, leaned back, and sighed.

And beneath his desk, under the most distant leg, lay a small, yellowing obituary.

The Hamptons

"Great to see you again, son. Wonderful stories. Just wonderful."

Mr. Rikler, as expansive as ever, drew Jamison into his summer manse and did not stop talking until they reached the veranda overlooking the sea.

"Have you had enough of sea vistas? Shall we retire to the smoking room?"

Jamison waved his offer away. "Viewing the sea from the land is a great deal more comfortable than watching the sea while being upon it."

"My sentiments exactly."

Jamison sat on the wicker couch and took a deep breath.

"You're tired—right, son?" Rikler asked. "Fatigued from the journey? Spend a few days here. Take it easy. I want my star journalist to be well rested. Relax some. You deserve it."

Jamison simply smiled.

"You want tea? We still have ice from the winter. Or a drink? Bourbon? Whiskey? Whatever you desire, I'll order."

Settling into the deep cushions, Jamison politely refused. "Well . . . maybe a cup of good coffee. With cream. And sugar. Out there," he said, pointing to the ocean, "there is such a dearth of life's little pleasures—like properly prepared coffee."

"Harper!" Rikler shouted toward the kitchen. "Get out here! We need a pot of fresh coffee. Now!"

Jamison shook his head. Clearly Rikler had not polished his household management skills since Jamison's last visit.

Harper shuffled in a moment later with a coffeepot and cups rattling on a large silver tray. He poured a single cup. "Shall I add the cream and sugar, sir?"

"No. I am pretty sure I can manage from here. Thank you, Harper."

Rikler was at the sideboard, cutting the end of a cigar.

"Though why you stay with him is beyond me, Harper. Surely you could have other employment," Jamison whispered.

"He pays me double of what any man makes in the Hamptons," Harper explained. "If I have to endure a few screams, so be it. A small price to pay for double wages. And I trust you will not give me away, will you, Mr. Pike?"

"Your secret is safe," Jamison replied, smiling.

Rikler returned to the couch nearly hidden in a great cloud of smoke. His hand shot out from the cloud. "So, Pike . . ." He coughed. "Where will you go next?"

Jamison slept until noon the following day. He had eaten very little the night prior. He and Rikler had shared a dinner at the massive table. Rikler had made no apologies for the lack of other guests nor offered any explanations.

Jamison sat up and blinked at the bright sun, debating in his groggy state whether or not it was advisable to stumble out of bed and draw the shades. When he drew his pocketwatch close to his face, he tried to focus on the dial. That's when he realized he had been in bed nearly fourteen hours. He stretched and yawned, then stumbled toward the open window. Filling his lungs with the fresh sea air, he rubbed his face with his hand and blinked, attempting to clear his vision.

From the door of the bedchamber came a soft tapping.

Must be Harper . . . or the upstairs manservant. With coffee, I hope.

He cleared his throat. "Come on in. The door is open."

The hinges creaked softly and Jamison turned back to the sea, staring at the rolls of waves on the sound. A sound of clanking and stirring came from the sitting area of the bedchamber. Then the sound of footsteps. As Jamison took another breath, there came the soft touch of a feminine hand to his shoulder.

When reality sank into his consciousness, Jamison nearly leaped in a not-so-graceful pirouette and threw himself into the far corner of the massive windowed balcony.

"Eva!" he whispered at the edge of panic. "What on earth are you doing here? I am still in my pajamas!"

"So I have noticed. I like a man in pajamas."

Jamison turned and ran to the door to retrieve his robe. "You have to leave. What if your father finds you here?"

She shrugged. "He sent me to wake you with your coffee. He thought you might be dead. And for his star reporter, dying in his bed will simply not do."

"Miss Rikler," Jamison said furtively, "you cannot be here. It isn't right."

Eva laughed, the sound of thunder at a distance. "Mr. Pike, how quaint. I think you doth protest too much."

As she talked she drew closer to him. There was something in her eyes, some hunger Jamison had never noticed before. Perhaps it was new or perhaps simply rekindled.

"Allow me just a moment, Eva. I must dress."

She slumped into a chair and placed her hand on her chin. "I have nothing to do today," she pouted.

"Miss Rikler, please!" he called out, louder than he needed to.

"All right," she finally said in acquiescence, but with a perturbed pout. "I will leave . . . for now. But hurry. We have much to catch up on. Don't keep me waiting. There are other fish in the sea, you know."

As she passed him she placed her forefinger under his chin and held it there for a heartbeat or two. "Hurry," she whispered.

There was no mistaking her softness for meekness.

Jamison sank in relief against the door as she left. Walking to the coffeepot, he poured a cupful and swallowed it nearly in one gulp.

Then he dressed in a most hurried fashion.

Jamison stayed in the Hamptons until Tuesday of the following week. He was grateful that Eva had prior commitments, so her intense visit was brief. On his last morning there, Jamison asked if Mr. Rikler had any preference as to where Jamison might travel next—if indeed he was to travel at all.

"Well, son, I wish you would spend a few months in town. My daughter says she needs time for the two of you to get reacquainted—and I am not in the practice of refusing my little girl anything."

Jamison stirred the cream in his fifth cup of coffee. "And how long would that require, sir?"

Rikler brayed out a laugh. "A month? Two? As if I know anything of the feminine wiles and sensibilities. Though it appears you are much more adept than I. But I must tell you, she has been seen in the company of a fellow from some bank uptown. Several times. I would act quickly if you want to prevent any alienation of affections. So stay as long as you like."

"A month, then," Jamison replied, setting the delicate spoon on the delicate saucer, then drinking the entire contents in one swallow.

"And I think it matters little where you go," Rikler continued. "Danger and drama have a way of following you, it seems. Pick a place. The paper will stand behind any choice." He reached for his cigar. "Within reason, that is. Within reason."

New York City

Jamison spent several days in the office, mostly responding to correspondence that had piled up in his absence. He also spent several afternoons with a wiry, angry artist who had been commissioned to do a series of sketches that would accompany his Berber adventure piece. The artist listened to his descriptions, began sketching, and in a moment would turn an accurate drawing of their room at the palace into a fanciful dreamlike vision with turbaned guards brandishing their spears, holding snarling lions, and surrounded by a bevy of harem women. It did not matter that Jamison objected to the final drawing—the artist sniffed that his descriptions were bland and pedestrian and that no reader would believe them.

Jamison visited clothiers. If he was to travel again, he wanted several sets of sturdy coats and pants with warm jackets and well-fitting shoes. When the tailors and cobblers learned of Jamison's renown, they all promised that his new garments or boots would be ready in half a fortnight or less.

He spent much time in his apartment as well, sitting in a comfortable chair, staring out the window at the park across the street, watching mothers and nannies push carriages laden with laughing children. He watched as they sat on park benches, gently rocking and soothing the small ones.

One afternoon his reverie was interrupted as the door opened. Benjamin stepped in with an armful of packages and books.

"Shopping again, Benjamin? You are quite the clotheshorse, it appears," Jamison said without rising.

"It's all yours, I'll have you know. Packages kept arriving all day at the office. Why didn't you have them delivered here?"

"I wasn't sure I would be here. And thanks for bringing them. You could have left them there. I would have gone to retrieve them."

"With that dubious group of reporters there? No. It's better this way."

Benjamin dumped the boxes and parcels on the entry table, then slumped into the chair opposite Jamison. He sighed.

"Busy day?"

"No more than most. I bought the book you asked for—the one on the Pacific Islands."

"Thanks."

"Have you decided where you might head next?"

"Not yet. There was that fellow who said to 'go west, young man, go west.' Or something like that. I heard the quote and thought it summed up a lot of dreams for a lot of young men. So I may head west again. There's a lot of adventures left, I imagine."

Benjamin's voice was quiet when he spoke. "You know I am not going with you."

Jamison smiled as he nodded. "I know. Some men are made for travel. Some are not."

"That's true. You don't mind? It is safer to travel with someone, isn't it?"

As Jamison turned and draped his legs over the arm of the chair, lacework doilies on its back fell off in a dainty heap. "Sometimes, I suspect. Not always."

"Will you be lonely?"

"No. Being alone has never bothered me."

"It would me," Benjamin said softly. "But that's the difference between you and me."

"One of the differences."

Without standing up, Benjamin removed his coat and laid it carefully at his side. "Are you seeing Miss Rikler tonight?"

"No."

"I thought she mentioned she had an invitation to a gallery opening. That outlandish fellow—Leutze—the one who does those historical paintings."

"Yes, but I'm not going."

"She knows that?"

"Yes. I sent her a note."

Benjamin loosened his top collar button. "That does not mean she will not be here. You've sent other notes. Not the most effective means of staying away, if you want the truth."

Jamison stood and walked toward the fireplace mantel. He stopped, placed his hands on it, appearing to study a framed daguerreotype of his mother and father. They did not look happy.

And as Benjamin busied himself in the kitchen, Jamison slumped down into the chair again.

After a dinner of pork chops with beans—a dish Benjamin prepared with great regularity—he stopped suddenly as he carried the plates back into the kitchen.

"Jamison, I forgot to mention it earlier. In the packages out on the table, there are two letters from Pittsburgh. One is from your father. The other is from Miss Hill. They came to the office today."

Jamison closed his eyes. His heart began to beat faster, and there was a nudging tightness in his stomach.

He held Neta's envelope to the lamp. It was thin—it could contain no more than a single page. Its brevity filled Jamison with a terrible sense of foreboding. Using his penknife, he slit the envelope with a papery hiss. He would read where he stood.

> *Pittsburgh, Pennsylvania*
> *February 1852*
>
> *My dear Jamison,*
> *I do not know how to begin this letter. It pains me to know how much I am forced to hurt you.*
> *I have found someone. You do not know him. I never wanted this to happen. I feel so horrible. I know that you deserve a woman much better than I—someone smarter, someone who can live with your absences.*
> *I want all the best for you. You deserve it.*
> *Please don't hate me.*
> *Neta*

There was a loud pounding in the hollow spot in his chest when he tried to breathe. And yet . . . he expected the news to hurt more than it did. Instead all he felt was emptiness. No pain. No grief.

At least not now.

He took the other envelope and tore it open.

> *Pittsburgh, Pennsylvania*
> *February 1852*
>
> *Jamison,*
> *I am writing this as your mother cries in her bedchamber.*
> *You have turned your back on the truth and her heart is broken. I am angry—more indignant than I could imagine a man feeling.*
> *We purchased your book. I read it through in one night. There is no mention of God in any of the pages—but instead there are long, lyrical descriptions of saloons and drunkards and women whom I can scarce imagine.*
> *Is that how we raised you? To inhabit such sinful places and to speak with drunks and gamblers and prostitutes?*

What are you, Jamison? A man of God would shun that type of life, yet you revel in the filth and degradation of man.

And then the gold—you write as if it is a mistress.

If a man writes about what he knows and his words show who he is— then you have become another creature altogether.

How will we face our friends when they read those same words? How will we explain what you have written?

At times I think it would be easier to claim we are childless.

You must repent. God will harshly judge a man who falls so far from the truth he knows.

The letter was unsigned, as if his father were simply unwilling or unable to add that one single note of relationship at the end. Jamison read it only once. He folded the sheet back into thirds and slipped it into his pocket.

Benjamin came out from the kitchen, looking for errant glassware. "It was from your parents? How are they?" he asked. "How is Miss Hill?"

"Fine," Jamison answered with deadness in his voice. "Same as always. They are all just fine."

And then he was alone again.

Condemned. Judged and condemned. And then there is no reason to be moral, is there? If there is no hope, then there is no truth, and there is no reason.

His thoughts were interrupted by a jabbing, persistent knock upon the door.

He knew who it was.

On his way to the door, he fetched his jacket and began to tighten his tie. Perhaps an evening at the gallery would be a good place to stop thinking.

FROM THE JOURNAL OF JAMISON PIKE

PARIS, FRANCE
JULY 1853

Before I left New York, I saw Eva one last time. I told her I did not plan on seeing her again when I returned. To my surprise, she seemed not the least upset, almost as if an obstacle had been removed from her path. She protested, of course, and even shed a tear or two, but I could tell her heart was not truly in it. As we parted, I believe we both felt a sense of great relief. She pecked my cheek, bid me farewell, and never looked back.

Why? I simply could no longer generate any enthusiasm when I was with her—and I am certain she felt the same.

I have spent the last months traveling—Japan, Russia, and countries I have scarce heard of before I stepped foot in them.

It is a whirlwind of recollections. Thank heaven for my journals.

I am now in Paris and it is indeed a city of light.

The food here has made me forget all my recent privations. I do not understand what the chefs do, but common chicken drowned in the right sauces and herbs constitutes a magnificent dish.

Most waiters sneer at my bad French, but I am able to make my desires known to them. And I must say, that of all the people who have realized that I am an author, these folks seem the least impressed. They nod, shrug, then return to treating me with calculated neglect. Yet despite the citizens, the city is magnificent. I have toured the church they call Notre Dame, an ancient structure laced with gargoyles and spires, plastered with carvings and sculptures, packed with a moody sense of mystical history, wrapped up in such an awe-inspiring place.

Dark, gray clouds drifted past that afternoon, hugging the earth. I walked from my room on Quai Voltaire overlooking the Seine River, which slices the city in two. (The rich live to the north. Artists and the working class live to the south. Or is it the right and left banks? My French is not that good.)

I found the church, the square in front nearly deserted save a few peddlers and beggars and some couples oblivious to everything but each other. I am not of the Roman Catholic faith and was unsure if the church would be in use all day. If some worship service was transpiring, would they let non-Catholics in? Was there a charge at the door?

There was a smaller door within the massive wooden door. I tried the handle and it swung open with no resistance. I stepped into the very dim interior. I blinked as I adjusted to the lack of light. Only a few people huddled about inside. A trio of old, bent women, heads covered in somber scarves, stood to my left, bathed in the warm glow of candlelight. Each was bowed and mumbling soft prayers in French. From above came the first notes of a most somber organ piece. It was neither loud nor soft, but at the level of speech—pervasive, intrusive in a most benign way.

I found a place in the back-most pew. I sat and remained still. There was no activity at the altar, just the flicker of hundreds of red votive candles. I heard the clink of coins being dropped into a nearby metal box. I do not know if prayers are to be said as this is done, or if it is simply the act of lighting a candle to fight back the darkness.

All was just so—just as it should be.

I have been gone a very long time, and as I sat there, my heart began to hurt—in an actual, physical way. It was not a constriction or illness, but a pain of a spiritual nature, perhaps.

I closed my eyes and in that amplified darkness, I saw Hannah's face. I have thought little of her these past months—or at least they were times of little duration. Every day her name enters my thoughts, and every day I drive it from me. Such banishment is a regular activity.

This was the first time in months and months that I let the image stay. I focused on it and saw again her eyes and her mouth and her lips. It was as if she were real again and before me.

I am not a man who believes much in spiritual things. My father has condemned me and claims I will never enter the gates of heaven. If such is the case, then why should I worry about morality and rightness?

Yet this is a spiritual matter. It is a matter of the heart.

I let Hannah's image stay and it comforted me. And in that

moment, she became most tangible. Not in the pretend manner of a child. Not even in the ethereal manner of a vision—but real flesh and blood before me. My lips moved, and yet I could find no voice for my words. I tried to raise my hand to hail her but could not. Tears swelled in my eyes.

I was snapped back to this world by the touch of a hand. I turned. It was a young girl.

She touched my shoulder with the same gentle force Hannah had used. There was a spark and a flame, and my eyes were at once wide open. It was not Hannah, and yet it was, at least for that singular, perfect moment. She had the most beautiful, innocent smile on her face—a smile that seemed to hide a great sorrow, a deep pain. I moved my lips. Eventually I mumbled a few words, all in halting, stumbling French. "What? What do you want?"

She smiled again and looked away. "I thought you were in pain."

"I am not," I replied, hoping my words were correct.

She let her fingertips graze the top of my right hand. I nearly jumped. "That is good," she replied. "In God's house there should be no pain. There will be no sorrow. God will see to your needs."

And I closed my eyes for the briefest of moments. When I opened them again, she was gone. I jumped up and scanned the church. There was no young girl near me.

I hurried out the doors into the gray of the afternoon, and there was no one in the square, save the same peddlers, beggars, and lovers.

I came away, harrowed and flushed, and could not put pen to paper for nearly a week to describe what had occurred.

When I finished the account, I knew it was time to return home.

New York City
October 1853

"He is dead? When? How? Robert Keyes is dead? You're sure of it?"

Jamison paced back and forth by Benjamin's desk. He was back at his office after many, many months of travel and reporting.

"April 1852. A year and a half ago."

"But I . . . ," Jamison stammered, stunned. "I was in New York then—or soon afterwards. Why was I not told?"

Benjamin almost bowed his head. "The office boy said he recalled very clearly clipping the obituary. He said it must have fallen out of your box."

Jamison flailed his arm in the air. "Then why did she not write? Or Gage? For God's sake, someone should have told me!"

Benjamin let him shout for a moment, nodding. "Please, Jamison, sit down. You've had a long journey. It's been a long time. Please."

Jamison's eyes were wide and his breathing fast. Eventually he stopped moving, then sat at the chair next to Benjamin's desk. "How did you find out?" he asked in a small voice.

"She sent a note. I wrote a piece on the yellow fever epidemic in New Orleans. She saw a copy and wrote. I wrote back. Asked how she was. She wrote about Robert. She mentioned she sent you a letter about it. But you must have missed it. You know how unpredictable the post is."

Jamison examined his trembling hands. "How is she?" he finally asked.

"Her words indicated she was fine. I had a friend call on her. Beth Ann. Beth Ann from Newark. You remember Beth Ann. You met her a few years ago at that opening of Bellini's *Norma* at the opera house."

Jamison looked up. His eyes had suddenly grown moist. "Yes. No. I mean . . . it doesn't matter. How was she?"

Benjamin sighed deeply and placed his hands flat on the desk. "She said Hannah looked fine. Thin perhaps, but then you know how women judge differently than men."

"Thin? Is she well?"

Benjamin spoke clearly and slowly. "She is very well. And happy. She still works at the clinic. She has a small apartment nearby. And she has friends. Beth Ann said she appeared very content."

"Hannah," Jamison whispered to himself, staring at the floor.

When the silence between the two men had grown long, Benjamin touched Jamison's shoulder. "Friend, why don't you go see her? All these years. A lot of history is now forgotten. Go see her. Go to Philadelphia. Or invite her to New York. Take her to the Crystal Palace Exhibition—a World's Fair is a good reason for a visit."

Jamison's head came up, and his eyes were filled with tears. His mouth moved, but no words could be heard.

"What, Jamison? What are you trying to say?" his kind friend urged.

Jamison let the tears streak down his face. "I can't. I can't," he said despairingly and then walked carefully, deliberately, out of the newsroom.

Jamison walked down Fifth Avenue for blocks and blocks. The autumn chill had given way to a more wintry wind. As he approached Canal Street, he shivered as the cold air slipped into his coat.

To his left was a tavern. He entered, peered about, then walked to the bar. The room was nearly deserted.

A tall, pallid fellow walked up behind the bar. "Whiskey?"

Jamison shook his head.

"Beer?"

He shook his head again.

The colorless man eyed Jamison closely. "Then I take it you're a man for some bourbon."

Jamison shook his head again as if he could not find the right words. "No . . . ," he finally said. "I guess . . . I know . . . I mean this is a tavern, but do you have any coffee?"

The fellow grinned. "Hard night? Sure, I got coffee. In back. You want it black or a little of the hair of the dog?"

"Black," Jamison said.

Much later, as he sipped his third coffee, Jamison asked the bartender, "What's your name?"

"Ethan," the fellow replied. "Like Ethan Hale—the patriot."

"Isn't that Nathan Hale?"

"It is?"

"I think. But maybe I'm wrong," Jamison said.

Ethan shrugged as if to indicate it truly did not matter.

"Why so empty?" Jamison asked.

"We're between times. Come six, we'll be crowded. And later, too. World's Fair and all—good for business. But right now, it's always quiet like this," he said as he wiped out glasses. "And what brings you here today? This ain't your neighborhood, is it?"

"No, it isn't. And I've just been walking."

Ethan's face loomed closer. "'Cause of a woman, I would wager."

Jamison couldn't hide his surprise. "How did you . . . ?"

"You stand back here long enough and you know. Sort of a look that is a bit sick and a bit angry and a bit . . . well, a bit like you ain't never going to see her again."

Jamison nodded. "That's close to being right."

"Oh, it's more than close. I've seen that look before."

Jamison slid the coffee cup to the edge of the bar. "But it wasn't like I had any claim to the woman. She was married, after all."

Ethan nodded and kept on wiping. It was obvious he had heard it all before, for he showed no surprise.

"Now he's dead. All these years I loved her. And while she was married, I still loved her. Now he's dead and I could jump on a train and go down to see her. I could see her and have dinner with her and . . . well—"

Ethan walked up with the coffeepot and topped off Jamison's mug. "Then why don't you?"

Jamison focused on a spot that was a thousand miles away. "All these years, I prayed she would rather have chosen me. That she wanted me instead of him. I couldn't be with her, but if things were to change—then we could."

"He's dead, right?"

"For over a year."

"Go see her then."

"I can't." Jamison's voice was no more than a groan.

"Why not, friend?"

Jamison took a deep breath. He fought away a tear. "She could say no, that's why. She could say no. I have lived without her for all this time—and now she would simply tear my heart out and throw it on the ground if she were to say no. I can't. I can't risk that. I just have to . . ."

"Have to what, man?"

"I have to keep moving. Then she'll never know. She'll never know. . . ."

CHAPTER SIXTEEN

New York City
January 1854

On this New Year's Eve, Jamison remained at home, preferring solitude to the often-frenzied attempt at levity and gaiety. In all the years since Harvard, he had availed himself to many different events on the last day of the year, and in his recollection, never once did the party live up to its promises.

Over four thousand people. Too many fellows well into their cups, too many women tilting about with shrill laughter–laughter not of merriment but of one too many libations.

Instead he thought he would pursue a quieter evening of a solitary dinner–Benjamin was taking his holidays with relatives in Albany– and a stack of books he had intended on reading.

He had requested of Mr. Rikler a less strenuous role on the newspaper for a time. He was obliged with the position of the reviewer of new books, a task that well suited his current temperament. The job could be done at home and required little interaction with any person. And spending the night with Mary Jane Holmes's novel *Tempest and Sunshine* felt right.

Since finding out about Hannah's widowhood, Jamison had

remained in a fog of sorts. Not dazed, not befuddled, but unsure of his surroundings, having no certain mooring place for his emotions and thoughts. For years, it had been Hannah, the married woman. In some odd way, that fact was set and sure, comfortably uncomfortable. He had dealt with that reality, and his life had been molded within that set of parameters.

But now all that had changed, and he was groping in the dim light, trying to ascertain how he must now live.

In truth, he thought little about it—or tried not to. Every time he ventured to let his mind go there, his thoughts would race and tangle into a Gordian knot of conflictions.

No, he decided, it was best, at least for now, not to think of it at all. Let the emotions become dormant. Read the books and escape.

In November he had written a short note of condolence to her, apologizing, then explaining the delay in his response—and then added that he was set to do much traveling out of the country for the next few years.

He was not. There were no such plans in existence. Yet that small falsehood lifted a great weight from his shoulders. He no longer felt his very breath catch in his throat at the thought of Hannah.

If I am gone, she will have no reason to think I may visit or call. And being gone, it would mean that any correspondence would be erratic. Yes, that is what is best.

July 1854

"I am still receiving offers for lectures," Benjamin said as he returned home one evening.

Jamison was all but lost behind a great stack of books and papers. "Lucrative offers?" he asked as he closed a volume and tossed it into a pile in the corner.

"Lucrative enough," Benjamin added. "Since you no longer draw a full reporter's salary, perhaps you had best reconsider your immediate refusals."

Jamison stood up and stretched. His outfit today consisted of a thin plaid shirt, workman's trousers, and a threadbare pair of felt slippers. It was obvious his hair had not been recently visited by a comb or brush.

Benjamin took off his waistcoat, undid his collar, and placed it on the door hook with his jacket.

"I hate to come home and admonish, Jamison," he said with some reluctance, "but you look no better off than the beggars I pass on Fifth Avenue. Ever since you ceased visiting the newsroom on at least an occasional basis, your appearance has taken a terrible downward turn."

Jamison examined himself, as if seeing his image for the first time. "Downward? Truly? This is not an acceptably dashing outfit?" Doing a pale imitation of a pirouette, he began to laugh. "But who do I dress up for? You have seen me worse, and you are the only other eyes that will look upon me today."

Benjamin shuffled through a stack of correspondence on the front table. "Then so much more the pity. You should get out. This is no life for a vibrant fellow like you. Doing book reviews alone in a dark room on a beautiful day such as this."

Jamison did not answer. He had no answer.

After a long moment, marked only by the careful slice of a letter being cut open, Jamison coughed, then asked again, "How lucrative?"

Benjamin smiled as he put down his letters. "Most equal to or better than our first trip to England." He went to his desk and extracted a slim ledger. "There are offers from Boston, Cambridge, Philadelphia, New Haven, Albany. . . ."

"Any offers from the Continent?"

Benjamin flipped several pages. "Bath, Cambridge, Greenwich, Bristol, Portsmouth . . ."

"If I go, will it be lucrative enough to keep away whatever wolf is at my door?"

Benjamin laughed. "It is not that precarious. Rikler would have you back in the blink of an eye to do your column again. Or travel at his expense."

Focusing on his reflection in the mirror over the mantel, Jamison said, "Then make arrangements for a short trip to England. Will you go with me?"

"Only under threat of death, Jamison. You saw how I was on the open seas. You can do this just as well without me. And then there will be more payment for you. I will take care of all the details before you leave. All you will need to do is read your itinerary."

"How long till I leave?"

"Two months. Maybe ten weeks."

"How long will I be gone?"

"Two months. Maybe ten weeks."

"It is a deal consummated," Jamison said firmly, then looked once again into the mirror. "Do you think I need a new wardrobe before departing?"

Benjamin laughed.

"And if I write a piece or two for the paper—can I get Rikler to pay for it?"

From a Letter to Hannah Collins Keyes

Hannah,

I am dashing off a note to you before I depart. I have been asked by my newspaper to head off to England for a spell, and while I am there I may present some lectures as well. The English continue to be keenly fascinated by the Indians and tales of savages and cowboys. I do not know how long the paper will have me serve there. I may head over to Gibraltar for a short duration. The benefit of this is that I will be able to return home for short visits—the only problem being that they are seldom planned in advance. Of course, I will attempt to contact you beforehand, for it would be nice to see you again—though I do not hold a great deal of hope for such a meeting taking place in the near future.

All the best to you. I trust that all is going well.

If there is a time you are in New York City and you need a special favor

or advice—please see my friend Benjamin Grossman at the newspaper.
He will act in my stead.

    As always,
    Jamison Pike

From the Journal of Jamison Pike

LONDON
NOVEMBER 1854

Again I have found myself in the coldest, most damp and dreariest climes known to man. My series of lectures has gone quite well. Benjamin had the inspired idea of adding scenery to my presentations. Before I left, I had a fellow who designs beautifully detailed backgrounds at the new Academy of Music Opera House on Fourteenth and Irving Place paint a special background for me. It is of a Western scene, with sagebrush and wide-open vistas under the bluest of blue skies. Then, in a manner of stage trickery, a second background is unrolled, with lighting from the rear. This background contains the figures of several savage Indians, in war paint, brandishing bows and arrows, riding on their nimble-footed ponies. It is as if they are descending on me, the speaker. Finally a third background is unrolled, this time with the body of poor Mr. Lambers lying on the ground in a pool of red, with one of the savages holding up his bloody scalp, shouting out a war cry of triumph.

It is magnificently gruesome.

I trust that his memory is not offended by these theatrics, but when Benjamin watched my first practice with the backgrounds, he was astounded by the power manifest in the presentation. He said he had tears in his eyes when I described poor George's death—and this from a man who has heard the story more often than any man on earth.

While on my short lecture circuit, I found myself returning to the position of that of a reporter. I interviewed some local folk, sat in on a meeting of the House of Commons, watched the changing of the

queen's guard outside her palace—all sorts of fascinating things that
readers back home might enjoy reading about.

I will file the stories when I return home, for my trip over here is
not that long in duration. I think that once I return to New York, I
will also return to my job as reporter on a full-time basis.

New York City
June 1855

"What do you mean, 'Hannah was in the office'?"

Jamison's face was a shade lighter than ash as he faced Benjamin
across the table.

"It happened just as I said. I was at work. This was a few weeks
ago. You were still in Charleston. I looked up and there she was.
She is much more striking in person—you never described her as she
really is. She said you told her to look me up because I'm the only
person who might be able to track you down. And that she understood you've been stationed in Gibraltar—and might be there for
years."

Jamison bent over and placed his head in his hands. He groaned
softly.

"Why did you tell her you were in Gibraltar?" Benjamin asked.

Jamison did not look up. "What did you tell her? You didn't tell
her the truth, did you?"

Benjamin pulled his chair closer to the dining-room table. Jamison
had returned home the night prior—very late in the evening—and
Benjamin had not wakened him when he had left this morning.
When he had returned home after work in the evening, Benjamin
had found Jamison sitting at the table, with a coffeepot and a plateful
of crumbs, reading through a stack of recent newspapers.

"The truth? Of course I told her the truth . . . even though I stumbled with it, almost lying at times, trying to cover your lies while not
lying myself."

Jamison let his head fall to the table with an audible thunk that sounded painful as well. "Why?" he moaned.

"Why? Why did I tell the truth? Was I expected to lie for you— about something that I had no knowledge of?"

Jamison pushed away from the table with a rush. His chair toppled over behind him and clattered to the floor. He did not speak but paced about, staring at the floor or out the windows.

Silence reigned for several minutes. Then Benjamin said quietly, "What would you have had me do? Why at least didn't you tell me what was happening? Why didn't you tell me what you wrote to her? It made me look like I was an accomplice to your lies. And I wasn't."

Jamison did not stop nor look up. "Sorry."

"Jamison, what's going on? What is this all about? I thought you held this Hannah in high regard."

"I do. I did. I mean . . . I still do. I just . . . I don't know. It's not something I want to talk about right now."

Benjamin took off his coat and placed it carefully on the hook by the door. He set his collar there as he always did. He scanned the small stack of envelopes on the front table. He removed his shoes and placed them neatly by the door. Then he turned back to Jamison, who now paced in the drawing room.

"What would you have had me do?" Benjamin asked again.

Jamison stopped and slumped into one of the two chairs by the front windows. "What did you say, exactly?"

Benjamin sat on the arm of the chair opposite. "She thought you were in Gibraltar. And that you had been gone for years. I said you were in England last year and may have stopped in Gibraltar on the way home. I said that you were doing lectures and articles. But that you've been in New York all along, save a few trips here and there."

Jamison sighed hard. He ran his hand over his hair, cut shorter now than it had ever been, almost tight to his scalp.

"I'm sorry, Benjamin. I didn't mean it to happen this way. I never thought she would come to New York, let alone try to see me unannounced. You shouldn't have had to lie for me."

"I didn't, really. I simply told her you weren't the type of man who would hurt anyone. I said there must be an explanation for it all."

Jamison looked at the short, curt note that Hannah had left.

Jamison! What falsehoods have you told me? Gibraltar? As a friend, I demand more honesty. If you can, come to Philadelphia before I sail on June 15. If you miss me, I expect a letter and a full explanation. If not, I will no longer consider you my friend.
H.

"She doesn't sound like she understood it."

"She was angry. She was upset over being misled, I imagine," Benjamin said. "To be lied to for so long–that has to be dispiriting."

"I didn't mean for it to go on so long. I didn't. It just felt easier– so I wouldn't have to deal with rejection."

Benjamin nodded. "From what little you have said, I had pieced most of this together. But you could have come clean. Long ago. Life is too short to carry so much pain."

Jamison slumped even farther into the chair. "I know. I know. But once it starts, it is very difficult to stop."

Benjamin leaned forward. "Jamison, if she is such a wonderful person–at least as wonderful as you have described–why do you think she would reject you out of hand? It doesn't make sense to me."

Jamison closed his eyes and sighed again. "I don't know. Maybe . . ."

"Maybe what?"

Jamison struggled back to a sitting position. "Because I am not good enough for her–that's why."

Benjamin narrowed his eyes. "Surely you don't mean that. You're a fine person."

Jamison's voice became a whisper. "Ever since Harvard . . . well, I have known that Hannah placed a lot of value on financial security. I was told that was the reason she married Robert Keyes in the first place. And you know I am not a wealthy man–you of all people, Benjamin."

Benjamin shrugged. "You could have saved more, that's true," he said reluctantly.

"And then . . . well, Hannah is such a wonderful woman. She deserves so much better than what I could offer."

"Nonsense, Jamison. You are a good man."

Jamison looked out the window, watching a man and woman push a baby carriage through the park across the street. His words sounded distant and hollow. "I am not good enough for her. She is a pure and honest woman. I am not. Not for many years. I could never hope to be good enough for her."

"But, Jamison, that is all in the past. Surely she could not expect more."

"I don't think I will ever be worthy of her. Not now. Not after all I have done."

Benjamin sighed. It was obvious he knew of Jamison's failings. "But she seemed like such a wonderful woman."

Jamison stood by his chair, not knowing what to do next. "How did she look, Benjamin?"

"Look?"

"Did she look happy? Is she still beautiful?"

Benjamin hesitated.

"Tell me, please."

"Yes, she is quite beautiful. Not in a gaudy way. But there is something about her. Everyone in the newsroom stopped what they were doing when she came into the room. They simply stared at her."

"She does that to people," Jamison agreed. "Is she happy?"

"I think she is. She was angry first. But I think she is happy as well."

Jamison nodded. "I am pleased."

"She's a believer, you know."

"A what?"

"I mean she believes in God. Faith. You know, like me."

"How could you tell?"

"Something about her eyes, I think. And that she was carrying a Bible with her. No one does that unless they mean to use it."

"A Christian," Jamison said under his breath. "All the more reason. All the more reason."

FROM THE JOURNAL OF JAMISON PIKE

Benjamin explained to me that Hannah was on her way to California. Gage Davis, my friend and Harvard classmate, was setting up a hospital—and asked if she might be willing to head the staff there. Eight years ago, Gage left the East Coast under a cloud of suspicion over alleged illegalities and stock manipulations. In the succeeding years, he built a second fortune, found love, and lost it to death. Now, in an effort to make amends somehow, he was using his considerable wealth to do good things.

When Hannah visited my office and Benjamin told her the truth—uncovering, I daresay, years' worth of lies and falsehoods—part of my carefully constructed world crumbled with those lies.

I truly felt those lies were what was best at the time.

Now I know they were not. But such is how vision and judgment become perfectly clear after the fact, not before.

I muddled about the apartment in a stupor after being exposed. I did not know how to continue or even if I could.

Then, like lighting a match to tinder, I had my solution.

I asked—no, demanded—an exotic assignment from Rikler. I asked if I might travel to the Sandwich Islands for a look at their royal family—the Kamehamehas.

Then I would head to China.

He agreed.

My stories sell papers.

I am trying to persuade myself that I am not pursuing Hannah to California. But in the darkness, my heart says that I must.

Benjamin said that God will forgive us if only we ask for that forgiveness.

And the only people who truly understand that are people who have been forgiven. It was apparent to him that Hannah understood that. And those who have been forgiven much often are the most forgiving. Or at least they should be. I am guilty. I should ask for her forgiveness. That is what Benjamin advised.

And that is what I find myself attempting to do.

FROM THE JOURNAL OF JAMISON PIKE

SAN FRANCISCO, CALIFORNIA
SEPTEMBER 1855

I entered into the harbor of San Francisco in a gray and somber mood. The weather matched my emotions. I found a hotel where I had foolishly intended on waiting for her arrival. San Francisco is no longer a modest fishing village. It is well on the way to becoming a true city—complete with opera houses and theaters and all manner of diversion.

I searched the docks for that forgiveness, I think. I did not find it.

Benjamin made it all sound so simple and achievable. As if God forgives that easily! He does not. That much I know. My father repeated often the exactness as to how God judges. I have fallen so many times and in so many ways. And I have not ever turned to God, for I am sure of his answer: too many sins, too far astray, too lost to find.

I care not to hear quoted the verses that indicate otherwise, for my time in my parents' home and in my father's church have so been drummed into my consciousness. The way is narrow and few are righteous enough to walk thereon. I know that I have fallen from grace—with both God and Hannah.

And I know, after days of anguish, that I can no longer remain on this soil.

I have written a letter to Hannah that I will post on the morrow. It is in care of Gage Davis. I saw him for an afternoon. Of all of us— my friends from Harvard—I'm convinced he should be the one whom Hannah marries. His eyes looked lost, and his sweet daughter needs a mother.

I know Hannah will look on my poor words with disdain. It is better this way, I am sure. I have not told her of all this in the letter. In time, perhaps I will.

Two days hence, a ship leaves this port heading first to the Sandwich Islands.

I have booked passage on that vessel.

CHAPTER SEVENTEEN

FROM THE JOURNAL OF JAMISON PIKE
DECEMBER 1855

There is both a sweet, satisfying side of travel and a bitter side.

The sweet side is dawn over a vista yet unseen, a new geography to explore, a new set of sensibilities to examine.

What is bitter, in a way, is that such travel occurs at such a languid pace. Weeks and weeks go by, and all I am able to do is sit on the deck of a ship, watching the endless parade of clouds and waves. I have much time in which to drown in my thoughts. And drowning in them is a particularly apt analogy.

As is the case on most journeys, this excursion has not gone as I had intended. Our voyage west from the California coast went well. Winds were moderate and rain only dogged us for a few days. Otherwise, the weather was most benign. I sat at the prow of the ship, out of the way of the sailors, and read some, wrote some, but mainly stared out at the vastness of the open water before me.

We neared the Sandwich Islands—Captain Leiters had said we'd reach them in no more than another day or two of sailing. Off to the horizon we spotted a sail. That in itself is an odd occurrence, since a ship rarely encounters another on open waters. In tighter areas, such as the Caribbean, encounters are more frequent but certainly not typical out here on the vastness of the Pacific.

Flying a French flag, the other vessel sailed close to us and hailed us. No sailor on board our ship spoke French, save me, and no one on the French ship spoke English, so I was pressed into service as translator; however, I suspect we could have found a mutual tongue had we polled both crews.

The French captain clearly acted as if in a great hurry, so he and I shouted back and forth in my best third-level language. What I gathered was his ship had just left one of the Sandwich Isles. (I could not ascertain which of the four main islands.) They encountered some manner of epidemic occurring there. I understood the word for "sickness" and "disease" but did not understand what specific type of sickness it was. I conveyed back to him our thanks for the warning. As soon as my *merci* was shouted, the captain spun his wheel and tacked away from our side.

The crew all then turned to me for explanation.

I remained collected, yet mentioned the word *epidemic.* That was all it took for a near panic to sweep through the ranks. The captain shouted out an order for calm, yet no calm was forthcoming. He also shouted out orders for the crew to tally the available stocks of fresh-water and food. When the amounts were shouted up from below the decks, he scribbled some notes in his log, doing sums and subtractions. Only then did he sigh with obvious relief.

He shouted to the crew to change course immediately and head in a southwesterly direction. Then he turned to me to explain.

"We suffered through a plague in a small port in the Maldives. Against my best judgment, we took to port for water. Bodies had been tossed into the harbor and bobbed about like apples in the fall. The smell be enough to cause any man to wretch. We was short on water—not empty—and should have sailed on to Madagascar. The water we took was foul and nearly a dozen men took powerful sick and died before leaving sight of land. No sir, we'll not be risking our hides. We be skedaddlin'. We set sail for Ratak. Water we'll be fine with. Food will be sparse—unless we catch a few dolphin on the way."

And that is what we did. No matter that we were holding some cargo bound for the Sandwich Islands, there would be no stopping there now. There would be no chance to write on the royal family either. But there was nothing I could do to prevent the change in itinerary.

So off to Ratak it is.

I asked the captain if I might examine his maps and charts to gauge the island's approximate location. He pointed it out. The small chain is indeed far from anywhere, but the captain offered me his private, uncensored evaluation that we have more than enough food and water to last the journey—providing the winds hold strong and true.

Yet as I listened I found no great conviction in his words. It was as if he were trying his best to convince me, and then my ease with the situation would pass on back to him.

I do not think that happened.

If I were a praying man, I would have gone to bended knee.

But I am not, and I did not.

FROM THE JOURNAL OF JAMISON PIKE
THE RATAK ATOLL, SOMEWHERE IN THE PACIFIC

The small island, surrounded by a wide circle of coral and stone that lay only a few feet above the sea, appeared to us at dusk one evening when the winds had died to a breath and the air grew humid, nearly fetid. The crew had been languishing on deck, despairing in a most vocal manner. Their spiritual malaise was as epidemic as any illness, for I have seldom felt so black and lost.

Then one member of the crew shouted that he saw a slim halo of green shimmering to the south. The captain spun the wheel and trapped a sliver of a breeze. By moonrise, we were sailing into the welcoming arms of the atoll, celebrating and shouting in the gray moonlight. We set anchor, drank the last of our water, and cooked the last of our flour and bacon, knowing that in the morning all manner of fresh food would be pouring into our near-depleted stores.

The Port of Shanghai, China
April 1856

"So, you'll be getting off here? It be a long way from anywhere."

Captain Leiters scratched his ear as Jamison watched his two trunks being unloaded and placed on the dock.

"This wasn't part of my original routing, but we missed the Sandwich Isles, and I am still under obligation to provide some exotic stories for my newspaper. And this," Jamison said, indicating the harbor of Shanghai with a broad sweep of his hand, "seems exotic enough, don't you think?"

"I suppose . . . but I ain't the one to ask. All the world, to me, is just a series o' harbors where men speak different tongues and they all be tryin' to cheat an honest man. So be careful, Mr. Pike. These Johnnies are a powerful crafty bunch. I bet they'd as soon slit your throat as to answer any of your questions."

Jamison tried not to look worried, even though he was. "I'll be fine. I'm told I can find an interpreter at the end of the docks. If I can be understood, I'm sure I'll be fine."

"Then the best o' luck to you, sir. It's been a privilege havin' you on board—bein' a man who wrote books and all, that is."

"Pleasure is mine, Captain Leiters. Perhaps our paths will cross again."

And with that, Jamison waved again to the captain and set off up the rickety, narrow docks and headed inland.

December 1856

Jamison wound up spending eight months in China. He found the land fascinating, filled with beautiful and terrifying contradictions. The lot of the peasants was harsh, yet they seemed to have such a spirit of peace and contentment.

He traveled about some and found evidences of Englishmen nearly everywhere he went—from schools to hospitals to seminaries. Despite that fact that he towered over most Chinese, he felt an odd sense of serenity as he spent his weeks roaming about the land.

But the pain in his heart grew. He knew he could no longer escape his reality by hiding in a foreign land. He made his way back to Shanghai and sought out a ship heading east. He ended up sailing on a Portuguese ship hauling tea, opium, and dishes.

He had decided to return to the Sandwich Islands via Hong Kong. After all, he had promised Rikler a story on the islands' royalty and would make good on that promise.

The Portuguese captain had no qualms about stopping on the islands. He claimed that the French inflated the claims of an epidemic. "Only the natives be dying," he explained. "No need for sailor to worry."

Upon arriving on the island of Maui, Jamison found lodging at Fodor's, a small inn overlooking the harbor, and set about trying to find and file some stories for the newspaper. The epidemic, such as it was, did indeed seem to be most virulent among the natives. In fact, innkeepers claimed that no white man had yet died from the illness—at least none on this island.

From south of Lahaina a pallor of smoke arose from the shore.

"Them poor sods take a heap of wood to burn, I hear tell. Something about the illness that holds the flesh from the flames," said Amos Houlet.

Jamison looked at the large black man in disbelief.

Amos, who seemed to be the bartender, waiter, and cook for the inn, added, "It be what they say. Now for me, I never draw near to them islanders. No sense poking a finger at God now, is there?"

Jamison shrugged and turned in his seat, facing his plate of freshly caught and fried fish.

"The sad part be the children dying most often."

"What do the doctors say?" Jamison asked as he stabbed at a portion of the delicate meat.

Amos wiped the counter and laughed. "That be funny, Mr. Pike. Funny indeed."

Jamison chewed, then looked up. "Why?"

"This island ain't got no doctor. Maybe one on big island, but never be coming here."

Jamison paused in midbite. "No doctor, you say."

Amos leaned close. "You know a doctor?"

Jamison nodded.

"A doctor who come all the way to this lonely place?"

"Perhaps," Jamison replied.

"If that be so, then you best not telling them poor island folk till he gets here. Many lost children and don't like hope being given and taken away."

As he ate, Jamison began composing a letter to Hannah.

He was certain she would come—despite whatever gulf might exist between them. It was not a truth as much as an overwhelming feeling.

CHAPTER EIGHTEEN

Maui, Sandwich Islands
February 1857

Jamison left his horse at the small livery stable at the edge of Lahaina. From the highlands he had spotted a ship entering the harbor. Since the beginning of the month, he had rushed to the docks to meet every vessel of size entering the calm waters of the port of Lahaina. To date, twelve vessels had entered the harbor and none of the twelve had carried Hannah. He remained disappointed but had not given up hope.

There was something in his heart that forced him to watch the seas for a canvas sail. He imagined a hundred different scenarios–and all had Hannah arriving to help stem the tide of the mysterious malady. He knew she was a compassionate woman and hoped his plea had appealed to her heart.

This day it had taken him nearly two hours to ride down off the slopes of the massive volcano that dominated the southern half of the island. He had been searching for one of the local shaman who claimed to have cured the sickness. But everywhere that Jamison visited, all the villagers claimed the man had not been seen in recent weeks.

By the time he walked down the wooden ramps to the docks, he was sweating. A hot wind blew in from the west. The ship that had entered the harbor this morning was no longer at dockside nor at anchorage.

They don't stay because of the sickness.

He stopped midstep.

On the far pier was a jumble of boxes and crates. A stack of Saratoga trunks was off to one side. He closed his eyes tightly.

If I were a praying man . . .

He ran down the dock, eyes searching for a label or address. He knelt beside one of the boxes and wiped at a thickness of dust.

Then he blinked again.

He stood and began to run back toward town.

When Jamison reached Fodor's Inn, he slowed his frantic steps to a walk. As he climbed the wooden steps in front, each step creaked a different key. Placing his hand carefully on the knob of the front door, he pulled. The hinges squealed in a comfortable song.

His eyes swept the darkened room and only stopped when they reached a large chair in the far room by the window that over-looked the garden. A shaft of sunshine found its way into the room and lit the chair from the side. He took a great gulp of air. He smoothed his hair with a brush of his hand. He tidied his shirt. Then he took another step.

It was Hannah! She must have fallen asleep. Her hair cascaded about her face like a golden waterfall.

Her face was the same as Jamison remembered. Perhaps a crease or two had grown deeper, but none of that mattered. Her mouth was slightly parted.

She is as beautiful as the first day I laid eyes on her.

"Hannah," he said, almost breathing the words. He touched her shoulder. Her eyes blinked wide as she jostled awake, and the teacup in her hand chattered, spilling the remaining swallows of tea into her lap.

They both stared at each other for a long moment, as if time weren't passing.

Finally she broke the silence. "Hello, Jamison." Her eyes never left his. "It is so . . . it is so good to see you again."

Jamison's apprehension and joy created such tumult inside him that it was difficult to speak. "And you, too, Hannah. It is . . . nice to see you as well."

A dozen heartbeats passed as their words faded into silence. Only the distant sound of the waves breaking on the rocky waterfront could be heard.

Hannah looked down at her hands, then up. Jamison held out his hand. She placed her small hand within his wider, broader one. He wondered if she felt the same manner of jolt that he did when their flesh met.

He took a half step toward her and without thinking, without analyzing, opened his arms. And in a likewise manner, she opened herself to him and they met, in the cool darkness of the small inn on an island at the edge of the Pacific, in each other's tender and intimate embrace.

FROM THE JOURNAL OF JAMISON PIKE
LAHAINA, MAUI

How I wished that single moment might stand forever frozen in time. Hannah was in my arms and her arms were about me. How more perfect could a situation be?

I simply let that moment be and banished all other thoughts and worry and concerns from my mind. I held her, and that was all that mattered.

Eventually I released her, and we spent several hours catching up on the news of our lives–all told in the briefest of fashions. Then I showed her the small storefront I had rented for her. Having her stay at any inn or boardinghouse in town would not do. Even the girl's boarding school has been the subject of great speculation and gossip. On the second floor of the storefront, there were small, but very functional, living quarters. Hannah will have her privacy without having to deal with rowdy sailors and the various malcontents that make up the population of the inns in this town.

She asked me how I knew she would answer my plea in a positive way. It was a most valid question—and one I struggled to answer. To be sure, there was every reason she might not come, but I told her I somehow *knew* she would make the journey. Much in my life, it seems, is in response to something I have known—not from facts or reason, but simply known deep inside to be true.

Hannah's coming to Maui is one of those knowns. She would not do otherwise.

And therefore, she, in flesh and blood and softly scented perfume, is here with me, standing next to me, having dinner with me.

How amazing is this turn of events.

A month later, on one of their island treks, Hannah and Jamison were nearly surrounded by a band of natives, scarcely clad, with feathers and masks and spears flashing. They had been exploring a narrow cleft, a short, steep valley, as it sliced deep into the island's center and had taken a short rest by a stream.

From the jungle around them came noises. Jamison held his finger to his lips, bidding Hannah to be quiet. There was a snap and a rustle from the darkness around them.

Hannah shrugged and whispered, "There is nothing out there but your imagination."

But she was wrong. For at that moment the natives descended with a singular whoop, trapping Jamison and Hannah in a great circle of clubs and threatening gestures. Hannah screamed and fled to take refuge behind the moss-covered trunk of a tree.

Jamison stood tall without flinching. He had had some dealings with natives in the past months and had come to recognize that their bluster was mostly bluff. When in combat with other natives, they became fierce and deadly, he was told, but had seldom attacked a white man without cause.

Jamison hoped what he had heard proved to still be correct.

He waited as they danced about, making fierce charges to within a few feet. Jamison looked for the man who might be the leader. Judging from the number of feathers and deference granted to him, Jamison thought he had the man selected. He called out and pointed, shouting, "You there! Come here."

It took a few moments of pantomime to have the fellow stand near him. Then he called to Hannah. She hesitated from her place of refuge.

"Hannah, please. You have to come now!"

It was a firm and commanding side that Jamison seldom showed. She obeyed and came to him. It was obvious she was quaking as she walked.

Then he whispered the most curious set of instructions to her. "Take a hatpin from your head. Show it to them. Show them how sharp it is by touching it to your fingertip."

She nodded, clearly not comprehending what Jamison might want.

"Now with your other hand, find that fleshy spot on my forearm. The spot with few nerves and bone."

She appeared greatly puzzled but did as he said. She found the spot, midway up his forearm.

"Now take the needle and plunge it through there."

"Jamison," she protested, "have you lost your mind? Sticking you with an unsterilized needle?"

He grabbed her arm as she was about to pull away. "I've seen the trick done in barrooms. Surely a surgeon as good as you can do it."

"But . . . but why?"

"Just do it. Now."

She felt for the spot again, searched Jamison's eyes, and then plunged the needle into him. The tip protruded an inch or two from the opposite side from where it entered. Because she was skilled, the pain was no more than a pinprick.

The natives stared in wonder as Jamison held up his arm showing the needle cleanly through his flesh, with nary a murmur on his part. The leader came closer. He touched the needle still in Jamison's arm. Then Jamison pointed to Hannah and back to the leader, then finally to the needle. "Do any of you wish to confront the powers of the great white doctor?"

Jamison cackled then, and in an instant, the entire group of natives stared, then turned on their heels and tore off into the dark green foliage. In a moment, silence returned.

"You can take it out now," Jamison said, wincing. "It has begun to hurt."

Hannah did so with dispatch. "Why on earth did you make me do that? You are truly crazed."

"No, I am not. It scared them off. And your reputation as a shaman is now being spread all over this island."

She held his arm and wrapped the wound with a strip torn from the hem of her dress. As she did, he closed his eyes and simply enjoyed the touch of her hand on his skin.

FROM THE JOURNAL OF JAMISON PIKE
MAUI
MARCH–JUNE 1857

It appears Hannah has found the source of the illness.

We were on a trek through a high jungle when we came upon a feral boar. It charged us, so I was forced to fire. Hannah asked if the natives ate the animals and, of course, they do.

She surmised that whatever illness had afflicted the boars was afflicting the native children as well. She postulated that the bad blood somehow carried the ill humors that were the cause of such death. After a few weeks of being told to avoid eating the flesh of the boars, deaths among the natives have begun to decrease.

My decision to ask Hannah to this island was indeed a most profitable one.

With Hannah in residence and performing her medical duties, I hurried on to the island of Oahu—and the larger port of Honolulu—in June. It is there that the royals have their formal residence, the *Hale Alii.* It is constructed of blocks of coral and in the sun glows with a sharp pink color.

The town resembles a New England whaling village, for that is what it is, in essence—save for being warm all year and populated with brown-skinned natives.

I arranged to have tea with the queen—Queen Emma—a beautiful and refined woman with a quick, gracious smile. She laughed easily and often and was most generous in her time with me. Her anecdotes of her English education and her extended family were truly fascinating. But all the time I visited in the royal court, I imagined Hannah, back in Lahaina, alone. I have never felt more pressure to conclude a story and interview as I did this one.

I stayed on in Honolulu only long enough to finish my article—multiple copies, of course, and packed them off on three ships bound for New York. I am certain that our readers will take note of the temperate weather and the scantily clad natives and think this land a paradise. And, in some ways, it is.

Now I am on deck of a small schooner that sails the local waters only, and the twinkling light of Lahaina's torches are once again in view. My heart has leapt in my chest.

Jamison imagined it to be near midnight by the time the vessel was secured at the dock. Had the hour been any earlier he would have run to Hannah's to tell her of his return. Instead, he made his way to Fodor's Inn. The kitchen was often open at all hours, and it had been hours since he last ate.

Amos sat behind the bar, head resting in his hands, softly snoring. Jamison gently nudged him awake. A few sailors sat in a far corner, each cradling a large ale, and mumbling in the dim light.

"Amos? I'm hungry. Is there any decent food in the place?"

It seemed that Amos was never startled. Slowly he opened his eyes, blinked, then smiled his great smile. "For you, Mr. Pike, we got food. Some snapper this morning. You want snapper? I fry it with plantains. Little brown sugar. Mighty good."

Jamison smiled back and nodded.

In a few minutes, a huge side of a snapper was on a plate before him.

"Delicious, Amos. I should take you back to New York with me. You could open up a restaurant. You could be rich."

"If I be rich, what I do then?"

"You could have servants then. You could laze about and enjoy your life."

Amos leaned backward to laugh. The sailors turned to listen. "I do that now, Mr. Pike. And not rich. I enjoy life now. No. New York too cold. They got snow, don't they?"

"Yes, it snows in New York."

"I never seen this snow, but I know I not like it. I not going."

Jamison took another forkful of snapper. "Have you seen Hannah?"

Amos whistled. "I like Hannah. She good woman. She been here lots. Dinner. Work at doctor mostly. She pretty woman."

"She is indeed."

Amos laughed again. "And then why she with you, Mr. Pike? That be big question. Beautiful woman–not-so-handsome man."

Jamison grinned. "She . . . well, she is not 'with' me, Amos. She's here as a doctor. She's an old friend. That's all, just a friend."

"And I be a tiny mouse," Amos whispered, then winked. "She may be friend, but she be more. Amos sees your eyes. I can see more."

Jamison offered a playful grimace, then held up his coffee cup. "Make your eyes useful, Amos, and find me a cup of coffee."

The black man sidled away from his perch to the kitchen, laughing softly and muttering something about "old friends."

After pouring a cup of hot coffee, Amos disappeared back into the kitchen again. Jamison was sure the man never slept in a bed but just wandered about the inn at night, cleaning or cooking, or fishing off the docks, then catching sleep as needed.

He stirred a large tablespoon of sugar into his coffee and stared out at the dark night. Down the beach small fires bobbed above the surface of the water. Natives would wade into the quiet surf holding torches. The light would attract small fish. It made spearing them an easy matter.

Jamison took a large swallow and watched the flames in the darkness a long time, thinking about the gulf that still existed between Hannah and himself.

Jamison left the inn that night under a full gibbous moon and walked down the quiet and deserted streets of Lahaina Town. A few lanterns flickered here and there, and the moon illuminated the rest of the landscape in deep somber gray.

It was a most nervous walk.

It was as if for the first time in his life Jamison had looked into a mirror without attempting to distort the image that gazed back at him. It was a new emotion, trying to accommodate who he really was, attempting to be comfortable in his own skin, within his own frame. For so long he had pretended to be something he was not— a carefree bon vivant, a world traveler, a cad, a man aloof and alone who preferred it that way.

He was none of those things. After so many years of pretending to be someone else, he was further away from knowing who he really was.

As he walked in the darkness, he thought of Hannah and himself and what their future might now hold.

When the road turned away from the shore, Jamison headed toward the water's edge, where the moon reflected off a million tiny ripples. He could hear the call of the whales well out into the channel between the islands. Even though the whalers killed so many, some were never dissuaded, because of eons of instinct and tradition, from coming to these warm waters to bear their young. Their high-pitched wails carried over the water like a child's cry in the night.

The waters lapped at his shoes. He kicked them off and stood barefoot in the surf.

He knew no one was near, so he gave voice to his thoughts. "Hannah . . . you are now real again. I have thought for a moment of seeing you leave this place, and I do not know if my heart could stand the loss. I have had so little in my life that I truly cared about—save you. What do I do now? Do I let you go home? Do I ask you to stay?"

He fell to his knees in the sand and bowed his head.

It would not be a prayer, for he was not a praying man, but his heart called out, *What do I do now?*

FROM THE JOURNAL OF JAMISON PIKE
MAUI
END OF JUNE 1857

Hannah asked me to find Nora's grave site.

It seemed so odd that three of us from that small group at Harvard wound up on this tiny island. Gage had been here first, of course, having pursued his beloved Nora to these shores. She had felt such guilt at having been instrumental in his financial ruin back in New York City that she had fled from his arms, intending to hide from Gage forever. It was here that he had finally found her—here where she had relented and accepted his forgivenessness. It was also here where they married and here where their daughter had been born.

And it is here where Nora lies now, alone and still.

The grave overlooks the ocean and is surrounded by a thicket of jungle. A caretaker keeps the wildness at bay. As we stood there quietly together, Hannah said that Nora's death was all part of God's plan. I reacted sharply, saying it was sad and did not make sense—a young mother being "taken" that way.

She countered that no one can be a "sundial" believer, coming out only in the joy and refusing to handle the sorrow.

It made me angry and I turned away. Love is not nearly enough to truly heal pain. Gage will never feel whole again.

But I remained silent.

We remained quiet for a long time, then she held her hand in mine and we returned to Lahaina. As we rode, I asked if she was planning on returning to California, now that the epidemic had passed. She nodded but did not elaborate further than that.

FROM THE JOURNAL OF JAMISON PIKE
BLACK ROCK, MAUI

Two days later Hannah said that we should take a picnic to Black Rock—a jetty of cold lava pushing into the sea. I was taken by surprise, but I agreed.

We found our way there with picnic basket in hand.

What transpired is still swirling in my thoughts. I do not know if I am recording it in proper detail or sequence.

She asked if I had ever been in love.

I did not want to answer. I knew I had been—but only with Hannah, and how could a man just blurt out that truth?

Then she claimed that in all my notes from around the world, I have implied that I had some manner of desire for her. I winced, for I had worked hard to prevent such from creeping into my words. Then she shouted at me, angry, about my letter to her concerning my recommendation that she marry Gage Davis. Like an overmatched boxer, I lolled on the ropes, trying to gain my bearings and wit.

I did not.

She then demanded that I answer. "How long do you think your life is?" she asked. "How many years will you have to not love?"

She said it was a pity that my parents were cold and unloving, but to allow that to cripple my life was wrong.

Then I grew more furious and passionate than I could ever have imagined. I accused her of seeking wealth alone–by marrying Robert.

She nearly struck me.

I am not sure of what we said then, except for my sudden admission. It shocked me more than it did her. All these years of silence were now broken. I could no longer hold back my heart. I am not sure why I said what I did, save I had no choice. To remain silent was to perish.

I told her that I loved her–from the first day I saw her. I told her that when I saw other women, I saw her face. I told her I was alone not because of mean-spirited parents–but because I loved her.

"You love me?" she asked.

As if in great pain, I extended my hand to her.

She raised her hand to meet mine.

"I love you more than the sun and the stars and the very air I breathe. Do you not realize how horribly difficult it is to be near you and not carry you off in a great passionate embrace? Do you not know how tempted I am to blurt out my true feelings every moment of every day? My heart has not known rest since I first saw you, Hannah. It is not your fault that I suffer such torment– it is the fault of my own heart."

Her eyes looked as if they would soon fill with tears.

"Do not cry, Hannah," I pleaded. "I will never want to make you cry. You must not cry."

"I'm sorry," she whispered. "I never knew. Not really. I may have . . . thought you did. But you never told me."

"I'm telling you now," I said.

And then, as if being pulled close by a slow-moving current, the two of us opened our arms and found each other in a long embrace, an embrace that had waited years and years for fulfillment.

And we remained that way–silent, together, locked arm in arm– as the sun gradually edged to the western sea and the crimson and gold of the sunset colored all about us.

❧

"So she say she love you?" Amos sprawled on the bar, his elbows forming the base of a hefty triangle, with his chin at the apex.

"Not exactly. But close," Jamison replied as he poured some cream into his coffee. "The problem is that she is a believer."

"Believer?"

"In God. She believes in God. I don't."

Amos shrugged. "No problem. Tell her you believe. She pretty woman. Worth saying."

Jamison slumped farther into his chair.

The winds had freshened from the south and the palm fronds rattled above them. He heard the groan and squeal of the tree's long trunk as it resettled into the wind.

"I can't, Amos. That would be telling a lie. Too big a lie, I am afraid."

"God not be happy?"

"More than that, Amos," Jamison insisted. "I won't lie to her anymore. I lied to her for years and years, and I have to stop now. And it would be a lie to myself. I'm tired of telling lies."

Amos sighed. "Big problem, then. What you do?"

"I don't know. I'm sure she wants me to find this God of hers."

"Then she love you?"

"I don't know. I think she will. She almost loves me."

Amos arched his eyebrows. "She pretty woman. She worth finding this God. How hard can that be?"

"I don't know. And she is indeed a pretty woman, Amos. She is indeed. The most wonderful and beautiful woman I have ever known."

Amos took Jamison's coffee cup without being asked and whisked it back into the kitchen. He returned with a fresh cup and a plate of something that looked like fried string. "Octopus. You look hungry."

Jamison squinted at the curled fingers on the plate. "Octopus?"

"No poison. Good. Taste."

Jamison lifted one tentatively to his mouth, then shut his eyes and chewed. Midswallow he smiled and reached for another.

"Told you. Amos knows secret." The big man scratched his belly, then tilted his head in question. "Where this place New Zealand?"

Jamison sighed again. "There are no secrets on this island, are there?"

"No. Too small. People talk. Nothing else to do."

Jamison pointed to the southwest. "About two months' sail in that direction."

"Whoo-ee. That be far. I hear some man will give you lots money if you go and write story. He write you letter. He want you to go to this place."

Jamison nodded. "Yes, my editor in New York, an old friend of mine, is in a bind. He knows his competitors are making their way to New Zealand. He thinks it will be a grand story. And he knows I could tell it very well. If he gets the story first, his newspaper makes lots and lots of money. So he has offered me more money than I could earn in five years to go and write it. The newspaper business has become much more cutthroat, Amos. I don't like it as much anymore."

Amos nodded as if he understood. "You go there? Take money? That be lots of money. Newspaper has that much money to spend?"

"Yes, Amos, my newspaper will give me lots of money. There is some sort of war going on with the Maori tribe. I could go, write the story, become almost rich, and live happily ever after. It would be enough to settle down with."

Amos whistled.

Jamison continued, "But if I take the job and leave now, I leave Hannah behind. That is a very hard choice."

"It be very hard, Mr. Pike. I wouldn't leave such a pretty woman. Not me. They hard to come by."

Jamison grabbed another piece of octopus. "I don't want to go, Amos. But I think I have to."

Amos nodded knowingly. "Pretty women take lots of money, don't they? Pretty women find rich man easy to love."

Jamison smiled, then reached for the last morsel of octopus on the plate. He chewed thoughtfully, then asked, "Is there any more of this in the back?"

Maui
Mid-July 1857

Jamison finally made up his mind. The newspaper's offer was indeed a small fortune—for just one trip to the wilds of New Zealand. Jamison imagined that after he left, Hannah would soon depart as well and travel back to Monterey and the hospital.

Their last two weeks were most idyllic, and yet as they reveled in each other's company, there was one monumental question that neither dared ask nor answer—and neither gave voice to either.

Save for the last evening they were together.

There was a nick of panic in Hannah's face that day, more so than before, Jamison thought, and of a different nature as well. They sat on the shore, not far from town, watching the moon over the water.

"I have no desire to leave you, Hannah," Jamison told her quietly.

"I know. I don't want you to leave either. But the world is not a perfect place, and our desires are not always to be fulfilled."

"I don't like this," he said. "Finally telling you the truth of my heart and being forced to let you go."

She turned to him in the darkness. He saw the moon reflected in her eyes. "Jamison," she said, "you must promise me one thing—for I know we face a farewell on the morrow."

"Anything you desire, Hannah, I will promise."

She looked away. "It will be difficult for you."

"More difficult than leaving you?"

"Perhaps."

She stood and walked a short distance away. He loved the delicate footprints she made in the sand and the way her hair looked like silver in the moonlight. He let her walk. He thought he knew what she was about to ask.

She stopped at the water's edge. "Jamison, do you believe in God?"

He stood and, for the longest moment, debated on what to do or say. Then he stepped into the sand after her. He was about to speak when she held her hand to his lips.

"I know your answer, Jamison. My faith keeps me alive. You do not share that with me, do you?"

Jamison did not reply.

"There is a gulf between us."

Jamison felt her hand on his arm, then on his chest, just over his heart. It was a light touch, yet pleading, demanding.

"Promise me that you will search for the truth. I am not asking you to change for me. But you must promise me that you will search."

Jamison nodded.

"You love me, don't you, Jamison?"

He stammered out a reply. "More than life itself."

"Then promise me," she said, almost with a harsh edge.

He waited only a heartbeat. "I promise, Hannah. I promise."

And as the dawn rose the next day, Jamison stood on the deck of the *Pride of Wisconsin*. He could barely see Hannah through the veil of tears in his eyes. He refused to cry where she could see him, wanting to face her one last moment as a brave man who did not wallow in self-pity.

But his heart was breaking.

He stared at her image on the dock, waving farewell, long after the ship slipped free from the harbor and sailed toward the western horizon and on to New Zealand.

CHAPTER NINETEEN

The Pacific Ocean
January 1858

The first half of Jamison's voyage from the Sandwich Islands to New Zealand had been far from pleasant. The ship had been beset by nasty weather most of the voyage—rain, winds, squalls, and cold. Jamison spent much of his time in his cramped cabin, holding on to the stays and rails as the ship pitched and rolled. He had little time to write but a great many lonely hours to think and contemplate.

Halfway through their voyage the ship put in at the island of Nuku'alofa, a smudge of land in the vast Pacific. After that stop, the skies cleared considerably. Winds blew favorably, and the crew was cheered greatly at the speed and comfort of the journey.

For the first time in weeks, Jamison left his cabin without having to hang on to rafters and straps and railings as he walked. The ship canted into the wind, of course, but almost in a languid way. He sat near the bow for most of the morning, feeling the warmth of sun on his face and letting the fresh air wash over him. Belowdecks, even in the best of vessels, was most often an unpleasant place. It was dark, with little fresh air to be had, and the aroma of an unwashed crew coupled with animals and rotting food was enough to make most men long for *terra firma.*

This ship, the *Pride of Wisconsin,* was a bit better than most. Food, while never good, was edible. She carried enough freshwater, and the captain insisted on sufficient rations for an extended voyage. While on the island of Nuku'alofa, the captain bought several goats and chickens and installed them in pens belowdecks. They, too, added to the foul ambience that drove Jamison to the top deck.

He found himself near the stern of the ship, overlooking the navigator's station, with its compact desk, well shielded from the wind and ocean spray. Along the desk were small covered alcoves for the ship's compass and sextant, with charts and maps on thick oilskin, impervious to water. Jamison leaned at the rail and watched the navigator, a thick-necked blond fellow from New Bern, North Carolina, aim his sextant at the sun, then transfer markings to the sea chart. With protractor and rule, he made several notations and drew lines across the oilskin paper.

"Are we on course?" Jamison asked.

Andy Messlet turned to Jamison and shrugged, a blank look on his face. He waited a minute, as if anticipating Jamison's response, then chuckled. "No one ever laughs at my humor. Of course we are on course. Why else would they pay me?"

Jamison grinned. "Not disparaging your abilities. I'm just anxious to get off this boat."

Andy stepped away from his desk. "I am, too. I have to be honest— I really don't like being on a ship all that much."

Jamison was surprised, to say the least. "Then why do you do it?" he asked.

"Ever been to New Bern, Mr. Pike? It's on the North Carolina coast."

"I've traveled some down south—Charleston, Savannah—but never through New Bern. Is it a nice place?"

"It's nice enough to make a man like me who doesn't like the ocean stay on a boat most of his life. New Bern is a nice place to be from, and even that is stretching the truth."

"So you stay on a ship even though you don't enjoy it?" Jamison asked in an incredulous tone. "Pretty harsh payment for freedom, isn't it?"

Andy shrugged. "I guess I don't hate the sailor's life all that much. All I know is it is a whole lot better than watching cotton grow back home." Walking back to his desk, he made another set of notations.

Jamison pointed and asked, "Where are we?"

The map, marked with square grids, had neither landmass nor island to interrupt the entire surface of blue. Andy pointed to one quadrant. "Here. But we won't see anything till we get to Auckland. A stretch of blue as far as you can imagine."

"You've sailed this before?"

"A few times. It ain't that bad of a run, really. Winds have always been good, and we make fine time." He picked up the map, rolled it back into a tube, and slipped it into a metal cylinder. Then he screwed the cap back on. "Not much more for me to do than to keep us pointed south by southwest. And in a couple of weeks, we run into New Zealand."

Jamison examined the sheet of rolling blue that stretched away to every horizon around them.

"What brings you with us, Mr. Pike? We've talked some, but you never got around to explaining yourself. And I know no man goes all this way without a purpose."

"You're right about that."

"So why are you here? I mean, on this ship, Mr. Pike?"

Jamison ran his hand through his hair. "I work for a newspaper. There is some trouble between the Brits and the natives in New Zealand. They want stories—exotic locations, danger, the normal sort of material for the papers."

"Oh, them Maori are indeed a nasty lot. One reason I don't spend much time on land there. Auckland's fine. But the rest of the country—well, I have no desire to be a target."

Jamison stared off into the distance. At that moment, his sensibilities had shifted. He had no desire to be a target either—now that he had someone waiting for him at home.

The navigator must have recognized a change in his expression. "Mr. Pike, something bothering you? All of a sudden you look, I don't know, sad, I reckon."

"No. It's not that. Not exactly." Jamison watched a gull flap past, cawing loudly. "Andy, is there anybody back home? Back in New Bern, I mean. Anyone waiting for you?"

Andy's face tightened. "No. My folks passed on a few years back. There are some cousins and aunts and uncles. But none of them are waiting for me." He stared hard at Jamison. "That fret. You've got the look of someone in love. Somebody is waiting for you. All of a sudden it came on you, right?"

Jamison nodded.

"Is she pretty?" Andy asked.

"The most beautiful woman I have ever known."

"Will she wait? No disrespect, but waiting is harder on a pretty woman. They have choices, you know."

"I think she'll wait," Jamison answered softly.

Andy settled back in his small chair. "The look is still there, Mr. Pike. If she'll wait, why should you fret?"

Jamison stood up and walked to the rail. The ship nosed into a wave and a fine spray danced about the deck, flickering in the sun like a thousand tiny jewels. "She made me promise something."

"Like to stay away from the ladies in port? You a wanderer, Mr. Pike?"

Jamison laughed. "No, nothing like that. It was more . . . well . . . spiritual." He paused. "Are you a believer, Andy?"

"In God? Sakes alive, yes. A man out on the sea without faith . . . well, that's like being on the ocean without a compass. Yes, sir, Mr. Pike. I do believe. May not be the best follower, but I follow best I can."

Jamison sighed.

"And I take it that you might not be one?" the navigator went on.

Jamison held up his hands in surrender. "I just could never see that faith did much for a man except make him judgmental and self-righteous. And most of the folks I know who depended on the

Good Book had to because they couldn't face life on their own abilities. No offense, Andy, but I always thought myself too smart to hide behind God."

"No offense taken, Mr. Pike. And the reason I ain't taking offense is because I know it's not the truth. Never was. Never will be. That's what a man says who is just plumb afraid."

"Afraid?"

"Afraid, indeed. You're afraid that God won't want someone like yourself. Or you're afraid of looking foolish. It ain't that way at all, Mr. Pike. It ain't."

The ship caught another rounded wave and dug into the sea again, splashing a heavier mist about the sail bottoms.

"She wants me to keep looking. She says I have to settle this matter or she and I can't be together," said Jamison.

"Sounds like a smart woman."

"She's a doctor."

Andy whistled. "You don't say. Like with knives and potions and all that?"

"More or less."

They stood on the deck facing the stern. When the ship rolled to the right, Jamison flexed and balanced as it did. "Can I just tell her I settled it? Without settling, I mean? You're a believer. Would that work?" he asked.

Andy stood up and faced Jamison. "You can, Mr. Pike. You can indeed. I bet there are many such folk who do that and show up in church every week, saying that they been saved while all the time knowing it's a lie. But for the life of me, I do not understand how those folks sleep at night. Lying to me is one thing, but lying to God is something else indeed."

Jamison nodded. "That is how I perceived it as well."

Andy put his hand on Jamison's shoulder. "Listen, Mr. Pike. It appears to me that you are one smart fellow. You speak real good and all. I bet you know all there is to know about God, but you ain't seeing it with your heart. Like that saying about not seeing the forest amidst all the trees. That's what it sounds like."

Jamison did not reply.

"Mr. Pike, my life has been changed since I decided that I best live for God and not for myself. It weren't a real hard choice. It weren't. Don't be making it harder than it is."

Thoughtful silence reigned.

Then Jamison said softly, "Thank you, Andy. Thank you."

"My pleasure, Mr. Pike. And now, I need to go below the deck and see what's being planned for suppertime."

And Jamison was left alone.

Maybe the choice wasn't hard for you, Andy. But I find it a sheer wall a hundred feet tall.

From a Letter to Benjamin Grossman

Auckland, New Zealand

Benjamin—

I trust you will be properly shocked when you get this letter—if you get this letter at all. As you know, I usually send duplicate letters on duplicate ships, but I do not have the time to do such with this letter.

I am in Auckland.

Auckland is a perfect English seaport. It simply happens to be on the other side of the world. It is so far from anywhere that I scarce believe that anyone discovered it. I have much more respect for the early explorers. To sail for weeks and weeks on a chartless sea—with nothing to view save water and sky and clouds.

I am not being paid, of course, to sightsee but to write a series on the "troubles" between the Brits and Maoris—the natives on these islands. I have included the first several installments with this letter.

This is an amazing land. It is so varied from north to south, I am told. I have seen what hell must appear like, for there are huge sulfurous mud pits that bubble and belch out noxious fumes and gases. From hidden pits and cauldrons the earth oozes and flows like a devil's kitchen. And I have seen what heaven might be like. I was taken to a cave via a boat and in the darkness, in silky filaments hanging from all over the ceiling of the cave, were suspended thousands and thousands of small glowing insects—giving off an unearthly blue light, as if the celestial skies were captured in the earth.

And then there are the Maoris themselves—large men, with bizarre designs tattooed directly onto their faces—swirls and points and shapes that are seen only in nightmares. They come boldly at their enemies—legs spread, tongues out, battle clubs at the ready.

Such is the everyday experience in this country.

Rikler was correct. Our readers will think I am creating this story out of thin air. But none of what I have written is fabrication, in spite of the outlandishness of it all. Please do not let them edit this at all, for I have not embellished a single fact.

I swear it.

We are to tour some of the farms set up on the south island. That land, I am told, comes complete with alpine mountains, fjords, and glaciers, in contrast to the tropical forests here in the north. My host is the consul general to this land, a gregarious fellow from London. I was surprised to learn he had seen me in lectures there—and all but demanded I tell the tales again to his staff.

Because of his gracious hospitality, I could not refuse.

How odd was it to tell tales of Indians in the land of Maoris.

Jamison

On the Ship HMS Constant Endeavor
July 1858

"I cannot tell you how privileged I feel to have you take me along on this voyage," Jamison said in his most proper manner. He was speaking to Major Ian Blackwell, the third-ranking military attaché of the English governor of the land.

"Mr. Pike, your presence will prove no hardship. And Her Majesty would welcome a bit of positive press on your side of the Atlantic."

Jamison did not answer. After interviewing his fair share of military men, he had concluded that the one thing Major Blackwell desired was positive press about his own exploits and achievements.

"I daresay it is most fancy of you Yanks sending a representative of a major newspaper to this godforsaken place—when none of the London papers have done so."

Smiling, Jamison replied, "We take pride on being first, sir. And I will be sure to mention your gracious accommodations."

Major Blackwell presented Jamison a short nod, pulled his tunic tighter, and stepped away to return to his small coterie of officers at the stern of the ship.

As Jamison understood their plan, the British soldiers were set to disembark on one of the narrower sections of North Island, north of Auckland. There had been Maori attacks on a small English settlement in Matauri Bay, and the major seemed most anxious to exact revenge.

Jamison had been allowed great freedom to mingle with the soldiers—more than any American military officers had ever given him. He surmised it was due to his nationality. If he wrote a positive article, the officers would point to it with pride and insist on multiple copies. If it was negative, the same officers would claim he was only a foolish Yank and dismiss it out of hand.

A handful of the soldiers, striking in their red-and-black uniforms, lounged at the bow of the vessel. They appeared genuinely interested in Jamison's stories—especially his battle with the Indians back home. He retold it several times on ship, each time finding a most receptive audience.

As usual with soldiers, many tried to top Jamison's exploits with their own. Some told of nasty encounters with the Maoris on South Island.

"Blighters soon slit your throat as take their next breath," one soldier explained. "A band of them, maybe dozens, came on us at night. Nearly took some of the fellows' heads clean off."

"Or bashed in their brains with those clubs they all carry," another soldier added. "Devious sods, all of them. The more we put six feet under on this campaign, the better I sleep."

But the Maoris were not the only ones tied with brutality. Some of the soldiers took great pride in describing how they slaughtered some of the warriors, and even the women and children.

Jamison had been glad to disembark when the ship came to a small harbor a day's sail north of Auckland. He boarded another ship—a commercial vessel flying the British flag—and sailed on farther up the coast. The regiment planned to march north along the shore, pushing the Maoris before them. The major wanted Jamison to be in position to describe the final battle in great detail—and be well out of the line of fire as he did so.

Therefore, the ship he was on would anchor just offshore, next to the expected field of battle. Jamison was given a fine-quality British telescope to more closely make observations, as well as a map of the regiment's proposed march.

"We'll be marching there in a fortnight, Mr. Pike. You have plenty of paper and pencil ready, for you'll see a fine battle. You'll see how an army takes care of these ignorant savages."

With that he placed his feathered hat on his head and set off for the shore, then stopped. "And perhaps," he added, "you might offer some notes to your own soldiers. I understand they have their own problems controlling the savages in America, too."

The vessel, designed and built to ply the calmer waters around the island, slid quietly into the protected harbor of Bland Bay. The air was cool this day, the summer and winter of this strange land reversed from what Jamison had always known. Yet even in the cool air, the jungle and greenery were most intense. From the deck, even with the telescope, he could only make out a thin strip of sand and brush. Then it became a wall of solid green.

Jamison marveled at the diversity of the New Zealand landscape. On South Island, there were open plains between mountains and glaciers; here on the northernmost part of North Island, it was a jungle, with the thickness of green standing hard by the edge of the ocean. All the land beyond was bathed in green, dark shadows, and the world grew mystical and dangerous.

Jamison spent a half day on the shore as they waited and managed to get only a dozen yards into the brush before he lost all sense of direction, so deep were the shadows and tight the vines and vegetation.

How will the British fight in such a thicket? he wondered. *Did the major truly know this terrain before he set out?*

"Captain Longstreth," Jamison asked, "is this bay well known to the British commanders? It seems terribly dense for a battle."

The deeply tanned captain held back a brittle laugh. "The major picked this off the map because it looked like a gentle piece of land. I tried to tell him there isn't going to be any fields of Waterloo out there. He waved me off. I'm just a sailor. He said I know nothing about marching and fighting savages."

Jamison brought his telescope up to his eye again and scanned the shoreline. He saw nothing. "They should be here today, shouldn't they? He said a fortnight, right?"

The captain nodded. "If they didn't get butchered on the way, that is. But that isn't like the Maori. A pence to a pound they're all out there in the jungle, waiting till them poor sods get here–tired and hungry and all. That's when they'll come on them. At night. That's the way them savages do it."

Jamison brought the telescope down. "Have you ever seen a Maori attack?"

The captain spit, then said softly, "I haven't. And I don't want to. But I heard enough about them to last me for a while. Savage beasts, they tell me."

Jamison scrutinized the angle of the sun. "An hour or two till nightfall."

"Yep, Mr. Pike, and I don't have an easy feeling about any of this."

And with those few words the captain turned away and scuttled down the steps to his cabin.

"You be writin' 'bout all this, Mr. Pike? For a newspaper and all?"
one of the sailors said as he tied off a rope near where Jamison stood.
"That's what I heard tell from the other fellows."

"I am."

Bander Sowiss had an easy smile and a loose-limbed manner.

"I'm called Bander," he had said when they first met. "And I don't
know what it means. I never asked me ma about it."

"I take it everyone asks," Jamison replied. "I would have."

Bander had laughed. "I'm used to it. I sort of like it, if the truth be
told. Makes it a simple matter to meet folk."

Now he stood before Jamison, watching the sea spray glisten in
the sun. "You meet a lot of folk in your business, don't you, Mr. Pike?
Interviewin' and askin' questions and all?"

"I do."

"Must be grand, travelin' all over and seeing the world."

Jamison leaned against the rail. "Isn't that what you do, Bander?"

The sailor laughed, nearly doubling over. "Land sakes, no. Once
I got to this place, I swore I would never cross an ocean again.
And I ain't. Too far from land. So I do this and we hardly ever sail
no place where I can't lay my eyes on a mountain or shoreline."

"You're the second sailor I met who doesn't like the sea."

Bander nodded. "There's a lot of us out here. It be a job to earn
a pound or two. That's all. Do the job and get the pay and that's the
lot of it."

From somewhere far inland there came an unearthly scream—as
if an animal were being torn in two by a predator. Jamison jumped,
then calmed himself and pointed out toward the darkening jungle.
"Bander, are you afraid? Of the Maoris? Captain seems to think the
jungle is filled with them—just out of eyesight."

"Afraid? I suspect I am some. But . . . then . . . no, I'm not."

"You're not?"

"No. I used to be afraid all the time. But then I found the way."

"The way?"

Bander stepped closer to Jamison. "The way, Mr. Pike. With

God. I heard this fellow—just before I left England—Spurgeon, his name was."

Jamison blinked in surprise. It was the same preacher who so touched his old friend Benjamin.

"I'm not even sure what it was that he said, except I knew I was a sinner bound for hell unless I gave in to God. And I did. And since then . . . well, there have been times I've had a fright or two, but I ain't never been afraid—really afraid."

Jamison slipped the telescope into the leather pouch at his belt. "Bander, how did that happen? I mean . . . why decide for something that you can't see or hold? I've had people tell me about God. Lots of people. But none of it makes sense to me. I look at my father—he is a pastor—but he is a hard man with a cold heart. God didn't make any difference in his life for the good. I bet good people will be good regardless of God. And mean folk will be mean—even if they claim that God is with them."

Jamison had no idea why he was going on about such matters, but once his tongue was loosed, he found it impossible to rein it in. "I don't understand why a strong fellow like yourself gives up and thinks that God is interested in your life," he continued, eyeing Bander. "It doesn't make sense, that's all."

The sailor's expression was kind, not upset, and almost bemused.

"I'm sorry, Bander. I don't even know you and I have called your faith ridiculous. I'm sorry." Jamison held his head down, as if ashamed, and turned to go.

"Wait, Mr. Pike. I ain't takin' any offense. God is a bigger God than to be offended by a fellow like you. And if he ain't offended, then I ain't either. Sit down, Mr. Pike. I'm done with me chores for now. It's gettin' dark, and I bet them Maoris are all in bed by now, tucked in their palm-leaf mattresses and all."

Reluctantly, Jamison turned back and settled against the railing.

"I ain't the one to be explainin' any of this," Bander began. "I ain't had much schoolin'. I ain't heard that much preachin'. But I know that me heart be changed."

Jamison found it hard to look in his eyes.

"Mr. Pike, you can say you don't believe in anything. But by sayin' you don't believe in God, that is sayin' you believe more in yourself. And I don't know you much, but I would say you ain't always happy with your own heart. If you ain't happy with God and you ain't happy with yourself, then where are you, Mr. Pike? I say your chances are better with God than yourself."

Jamison did not look up. "Perhaps, Bander. Perhaps."

"And don't go lookin' at other fellows to see God. Don't look at me to see him 'cause I ain't that good of a mirror. You want God? You look for God in the Bible. That's where he is. And then in your heart. Sorry about your father, but maybe he done the best he could. Maybe his father was a mean fellow, too, and that be all he knows."

The image of his grandfather's dour portrait loomed in Jamison's mind. There was not even the hint of a smile on that face.

"It don't make sense what God done for us. Givin' up his Son to die and all that. I don't think I could do that. But God did. And all there is for us is to take the gift. Simple, if you ask me. You say no— and then there is only hell that waits for you. You say yes, and all of heaven is open. A foolish man be the one who says 'no thank you' and picks hell instead of heaven."

Jamison took a deep breath. From the calm harbor came a soft splash and a rippled sound, as if a fish had cleared the water leaping into the cold surprise of air.

"A sacrifice, Mr. Pike. A strong, smart man like you don't want to be acceptin' free gifts, I bet. But there it is. You're goin' to live forever. Choice is—where do you want to be forever? Like I said, a foolish man goes about ignorin' the gift."

A louder splash came from the water just near the ship. Jamison had his back to the waters and Bander leaned against the deckhouse. The moon was at his shoulder, a small wedge of gray in a night darker than Jamison had ever seen before.

He looked up and, in the corner of his vision, saw the tiny white smudge of a shooting star. He turned to see if Bander had noticed it—and in that one small instant he knew that something had gone horribly wrong.

Bander leapt to his feet, shoving past Jamison, shoving him back to the deck, back toward the deckhouse. From the bow of the ship came a scream–an English scream, Jamison was sure. His shoulder bounced to the wooden deck, and as he fell, he turned. On the bow, silhouetted against the moon, were the figures of three men swinging clubs in an arc of deadly evil. There was the thudding sound of flesh stopping that trajectory. Then another scream and a shot, and from the stern of the ship came a booming roar. A rifle discharged and the smoke and flash illuminated the entire deck.

Maori warriors leapt about, screaming and clubbing. Another shot sounded, then another.

A Maori scream this time and a splash into the waters below.

Jamison turned on his side and watched in mute horror as Bander leapt in between a Maori and Jamison's prone figure. Bander held his arm up as faint protection, and it stopped the Maori club with a crunching rending of flesh. Jamison could see only the ball of the club rise and plummet again, this time Bander taking the full force. Jamison did not see the injury, yet Bander stayed upright.

"Get below, Mr. Pike!" he screamed.

A third and fourth blow brought him to his knees.

A volley of shots rang out as sailors from below swarmed out on the deck. The Maori over Bander spun backward, nearly flying in an arc to the waiting sea below. A third and fourth volley boomed out, like thunder from a cloud only inches from a man's head.

And then, as quickly as it had all begun, silence returned–save the moans of the injured and the scream of birds awakened by the noise.

The captain called out for torches and the ship's doctor.

Jamison crawled to Bander, crumpled on the deck beside him. His hands and face were sticky with blood. Jamison turned him over. There was a jagged whiteness at his temple. His lips were moving slowly.

"Bander," Jamison pleaded, "why did you do that? Why did you protect me?"

Bander's lips moved and Jamison leaned close. "I was ready to die, Mr. Pike." He coughed. "And you were not."

Jamison lifted the sailor's head and called out for help, for the ship's doctor.

"Don't," Bander whispered, then coughed again. He shut his eyes, wincing. "Don't look to men, Mr. Pike. Take the gift. Choose . . ."

And then Bander slumped, loose and lifeless in Jamison's arms.

And from the stern of the vessel came a cry, "Don't drop the sails! The heathens sliced off our rudder!"

Jamison stared into the darkness and wondered where God might be.

And he wondered if God might hear one more desperate prayer.

CHAPTER TWENTY

New Zealand
July 1858

Them heathen will wait till darkness is complete with the downing of the moon. That's when they'll try and finish us off," Captain Longstreth shouted. Jamison was sure he had tried to make his voice harsh and firm, but there was a trilling in it that indicated to all listeners that he was near to panic.

"They be calling on their spirits and magic to help them. Well, fellows, it won't be of any help. We'll defeat them now, won't we, men?"

If they heard his question, they chose not to respond.

The ship was in desperate waters. The rudder was useless–the thick leather cords had been sliced through and the iron gears jammed with metal spearheads. She could be repaired, but they needed daylight or torches to assess the damage. Torches would bring Maori arrows like deadly rain. If the crew lowered the sails, the winds would take them directly into shore where they would be instantly overrun.

Perhaps two hours remained until the moon dropped behind the hills to the west.

From the shores came an eerie chanting. *Like the sound of demons,* Jamison thought, *calling up their spirits for the battle.* Captain

Longstreth distributed the few weapons on board. A civilian ship carried few armaments—and on this ship there was no cannon, only hand weapons. There was a scattering of rifles and pistols and a handful of bayonets. Those who did not have a true weapon grabbed wooden rope stays or hammers or sledges.

Jamison hurried to his cabin and took out a sheet of oilskin paper. He remained below deck, lit, then hid his candle from any porthole or opening, and began to write hurriedly.

My Dearest Hannah,

I have but a few minutes to write this. Our ship is trapped, and there are natives gathering at the shore. The captain says they will attack at nightfall—when the spirits of victory are most intense.

There is magic in the world, Hannah. There is. But I now believe with all my heart that God is greater.

I have held to my promise.

And now I will promise you once again. I will return to you. I will fight through all the demons of hell to once again hold you in my arms. I will continue to draw breath until my eyes once again gaze on your most lovely countenance. Without you I am as empty as the dark.

Promise me, Hannah, that you will wait for me. Promise me that your arms will be open for me when I return.

And until I do, listen for my voice on the wind. With every breeze you will hear the trees' branches and leaves calling your name and declaring my love to you. My heart will be carried by the clouds. Look up to the sky, and I will be there, Hannah.

Promise me you will wait.

Promise me your heart, my sweetest Hannah—my love, my life.

Always,

Jamison

When he had completed those few lines, he sealed the letter carefully in a tight leather pouch and climbed the ladder to the top deck. The sailors had stacked bags and crates and barrels about the deck, making a small fort. But there were not that many sailors and more gaps than defenders.

Jamison hurried over to the captain. "Captain Longstreth," he said quietly, "I have a letter here. I want you to take it. And take it to the address on the envelope."

The captain narrowed his eyes. "What? There are savages out there waiting for our blood. I have no time for such trivialities."

Jamison shook his head. "No. This is no trivial matter. And you'll escape all of this."

The captain grabbed Jamison by the shoulder roughly and pulled him close. "You're talking like a madman. What do you mean? You have a vision or something?"

Jamison whispered his reply. "Something like that. I looked at you just now and somehow know you will be back in California safely before this year is over. I don't know how I know that—but I think . . . I think . . . that God told me."

The captain backed away a step and stared into Jamison's earnest eyes. "Give me the envelope," he said gruffly. "And don't say a word of this to any man on ship. We'll be getting out of this. We will. Them heathens . . . well . . . we can fight them off."

Jamison handed him the envelope. "We won't. And promise me you will get this to California."

The captain squinted at the address. "I can't read all that well, Mr. Pike."

"Monterey, California," Jamison instructed. "Just south of San Francisco."

He nodded. "Them places I heard of. And I've been in San Francisco, I believe . . . once, a long time past."

"But you must promise me." Jamison's words were tight and heartfelt, demanding a truthful answer.

"I promise you, Mr. Pike." He was about to step away when he turned back to Jamison and whispered, "Your vision . . . that voice . . . it truly says I survive?"

Jamison smiled and placed his hand on the captain's shoulder. "You will survive, Captain. I assure you of that."

And that was when the first scream began.

As the darkness blanketed the sea, the Maoris had evidently slipped into their canoes. Like a silent shudder, they came up alongside the vessel. It was but a jump to the rail and, in a heartbeat, many had cleared the first obstacles.

"Light the torches!" the captain screamed, and flints were struck in unison. Numerous flames flickered on. In the time it took to spin about, half of the men carrying the torches lay bleeding or dead on the decks. Those who had weapons fired, often blindly into the dark. Flashes tore through the night like lightning and thunder, tightly closed in a fist.

Men screamed and fought at the demons in the dark. The sound of whooshing clubs, like tearing velvet, seared the silence between the screams.

A torch fell to the stern and puddled into a coil of greasy rope. Like an explosion, the rope took fire and the echoes of that flame lighted the scene. Licks of fire shot up the rear mast and soon the snugged canvas was on fire as well.

Men screamed and dodged the Maori clubs, only to fall into a sea of flaming canvas. Jamison, holding a long pike in his hands, fended off one attacker. Another sailor came from behind and thrust a bayonet through the man's back. Jamison saw the sharp tip protruding from the native's stomach and then the shocked and pained look in the dying man's eyes.

Another scream and the center canvas took to flames. Men abandoned their defense and leapt into the water. Maoris in canoes paddled about, watching and waiting and quickly dispatching anyone who attempted to swim to shore.

The deckhouse, now wrapped in flames, lit the shoreline as well. Jamison turned and saw a hundred men, maybe more, dancing and shouting and waving their clubs.

It is finished, he thought as he held his pike ready to deflect another blow.

A small explosion rocked the ship. A barrel of oil must have taken to the flames. And then another, much larger, explosion nearly tore the deckhouse asunder. Jamison was tossed about; he felt himself tumbling and tumbling into blackness.

The cold waters grabbed at him as he splashed down into the sea. He gulped at air and ducked under the water, attempting to swim as far from the battle and the marauding canoes as possible. He turned faceup in the water, opening his eyes to the salt, trying to see shapes or figures before he surfaced. He had to find air. He popped out of the water, gulped in deeply, and pivoted to see the ship nearly consumed in flames. He took one more breath, dove under the water, and swam until his lungs were near to bursting.

Dear God . . . I have never prayed to you before . . . but, please . . . help me. Help me. Help me.

And with that, all was darkness.

For a long moment Jamison imagined himself as drowned and lying at the bottom of the sea. Then his eyes began to throb, swollen shut and pained. His right side hurt as if he had taken a blow from a club. His arms ached, as did his shoulders.

If I were dead, would I be in this much pain?

He raised his head. There was the faint sound of water lapping about his legs. He forced one eye open.

The dawn was perhaps an hour distant, and all was a golden gray. He pushed up on his arms and winced. He lay on the shore–some shore–alone and alive.

Turning, he cried out in pain and clutched at his side.

Perhaps a rib is broken. Hannah should be here to help.

Then it all came rushing back in a tidal wave–the attack, the desperate battle, the screams, the letter, and his black swim through the night.

He sat on the shore and squinted. The first rays of sun yielded little. He knew he was not on the beach where the Maoris had danced in the darkness. He would not have been left alive if he were. And the sun was rising over his back. He stood and squinted into the west.

I must have caught a current, he thought. *And I swam or floated to one of the islets that lay to the east of us as we sailed north along the coast. The captain called these the . . . the Bay of Islands, I think. What did he say about them? . . . That they were small, scattered, and deserted.*

He looked down at himself.

His clothes were tattered, his boots long at the bottom of the sea. His injuries, while very painful, did not seem life threatening. He saw no open wounds. He had no food, no water, and no matches. He had nothing in his pockets.

But he was alive.

He stepped onto dry sand and sank to his knees.

Thank you, God, for your protection. Take those who were not as fortunate as I have been into your arms. Be with Hannah.

He fought back a sob.

And somehow–help me return to her side.

He remained in the sand for several minutes, then stood, brushing the sand from his knees as if he were attending a party and had kneeled to speak to a child. He took a deep breath. "I'm alive. And I am on my way home."

It was the second time another person had sacrificed his life for Jamison's.

Lord, have I been so blind that you have had to take two of your own to make me see? Could not there have been a less costly way?

The pieces had been there all along. But it was not until that fateful night that they had finally fallen into place–because of Bander's honest words. Jamison knew the stories. He had heard the sermons. He had read the Scriptures. But he had never once considered admitting his weakness in order to take God's perfect gift.

Two men–two sacrificial deaths–and finally his eyes had been opened. Before he'd gone belowdecks to write the letter to Hannah, he had whispered to the dark sky and heaven above, "Lord, I am so sorry that I did not see. I am so sorry that others had to die for my life. Accept me now, Lord, an abject sinner; accept me as your child. I accept the gift. Take my life, Lord. Take it now."

And his faint sobs had hung on the dark breeze.

Now, on this unidentified shore, Jamison knew he was lost and yet found.

He was in peril, yet he was safe.

He was now a child of God, and that made all the difference.

He sat on the curved trunk of an upturned palm, his arms wrapped about himself for warmth, waiting for the sun to rise. It finally showed its face, ever so slowly. He waited until the rays warmed him some. Then he rose, stretched, and determined to take stock of the situation, precarious as it might be.

He walked south for nearly an hour, until the island began to turn. As he trudged through the sand, he could see the mainland—or at least what he thought was the mainland—well off to the west. It was beyond his capabilities of swimming, to be sure—beyond any man's strength, he imagined. And if a current had brought him out to this speck of land, it would also prevent him from paddling back to shore. He stopped at the southern tip of the island, then turned about and headed back. He did not imagine that anyone would place a settlement on the eastern edge of the land—especially if all the current English settlements and towns lay to the east. *Something about facing your friends,* Jamison thought. He walked north and came to the spot where he had washed ashore. There was nothing remarkable about the spot—a few downed palms, a cupping of shoreline curving inland a bit, like a smallish harbor.

He walked farther north.

When the sun began to grow more intense, he veered closer to the tree line. Not certain what he was intending to find, he knew he must search. As the island began to turn again, there was a sight that gladdened his heart. Running to the sea, through a channel in the sand no bigger than a man's outstretched hand, was a narrow stream. He hurried to it, found a quiet pool, and lay down and drank deeply.

At least he would not die of thirst.

Ten minutes later, as he neared the island's most northern point, he discovered one more item that truly gladdened his heart. It was a barrel in the surf, being nudged toward the shore. He ran to it. It was empty, yet more or less watertight.

"I have found my way home," he said softly to himself. And then, only a heartbeat later, he yelled into the silence, "Thank you, Lord, for your provision!"

He pulled the barrel well up to shore, then continued his reconnaissance. From his estimation, he could have circled the entire island in less than a half day. It rose only slightly, from what he could determine, and to the north lay a series of sharp precipices and jagged shoreline.

He dragged the barrel back toward the stream.

"If I wait longer, I will simply grow weaker," he said, again to himself. Finding some flexible green vines the diameter of a man's thumb, he used them to lash two lengths of driftwood to the barrel. To that, he lashed a crosspiece, forming a primitive outrigger canoe.

"It's not what the natives in Maui used, but it will have to do," he said aloud.

He knew the barrel would provide flotation, but if it turned and spun in the water, he would waste time and energy holding on. He found a flat piece of driftwood that was as close to a paddle as he might hope for. He ladled freshwater into the barrel with a dense, scoop-shaped leaf, filling it a quarter full.

"Water's more important than food," he said to himself.

By the time he finished his rudimentary preparations it was only hours from dusk.

"Setting out now would be the act of a foolish man," he said quietly. Instead he ventured only a short distance into the brush and pulled back with him an armful of jungle grasses and fresh palm fronds. With the barrel, he fashioned a simple lean-to, using the fronds as a roof and the grass as a bed on the sand.

And as he watched the sun draw to the west and the darkness fill the sky, he imagined holding Hannah in his arms again. It was her face that he dreamed of that night.

As dawn broke, he waded into the surf. "The water is not too chilled."

The barrel was cumbersome to drag, with its driftwood arms in place, and the waves conspired to push him back toward the shore. With every kick of his legs, he felt again the ache in his side and the soreness in his shoulders.

After nearly an hour of swimming and paddling, he was only several hundred yards from shore. It was not a great distance, and the current still pushed against his legs. Even with all his concerted efforts, he had made little progress toward the far shore, perhaps two miles distant.

As the day progressed and the sun climbed directly overhead, Jamison grew more and more weary. Removing the small opening from the top of the barrel, he extracted a few handfuls of water and sat, bobbing in the water, breathing hard.

"Perhaps if I paddle parallel to the shore . . . maybe farther south the current will be lessened."

He looked about. If he did that, there would be no island to drift back to. To the south was simply open water. If the current traveled strong, he might simply be washed out to the Pacific.

"But if I stay here," he said, "I will die between land to the front and land to the back."

He turned the barrel and began to paddle south.

By midafternoon, he turned toward the mainland, feeling only the slightest of currents. By the edge of dusk, he was within a half mile of the other shore. He began to feel a great sense of victory—and a great sense of God's protection as well.

He could no longer see the sun as he at last pushed into the first waves of the mainland's shore, paddling harder than he had paddled all day. And as the darkness began to slip in from the east, he rode the barrel in and rejoiced as the surf and shore snapped the arms of the outrigger off like twigs. He waded and swam the last few yards, collapsing in the hissing surf.

The pain in his arm grew more intense, and now that he was safe, his body appeared to give itself permission to fully articulate that pain.

A Day Later

"But am I safer here than on that deserted island?" Jamison asked himself when he awakened the following morning. "The Maoris are here—but I would be a dead man had I remained there."

During the voyage from Auckland, the ship had passed a handful of small settlements and farms along their route. Jamison had not paid close attention and was not certain how far south they might be, or if there were any obstacles along the route. He recalled seeing a small farm on the coast—perhaps half the distance from Auckland to Bland Bay.

But he had no alternative. So on the morrow he began to walk along the shore, heading south.

And God must have been offering his continued protection, for at the end of the following day, Jamison—dirty, exhausted, and nearing the end of his strength—wandered onto the small farm owned by one Alton Greffson, most recently of Portsmouth, England.

To say the man was shocked to see Jamison march up from the shore would be a most obvious understatement.

When Jamison stumbled onto the Greffson farm that day, he simply passed out a hundred steps from their front door. It was to become his home until he recovered.

He insisted, as Greffson and his wife carried him inside, that he was fine. Yet it was soon obvious he was not. The bruise on his side was purpling, thick and angry, and Mrs. Greffson, somewhat knowledgeable in matters such as these, was most afraid that his organs might have been damaged. Jamison coughed up blood for the first week he was in her care, and despite his pleas to continue his journey, she would not allow him to rise from his sickbed.

In the attack he had suffered a large welt and deep cut on his back that soon turned hot and painful and filled with yellow pus. Mrs. Greffson attempted to cleanse the wound with brandy, causing Jamison to scream in pain. His arm, she thought, might also be broken, so sensitive was it to touch and movement.

News of the Maori attack had spread quickly among the settlers, of course, and in retaliation to the brutality of the natives, the British military governor sent a full battalion of well-trained British troops northward. The settlers gossiped that these soldiers simply slaughtered any Maori they happened to meet—man, woman, or child.

Late September 1858

"I'll have to be leaving soon," Jamison said as he sat on the Greffsons' porch overlooking the sea.

"Back to your Hannah?" Mrs. Greffson asked with a blush to her cheeks. "The way you have gone on about her, perhaps that is why your body healed faster."

"If wishes were reality, I would never have left her side," Jamison said. "And I will thank you for the rest of my days for the kindness you have shown me these long weeks."

"It is nothing that God has not asked us to do," she replied, then blushed again.

New Zealand
October 1858

He returned to Auckland, anxious to leave.

More than healing, he wanted to return home. There was a dearth of ships in Auckland Harbor this year, the locals told him. Whalers usually stopped there for the winter months, but whaling had been poor this year, and many ships had stayed in the Sandwich Islands instead.

He was forced to tarry in Auckland until December, when the first ship bound for the east appeared. He boarded the merchant ship flying a Portuguese flag and began to pray that the weather would be favorable and that the ship's captain would maintain his promised itinerary. Traveling on the vast Pacific could prove vexing no matter what direction, for the winds could often be most capricious, causing a long journey to grow into an epic voyage.

Jamison spent the hours writing and reading. He had found a Bible in a small shop in Auckland and began to read it in earnest. He spent hours in conversation—imagined, of course—with Hannah and Gage and Joshua, reliving their times at the Destiny Café in Cambridge.

He learned enough Portuguese to ask the navigator, on a daily basis, the ship's progress. The thin red line the man drew upon the sea charts grew at an absurdly slow pace. But finally he unrolled the one chart Jamison had been praying to see for months—the chart that included the image of the western shores of America.

Monterey, California
June 1859

It was a hot day in June when the California coast actually appeared in the captain's telescope. Jamison grew so excited and anxious that he paced the deck for hours and hours, unable to sit still for even a moment.

He had pleaded with the captain for days prior to make Monterey their first port of call. The captain had no reason to do so but took pity on Jamison's heartfelt entreaties.

The Monterey harbor had never looked so inviting and welcoming as it did that day. Jamison did not wait on ship for his few possessions to be unloaded. He jumped to the pier even before the ship was fully tethered to the iron rings on the pylons.

He ran inland, knowing only where Gage's home was located.

The town had grown much since he last saw it. More buildings shouldered along the bay and more homes dotted the hillsides that surrounded the gentle harbor. He ran up the street—Gage's massive home was nearly impossible to miss. He threw open the gate and ran to the entrance, calling out for Gage, knocking on the door, calling out his old friend's name again.

The door opened slowly and a woman's face appeared. It was Rosala, Gage's Mexican housekeeper. From behind her came a loud male voice saying, "Who is it, Rosala?"

The woman did not answer but opened the door wider. Gage was bathed in the cool shadows of the interior, yet his eyes found the eyes of his visitor.

There was a long silence brought on by the shock to both men. Gage had grayed, and the lines in his face were more drawn than before.

"Jamison?" he managed to croak out. "Is it truly you?"

"Gage!" Jamison cried, near to tears. "I am home."

And with that the two men ran to each other and embraced in a fierce hug.

Gage was near tears as well. "We thought you perished for certain. Captain Longstreth held out little hope for your survival."

"God's grace! He made it, did he? And I survived as well. God offered protection and blessings."

With those few words, Jamison conveyed to Gage that his life had indeed changed.

When Gage smiled, a new light in his eyes, Jamison knew that his friend had understood the briefest of explanation.

Jamison stepped back and wiped his cheek with his palm. "Gage, old friend, where is Hannah? I have to see her. Where is she? Where is her home?"

A look of surprise would not describe Gage's face. It was surprise and sadness and great pain.

"What? Gage? What happened? Where is Hannah?" Jamison cried.

Gage moved his lips but made no sound.

"What? Tell me!"

"Jamison," Gage said, his voice no louder than a prayer, "she is not here."

"What?"

"She's gone."

CHAPTER TWENTY-ONE

Monterey, California
June 1859

Jamison would have fallen to the ground had Gage not been at his side to provide support.

"Rosala, send for Dr. Neuman! Help me get Jamison into the drawing room. Then get me some brandy!"

They shuffled and dragged the unconscious Jamison to the large couch in the drawing room. Gage, usually unflappable, paced about, almost at a run, and close to the edge of frantic. Rosala brought a decanter of the finest brandy and a damp cloth for Jamison's head. She knelt by him and held his hand, offering whispered words of comfort and prayer.

Dr. Neuman rushed in, his white coat nearly off his shoulders. He bent to Jamison's chest and listened, holding up his hand, bidding Gage to stop his muttering and pacing. The doctor picked up Jamison's wrist, placed his thumb on it, and counted silently to himself as he checked his watch. He felt Jamison's forehead. Then he turned to Gage with a somber glare. "What happened?"

Gage, frightened at the doctor's seriousness, quickly explained.

"When you said Hannah was gone–that's when he fell?" Dr. Neuman asked.

Gage and Rosala nodded.

"I don't think he was a well man when he came here. There is a rattle in his lungs–an almost liquid sound. Yet I don't sense a fever, and his heart and pulse appear strong. Where was he?"

Gage gestured toward the front of the house. "Out there. In the entry hall."

The doctor shook his head. "No. No. Where did he come from?"

Gage shrugged. "New Zealand, I surmise. That was the last we heard of him–that he was attacked by savages there, and no one knew if he was alive or if he perished."

The doctor sat back. "So this is the fellow? The fellow that Dr. Keyes . . . I mean . . . you know."

"Yes," Gage answered. "This is that man."

"Well, good heavens, then. Rosala–could you send someone to get a team of orderlies down here at once? With a stretcher."

She nodded and hurried from the room.

Gage took the doctor by the arm and pulled him far to one side. "Will he live?" he asked softly.

The doctor did not respond immediately. "I don't like the sound of his breathing. It could be pneumonia. Or consumption. Either way–he is not well. Not in the least."

Three orderlies, in white coats of varying degrees of cleanliness, rushed into Gage's drawing room, carrying a canvas stretcher.

As the doctor readied to follow them, Gage grabbed his arm one last time. "You have to save him. Hannah would kill me if I let anything happen to him."

Dr. Neuman did not smile, offering no silent encouragement. "I will do my best. But I make no promises."

Three days passed until Gage saw his old friend again. Dr. Neuman had been adamant that Jamison was not to be disturbed under any conditions. He was comforted with moderate doses of morphine and brought into the bright sunlight to allow the heat to penetrate his bones.

Gage could stand it no longer. After Sunday church services, he refused to allow anyone to deter him and barged into his friend's hospital room.

Jamison lay in the bed, partially inclined. His skin had a gray pallor, and a thin sheen of sweat marked his forehead. His lungs labored to catch the air.

"Jamison?" Gage whispered. "It's Gage. How are you?" he asked as he pulled up a stool to the side of the bed.

Jamison's eyes fluttered like a moth in the rain. He opened them, blinked again, then turned toward the voice. He recognized his old friend immediately. "Gage. I'm fine. How are you?"

Gage reached out and took Jamison's hand. He resisted the urge to pull it back because of the weakness of his grip. "Worried. You appear after all this time, only to disappear again."

Jamison coughed. It sounded like it bubbled up from a great depth. "I like a grand entrance. Theatrical." His voice was but a rasp.

"Too theatrical, my friend. Much too theatrical. You had Rosala worried to death."

The two men studied each other, as if trying to read the emotions behind each other's eyes.

"Hannah went back to Philadelphia," Gage said.

Jamison tried to offer a wan smile. "I know," he whispered. "I grabbed hold of the doctor in my first lucid moment. I made him tell me. I told him I would pass from this world if he didn't, and Hannah would blame him for it all."

Gage offered a great sigh of relief. "Oh, that's good. I thought all this time you thought she was dead."

Jamison coughed again. "I did. But she's not, is she?"

"No."

Jamison attempted to squeeze his friend's hand. "How is she?"

"Good," Gage said quickly, but his tone didn't convince Jamison.

"Tell the truth," Jamison insisted. "I may be dying. You don't lie to a dying man."

Gage stiffened. "You're not dying. You're not. And I am not lying."

"Then don't lie about Hannah."

Gage looked away, out the window to the sea. "She was sad. Is 'brokenhearted' a medical description? When Captain Longstreth left, she was as melancholy as I have ever seen a person. The light was gone from her eyes."

"She left Monterey. Why?"

Gage placed his hands on his knees. He tightened his lips in concentration.

"It isn't that complex a question," Jamison said softly.

"No," Gage replied quickly. "It's not. But . . . it was not just one reason. There was a letter from her mother in February. Her father had had a stroke, she thought, and the family finances were in shambles and she didn't know where they might live. Hannah had saved some money over the years. And she wanted to do what she could to make things easier for her parents."

Jamison nodded and tried to raise his hand to his forehead. He struggled to adjust himself on the pillows. Then he attempted a deep breath and replied, "You said it was complex. That is not complex."

"No. It isn't." Gage hesitated. "I think she thought you were dead. I think she was grieving. I don't think she could stand watching the harbor every day for a ship to arrive—and probably with bad news. I don't think her heart could take it."

Jamison blinked and nodded. "I know how loving someone and not knowing if they are alive or dead is painful."

Gage stood. "And she went back east to see a doctor."

Jamison struggled to rise from the bed. "Is she sick? What is the matter?"

Gage sat back down and put his hand on Jamison's shoulder. "No. Nothing like that. For . . . well . . . for female problems. That's what Doctor Neuman hinted at."

Jamison nodded.

"You knew she lost a child when she was married to Robert?"

He nodded again.

"I think there might have been some complications. I don't understand it. She's a young woman, after all."

Jamison managed a weak laugh. "Gage, you flatter yourself. None of us are young anymore."

To Jamison's surprise, Gage leaned over and embraced him in a grand, gentle hug.

"She left a letter for you," Gage said quietly and reached into his breast pocket. "She gave it to me and said that if you arrived, you were to have it."

Jamison sat up as best he could. He took the slim envelope and tore it open. It was a single page. He spent a long time staring at the letter. When he was finished, he lowered the page and wiped a tear in his eye.

"She says to wait for her." Jamison cleared his throat. "And she says that she loves me."

A sob welled up from his heart, and he covered his eyes with his hand.

Meanwhile, Gage stared out the window at the gulls, who wheeled and danced in the wind, until his friend's sobbing had ceased.

It was a long wait.

A few weeks later, when Jamison had regained some of his strength, Gage brought him back to his home. Rosala was adamant that she alone could provide the care he needed. Dr. Neuman protested, but even he could not keep Jamison in the hospital any longer.

Rosala fed and tended to Jamison with more care and compassion than any nurse could have offered.

As July neared an end, Jamison was rustling about the room, packing his few belongings into an old grip of Gage's. Rosala twitted about, almost shouting in Spanish, removing the clothes from the bag as soon as Jamison laid them in.

Gage stepped into the middle of the fray. It took him a few minutes to sort matters out. "So you think you're leaving?" he said as he stood between Rosala and Jamison.

"I have to," Jamison said, his words coming out in a slight wheeze.

Rosala responded in a torrent of angry Spanish. Gage listened patiently, then spoke back to her in her native tongue.

"What did you say?" Jamison asked as he dared to fold a shirt and place it in the bag, all the while Rosala eyed him with great anxiety.

"She said she would rather die than have you leave us as sick as you are. I told her to look at your eyes. I know we can't stop you—even if I wanted to. I know the power of love."

Jamison offered a brave smile.

Rosala chattered on in Spanish.

"She says you must now make a vow. You must promise to return to us."

Rosala spoke again, gesturing in wide circles with her hands.

"She says that if you do not, she will come after you herself. It is not an idle threat."

Jamison nodded gravely, and in his best Spanish, told her he would be back.

"And that is a promise," Jamison said as Rosala's face suddenly turned from anxiety to tears, and she rushed to embrace her patient with a fierce, almost painful, embrace.

That night, as the moon rose over the silent harbor, Jamison pushed himself out of bed. The air was warm and scented with the fragrance of lilies, blooming like a carpet on the hillside between Gage's home and the sea.

Out the window Jamison could see the moonlight, as bright as any lantern, dancing on the waters. And from where he stood, he could see the house where Hannah had lived.

He stepped out Gage's door and walked the short distance to the adobe house. Once inside the tight stillness of her home, he walked about the rooms, so recently inhabited by Hannah, and gently touched the things that were hers. In her room stood a small wooden wardrobe. Inside were a dozen dresses hanging on hooks. At the very front was the dress Hannah had worn on the last day she and Jamison were together—a flowered print, loose and flowing to the floor.

He reached out and gently touched the sleeve. It was as if she still animated the fabric, for his finger felt the sparkle and energy of her body. He had to close his eyes to regain his composure. With great care he lifted the dress from its hook and drew it to himself and embraced it—as if he were embracing the real flesh and blood of Hannah. His heart began to beat fast.

He whispered aloud, "Dear Lord, hear the prayer of my heart. I have to be with her. Please help me, Lord. Please help heal me."

And then he slowly made his way back to Gage's and to his room. He laid the dress next to him with all the tenderness he could muster.

When the dawn broke, he blinked his eyes open to greet the day and realized that he had not slept as well or as soundly in months and months and months.

August 1859

"So then," Gage said as he draped his arm over Jamison's shoulder, "this is farewell?"

"Nonsense," Jamison replied. "I will be back soon. We will be back. Hannah and I."

Gage embraced him. "You have promised me, friend. And I will hold you to that."

"I will write you."

Gage nodded.

Jamison hoisted himself into the rear of the carriage, then leaned out the open window for one last handshake. He hoped the pain in his chest would not be visible to anyone.

"You must return," Gage said firmly. "You promised."

"I will, Gage. I will."

"Promise me you will bring her back!" Gage shouted as the carriage pulled away.

Jamison smiled and waved.

And as he looked past Gage, he saw Rosala standing off in the distance, handkerchief to her eyes, sobbing, waving good-bye.

CHAPTER TWENTY-TWO

Pittsburgh, Pennsylvania
November 1859

What was once an epic journey—traveling across America—had become nearly commonplace in little more than a decade. Rail lines began to spiderweb their way across the land, and where the rails were not, stagecoach companies vied for passengers.

Jamison was heartened that the journey was easier, for he had not fully recovered. His chest hurt and he had trouble catching his breath at times, but he was determined to get to Hannah—and quickly.

She had left only five months before his arrival in California. As soon as he was able, he had sent word to her of his intentions. Yet despite the advancements in travel, it was never assured that a letter would reach its final destination. Hannah had no address in Philadelphia, for Gage said she would be searching for a new apartment or home for her parents.

Jamison had written several letters—to Hannah's relatives and to Dr. Copley, hoping that one of them would find its way into her hands.

Once again, Jamison was on a river in winter, on a paddlewheel steaming north as fast as it could. The weather had snapped cold, and the captain was fearful that the river would ice over before they made it to Pittsburgh. Jamison thought the cold more cruel than before and remained in his cabin huddled beneath a pile of buffalo pelts.

As the boat passed along the southern edge of Ohio, welcome winds from the south filled the valley, bringing wet warmth with them. It became warm enough that Jamison stood out on the open decks and watched the landscape slip by.

Despite the urgency of his journey, Jamison knew there was one thing he must do before finding Hannah—and that was to make peace with his father and mother. He now understood forgiveness, after experiencing God's forgiveness himself. There would be a cloud over his future if he did not settle matters in Pittsburgh.

It was not a journey that he anticipated with great joy. He would have to forgive, with no real hope of being forgiven. Yet he knew he must attempt to reconcile.

Dawn lit the three valleys of Pittsburgh with gold and red. Jamison took his small bag and made his way down the gangway and along the docks. The city had changed much since he had been here last. Tall buildings now edged the river, shouldering each other out of the way. Where a dozen wagons and hackneys had once competed for the muddy roadway, now there must have been hundreds.

Jamison swallowed once, hailed a carriage, then sat back and tried to collect his thoughts. There had been no communication between him and his parents for years.

And of all the fears and dangers he had faced in his travels in the last years, this ride up to his parents' home was the most terrifying.

The carriage clattered away and left Jamison standing quietly in the street. The neighborhood had grown larger. Many new homes had been built. Lots that were once left to thistle and weed now bore neat houses and white picket fences.

Jamison stood outside his family's home and stared for a very long time. He saw no movement inside the house. He knew his father was still the pastor, for the sign on the church still listed his name on the bottom.

He wondered what it was like for other children, long grown and returning home. Did they knock? Did the parents wait inside the door on the appointed day to swing the door open, unbidden? Were there children who simply walked in and called out their entrance in a happy and jovial voice?

He was sure there were but just as certain he was not one of them.

Slowly he made his way to the front gate. It squealed as he opened it—just as he remembered. The ironwork needed painting; chips had peeled and flaked off.

He climbed the stairs and waited again at the front door.

It was not as if Jamison had not rehearsed this meeting a thousand times over the last few years. In one scenario, he imagined the door being swung open, his father standing there, speechless, then opening his arms for a long embrace, with tears and pats. And his mother standing in the darkened hall, weeping as her husband embraced her only son.

He realized, of course, that would most likely not occur.

Would his father forgive him? Was he totally and completely disowned? Would they even recognize him?

His lines, too, were well rehearsed, but he had no idea which play might be presented this day. As he stood there in the darkened alcove, he had decided to simply be himself.

He raised his hand ten times until he finally took hold of the tarnished brass door knocker and let it drop against the dark wood of the door. He listened and imagined the knock reverberating through the house—almost echoing as it fell to silence again.

He heard nothing. No footsteps, no calls. No clattering of anyone slipping toward the door.

Taking a deep breath, he raised the knocker again. He turned to the door and leaned, hoping both that he would hear something—and nothing.

His heart clumped as he heard footsteps—not spry, neither weak nor shuffling. He felt his eyes growing wider as the doorknob slowly turned. It seemed to take an eternity, but the door eventually came away from its lock.

Jamison fought the urge to run.

His father stood there, framed by the opening.

He was much older than Jamison had ever pictured in his mind. His hair was completely white now and thinned to a wisp. His face had become jowled and heavy, and the skin folded on itself in great wrinkles. A pair of delicate glasses perched on his nose and were pinioned against his ears. His clothes were no different than Jamison remembered—dark, somber, with a slight heady aroma of mothballs.

Neither man spoke for the longest minute.

Jamison could stand the tension no longer. "Father," he said simply, hoping that he betrayed little of the juggernaut of emotions he was experiencing.

The elder Pike nodded, almost as if he had expected Jamison to be at the door this very day and at this very time—as if he were not surprised in the least by his presence. "Son," he replied.

Again the silence exploded around Jamison. His ears began to ring and throb from the sheer absence of all sound. "I have come back," he said softly; then his selection of words, rehearsed or otherwise, simply ran out.

His father attempted a smile. On him, smiles usually appeared as a pained acknowledgment of some humorless truth. Such was the case this day as well.

"Please, come in," his father said just as softly.

The elder Pike turned and walked toward his study, implying with a small wave of his palm that Jamison should follow. He did so.

He watched as his father took a seat behind his old desk. He indicated that Jamison could have a seat on the small sofa by the window or the hard-backed chair by the desk.

Jamison chose the hard chair.

"It has been some time," his father said.

"Years."

"And you look well."

"And you," Jamison said, hoping he sounded truthful.

His father turned away. "I know I do not. Vanity, thy name is man, I have said, and now that I have become an old man, I know it to be more true than ever."

Jamison listened to the sound of the words, the tone, the pitch. It was one of the longer sentences, other than preaching, he had heard his father utter.

"We all grow old."

His father nodded. "Indeed."

Jamison scrutinized his hands. "How is Mother?"

His father paused before responding. "She is . . . she is well. She lives at a small residence down by the river. Hollyhock Place, they call it."

"What?" Jamison asked, not wanting to express too great a surprise. "Why?"

His father looked directly at him. "She no longer knows who I am. Or who she is. Or where she is. I found her wandering the streets too often. I could no longer do God's business while I worried over her condition. She is safer there."

Jamison took a deep breath. "How long?"

"A year or two after you finished Harvard. I saw small things at first. Then it was more and more."

"Does she know anyone? Is she happy?"

His father shrugged and did not answer.

It was perhaps the first time as an adult that Jamison saw his father not be certain and dogmatic about anything.

Jamison drew another deep breath. The house smelled as it had always smelled—of coal and chicory and paper and the odd breathing potion with a hint of mint and sassafras and the anise candies in the dish on the dining-room sideboard.

"You still preach?"

"I do. But I have a young fellow—your age, I guess—who steps in when I . . . when I have run out of ideas. He'll take over soon enough."

Jamison closed his eyes. *Run out of ideas?* "Father . . ."

The elder Pike sat and waited as if he was expecting something else.

"I did not write of this—but while in New Zealand . . . I found God . . . or he found me. Faith. For so many years I scorned what you believe. Now I do not. I have given myself to God."

His father actually smiled. And he nodded. And he smiled again. Then he rose from his chair and walked slowly around his desk. He looked at his son, then opened his arms. Surprised nearly to immobility, Jamison at last stood and spread his arms as well.

In that moment Jamison felt the weak and tired arms of his father about him, holding him as tight as his aged frame might allow. And as his heart seemed to stop in his chest, Jamison caught his breath and listened.

It was a sound he had never once thought he'd hear, never once imagined it in any of his possible scenarios. It was the sound of his father crying, great whispery sobs, welling up from the very bottom of his soul.

Jamison could scarce hear his father's words, mixed with tears.

"I have prayed every day of my life to hear those words. You will never know the depths of my anguish over a son whom I thought was lost. My dear God, you are faithful. You have given me what you have promised. Oh, God is so great. I can die a happy man now."

Jamison held on to his father and let his own tears fall.

It was not that his father was now the epitome of a sensitive, caring, loving parent—far from it. He was still judgmental and cantankerous and gnarled. But his hard spirit had been softened.

Perhaps it was his mother's absence. Perhaps it was maturity in the faith. Perhaps it was Jamison's rediscovered belief. But for whatever the reason, Jamison knew that his life would never be quite the same. He would no longer have a flinty childhood to blame for his actions. He had found forgiveness in Christ and was able to forgive his father for his shortcomings as well.

He did the best with what he had been given, Jamison reasoned, *and if God has allowed him to serve all these years—then I should allow him to be my father once again.*

Jamison spent two afternoons at Hollyhock Place. It was not his mother that he saw but a vacant shell, holding only the animation of what she once was. Her soul had departed, he was sure. There was never even a flicker of recognition in her eyes as Jamison entered the room. Even his name brought no awareness.

Jamison was even sadder that she could not be made aware of his journey back to God.

After only three days in Pittsburgh, Jamison stood at the front door holding his bag.

His father did not plead with him to stay. "If you love Hannah," he said, surprising Jamison, "then you must find her. God does give you what you need."

And with a hug the two men nodded to each other, and Jamison turned away and walked down the sidewalk to the waiting carriage. He waved once again as he closed the carriage door. He did not see his father's tears. But he knew the door stayed open until the carriage had rolled out of sight.

CHAPTER TWENTY-THREE

Pittsburgh, Pennsylvania
December 1859

When the carriage turned along the riverfront, Jamison leaned forward and tapped at the glass partition between himself and the driver. He had made arrangements to take the early morning eastbound train.

"Driver, I said the train station. The one on Sixteenth Street."

The carriage was blocks west of Sixteenth.

"Can't take you there, sir."

"What do you mean, you can't take me there?"

The driver, an elderly man with large gaps in his teeth, turned toward Jamison. "Tore it down two years ago. Built a new one over on Liberty. That's where we're going."

"They tore it down? Why?"

The driver faced forward again and shrugged. "Old one was old, I guess. The new one is a sight bigger, and there's even a restaurant inside."

Jamison craned his neck as the carriage turned the corner onto Liberty. The new station was three times as big, Jamison thought, and faced with some manner of polished white stone. Steam from the trains filtered into the chilled air, masking the building in wisps and vapors, almost making it disappear in the dawn.

Jamison made his way through the cavernous main hall. Shouts and laughter and conversations and calls echoed about. His footsteps sounded harsh on the polished marble floor. He checked the large board over the bank of ticket counters.

There were more than two dozen trains listed with dozens of destinations and times.

Why, a man could get to anywhere from here!

He was headed for Philadelphia. He trusted that once there, he would be able to find Hannah. That is, unless she had taken her parents to New Jersey or some other location. Still, someone in town would have to know her whereabouts.

The large clock read half past eight. Scanning down, he located his destination. The eastbound train would not be leaving for another forty-five minutes. He and his father had eaten breakfast together before he left, but he decided to buy a newspaper and order a cup of coffee as he waited. His father, ever the frugal pastor, made coffee weaker than tea.

The restaurant occupied a corner of the great hall, its tables and chairs spilling out into the open space in a great circle. Waiters scurried about and called out orders into a small window on the east wall.

Jamison sat at a table at the edge of the circle. He ordered a sweet roll as well, thinking that coffee might be too slight of an order. He thought he could take it with him if he chose not to eat it.

He folded the newspaper in fourths and smoothed the creases. His hand came away with a great smudge of newsprint, and he wiped it on the napkin at the table.

All his actions betrayed his inner turmoil. He was on the journey of a lifetime and thus repressed his nervousness and anxiety as best he could. It was as if a coiled spring had been wound tighter and tighter—just south of his heart.

He glanced at the clock every few minutes. Now that he wanted the time to hurry, it seemed as if it slowed to a glacial pace.

From the corner of his eye he watched a young man enter the station from the train platform. From the opposite end of the hall, a young woman shouted out a name. She waved her gloved hand and called out again. The young man dropped his satchel and ran toward her, embraced her in a great hug, and twirled her about in a circle. Jamison could not hear their words, but her face beamed with laughter and joy.

The young man let her down yet did not relinquish his grip on her.

Jamison tried to smile and returned to his paper.

A minute later a red ball bounced along the floor, coming from somewhere behind him. With a deft move, he bent over, caught the ball on a bounce, and sat back up, all without spilling a drop of coffee.

He searched about for the owner of the child's toy.

A young girl in a deep blue overcoat came running toward him. "You caught it. You caught it. Thank you," she said as she slid over the slick floor.

Jamison smiled and presented the ball to her. He saw her mother and offered a slight wave of acknowledgment. Pushing an infant's carriage, with another smaller child in tow, she waved back.

"You should be careful with your ball," he said as the little girl bounced it up and down.

"Oh, I am," she replied. "It wanted to know how high it could bounce and I was letting it go."

Jamison smiled. "What's your name?" he asked, seeing that the girl's mother was fussing with her other child. At least he could keep the young girl from wandering off by conversing with her.

"Emily Ann Wilson," she said as if he should have known it.

"Where are you going, Emily Ann Wilson?"

She turned to him and beamed. "To my daddy's new house. He has been gone since Abraham was borned. And now we're going to live with him."

"That's wonderful, Emily Ann. Where does he live?"

"In a house, of course."

Jamison realized that a child her age might not know the name of the city. "I bet you're glad to be going to live with your daddy."

"I am. But we knew we would. Mama promised."

Jamison leaned closer. "She did?"

Emily Ann rocked back and forth, holding her ball in her folded arms. "Yes. She made us pray every night. She promised that God would give us what we needed to be a family. And he did. Just like she promised."

Emily Ann's mother and younger siblings rolled up next to Jamison. "Thank you so much for amusing her," the mother said. "We're all in such a state."

"It was my pleasure. I hope you have a safe trip to your husband."

Emily Ann's mother stopped. She brightened. "She told you?"

Jamison nodded.

"It's a miracle. We thought he was dead. We hadn't heard anything in months and months. Then a letter saying he found work and a house with a picket fence and a school nearby."

She watched as Emily Ann ran in great childish circles in the open space. "I prayed harder than they did. If he had died, I don't know what I would have done. But God has given us what we most needed."

She smiled and pushed the carriage in the direction of the westbound train platform, calling out for her daughter, a smile in every step and word.

Jamison had purchased a ticket allowing him access to the second-class passenger car. The seats were comfortable enough, he told himself, and the journey was not that long or arduous. The second-class cars were less luxurious than first and the windows smaller and often dirtier.

As he stepped aboard, the conductor eyed him and then his ticket with great care. He removed his silver punch from the holster on his belt and punched the ticket. Leaning closer to Jamison, he said in a low tone, "Grab your bag and follow me."

Puzzled, Jamison picked up his satchel and followed the conductor. He worried that something might have been wrong with his ticket or that this car was not the second-class car he thought it was.

The train pulled out from the station within a minute of its posted departure. They both wobbled between the cars as the train jostled over a crossing. Jamison followed him through two cars. The conductor looked around as he opened the door to the third. The small plaque above the door read First Class Only.

"But I didn't pay for . . . ," Jamison explained.

The conductor smiled. "You looked like you could use the extra cushioning. You seem a mite fatigued. And this car ain't near filled and if nobody's using the seats, then why should I let 'em go to waste? And it's nearly Christmas. Sort of a gift, you know?"

"Why, thank you," Jamison said. "I can sit anywhere?"

"Anywhere in this car. The seats are better and bigger, and the windows are much cleaner. See the countryside."

Jamison tried to offer the conductor a coin, but the man waved him off. "Just enjoy it," he said as he tipped his hat and disappeared into the car behind them.

Jamison settled in. The conductor was right. The seats were much more comfortable, and the car was warmer. The route and the scenery were familiar to Jamison. He had traveled this line dozens of times between his home and Boston and then to Harvard. He marveled at the growth of the towns the train rolled through. What had once been sleepy hamlets were now bustling with entire streets filled with shops and carriages.

The village of Johnstown had grown into a proper city. Street after street ran at angles to the tracks. Smoke poured out of ten or so tall smokestacks, and there were neat rows of houses radiating into the distance.

It was a scheduled stop for passengers and the train took on freshwater and coal as well. Jamison stepped out from his car. Peddlers manned pushcarts, offering lunches, fruit, and all manner of beverages. Jamison knew he should be hungry but was not. His stomach felt in knots, as if he knew something untoward were about to happen. Yet he bought two apples and a small wedge of cheese, in case his hunger returned. He heard the jostle and clank of cars being added to the end of the train. Jamison stepped to the end of the platform, stretching his legs. Dozens of open-topped cars, now part of the train, brimmed with black coal.

The train, noticeably slower with the new load, lumbered on through the afternoon. Jamison could almost feel the surging of the engine as it labored up the steep grading. Once they cleared the mountains, he knew they would make fast time, heading east down the slopes. But until they reached the highest elevation in the Allegheny Mountains, their progress was not much faster than a speedy carriage.

Jamison looked at his watch. It was nearing four in the afternoon. What shadows there were had disappeared under a thickness of clouds. The air was wet with the promise of snow. As the train huffed past the last bits of Altoona, great flakes of snow appeared, swirling about the train as it pushed upward. In the span of a few miles, the ground began to take on its white blanket.

"When's our next stop?" Jamison asked the conductor as he slowly made his way through the car.

"It should have been Mount Union. That's where we normally stop. But we're stopping in Huntingdon. The westbound train lost a gearing last night. A simple five-minute repair—if you got the part. Them unlucky passengers had to spend the night there—most of them huddling in the small station. We got a repair crew on board with the gear. Actually the stopping makes no big difference. There's only a dozen miles between the two stations."

The snow flew now in exuberant earnestness and etched trees and fences in whiteness. As the horizon shrank from miles to a few hundred feet, the rest of the world was lost to white and the coming of the dark.

The train jostled left-right-left. Jamison peered out the window.

A well-traveled passenger could tell when the train was coming to a village or town, even if there were no lights to guide him. The train often crossed a road or two, and the crossings seemed to be at odd angles to the rail bed, jostling the passengers alert. Huntingdon, though a small hamlet nestled along the banks of the Juniata River, was no exception. The train jerked again to the right, then hard to the left, and Jamison grabbed at the armrest to steady himself.

Outside, the flakes of snow seemed as big as a child's hand, crowding their own way to earth, slipping and falling in the cold air. A light shone in the growing dusk, then another and another, each flame exclaiming the existence of a homestead or farm or house nestled by a stream. The train slowed; the wheels took hold on the steel rail and squealed as the brakes tried to gain purchase on the slick surface.

A great hush of steam billowed up from the engine as the engineer released the pressure and the train lumbered to a patient stop. When he felt the last shudder rock through the cars, Jamison stood and stretched. His bones themselves felt a fatigue.

"The price one pays for aging," Jamison quipped to himself.

He stared out the window, toward the south and the river. On the riverbank was a tall bluff of open rock and shale facings. The snow caught the ledges and outcroppings, like chalk highlights applied by a giant's hand.

The conductor called out the name of the town as he walked through the car. He paused by Jamison. "We're only stopping for a minute or two. I would stay on the train if I were you."

Jamison nodded his thanks and sat back down, pulling his coat closer. When the train stopped, the heat seemed to stay huddled at the far front of the car.

Jamison peered out again, to the north, across the tracks, to the open, wooden platform of the Huntingdon station. There may have been fifty people huddled about, all of them gathering a dusting of snow as they waited to be called to reboard their train. A team of workmen in blue canvas dusters clamored about the engine, shouting in the cold, some pointing, some on their knees, holding great wrenches and hammers.

Breakdowns were a regular occurrence for any train. Those that labored through the mountains seemed to be hardest affected. In the past Jamison had spent a number of nights sleeping on uncomfortable train seats as he waited for repairs to be made to an engine or tender or coupling.

The disabled westbound train consisted only of an engine and a coal tender and two passenger cars. Most of the station's platform was visible to Jamison. In a moment the workmen stood back and shouted to the engineer. A cloud of steam hissed and the train jerked forward a foot or two. A few of the workers shouted, clapped each other on the back, and picked up their tools and headed back to Jamison's train.

The crowd of tired passengers began at once to mill in an untidy wave toward the last car. Jamison's train now hissed and jerked hesitantly to its start.

Jamison smiled and recalled how relieved they all must feel–happy to restart their interrupted journey. Perhaps they all might arrive at their homes in time for Christmas, now less than eight hours distant.

Jamison reached for his bag and extracted a slim book. He had tried to read it myriad times between Pittsburgh and here and never had found the patience.

The train shuddered again and pushed forward another ten or so feet.

As he opened the book and pressed the two pages apart in his lap, something from the platform across the way caught his eye. Something unusual in the milling crowd of folks waiting to reboard caught the periphery of his vision. What it was, at first, he could not be sure of. He was not even sure why he turned back to look.

At the edge of the crowd, there was the smaller figure of a woman dressed in a green coat, the color of ivy found deep in the woods. Her hair was covered by a scarlet burnoose. Her face was hidden in the shadows, half turned from Jamison's eyes. He could see only the gentle curve of her cheek and the very tip of her nose and perhaps the flutter of her eyelashes in the snow.

That must not have been it, he thought.

He scanned the crowd again.

There was . . . something that he saw without seeing. There was something that caught his eye for a brief second.

Then he realized what it was. He turned back to stare at the woman in the green coat.

It was what the woman was holding in her right hand.

A dark leather satchel.

A doctor's bag!

And then, in the glowing darkness, a shaft of light from the gas lantern on the platform illuminated only a sliver of the woman's face. Her eye, her cheek, her lips were lit by the lamplight for a heartbeat.

Jamison's eyes widened. His heart tightened into a knot. He grabbed his bag and coat and ran toward the rear of the car and the open steps between the cars. The south platform at Huntingdon was not very long. His train pushed slowly forward. Jamison scanned to the east. Only a dozen feet remained before the platform ended and the rocks and cinders of the rail bed began. To wait was to lose any opportunity to exit. Jamison did not hesitate. He jumped. The snow-covered platform was slick as ice, and Jamison nearly fell back into the train. He slid about like a skater, searching for balance, trying to avoid contact with the train he had just exited.

He spun about, flailing his arms, almost throwing his bag into the air. Finally he managed to find his steps, took a deep breath, and began to run in the opposite direction the train was heading. His car had been near the first cars of the train and there was a long length of boxcars and coal carriers between him and the opposite side of the station.

In a moment he was at the far end of the small platform. In the few seconds' gaps between passing cars, he could see the crowd on the opposite side of the station growing smaller and smaller. They were boarding their delayed train and anxious to restart their journey. Steam billowed from the engine, ready to start the slow chug west. He saw the engineer waving to the brakeman, giving a clear go-ahead signal. As soon as the last passenger boarded, Jamison was certain the train would start up.

Jamison ran back and forth. He would have screamed, but no one would be heard over the clacking cacophony of the two trains. Near panic, he looked west. There were but six cars left to his train. As the last one rumbled past, he jumped from the southern platform to the train track, strewn with cinders and slick with ice and snow. He sprinted across the five tracks and dashed to the end of the west-bound train. When he leaped up onto the platform, only a mere handful of passengers waited there, in the snow, in the cold, to board their repaired train.

Was she a passenger on that train? Could she have been? Was she heading to California as he was heading to Philadelphia? Were they about to have crossed each other in the cold and darkness?

He glimpsed that green coat.

His heart turned about in his chest.

"Hannah!" he screamed.

The figure in the green coat turned back toward him.

He dropped his bag. It was her! Her eyes, her face, her lips. It was her! Her hand fluttered to her throat. He saw her lips tremble. For a heartbeat, neither could move.

Could a mathematician calculate the odds of such a serendipitous reunion?

She dropped her physician's satchel and began to move toward him as he moved to her. The last few passengers edged aside, and she began to run, as did Jamison.

They met there, on the open wooden platform of the Huntingdon station in the Pennsylvania mountains, as the snow of Christmas Eve fell in a great swirling, joyous symphony of colors and sight and sound.

She threw her arms open as did he, and they embraced. Neither had the power of speech as they clung to each other with great passion.

Jamison did not hold back the tears that began to streak down his face. He had Hannah in his arms again and no power on earth, he vowed to himself in that instance, would ever separate them again.

"It is you, is it not, Jamison? This is not some Christmas appari-tion, is it?"

He caressed her cheek with his lips. "No. And you are no appari-tion either."

She reached up to his cheek and touched his face, tracing the path of his tears with a trembling fingertip. "I have waited for you. I told you I would."

"And I have returned to you," he said, "as I promised."

And in a perfect moment of enduring love, time stilled as their lips met.

All the pain in his life dissolved like snow on a warm kitchen window, the droplets of water washing away his hurts and bitterness and cynical thoughts. For Hannah, her eyes told the story—that she, too, had found the love that would bind up her tattered heart.

He embraced her tightly, never wanting her to leave the protection of his arms, and she pulled toward him, seeming to echo his desire.

The snow continued to fall, clattering softly against itself, dusting them and the world around them in a magic stillness.

CHAPTER TWENTY-FOUR

Huntingdon, Pennsylvania
Christmas Eve 1859

Jamison, when asked about this moment in the future, would smile and shrug. He had no firm recollection of how long he and Hannah stood there on the train platform, lost in each other's embrace.

The conductor had called "All Aboard!" several times, and neither Hannah nor Jamison had moved. He called out one last time, then shrugged, climbed back on the train, signaled the engineer, and closed the door of the passenger car.

Jamison had closed his eyes, trying not to cry more than he had. The rumbling noise of the train at last died out, leaving the two of them standing in the silence of the snow.

"Where were you going?" he whispered finally.

"To find you. To California. Gage sent a telegram. Somehow it got through and they found me. When I knew you were alive, I had to find you. He wrote that you found faith in New Zealand."

"I did as you asked. I kept searching." He kissed her again and continued. "And I was searching for you. It's been a quest I think I have been on my whole life. And now I have you in my arms."

She laid her head on his chest. "I can hear your heart," she said. "It's pounding so fast."

He smiled into the darkness. "I finally feel alive and whole, Hannah."

She leaned back and offered him a beatific smile. "And I am whole again as well, my sweet Jamison. I am alive and whole. I have prayed for this moment every day."

He reached to her and brushed away a soft piling of snowflakes that had gathered on her hood. Some fell to her cheeks.

"We need to get out of the snow," she said softly. "I don't want them to find us here tomorrow, looking like snowmen."

He stared as she spoke, watching every move of her lips, watching the delicate sparkle in her eyes, the gentle curve of her lashes, the glow of her cheeks. Then, tenderly, he placed his hands at the sides of her face and pulled her lips once again to his own.

After a long meeting, he leaned back. "There is one more thing I must do before we leave here," he said, lowering himself to one knee. He took both her hands in his and smiled up into her radiant face. The snow danced about them both, trembling like chilled butterflies, alighting for a heartbeat, then fading from sight.

"Hannah," he said, "I have practiced these words a thousand times since we parted on Maui. I have my part perfect and now the rest is up to you."

He lowered his head, then spoke the words he had prayed to be able to say. "Hannah, you are my love and my life. Will you marry me?" he asked in the warm glow of the lamplight.

Her fingers trembled to her lips. She blinked her eyes several times, as if to clear the mist in them. "Yes, Jamison, I will," she said, her words masked by a joyous sob. "I want to be your wife. I want that more than anything in heaven or earth. Yes, Jamison, yes."

He stood and embraced her as tightly as he had ever embraced another person. "I don't have a ring," he whispered.

"That's all right, Jamison. There is plenty of time for a ring."

The furious pounding would have been enough to wake the entire neighborhood had the snow, now falling in majestic abundance, not muffled the sound.

"I'm coming! I'm coming!" came the garbled reply from somewhere inside.

In another instant, Hannah and Jamison, wet from the snow, stood grinning and dripping in the front parlor of Mr. Edwin Leath, justice of the peace for Huntingdon Township.

It only took a few minutes for Jamison to explain the rudiments of their story.

Mr. Leath scratched his head, puzzled as a man might be. "But it's Christmas Eve. Don't you two know that?"

Both Hannah and Jamison smiled and nodded.

"We will waste not one more day apart," Hannah said with finality.

Mr. Leath sighed, then turned and called up the stairs, "Hazel! Come down please. We need a witness."

Mrs. Leath, wrapped in a tattered, faded robe that pooled about her feet like a drapery, stood a step behind her husband. She was grinning. There was a kerchief about her head, pulled tight enough, Jamison thought, to be painful.

Mr. Leath was better assembled, with black formal trousers, a white nightshirt almost tucked fully in, and red suspenders. He even fastened the top two buttons of his nightshirt, adjusting it carefully. He turned up the wick in the lamp, and soon the parlor was filled with a flickering glow. From the mantel above the fire, he took a slim volume.

"This book has all the proper ceremonies," he explained as he flipped through the pages. "Births, deaths, swearings-in, marriages . . . ahh, here it is. Marriage." He stopped, lowered the book, and peered over at Jamison. "You got a license, don't you?"

"License?" Jamison managed to choke out.

"To get married. You need one of them. Else it ain't legal in the eyes of the state."

Jamison took a panicky, shallow breath. "Where do we get one of them?"

Mr. Leath cackled. "Well, son, you're in luck. 'Cause a justice of the peace be the person who sells them. And I can draw one up in two minutes—if you got three dollars on you. You got three dollars, don't you?"

Jamison nodded, relieved, and reached for his billfold. He followed Mr. Leath to a small desk in the corner of the room, and the man began to fill in the blanks on a license form.

Mrs. Leath nodded and smiled to Hannah. "Nasty weather."

Hannah, who had not stopped smiling since seeing Jamison again, said, "I hadn't noticed."

"That's a pretty dress," Mrs. Leath continued, evidently trying to make small talk.

"Thank you."

There was a short silence, then the low murmuring of Mr. Leath.

"Would you like a flower or two to hold for the ceremony?" Mrs. Leath asked sweetly.

"But it's winter," Hannah said, surprised.

Mrs. Leath scurried away. "I have some narcissus that I forced. I was saving them for dinner tomorrow—but I think this occasion is more special."

And as the four of them gathered in the middle of the parlor, Hannah held a small bouquet of flowers in her hands. Jamison carried his Bible, and the two joined hands.

Mr. Leath read the vows slowly, as if he took great care to include every word, fearing that one overlooked term would invalidate the entire ceremony. All the while he talked, Jamison gazed at Hannah. His eyes told of his wonderment at the fact that she was standing beside him, repeating the vows that would join them together forever.

She looked away, as if shy for that moment, as if taking these steps and repeating these words for the very first time in her life.

Later she would tell him that never before had she been so moved by a man's promise to love and cherish a woman.

At the end of the short ceremony there was a short silence. Mrs. Leath gave a loud sob and buried her face in her hands, bunching her robe about her eyes.

Mr. Leath smiled. Jamison was not sure, but he thought he saw the old justice of the peace blush.

"I now pronounce you man and wife," Mr. Leath said happily. The very words seemed to dance in the air. "You may now kiss your bride."

Jamison waited, almost breathless, as Hannah turned her face to his.

"I will never forget this moment," he whispered and then brought his lips to hers.

And their marriage began to the great, heartfelt sobs of Mrs. Leath and the quiet crackling of the fire.

As the clock tower began to toll midnight, Jamison placed his hand under Hannah's chin and drew her face to his.

"A Christmas kiss," he said, as if neither were in any hurry to finish the unwrapping.

They had been married for all of an hour. On Mr. Leath's recommendation, they found a room at Holtzer's Inn on Spring Street. It was a large room with a fireplace on the second floor. The bowed window peeked out over the town's square. There was a huge canopied bed draped with lace and scarlet silk that flowed down like a river from the top of the frame to the floor.

The manager, when he found out that Jamison and Hannah had just been married, hurried to the room before them and started a warming fire. He had lit a dozen tapers about the room. He fussed about for several moments as he set everything just so in the room.

Jamison thanked him and offered him a tip, which he refused.

"A wedding gift. But you must promise me one thing," he said.

"You must promise to tell me how you happened to get married here in Huntingdon on Christmas Eve. But the story can wait till the morrow," he added quickly, smiling.

Jamison wondered if the kindly manager had seen the note of nervousness in the groom's eyes.

Hannah stood in the bow of the great window, staring out, still holding her flowers to her chest. Jamison closed the door and came up behind her, encircling her in his arms. The world had gone still and quiet from the snow. Even their footprints, the only ones in the snow, had been covered again.

"There has been no more perfect day in all of history," Jamison said as he held Hannah tight. She agreed by snuggling deeper into the protection of his arms.

After a long embrace, she broke away and set the flowers in a pitcher. She splashed in some water from a jar by the bed.

Jamison reached over to his bag. He pulled out the two apples and cheese that he had purchased that day. It seemed so long ago, he thought.

"It's not much," he said as he offered her an apple, "but it is all I have."

She took a delicate nibble. "It is the grandest, most wonderful banquet at which I have ever been in attendance," she said, her words such a musical lilt that Jamison could scarce prevent himself from embracing her once again.

And then a second later, he did exactly that. As he felt her heart beat next to his, he, for the first time in his life, felt truly at peace. His quest had ended . . . for he had truly found his home.

From where I sit I hear the gentle swish of the waves on the rocks below. The scent of the sea is all around us, and the flowers on the hillside below are but sweet amplification for the senses.

It is just dawn. Sunsets are the more showy part of the day, but I prefer the flinty light of dawn—quiet, reserved. A prelude, and not a finale volume.

I have written three such final pages—one for each of my Harvard friends' stories. This will be my fourth and final . . . my own.

It seems I have spent a lifetime taking notes, jotting down snippets of conversation, copying bits of letters—all to document my life and the lives of Joshua Quittner, Gage Davis, Hannah Collins, and myself. I knew when the four of us met at Harvard, now so long ago, that our stories would be special in some manner.

Fate, or perhaps God, has not proven me wrong. I have written their stories with as much truth and honesty as I can muster—in *The Price, The Treasure,* and *The Promise.* I am now within a few pages of completing my own. I believe each story has conveyed a life, complete with pain and joy, complete with sin and redemption.

A few years have passed since I penned the first volume, and I think it's wise to retreat slightly and let the loyal reader know the continuations of each person's story and life.

Joshua Quittner was the subject of *The Price*. He came to Harvard brimming with faith, fated to follow his father's footsteps in a small pastorate in the wilds of Ohio. It was I, before I knew how wrong it was, who led him to abandon his calling. He set out to California to find his fortune, nearly throwing his life and salvation away at the same time. I shudder to think what would have been my punishment for causing a man of God to leave the path.

He lost it all and yet gained it all. His life, perhaps, is the most full and rich and joyous of us all. Perhaps being in God's service provides those rewards—rewards no man can buy but are given freely by God.

Joshua lives no more than a few days' ride from me. He is the pastor of a large church in Stockton, California. The church is a wonderful, airy, bright, and worshipful place that overlooks a little valley. His wife, the lovely and gentle Quen-li, whom he met while in the goldfields, has given him five beautiful children and is conversant in English as well as Chinese. I laughed the first time I heard Joshua speak in his wife's foreign tongue, but he tells me he is nearly fluent.

He is not a rich man, of course, but they have a large home filled with children and laughter and love.

His father passed on many years ago, sadly before Joshua had any chance to make peace. It took dozens and dozens of letters, but he has at last reached an understanding with his mother. He has not returned home to Ohio, for the journey is indeed costly and dangerous—especially as one ages—which we all have done. But he is settled in place and in mind, for his mother has forgiven him.

I, of all people, know how much a burden such unresolved relationships can be.

The congregation at his home church in Shawnee is still small, as is the town. Through the largesse of Joshua and others—Gage, for one—the church has a wonderful organ and has been endowed with a scholarship. For outstanding young men, the fund pays their college tuition, providing they return to preach for three years in the pulpit of the church.

By the way, Constance, the Ohio woman whom Joshua's parents had earmarked to be his bride, is married, Joshua learned, to Spider Jeffreys, a rich, reclusive fellow. People claim that the match is odd, but they are said to be content.

Gage Davis was the main character in the second volume in this series, titled *The Treasure*. The son of great wealth, he was destined, even while at Harvard, to become a titan of industry, a Prometheus unbound in the financial worlds.

He did, for a moment.

Then, like Icarus, he flew too close to the sun and plummeted to despair. Caught in a business matter of dubious legality, his evil brother, Walton, forced him out of the family business. A broken man, Gage headed west.

Yet his fine intelligence and business acumen did not desert him. In short order he became a man of substance again. Nora, the woman who was partially the cause of his downfall, never left his heart. He pursued her west and to the Sandwich Islands. For a short idyll after their marriage their lives were blissful and serene. A child was born.

Then God took her from Gage. I still do not understand the why of this, but I have learned that God is indeed sovereign.

Gage returned once again to California—to his home in Monterey. He is not poor, not by any means. He is a rich man—very, very rich. Many urged him to run for governor or senator after being so loved as mayor of our town. He declined all their entreaties, claiming it would restrict his freedom.

In the ensuing years, he has endeavored to give much of his fortune away. He has built hospitals and libraries, mostly.

Gage has not married again after the loss of the love of his life, Nora, and those of us close to him think he will ever remain single.

He has experienced too great a loss, I think, and had too pure a love to be muddied by another.

His daughter, Hope, is becoming a charming and beautiful young woman. He tells all that she is the image of her mother, and one can easily see why Gage will not find a woman to compare.

Yet when I look into his eyes, I see sadness there.

Gage has had the most of any of us—and he has lost the most of any of us, I believe. He had so much growing up—and treated it as a right, rather than a gift.

He says the fact that he is now a believer has helped him deal with the pain in his life.

His father died many years ago, never recovering nor even coming to an awareness of reality—that his younger son, Gage, had left the family business in disgrace. He never once more called Gage's name after Gage had left New York. The Davises' former servant and loyal friend, Edgar, also passed on, only two months after Gage's father. Influenza took him quickly. I believe that Gage found Edgar's passing a harder blow than his own father's death.

Gage's greedy brother, Walton, is very, very rich and has prospered in the family business. He sends one letter a year to Gage—as does Gage in return—very brief, very businesslike, at Christmas. His mother has yet to write a single word.

As I said, there is sadness in his eyes that money cannot erase.

And then we come to Hannah . . . and to myself.

Hannah and I were married on Christmas Eve in 1859, in the small parlor of a justice of the peace in Huntingdon, Pennsylvania. We joined our lives together and with God.

After the wedding, we set off for California.

Being with Hannah was all the balm my soul required. I scarce can believe my wondrous fortune at waking and seeing her angelic face on the pillow next to mine. God is good and we were kept safe.

As for Hannah's family, her father, who had lost the family fortune in bad dealings, passed away last year. An ill humor of the lungs was the cause. He was angry and unrepentant about his role in his family's downfall to the end. Her mother continues to complain bitterly about everything in her life in every letter. She has gone on to live with her sister, whom she also used to complain about.

My own mother passed on in 1862. It was indeed a mercy of God since she knew no one when she closed her eyes that last time. My father, with whom I have reconciled after many bitter years, still lives in the parsonage in Pittsburgh and continues to preach on a regular basis. I have invited him to live with us here in California, claiming that the warm air would be good for his bones. Recently he has written that he is considering the offer—especially since the young preacher of whom he spoke is now ready to shepherd his church flock.

Hannah teaches medicine and does doctoring when needed—sometimes here in Monterey and sometimes at a new college in San Francisco.

I manage, so to speak, a small newspaper in town. I write a column or two, I edit some, I take my luncheon at a local café where my face is well known. I greet advertisers in the afternoon. Hannah and I read much; we swim in the ocean. She and I take walks along the shore most every day, for the weather here is nearly always delightful.

It is a pleasant life.

Speaking of serendipities, Hannah found her old friend Lawrence, who had been such an encouragement to her when she had begun to work as a partner with old Doc Copley. After years of wondering what had happened to Lawrence, who had had to leave Philadelphia quickly, they literally bumped into one another on a corner in San Francisco. He was there on business, and she was there teaching for a week. She says they cried for an hour after recognizing each other. He lives in Seattle, where he owns a men's clothing shop. It is a profession that Hannah says is well suited to his sensibilities. No mention was made of why he'd had to flee on such short notice, and Hannah did not think it proper to bring the subject up.

Hannah and I are older now. We have no children, and that reality is often painful to Hannah, especially as she sees the lines in her face deepen. I blame Robert Keyes and his brutality for her barren condition, even though I know it displeases God for me to be revengeful.

I look back at my life and am amazed. As a young man, I was a foolish cynic–blinded and ignorant. Yet God chose me and refined me in a blazing fire.

I may not tell everyone I meet of my faith in him, but those I get to know, I do.

Life is an odd journey, is it not? A curious unfolding, hour by hour, day by day. Yet I know God has blessed me greatly. And every day I praise him for all that he has done.

We started off as four callow youths. We are all older now, and a little slower, perhaps–but by God's grace we have all become children of the living God.

That is the most amazing miracle of all.

I have heard so often that God gives us what we need. It is a great sadness to me that I took so long to recognize that gift.

The dawn is hours past, and Hannah has returned home from an early walk. She has brought in a bouquet of brilliant blue flowers, picked from the hillside below our home. They are now in a vase on the table by the door.

She enters the room and I smile, for she is the light of my life and my reason for living. Without her I would be lost.

She bends to me and wraps her arms about my neck and shoulders and kisses my cheek. I reach up and touch her face in return.

She smiles.

Life is good.

Jamison Pike
Monterey Bay
The State of California
May 1863